'In its fairly irresistible combination of transgressive sex and a
richly layered evocation of history, *Sedition* demands comparison
with Sarah Waters' untouchably brilliant novels ... a properly
subversive and quite unforgettable novel' *Guardian*

'Packed with colourful characters ... this is an original, winningly
imagined tale' *Daily Mail*

'A sly, witty, deliciously knowing treat ... [a] fascinating debut'
Metro

'You will be seduced as surely as Katie Grant's young ladies in this
masterpiece of salacious wit. This is one of those precious novels.
The kind that bookworms burrow inside to devour with relish
from cover to cover. The kind you'll secrete behind all the other
books on your shelves in case friends steal it and somehow
"forget" to give it back. The kind from which you'll read chosen
snippets to your offspring when they're old enough. An induction
into the magical unruliness of words. Not a dull or superfluous
page' *Scotland on Sunday*

SEDITION

Katharine Grant

virago

VIRAGO

First published in Great Britain in 2014 by Virago Press
This paperback edition published in 2014 by Virago Press
Reprinted 2014

A CIP catalogue record for this book
is available from the British Library.

ISBN 978-1-84408-986-4

Typeset in Caslon by M Rules
Printed and bound in Great Britain by
Clays Ltd, St Ives plc

Papers used by Virago are from well-managed forests
and other responsible sources.

 MIX
Paper from
responsible sources
FSC® C104740

Virago Press
An imprint of
Little, Brown Book Group
100 Victoria Embankment
London EC4Y 0DY

An Hachette UK Company
www.hachette.co.uk

www.virago.co.uk

To William, for never doubting
and to Michael Schmidt for never saying
he was too busy, though he was.

Acknowledgements

ALL novels benefit from the following: an enthusiast, a generous expert, a poet, a keen agent, a sharp editor and the provision, by a kindly agency, of time. *Sedition* had all of these. The enthusiast is my husband; the generous expert, musician Keith Jacobsen; the poet, Michael Schmidt; my agent, Georgina Capel; my editor at Virago, Lennie Goodings; the kindly agency, the Royal Literary Fund. Take away just one of these and I would have been in trouble. I couldn't be more grateful to you all.

Any mistakes readers find in the text will be mine, and not the fault of any of the people or agencies above, or of the many sources I consulted. If you do spot a mistake, I apologise, and hope it doesn't spoil your enjoyment of the book.

SEDITION

Prologue

IT was a month after her mother died that Alathea Sawney-ford's father first took her to the coffeehouse. Mr W, the proprietor, sucked in his cheeks: children irritated customers. But Mrs W simply set a small chair below the counter to shield Alathea from the pictures Mr W favoured for the walls. He called them 'artful'. Mrs W called them nothing at all and would have blushed were she a blushing type of woman. Anyhow, despite the pictures, she never thought of turning the little girl away. With no children of her own, she had love to offer – rough love, maybe, but love all the same – and though Alathea has long since outgrown the small chair, Mrs W's welcome has never been withdrawn. Mr W can suck in his cheeks all he likes; it pleases Mrs W to encourage Alathea to look on the Virginia & Baltick as a haven, and occasionally Alathea chooses to do so.

She is on her way there now, drawing behind her the latest in a long line of stalkers set on her trail by, she guesses correctly, her father. Never certain whether the surveillance is for her protection or his own, it's nevertheless always a pleasure to identify the wretch so keen to be unidentified. Today's tail is a poor specimen, exuding furtiveness. He might as well carry a sign.

Alathea is about to duck into the V&B when, through the low February cloud and city steam, she sees a crowd gathering at the top of Threadneedle Street. She pauses, then makes her way over and pushes to the front. A young woman is hanging. She is quite dead.

A man parts the crowd with his barrow. Bad luck to touch the hangman or his barrow. Alathea, unshrinking, sees the hangman is in a fury. He doesn't get paid for collecting suicides. 'Robbed of ten shillings,' he mutters, banging his barrow down.

Alathea pokes the corpse with one finger. 'Wire,' she says, with a nod towards the girl's neck. The hangman grunts. Unasked, Alathea holds the dead legs firmly and nods again. The hangman stares, then shrugs, climbs on to his barrow, levers the wire from the gantry and lowers the body. The crowd shuffle forward to have a look, then retreat when the hangman waves his arms. Alathea settles the girl's skirts and contemplates her face.

'Desperate, your friend,' the hangman says, momentarily forgetting his ten bob.

Alathea doesn't contradict, though she's never seen the girl before and wonders about desperation. The girl's hands are quite relaxed, her fingers spread as though to press the final chord on a keyboard. There is certainly evidence of pain in the bloated cheeks and bulging lips, but to Alathea physical pain is something squeezed out and wiped away. Despair, being more entrenched, is more worthy of note. She bends as though to look for signs of it but instead removes the corpse's shoes and tries them on. They don't fit so she returns them. 'Pity,' she says. Then 'Kiss her.'

2

'What?' says the hangman.

'Kiss her,' Alathea repeats. 'Like this.' She kisses the hangman full on the lips. It's not the unexpectedness he remembers, it's the feel of her tongue. He feels it from top to toe.

'If a hangman kisses a suicide, God forgives both,' Alathea says. 'Do it.'

Before the hangman can refuse, she is gone, and though their acquaintance has been short, he feels her loss like a view suddenly revealed and as suddenly cut off. He rakes the crowd with his eyes. She is nowhere to be seen. A gloomy day seems gloomier. As he trundles the corpse to its paltry grave, the only thing that cheers him is a notice tied to a horse-post just outside the Bank. It's a call to arms, brothers. Tax the rich! Power to the people! He counts six signatures. That should be six hangings this year at least. If all done at once, the authorities may ask for a discount. He'll be damned if he gives one.

I

THE girls were not consulted. Had they gone to the workshop of the pianoforte maker at Tyburn, things might have been different. As it was, Tobias Drigg, father to Marianne and Everina, made his way to Vittorio Cantabile's workshop alone, although not alone by choice. He could find his way easily enough: ten years after hosting the last wretch's execution, the Tyburn gallows remained, even the destitute superstitious about chopping the famous arms for firewood. Drigg did not want to be alone because whilst he had suggested the venture on which he, Archibald Frogmorton, Gregory Brass and Sawney Sawneyford were now embarked, he was not equipped to see it well begun. Like his friends, his chief interests were cloth, liquor, furs, leather, timber – anything to be bought low and sold high. A pianoforte was not on this list, yet this is what he had been commissioned to purchase. Drigg wished he had never mentioned the thing. He wished he had not even thought of it. He wished he was back in the Virginia & Baltick discussing plundered ships and the mulishness of Yorkshire jaggermen.

One of the gallows' arms pointed to the right, and after a brief meander during which he seriously contemplated abandoning his commission, Drigg found himself in front of two square storeys of black brick, the sullen hub of five narrow warrens. Lean-tos would have softened the workshop's appearance, but nothing touched it apart from the cartwheels that habitually clipped the cornerstones of the three sides where the road passed very tight. On the fourth side the road was wider, so a wooden pavement had been attempted. The building marked a boundary for local robbers. East-side, official thief takers and Bow Street Runners; west-side, devilry. The window and the door were on the east side, as was the attempted pavement. It was a good place for the alehouse it eventually became.

Drigg rat-tatted on the door. No answer, except for jeers from a crowd of beggars. Drigg pushed the door open and took a moment to shut out the street. For a second, he could have been in the V&B – that tallow tang – then his eyes readjusted and he found himself contemplating a scene of destruction. Of the fifteen or so instruments in the workshop, few were whole. Two single-manual harpsichords had vomited their innards, and from a spinet, a spew of shrivelled veins. Another, skeleton cracked, had lost two legs and was frozen in a crippled buck. Others were covered with shrouds. Over the lid of a lion-footed clavichord, keyboard missing, implements to pluck, hit, squeeze, stretch and force were spread in the manner of an orderly torturer. Directly in front of Drigg was a large desk, a stool behind it. Set in the right-hand wall a fireplace, fire unlit.

Drigg shuddered. Overlying the smell of tallow was a smell much more fungal – an undertaking smell, he thought, venturing past the desk, dodging the shrouds and further unnerved by the draughts that caused a permanent whispering and twanging, as though a concert was either finishing or just about to start.

Drigg stiffened his spine. 'Halloa! Halloo there!' He could feel dust spores in his throat and his nose prickled.

From somewhere emerged the proprietor, balding, thin as drawn steel and draped about with wire and ivory, felt and pivots, jacks, stops, mutes and pins. His hammer was poised for a burglar.

Drigg blurted, 'I wish to buy a pianoforte.'

Cantabile at once recognised a City creature, a coffeehouse man. Lloyd's? No, no Lloyd's man came here. Garraway's? No banker's sheen. Batson's? Possibly, though Drigg lacked a sawbones' smuggery. Cantabile kept the hammer raised. The Bedford? A man who shouted 'Halloa!' supping with poets? No. The Virginia & Baltick. That was it. Plain as plain. A V&B man. Cloth and furs. Thick thread and dead animals.

Cantabile did not see himself as a vendor of keyboard instruments. He was a musical craftsman like his late father and, also like his late father, had achieved renown in their native Milan but no fortune. London had promised more discerning customers, but in this Cantabile had been disappointed. Sales had been good – his reputation preceded him. It was the customers who appalled. It became painful to part with creations over which he crooned and laboured, to imagine them under the thumbs and fingers of buffoons, money grubbers and imbecile girls. He drove harder and harder bargains. Shortly before customers refused to buy from him, Cantabile refused to sell. Only when starvation threatened did an instrument depart. Cantabile did not care who saw him weep.

Starvation threatened today, but he moved sideways and gently closed the lid of the pianoforte he was currently refining. This pianoforte was not a work of art, it was a work of genius. Under-dampers of brass and a sounding-board of seasoned beech achieved resonances beyond anything Broadwood or Erard could boast. Innovation, materials and the dexterity of a master combined with uncanny precision so that every grain and splinter, block and hammer, string and pad, screw and hinge was perfect. Cantabile had gilded the small rose in the middle of the sounding-board as tenderly as an artist paints roses in a woman's cheek. He loved this instrument without reserve. It contained more of him than his child. It was, indeed, the child he should have had. He stroked it with spread fingers. Not a hint of the V&B should taint it.

Drigg gave it no more than a glance, since it was brown and unattractive. Cantabile saw the dismissal and took umbrage. This beauty, this divinity, passed over as nothing by a V&B man! He reached for the pistol under the counter, but stopped himself. He had a better weapon at his disposal. 'Annie, Annie!' he thundered.

His daughter materialised. Drigg was knocked backwards. Under her cap, Annie boasted lustrous chestnut hair. From wide forehead to sculpted nose, she was pretty. Below the nose, catastrophe. A hare lip created a whole new gummy feature in her chin, and Annie gave Drigg the full benefit.

Cantabile grinned. Ah, Annie. She was beyond price. He had vomited when she was born and ordered her swilled away with the afterbirth. His wife objected. The baby was a baby, she said, her baby. In a moment he counted as cowardice, Cantabile gave in. He had had no peace since. He did not get over his daughter's deformity as his wife had. The stabs of tenderness which caught him unawares mocked him when he looked at her face: a book with split pages, beauty above, monstrosity below. And ridiculously unstable. Annie's mouth drifted. He could not stand the smudginess of it. It tore him up, what the girl was and what she might have been. When Annie was three, he had sought help, but surgeons were afraid of adding to the damage. A hare lip was not dangerous, they said. Dangerous? Of course it was not dangerous! It was horrible. Was that not as bad?

Cantabile took her home again, a small, solemn, lisping child, forbidden to eat unless facing the wall.

She did have her uses. With Annie in sight, Cantabile could leave a pot of money in full view; and as soon as she could sit at the keyboard unaided, he set her to play in the window, a display that had helped custom fall away so satisfactorily that it was soon no longer necessary. Instead Annie buried herself in the brick fortress, absorbing music and the craft of instrument-making as other children absorb fairy tales and the craft of pickpocketing. Her presence agitated Cantabile, yet he could not do without her. When her mother had taken ill, Annie had turned nurse, and she was a natural instrument maker. She worked harder than any apprentice and played better even than her father. Cantabile might have been jealous, but as she grew, the lip grew more prominent and kept her meek, so father and daughter lived like porcupines, prickles always up, Cantabile's sharp with aggression and Annie's blunter, for defence.

The effect of Annie on Drigg, however, was not what Cantabile expected. The fool was too mannerly to stare and leave. At last, Cantabile was forced to say, 'Annie, this – this gentleman wants to buy one of our instruments.'

Annie stood boldly upright, tilting her chin, which, as anybody who got past her lip might have noticed, was dimpled. She did not smile – Annie's smile made even her mother blench and draw up her sheets. Apart from not smiling, Annie faced the world head-on. Her mother thought this brave, but it was not. Despite everything, Annie was a dreamer. Some girls might have dreamed of physical correction, but Annie never dreamed of that. Her dream was far more intoxicating. In it, she played her father's most sophisticated pianoforte to a public audience. This dream audience gawped at first, then it listened, marvelled and stood to applaud. In the audience was her father's only

9

friend, Monsieur Belladroit, met in Paris on Cantabile's journey to London, a regular correspondent and occasional visitor. In her dream, when the concert was over Monsieur took both Annie's hands in his, knelt at her feet and loved her. This was the intoxication, and this future audience was why she waited patiently for the man in their shop to find the words of farewell he was so politely seeking and why, when such words eluded him, she made herself pleasant. The man might buy a ticket to attend her recital. If he stared now, he would not stare then. Anyway, she did not share her father's horror of sales. Something must pay the rent and for the medicine needed to ease her mother's lesioned lungs. 'Are you familiar with pianofortes, Mr ... ?' she asked, wiping grimy hands on a large cambric handkerchief tucked into her belt. She had been scraping wood.

'Er, Drigg. Tobias Drigg.' He could not look away.

'Were you thinking square?' Annie took a lamp and led Drigg from the dingy front showroom to dingier storage, where the heavy structural work was done. Bony frames and belly-rails clattered together. 'Watch out!' Drigg ducked too late. His hat and wig were swept off. He retrieved them and followed Annie more closely. There were no windows. Drigg had only fleeting impressions of ivory sheets, bunched quills and the dull sheen of half-polished lids. So many unfamiliar shapes. So much unsilent silence. His shoulder caught on an iron hook. He pulled free, overbalanced and stubbed his shoe on a pile of curing leather. 'God's teeth!' he muttered. 'Is there to be no light?'

Annie lifted the lamp. Immediate transformation. The place was an ordinary workshop again, filled with ordinary instruments.

'These are very popular,' Annie said, pointing to three harpsichords. 'Many people find them highly satisfactory. All have cypress soundboards – my father follows the Italian way – and two choirs of strings. Listen.' She made her way to the nearest instrument and rippled out the scale of D major with her left hand. 'Try one yourself.'

'Pianoforte, not harpsichord,' Drigg said at once. 'That's what we want.'

'Really?' Annie lowered the lamp and padded over to a bigger square instrument sitting on its own. Drigg followed. Annie raised the lamp. Drigg's eyes locked back on to her lip. Annie kept the lamp high. Now he wished she would not. 'Here's a pianoforte,' she said. 'May I know the colour of the room in which your instrument will live?'

'Colour? Green, I believe,' said Drigg. He peeled his eyes away.

'Well then,' said Annie, her voice low and pleasant, her lisp not unattractive. 'This maple would do very well. As you can see, we don't go in for painted frames. Appearance should never take precedence over sound. You may like to know that we sold one of these only yesterday to the Duke of Granchester for his daughter Blanche to play.' She lied easily. She was a good sales-woman.

The mention of the duke had precisely the effect Annie sought. Drigg calmed himself. 'The Duke of Granchester,' he repeated.

Annie put down the lamp and lit a bright candle. 'Yes. Just look at the quality of the inlay.' They both looked. 'Lady Blanche is not a fine player,' Annie confided, spitting slightly. Drigg curled his fists. 'Your daughter will be more accomplished. If I'm not mistaken, your daughter is the person for whom the pianoforte's intended?'

'Two daughters,' said Drigg, trying to move inconspicuously away without bumping into anything. 'But not only for them. I'm purchasing a pianoforte for all our daughters – I mean to say

11

my two, Marianne and Everina, and for the daughters of three friends – Alderman Frogmorton, Mr Brass and Mr Sawneyford. They have a daughter each.' His sudden loss of colour had nothing to do with Annie and everything to do with the weight of his responsibility to these friends and all their daughters, this responsibility being the reason for his pursuit of a pianoforte in the first place. It was not an unusual responsibility. It came to every father with daughters, and with Marianne eighteen last birthday and the other girls close behind, these fathers' turn had come. It was time to think about their daughters' marriage prospects.

Some things were already established. For example, all their daughters were financially well accounted for – and not just financially, since doggedness, talent and unswerving ambition had made their fathers more respectable than their parents (not all of them known for certain). The men's trouble, much debated between them at the V&B, was that though commercial success offered easy acquaintance with the rank of people from whom they hoped to recruit sons-in-law – landed people, titled people – commercial gratitude was laced with social distaste, and no matter how large the profits engineered by Archibald Frogmorton, Gregory Brass, Sawney Sawneyford and Tobias Drigg himself – and the profits were substantial – there developed no deeper intimacy.

The men were determined to prevail. To achieve success, they needed the girls to stand out. It was then that Drigg had suggested something might be made of the fashionable rivalry between the harpsichord and the new-fangled pianoforte, a rivalry, he had been told, hotly dividing opinion up and down St James's Street. Since the pianoforte was currently the favourite, he had wondered aloud if their girls could be among the first to master this new instrument – soon, he had also been assured, to be a feature in every home – and whether this might not make them stand out very favourably. He had waxed quite lyrical. He had, in fact, gone on at some length. Even at the time Drigg knew he had been over-persuasive, allowing himself to be goaded by Brass's habitual derision at any suggestion Drigg made. Frogmorton, though, had been quite taken with the picture Drigg painted, and somehow the notion of a concert party at which the girls would perform in front of potential husbands took shape. In the faecal fug of the V&B, they had envisaged a grand evening, their girls irresistible, the uninvited feeling the loss. The picture had been so beguiling that in the end Frogmorton had turned to Drigg and charged him with setting the wheel in motion by locating and purchasing the necessary instrument. That was when Drigg had got cold feet, but when he tried to demur, suggesting they should all witness the purchase, Frogmorton argued that if they went in a group, they would be fleeced. Drigg should go alone. Drigg had given in, as he always did. Why was it, he wondered, not for the first or last time, that although he had once saved Frogmorton's life, it was always he, Drigg, who felt indebted?

'Five girls,' Annie said.

Drigg jerked. 'Er, yes. Five.' He thought he had better explain. 'They're to play at a concert.'

'A concert!' Annie echoed. 'My, sir, they must be accomplished.' The candle dripped and Annie, shielding it, curtailed the light. Drigg felt Annie was a nice girl. She would help him do the right thing. 'They *are* accomplished. They're to play for husbands at a concert party. That is, the concert's to attract husbands. After the concert, offers will be made for them, which is why we need a good pianoforte, one that can fill a large drawing room, or perhaps a saloon. We may have the concert at home, we may have it elsewhere, so we really need what I think is called a "grand". We want our girls to have the best. Our girls deserve the best.' His confidence grew as he spoke. Why shouldn't his idea be a success?

'Of course, sir,' Annie said. Her voice grew wistful. 'If your girls want love to flourish, what better way than through music?' Annie did not usually betray her soul's romance except at the keyboard, but she felt there was romance in what Drigg told her and was happy to encourage it.

Drigg was happy to be encouraged. 'Love?' he confided. 'Between you and me, I don't think they know much about that. It's not a consideration. Getting on's the thing.'

'Love's a good way of getting on, at least in music,' Annie said. 'To make good music you must know about love.' She believed this utterly.

Drigg was indulgent. 'My dear, I suppose girls like you set great store by love, since, as they say, love is blind. But you see, that's not the way our girls look at love. They've no need.' He closed the lid of the pianoforte with a thump.

'Thank you,' said Annie, her tone much colder. She could see the proposed concert now. This man's satin-skinned daughters, their rosebud lips; the fluffy playing, the false adulation, the offers, the ring, the wedding party and the faultless children to follow. After a long moment, she said, 'Come,' in her shop-keeper's voice. 'I see now that you need quite a different sort of pianoforte.' She blew out the candle, lowered the lamp and led into darkness.

In an alcove apart was a large instrument. Annie swept off the covers. Its brutally handsome frame bore no trace of the experiments with detachable hitchpins, gut liftrails and skin-packed hammers to which her father had subjected it. Inside, although everything was fixed, nothing was quite mended, and as a result the pianoforte was unpredictable as a nervy carriage-horse. The keys, when depressed, sometimes clanged, sometimes made no noise at all. Strings were always bursting and scraping over their fellows. This pianoforte was destined for butchery. Even Cantabile agreed.

'This, sir, is just the pianoforte for your purposes,' Annie said. 'We've been waiting for that very special customer. It was too expensive for the Duke of Granchester. But you, sir, with your marvellous girls so anxious to get on, won't begrudge the money. Would you like to hear it?' She did not wait for a reply.

Annie knew this carriage-horse. She alone knew how to coax it, drive it, steady it and, more importantly, how to weave its percussive hiccups into the counterpoint. Under her fingers, it would bend its head and accept a rein meant for a harpsichord. This was the pianoforte this Mr Drigg and his dreadful girls deserved. Annie chose to play Maria Barthélemon's sonatas, works that her father had come to admire after meeting the lady herself. He had sent Mrs Barthélemon his compliments. Mrs Barthélemon had sent these, with a dedication.

To warm the instrument, she spread a chord and executed two quick runs in thirds and sixths. Drigg clapped his hands over his ears. 'Mary have mercy! The noise! The clacking of those keys will bring the house down.'

Annie paused. 'You wanted a grand pianoforte,' she said. 'This is the sound they make.' She half got up.

'No – no,' said Drigg, removing his hands. 'Sit down. I was only surprised. I've never heard one' – he did not want to confess to 'ever' – 'so very close.' He stepped back.

Annie started again, the larghetto, not the allegro. She concentrated. If the music was to work its magic, she needed more from this pianoforte than a grudging acceptance of her instructions. She scolded; she flirted; she ordered; she cajoled. After fifteen bars, the pianoforte submitted. Together, they set to work on Drigg.

Drigg had no idea of music. There was none in the foundling

hospital in which he, usually snivelling, and Frogmorton, superior because his mother had left him with a name grander than her own, had been raised. There was no music on the lighters on which Drigg had spent five years coal-heaving before he pulled a drowning Frogmorton out of the low-tide slime of the Thames, a rescue that set him on the road to riches. His discerning expressions were entirely sham. Once he grew accustomed to the sound, dimmer and more clinging than the sharp pluck of the harpsichord, there was no sham in the trembling far beneath the skin, a trembling that increased to a nostalgic twitch as the music revived memories of Mrs Drigg on their wedding night. How shy she had been. The tone changed. Now he was reminded of Marianne's childish ringlets – sadly long gone – and the tiny eyelashes of his poor dead son. His mouth opened slightly. Through some trick of memory, he could hear a mother sing. Perhaps it was his own. His eyes pricked.

When the music stopped, he forced away the pricks and twitches and cleared his throat. One thing was clear: if Marianne and Everina could play this instrument as Annie had just done, so moving, so pure, there would be offers for them before the concert had finished. This was important. Drigg's fatherly affection did not blind him to the fact that his daughters were too like their mother for complacency. Currently, both were soft and plump, but soon they would be tough and fleshy – more likely to pick up a butcher than a baronet. Once thought, this could not be unthought. He spoke as soon as he was able. 'A glorious instrument, my dear, and after that first shock, how well it sounds. Shall we return to your father?'

It was dark. Annie may have smiled.

'I'll have the large pianoforte in the back, Mr Cantabile,' Drigg said, rhyming 'Cantabile' with 'crocodile'. He took a part-printed banknote out of his pocket. 'You know, the one too dear for the Duke of Granchester. Oh, and I'll need the name of the person who taught your daughter. She plays with great skill. How much shall I write?' He unfolded the note and picked up Cantabile's quill. He was in a hurry now.

Vittorio Cantabile ignored Drigg. He eyed Annie up and down. 'That black piano, eh?' Annie stared straight back at him. Cantabile thought, She's a wily one, this Annie of mine. Why not let the black devil loose to do its worst? Annie thought, Don't deny me this small revenge, Father. Surely even to you I'm worth more than this City creature. Cantabile offered the tiniest of nods. Annie felt as if he had embraced her.

'And a teacher?' Cantabile asked. 'Can't your girl play, Mr—?' He did not care to remember the name. 'Not much point in having a pianoforte, and certainly not that black one, if she can't play.'

Drigg bridled. 'Of course my daughters – I have two – can play. All the girls can play. Naturally, they'll need help moving from harpsichord to pianoforte, and I've heard that these instruments need to be well regulated. A teacher is skilled in that too, I believe.'

'All the girls?' Cantabile's face turned to stone. Like Annie, he saw a parade of girlish perfection. Perfect daughters for this man! Where was the justice in that? 'How many girls have you?' He spat the word 'girls' as though it were a disease. Annie took Drigg's note and removed the lid from the inkwell.

'The instrument is to be shared,' said Drigg, fiddling with his wig. 'Although perhaps my Marianne and Everina could have special tuition, at home, on our present instrument, as well as on this one, just to – well, to help perfect their technique?' He often forgot about Georgiana Brass, but Harriet Frogmorton's trim beauty and Alathea Sawneyford's disturbing charms

17

loomed. Marianne and Everina must be best at something. 'The girls are to give a concert, you see,' he said in tones he thought commanding.

Mr Cantabile watched Annie smoothing Drigg's note. 'If you want a good teacher, why not take Annie herself? There's no better player, and she can keep a pianoforte up to scratch. Believe me, you'll need her for the black demon she's sold you. She could help your girls at home and direct the concert from the stage. What do you say to that?'

Drigg dropped his wig-ends. 'Ah,' he said, 'I'm not – I'm not sure . . . I'm not – you see, they're – well, they're – and your daughter is—'

'My daughter's what?'

'She's . . .'

'Yes?'

'Well, you know what I mean. I mean – oh dear – I mean if she perhaps could cover herself up? Then, perhaps, it might be possible, Mr Cantabile?' – again pronounced wrongly.

'Why should she do that?'

Drigg silently appealed to Annie. She was as stony-faced as her father. 'Our name is Can-ta-bi-lé,' she said. 'The end does not rhyme with "vile". It has two syllables: *i* and *é*.'

Drigg felt he had doubly insulted her, but how could he apologise without saying rather more than he meant?

'I'm willing to teach your daughters,' Annie said. And how I'll teach them, she thought. I'll teach them their just deserts. Her eyes almost sparkled.

'But we cannot have you,' Drigg cried. 'You must see.' He could not look at Annie now.

Cantabile was waving his hammer. 'I don't see at all. You'll get no teacher as good as her, and you'll get used to the lip.' He cackled. 'Useful thing, in fact! If you've sons, there's no need to worry.' He glanced slyly at Drigg's crotch. 'No one will ever want Annie in that way, eh!' He lunged forward and poked Annie's ribs. 'Though I'm not sure she believes me. You don't, do you, Annie? You sometimes dream of marriage in that bed of yours?' He peered at her, suddenly realising he had hit a nerve. 'Well, well! I think you do! I really think you do!' He gave a little crow. 'Annie a wife! Why not?' He peered at her again. Yes, he was right. Well, he'd show her what he thought of that. 'I suppose you'd be happy with a blind man?' He threw this at her, then grinned at Drigg. 'Do you agree, sir? I mean, if a blind man heard Annie play at a concert he might imagine that only a beautiful girl could create such a beautiful sound. But oh, the horror of a kiss!' He could not resist. 'He'd think he'd married a squid or an oyster! The sogginess! The slipperiness! Leave a mark on a man like a snail.'

All sparkle was extinguished in the flood of Annie's flush. That earlier silent communion with her father over Drigg had been a trap. She should have known. Her concert dream tottered. Her belief that her music could triumph over her deformity began to shrink, her vision of Monsieur kneeling before her to fragment. She tried to blot out her father and bolster her belief, reminding herself that when she was twelve, Monsieur Belladroit had arrived at the workshop worn out and sad and she had played from Herr Bach's *Well-Tempered Clavier*. After, Monsieur had kissed her like a grown-up. Not on the lips, to be sure. Nearby. Eyes open. Certainly, Monsieur had not been back to London since then, but that did not matter. In the years of his absence, her dream concert had taken real shape. She knew what she would play and in what order. She knew what she would wear. She knew what she would say to Monsieur as he took her hands.

But no matter how hard she fought to keep her dream clean and clear, her father, with his guess, had poisoned it. Even as she struggled, she knew she would never again dream without his tainting intrusion, never again imagine Monsieur's words of love without hearing her father's mockery. Monsieur would never kiss her. She stopped struggling and stood helpless as her dream darkened and soured.

Drigg blustered into the silence. 'Of course Annie is – of course such a girl would be – of course there's no question ...' He was out of his depth. 'Now, look here. You must understand. Sorry as I am for your daughter, Can-ta-bi-lé, and really, her, er, her, her *affliction* is hardly that bad – I see worse, far worse almost every day. But we need everything to be perfect so we simply cannot have her.'

'Well then, you cannot have the pianoforte!' Cantabile twirled the hammer and shot Annie a bolt of pure malice.

Annie leaned hard on the desk. She was hardly aware of making a decision, but a decision was made. She refused to cry. She refused to shake. There would be no tremor in the floor as she crumpled, because she would not crumple. She went straight to her father's pride and joy. Cantabile, quick to understand, tried to slam the lid. Annie thwarted him with a shoulder strong enough to unbalance. She sat down. Haydn's Capriccio in C Major sprang from her fingers, spirited, charming, ruthlessly in time. Cantabile righted himself and tried to push Annie off the stool. Drigg, emboldened by the music, was quick. He rushed forward and knocked the hammer from Cantabile's hand. The men seized each other and rocked round the instruments, grappling and grunting. Drigg was short but strong. Cantabile, whose fighting method was the random flail and kick, wasted himself hurling abuse. In the end, and without much trouble, Drigg neatly crushed Cantabile's arms together and they stood locked in a wrestler's embrace.

All the while, Annie played. It did not matter that Cantabile continued to shout. The music drowned the man. Through the grunts and groans, Drigg listened with new wonder. This sound, this particular sound, was exactly what he wanted. Brighter than the black pianoforte, less smoky, less troubling, this pianoforte caused shudders, yes, but nothing discomfiting – more like shudders of joy. What had he been thinking? He almost blushed. Compared to this instrument, the other was improper. He saw that now. A narrow escape. This pianoforte was the one. It sang like a bird, flowed like water, fortified like wine, and its virginal innocence was just the thing for virginal girls. How could two instruments called the same name be so different? No matter. As Annie drew everything from the brown pianoforte that it had to give, the pauses in the music tantalising and teasing, Drigg dismissed the black pianoforte out of hand. Forget that one. This was the ship sailing into harbour, the path up the splendid aisle, the investment paying out.

He let go of Cantabile, who rushed at Annie and slammed the lid almost on her fingers. She got up and she and her father faced each other. Drigg said, thinking to be placating, 'This is a pianoforte, a pianoforte indeed!'

'Quite right, sir,' Annie said as she slid past her father and returned to the desk. 'It may not be as handsome as the other, which is why I thought it wouldn't appeal. I apologise. This is the best pianoforte in London, possibly the world. With the other instrument, your girls would amaze. With this, they'll astound.'

Cantabile once again seized his hammer. 'This pianoforte's not for sale. You can't have it.' He poked the hammer at Drigg. 'Nobody can have it.'

Drigg ignored him. 'We can pay,' he said. His note had fluttered to the floor. He picked it up and imagined himself telling Frogmorton, Brass and Sawneyford that he had secured the best pianoforte in the world. 'We'll pay top price.'

'And so you should,' Annie said, picking up the quill. 'You'll not get such a chance again. This pianoforte has six octaves and the pedals – well . . . '

'Six what? Never mind. How much?' Drigg blew sawdust from the note.

Cantabile was a dervish between them. 'I've told you, it's not for sale!'

Annie opened the inkpot. 'A small deposit, sir. You take the pianoforte and I'll send you my mother's doctor's bills.'

Drigg balked. He did not want that kind of a bargain. It was not what he was used to.

Cantabile was beside himself. 'The girl has no authority. The pianoforte's not hers to sell! If you lay a finger on it, I'll have you for theft.'

'The best pianoforte for your concert; the best husbands for your daughters; the best treatment for my mother. Is that not fair?' Annie asked, the quill held out.

'I'd rather just pay.' Drigg tried not to hear the increasing violence of Cantabile's threats.

'That's the bargain. Take it or leave it.' Annie laid the quill down.

'Well, I'm—'

'You'll not have it! You won't!' Cantabile's hammer whistled passed Drigg's nose.

Drigg suddenly hated him. 'We'll have it,' he said to Annie. 'We'll damned well have it on any terms.'

'You won't,' shouted Cantabile. 'This pianoforte goes nowhere.'

Annie locked eyes with her father. His were burning. Hers were cool. 'My father speaks ill of the King,' she said, enunciating each word carefully.

'What?' said Drigg. 'Everybody speaks ill of—'

Annie interrupted. 'My father has French pamphlets. Here

in London there are groups of foreigners who are no friends to England—'

'Be quiet!' shouted Cantabile. 'I'm not French. I've no sympathy with the chicanery going on over the sea.'

Annie leaned forward and whispered into Drigg's ear. For the first time in his life, Cantabile was afraid. Annie straightened up. Her father was silent. 'The pianoforte goes with you,' Annie said to Drigg.

'Shall we say next week for delivery?' Drigg crammed his hat on. He had heard not a word of Annie's whisper, if indeed she had whispered anything. He just wanted to get out.

'Certainly,' Annie said.

'And I'll pay a lump sum.' Drigg seized the quill and scribbled an amount on to his banknote, then, for want of more paper, turned the note over and scribbled down Frogmorton's Manchester Square address. He did not want Cantabile turning up at the Drigg establishment in Stratton Street. He blotted the ink firmly and made for the door. With his hand already on the doorknob, a noise caused him to turn. Cantabile had his mouth open. For a moment, Drigg wondered if the man was having some kind of seizure. Then he realised Cantabile was laughing. Drigg shook his fist. Cantabile held up his hands in mock-surrender. 'I won't have my pianoforte played badly at your concert. You do need a teacher.'

'We've been through that.'

'Not Annie. Forget her. You need a true master. I know just the man.'

The door was already open. Escape! Drigg tossed caution to the wind. 'I accept your offer, Mr Cantabile. We'll pay your man so long as he produces the desired result. Now, if our business is concluded I really must go. Good-day to you both.' He threw the door wide and was assaulted by the scrum of the street and a chorus of 'Wotcha, Frenchie! Fuzzy-wig! Fuzzy-wig!' He walked fast, without looking back. Thank God that was over. He took a cab straight to the V&B and sat at the long trestle with a bowl of coffee, treacle-thick. He felt cold and hot, then hot and cold. When Mrs W's tabby cat pushed against his leg, he pushed her away. The cat leapt on to the lid of the great water urn that swung and hissed above the fire. Drigg drank his coffee and, to steady himself, watched the cat pad round the lid before settling down to warm her behind. Swing, gurgle, purr. Swing, gurgle, purr. Gradually, Drigg felt more at ease. He got up and stroked the cat. Her life contained no pianofortes, no daughters, no Annie, no Cantabile. 'Just at this moment, I envy you,' he said before swallowing the last of his coffee, straightening his wig and heading back to the City to make up for lost time.

The second Drigg closed the door of the workshop, Cantabile slapped Annie hard across the cheek. 'What did you whisper to that man?' Annie said nothing. Cantabile slapped her again. 'Blackmail is not pretty in a woman.' He spun away from her, opened the lid of the pianoforte and blew gently over the keys. He closed the lid. He would not look at it again.

Grabbing a bottle from one shelf and a dirty glass from another, he poured wine and set the bottle on the desk with a thump. 'I'm going to send them Claude Belladroit as teacher,' he threw out. Annie still said nothing. 'I'll write to him today. He appreciates beautiful girls, *fully appreciates* them' – his lip curled – 'and even ugly girls if they're rich.' He gulped his wine. 'Do you know, I believe I might persuade him it's time he settled down with a wife. Why shouldn't he marry one of these concert puffballs, then leave her when the money runs out?' He drank some more. 'Wait! Why doesn't Claude seduce them all while he's about it? That would be a pleasant task for him, and the girls' ruin would be some revenge for my pianoforte.' He

24

finished his wine and crunched the glass until it splintered, a favourite trick. Annie braced herself against the rough finger he scraped down the back of her neck. 'Claude Belladroit with those girls. Dream about that, Annie.' He laughed as he headed for the stairs, but Annie knew he would sob for his darling pianoforte tonight. Once in her own bed, she did not dream about the girls: she thought about them, wide awake, and when at last she closed her eyes she dreamed of nothing at all.

2

THE girls were taking tea at Stratton Street, Everina Drigg their giggling hostess, Marianne glowering from double chin to thick eyebrows because she, as the elder sister, should have been in charge of the tea kettle. All five girls had been singing. Music was strewn on and between tables with barley-twist legs and sofas almost too plump for comfort. When the five girls sang together, the picture reflected in the long mirror was pleasing, mainly because all were young – only Marianne had reached eighteen – and when they sang, the pleasure in their eyes, the stretching of their necks and the rise and fall of silk-covered breasts softened their defects. This softening was particularly necessary for Everina, whose teeth had been expensively and unsubtly replaced when her real ones became painful and discoloured. But Everina was not alone in needing help. No amount of ribbon or skill could fatten Marianne's disappointing hair, and although it would probably do no good, Harriet Frogmorton, who by age came between the Drigg sisters, was right to clip her nose with a clothes-peg every night since its roundness spoiled an otherwise lively face atop a neat, trim body. Of the other two girls, Georgiana Brass's defects were difficult to pinpoint – since she had given up eating, it was difficult to see much of her at all – and Alathea Sawneyford was, as Mrs Frogmorton and Mrs Drigg often remarked, an astonishment. It was hard to pick out a single extraordinary characteristic. Her dark hair was remarkable only because it was cut short, and her skin, compared to Harriet's and Georgiana's, was sallow. Yet one thing was certain: men saw Alathea and wanted her, as men eating eggs want salt. In the eyes of Mrs Frogmorton and Mrs Drigg, this was a defect nothing could soften.

Harriet was not thinking of anybody's defects now, and certainly not her own. She wanted a cup of tea and Everina was being particularly slow. 'The tea is ready, Alathea. Come and sit with us,' Harriet said, aiming her remark straight at Everina. Alathea left the harpsichord from which she had been accompanying the singing and settled herself on a chair. 'Now we're all set,' Harriet said, and was relieved to see Everina pick up the tea strainer and begin to pour.

At once Marianne was on her feet. 'For goodness' sake! You shouldn't be in charge of the kettle! You don't even make tea properly,' she complained loudly, curling her lip. 'Just look at it. Slop-water.'

Everina, unabashed, carried on pouring. 'That's all tea is, expensive slop-water. You said so yourself when Mamma told us how much it cost.'

'At least I manage to pour it properly. Look at the mess you've made.' Marianne pointed at extensive puddles and drips.

'I'd pour much better if you'd leave me alone,' said Everina, still unabashed, 'and *we* don't have to clear it up.'

'Oh, do be quiet, both of you,' said Harriet, her patience

giving out. 'Are you going to give us some of this tea? I don't care if it's slop-water.'

Marianne, still glowering, sat down again, and Everina began to distribute dripping saucers. As soon as she'd had her tea, Harriet felt better. She turned to Georgiana Brass, sitting next to her on a sofa. 'I've brought a shade I think suits me.'

Along with her nose, Harriet had recently begun to worry about her lips. She found them too thin and was a keen experimenter with lip colour, sometimes to comical effect that she was not above acknowledging. She had at her feet a basket filled with powder and paste as entertainment after the music until the carriage should call to take her home. 'I know it's bright, but lips should be bright.' She put down her cup, picked a pot from her basket, smoothed on some grease, made a large *o* and laughed at her reflection.

Sulky Marianne offered an opinion without looking. 'You look like a doll. Lips should be natural.' Marianne disapproved of Harriet's new interest although she herself used rouge every day, Everina, with sisterly slyness, assuring her that whatever their mother's warnings, the look was sophisticated.

'I think our dolls always looked very fine,' Harriet said, frowning. She knew it was silly, but she could never shake off her childish notion that dolls could hear, and the girls were not so grown-up that all remnants of their childhoods had been tidied away. Behind the harpsichord, a large dolls' house was still installed in the corner where it had been unwrapped ten Christmases ago, Marianne ruling its miniature household until Everina kidnapped her favourite doll and refused to release her until Marianne's bossy grip was relaxed. The dolls, too, were still present, stacked in a painted chest next to the house. When Mrs Drigg, thinking to please, had tried to banish them, declaring the girls too old for nursery distractions, Georgiana Brass had begged her to leave them, or, if they must be banished, to be allowed to take them home with her. This set up an immediate clamour from both Marianne and Everina who, though they had lost interest in the dolls themselves, certainly did not want Georgiana to have them.

Even as she dipped her little finger into the pot of red paste Harriet held out, Georgiana Brass looked longingly at the chest. 'I wonder how they are,' she said and, unsure what to do with the paste, wiped it over the palm of her hand. Rouge would have improved Georgiana. In repose, she comprised only a wave of corn-coloured hair and a pair of empty eyes. There were bones inside her clothes, but little else. She could not remember why she had given up eating, or when. She knew only that she must not start again because if she did she would solidify into a person, and she had no idea what kind of person she could possibly be. When the girls were together, she always chose to be near Harriet because Harriet's stance on everything, from allocating singing parts to cutting fingernails, was reassuringly practical. Harriet was sometimes impatient with Georgiana's inability to decide even the best way out of a door. Nevertheless, she always made room for her, for which Georgiana was grateful.

'Do you remember the day we dressed your doll like the Duchess of Devonshire, Everina?' Harriet asked.

Everina laughed. 'The feathers Alathea stole from the draper are still in the box.'

Harriet put away her pots, went to the chest and opened it. 'Yes, look,' she said, kneeling down and secretly apologising to the dolls if their feelings had been hurt. 'She's still wearing them. Oh! And' – she delved right in and brought out a tiny wooden rocking horse – 'look, Georgiana! You gave this to Marianne the birthday she had scarlet fever.'

Memories, even for girls not yet old enough to have many,

are irresistible. Heads were soon bent over the chest, pulling things out and correcting each other's 'I'm sure this was mine' with an 'I'm sure it wasn't'. The dolls' clothes, tight-bodiced and square-necked, were declared hopelessly out of fashion and it was decided that new clothes would be made, although only Georgiana actually meant it.

Alathea held back. For a month or two she had coveted that little rocking horse, but she had never liked dolls. They had been given to her, of course, and were now in the chest with the others. She did not wish to reclaim or even look at them. Instead, she wondered how Mrs Drigg had ever imagined maroon velvet, lime-green silk, pink brocade and ochre paint would create a room in which it was pleasing to entertain. She flicked through a much-thumbed romantic novella that Everina had left lying about.

At last the girls closed up the chest and Everina called for more tea. 'Bring cake, too, Sam,' she said to the mulatto waiting-boy. 'The vanilla one with the cherries.' The boy vanished and came back laden.

'I'll make the tea this time,' said Marianne.

'Oh, do,' said Everina. 'I'll be counting the drips.'

Harriet settled back next to Georgiana. 'Look,' she said, twitching up her skirt. She had been waiting for the right moment to show off a pair of new shoes. To Harriet's disappointment, Georgiana appeared not to hear, and indeed Georgiana did not. Since Sam had arrived with more tea, Georgiana saw only the cake and heard only the imploring of her stomach. She could attend to nothing else. Food was the enemy. She must not give in. No cake. No cake. Why had Everina called for it? She waved away the plate Sam offered, and he took it to Alathea, who plucked out a cherry, held it between two fingers and licked it.

When Alathea's tongue was out, it mesmerised. In terms of

years, it was still a novice. In terms of imagination and experiment, it was quite advanced. Before the age of thirteen she had worked out that the tongue – the physical tongue, that is, not the wordy tongue – was a woman's unsuspected weapon, attracting and repelling, drawing in and excluding, and all without even touching an opponent – Alathea classified most people as opponents. She knew her tongue well and was getting to know it better. Servants like Sam were dull experimental subjects, though. Not like the hangman, the thought of whom made her smile. Her living flesh must have contrasted very warmly with the dead.

Harriet could wait no longer. She took off a shoe and thrust it into Georgiana's hand. 'See, Georgiana! Straight from the foot of a noble Frenchie. Aren't they fancy?'

Georgiana forced her attention on to the shoe. A small garden scene had been painted on the heel. 'How do you know they came from someone noble?'

'It was picked up at the guillotine, silly. There's lots of shoes like this to be had from France right now. Father gets them, though he tells Mother they were made in London. You know how she is about foreign things.'

'Can you walk in them?'

'Why on earth would I want to do that?' Harriet slipped the shoe back on. 'They're for parties.'

'Let me see.' Marianne peered over. 'Is that blood on the toe?'

Harriet whipped the shoe back off. 'Oh,' she said, nonplussed.

They all inspected the stain.

'Blood, for certain,' said Everina, scraping at a piece of cherry stuck between her implausible teeth.

'It'll wash out,' said Harriet uncertainly.

Alathea, tongue in, reached for the shoe and sniffed it. 'A

young girl's blood,' she said. The girls shivered. Trust Alathea to know. She knew everything, and if she did not know, she fabricated, her tales always purporting to be about one thing when afterwards they realised, or thought they realised, that the tales were about something else, usually something disquieting. Still, true or fabricated or somewhere in between, Alathea's tales always added spice to otherwise dull days.

'Take the tea away, Sam,' Harriet ordered the boy. 'Go on! Quick!' She never worried about assuming command, even in somebody else's house.

'Miss Everina?' The boy had learned not to cross either her or her sister. Everina's elbow was sharp and Marianne's foot heavy. 'Miss Marianne?'

'Oh, you heard!' Marianne brushed crumbs from her lap. She resented Alathea, but she wanted to hear the story. The boy collected the tray and slunk out, casting a last glance at Alathea. She blinked at him. For a second he was in heaven.

'Now, Alathea,' Harriet said. 'Go on. Tell us about the girl.'

Alathea picked up a dropped crumb. Catching Georgiana's eye, she crushed it between her teeth. 'A girl like you, Georgiana. Maybe she actually looked like you. I expect she was stripped to her petticoat before she faced the guillotine. Perhaps *of* it, too.'

'Honestly, Alathea,' said Harriet uncomfortably. 'Do you have to?'

'She'd have been wearing her best petticoat,' Alathea said, her face completely straight. 'Remember I told you of the girl I passed the other day, who strung herself up in the City? She was in her petticoat. It's obviously the fashionable thing to wear for death.' It was a lie. The dead girl had been fully dressed. Still, Alathea thought, she was wearing a petticoat under her skirt. That was truth enough.

'It's unseemly, you wandering about the City alone,' said Marianne. 'Our mother would never allow it.'

'I don't have a mother.'

Marianne reddened. How stupid to present Alathea with an opportunity to remind them. 'Father, then,' she said.

'What had happened to that poor girl?' asked Harriet, frowning at Marianne, who mouthed, 'Well, it *is* unseemly.' 'Did you know her?'

Alathea waited until all eyes were focused on her again. 'Her story's clear enough,' she said, sidestepping Harriet's last question.

'Is it?' said Everina with a shudder. 'Most stories don't end with a hanging.'

'It was a garrotting,' corrected Alathea. 'She did it herself and who can blame her?' She curled up in the chair. 'Her story's sadder than the guillotine girl's.'

Georgiana, Harriet and Everina gazed at Alathea in dreadful expectation, and, as one, left their seats and settled cross-legged on the floor around her. Marianne sat too, fooling nobody in her pretence of examining a stain in the carpet. She was as much in thrall to Alathea as any of the others.

'She was an only daughter,' Alathea began, 'much beloved of her parents. They lived – her parents still live – in a big house in Lincoln's Inn Fields, filled with with pretty things.' She paused.

'What kind of pretty things?' Everina prompted. 'Seashells and kittens, things like that?'

'Oh no,' said Alathea. 'I mean paintings and jewels and things that you buy. Things you don't throw away.'

'You don't throw kittens away,' Everina pointed out, 'or shells, if they've been given to you by a friend.'

'Do be quiet, Everina,' said Harriet. 'What was the girl's name, Alathea?'

'Her name was Raphaella, and the house was full of people and music and everybody was happy. It could have lasted for ever, except that a man came, a musician. He played many instruments, but when he touched a keyboard, everybody wanted to listen. And he was beautiful to look at – young and strong, with clear eyes and the kind of body you see in books on anatomy.'

'You've seen books on anatomy?' Harriet, startled, could not help herself.

'Of course,' said Alathea. 'Don't you want to know how men are made?'

'I – I—' stammered Harriet, for whom curiosity about men's bodies was restricted to private thoughts. 'I don't think about them,' she said lamely. Alathea raised an eyebrow.

'I once saw Sam relieving himself against the garden wall,' said Everina with an inevitable giggle. 'It was – well . . . '

'Oh,' said Georgiana, horrified.

'Don't be coarse, Everina.' Marianne was at her most reproving.

'You looked too,' retorted Everina. 'You said—'

'That's enough,' Marianne barked.

Alathea shrugged. 'All I'm saying is that if you'd been Raphaella, you'd have wanted him.'

'You mean, fallen in love with him,' Marianne corrected.

'As you like,' said Alathea. 'He and Raphaella began to play duets together. They were marvellous, and Raphaella soon found the two hours the musician spent at their house each day were the only hours that meant anything. The rest of the time was dead. But though she waited and waited, he never asked her to marry him. At first she wondered if he ranked himself too far beneath her. But he always came through the front door, never the servants' entrance. Then she wondered if he had too little money for marriage. But his clothes were respectable and

34

his horses shining. Then it came to her: he didn't know she loved him. She hadn't made it plain. She puzzled how to do this. It's hard for a girl. But she plucked up her courage and told him straight. And he did something terrible.'

The girls were agog.

'He laughed,' said Alathea.

Marianne snorted. 'That doesn't seem so terrible.'

Alathea said, 'She told him he was everything to her. She told him she would abandon family and friends for him. She told him she loved him more than music. She offered herself to him body and soul. And he laughed. He might as well have stabbed her in the heart with the heel of one of Harriet's new shoes.'

Harriet scrutinised Alathea's face. Was that a tremor of real pity, or a tremor of contempt at their gullibility? Had there been a garrotted girl at all? Harriet was never sure of anything about Alathea. She never spoke about herself. They were never invited to her house. All that Harriet knew for certain was that under that dark halo of hair, Alathea could seem saintly and demonic at the same time.

'Did she slap him?' Everina was asking. 'I'd have slapped him.'

'She didn't touch him,' Alathea answered. 'She felt the fault was hers. If a man who could make such music with her didn't love her, she couldn't be loved by anybody, so she cut a string from her harpsichord – it was bass A, a mournful note, don't you think? – and when the musician left, she followed him into the City. At the top of Threadneedle Street, he turned and saw her. They exchanged glances; Raphaella held out a hand. She held it out as far as she could stretch it. The musician raised his hand. He raised it high. Then he waved goodbye and ran away. That's when she twisted the wire into a noose, borrowed a flower girl's stool, slipped one end of the wire over the arm of a barber's sign and—' Sam returned for the cakestand just as Alathea raised her chin in imitation of the girl.

'The musician rushed back and tried to save her, surely!' implored Georgiana.

'Why?' Alathea's chin was still raised. 'He doesn't love her.'

'But she loves him so!' Georgiana cried.

Alathea's chin dropped. 'Snap,' she said gaily.

3

NO. 23 Manchester Square, March creeping in. The piano-forte materialised out of the morning, shrouded in blankets on an undertaker's cart. The complanatory vibrations were loud enough to alert servants and mistresses all down Spanish Place and into the square itself. There was a pause for gawping amid discussions about the removal of winter drapes.

Grace Frogmorton stood at her own window (whatever the temperature, she removed neither winter drapes nor woollen petticoat until May). She patted a new hairpiece and frowned. A bald turnspit dog, recently retired from kitchen duties, whined to be picked up. 'What's this, Frilly?' Mrs Frogmorton said, bending stiff knees to oblige. She had been expecting the pianoforte for the past four days and now she was mortified. An undertaker's cart! Typical of Drigg.

She often wished it had not been Drigg who had rescued her husband when his early apprenticeship with a corn merchant had ended abruptly. One moment sweet, dusty corn; neat figures in the ledger; a tutorly finger explaining the balance sheet;

two oat-fed daughters to ogle. Next a roar, a club, a charge of short shrifting, a smash and grab, yellow corn peppering black mud, the mob swirling and shrieking, the daughters shrieking and swirling, the corn merchant blustering, begging and finally hanging from a gallows made of his own rigged scales. Frogmorton and two other apprentices were lucky only to be tossed into the Thames. Mrs Frogmorton had to be grateful that Drigg's strong arms had hauled Archibald out, and it was true that Drigg's eyes and ears at the docks had proved indispensable to her husband's ventures. Nevertheless, Mrs Frogmorton had never thought much of him. She hoped the servants at That Place, as she called Spanish-occupied Manchester House, were not looking, or, worse still, The Spy (as she called the Spanish Ambassador himself). Didn't Drigg realise that despite the foreign element, Manchester Square was a world away from Stratton Street? 'A world away,' she muttered. Frilly yapped. And the thing now waiting outside her front door had cost enough, or so Mr Frogmorton had told her.

Neither Alderman nor Mrs Frogmorton knew anything of Annie Cantabile or her father. Drigg had meant to tell them everything next time they met in the V&B, but Gregory Brass had upset the whole afternoon, clattering in clutching *Spence's Penny Weekly* and shouting about votes and taxes and how Spence and his like should be hanged for traitors. When Drigg observed that Spence was already in prison, Brass had exploded. 'Prison! Bah! A public lynching's the thing. That'd teach him. I mean, the poor can't eat the vote, or fornicate with it, so what use is it to them?'

The alderman had quickly taken charge of the penny weekly, using it as a wedge to stop the table rocking, but Drigg had lost courage, and had declared only that he had bought a pianoforte and that the cost had been £80 – slightly more than quoted but less, he asserted, than the pianoforte's true worth.

A teacher would present himself in due course. Long friendship brings trust, and Drigg's story had been accepted without question.

Since nothing had been said of a man coming atop the instrument, Monsieur Belladroit's elegant dismounting took Mrs Frogmorton by surprise. She drew back and would have declared herself out, as Harriet really was, if a maid had not already indicated she was in by calling her name. She must go down. On her front doorstep, Monsieur seized her hand and kissed it delicately before raising a face finely boned, with remarkably straight eyebrows and shoulder-length hair tied in a plain brown bow. Frilly commenced a monotonous bark. Mrs Frogmorton pulled the dog closer, reducing the bark to a yap and two marble-eyes bulging from her bosom. 'I was not expecting a man,' she said.

'Just the pianoforte tuner and teacher, *madame*. Excuse me.' He hurled a torrent of invective at the kite-tail of urchins behind the cart, produced a pistol and fired. The urchins fled, except the one Monsieur managed to bring down. The boy howled and hopped, spraying blood. Monsieur wiped the pistol's barrel. He turned back to Mrs Frogmorton. 'I shall unload.'

Mrs Frogmorton was both impressed by his marksmanship and alarmed by his accent. A foreigner. She had never had one across the threshold. 'The boy—' she said.

'What boy? I have not brought a boy.'

Mrs Frogmorton raised her hand to indicate the shot boy, and found a beribboned note pressed into it. 'Claude Belladroit. My credentials.' French, that was it, thought Mrs Frogmorton. Those *th*s hissed into *z*s. Those rolled *r*s. This man was French. She felt quite flustered. He must be a Catholic, and probably part of the nonsense going on over the sea. Yet it was those neat, straight eyebrows that now gripped her attention. She had

39

never seen such eyebrows. Had they been plucked into shape? And his lips seemed to be quivering, as though waiting for her permission to smile.

'*Madame?*' He appeared very anxious for her approval.

Mrs Frogmorton stood straight. She understood at once that she was being charmed. That was what foreigners did. She resented it. The man did not appear to notice her resentment. A quick flash of small, even teeth, then a sharp berating of the muscle hired to shift the pianoforte. They must hurry, since Madame Frogmorton had emerged without overshoes or cloak, Monsieur said. Quick, quick now. Mrs Frogmorton was startled. Her husband would never have noticed if she was cold. Monsieur ran up the steps and Mrs Frogmorton could only follow as he zealously inspected the disposition of the downstairs rooms. In the street, the pianoforte was dismounted, body first, the mechanism groaning like an amputee, its wooden frame a set of prosthetic limbs carried behind.

As the pianoforte was brought indoors Monsieur verbally beat the muscle without cease. 'This is a home, you clowns, not a warehouse! Take care of the statuary. Mind the pillars. Do not even brush the paint. Do not displace a single speck of dust on any of this big brown furniture, should we find dust in this home, which I doubt. Get on! Do I have to carry the instrument myself?' Once the whole pianoforte was safely in the hall, he ran out and threw the carter a tip like a slap in the face. 'Get this contraption away. It is a disgrace.' He ran back into the house. 'Upstairs?'

Mrs Frogmorton meant to expostulate. Instead she said, 'Upstairs on the right. The harpsichord has been moved to accommodate.'

The only flaw was the fuss Monsieur made over the instrument's exact placing in the drawing room. Mrs Frogmorton wanted it under the chandelier, sideways to the door, the centrepiece to a room whose furniture, however she placed it, was never elegant, and whose welcome, despite a generous fireplace, never convinced. Monsieur wanted the pianoforte in the corner furthest from the fireplace, tail towards the middle of the room. Mrs Frogmorton could never remember how Monsieur won, nor why she forgave him. She only knew that she was being ushered out politely but firmly so that Monsieur could 'bed the pianoforte in' – a phrase Mrs Frogmorton had never associated with musical instruments. Foreigners, she thought. They turned even plain English upside-down.

Harriet arrived home just after midday; the other girls visited later to be told of the concert plan. Marianne and Everina Drigg were quick to say that pianofortes had not been thought well of by the Misses Lee at the Academy for Young Ladies where they had been expensively educated. Marianne also declared, with a stamp, that as the oldest of the girls and the one who knew most about music, she should have been party to any decision. Harriet had been dismayed at the thought of effort. Georgiana Brass had just been dismayed. Alathea had been curious, though she had not asked to know more. It made people uncomfortable if you found out things for yourself.

The following afternoon the girls and the three mothers were gathered in the Frogmortons' downstairs parlour, a room as unsuccessful as the drawing room though decorated more lightly, with chinoiserie on a pair of blue-veined marble-topped tables, and on a third a clock with a camel feature that Mr Frogmorton had received as a present for a favour he did not care to recall. The settles, solid and English, had come from the sudden sale of another Manchester Square house, the panelling too. Mrs Frogmorton had spotted the bailiffs from her bedroom window. There was velvet wallpaper above the panels, plain cushions, striped curtains and a fireplace that kept most of its heat to itself. Mrs Frogmorton never sat in this room when she was alone, preferring the little antechamber attached to her bedroom. There was a small stove in there which, once she had closed the door, she often tucked beneath her skirts.

Agnes Drigg was troubled by the fire. It told her she had made a mistake ordering the Stratton Street drapes taken down. The drapes should have stayed up, because in Manchester Square it was still winter and Manchester Square was never wrong. Mrs Drigg knew better than to look to Elizabeth Brass for reassurance, since Mrs Brass had no notion of drapes or anything else. Stuck in a poky house in Covent Garden for the convenience of Mr Brass's membership of Bedford's gaming club, Mrs Brass, like her daughter, found daily life a series of unanswerable questions, whether it be breakfast eggs or moving, which she longed to do, if only to stop the ladies of the night earning their money in her porch, some of it from her husband. The last question Mrs Brass clearly recollected answering was Mr Brass's proposal of marriage. She had realised soon afterwards that her own judgements must never be trusted again.

All the mothers were conscious of a pang. 'This will signal an ending of sorts,' Mrs Frogmorton had said while the girls were still upstairs admiring a music box bought for Harriet by her father and which she kept next to her bed. 'Our girls will fly away.'

'Surely we'll be welcome at their new hearths,' Mrs Drigg tried to comfort her.

'Of course, Agnes, but we'll be encumbrances. Mothers usually are. Mine certainly was.' Mrs Frogmorton could already see doors closed, secrets kept, grandchildren steered away.

'At least Alathea will be – well, you know . . .' said Mrs Drigg.

They nodded in deep understanding. None of the three had known Mrs Sawneyford. As a consequence, her looks and character were a regular subject of speculation, particularly as Alathea grew older and more bewildering. Mrs Frogmorton and

Mrs Drigg thought the girl should want a mother. It was only natural. They were both willing to shoulder the burden. She did not want a mother; that was perfectly clear. They thought she should want to be embraced. They tried. She resisted. They thought she should want to confide. Not a word. Yet they could not ignore her. They had agreed, with heavy hearts, that that would be unChristian. So she grew with their daughters, tolerated but never liked, included but never truly welcomed.

'We'll treat Alathea as if she was our own,' said Mrs Frogmorton with some effort.

'We'll try,' said Mrs Drigg, also with some effort. A mutual nod accompanied a mutual sigh.

Summoned downstairs, Harriet, Everina and Marianne sat on the settle, their skirts jostling, Harriet once again wearing the bloodied shoes which her maid had made some effort to clean. Alathea draped herself over a high-backed chair. On Marianne, spotted calico would have looked dull; on Alathea it created an intriguing map of curves. Georgiana, on another high-backed chair, had arranged her bones in a tent of figured silk through which her neck stuck like a flagpole. She had agonised over the choice of gown and now realised she had dressed for an entertainment, not an introduction to a music master. Her miscalculation consumed her.

Mrs Frogmorton, fully conscious of her advantage as hostess, moved about the room like one of her husband's larger freighters. 'Now, girls, you will be taught separately in the following order: Harriet, Georgiana, Everina, Marianne and finally Alathea. Sunday is—'

'Surely I should be taught first,' Marianne interrupted.

'Why?'

'I'm the oldest.'

'What difference does that make?'

'I just think—'

'For goodness' sake, Marianne, we're not deciding an inheritance.'

'I didn't say we—'

Mrs Drigg fell into a twitter. 'Now then, Marianne. But actually, Grace, isn't that a good idea? Marianne and Everina will need to come in the carriage and their father will want to get to the City afterwards, and although they could walk—'

'Walk!' Marianne was outraged.

'No, of course not. Oh dear. I wish we lived here, Grace. It's so nice in this square. When we moved to Stratton Street it was with the best intentions and now we're surrounded by Jews. Jews! Think of it! Better to have Catholics, I think.' Mrs Frogmorton frowned. 'Or perhaps not,' said Mrs Drigg hastily. 'I never quite know. What do Catholics actually do in their houses, I wonder? What view do they take on winter drapes, for example? Not that winter drapes are important. Though of course they are. Too early, yes, too early.' She subsided.

Mrs Frogmorton and Harriet exchanged a familiar look. 'I think,' said Mrs Frogmorton before Mrs Drigg could start again, 'that Stratton Street is hardly the end of Christendom. Still, if Marianne's so keen, I'm sure nobody minds if she has first lesson.'

'I don't want to go after her,' said Everina at once. She feared any comparison with Marianne's self-professed musical superiority. 'It will hardly wear out the carriage to make the journey twice.'

Mrs Frogmorton grew impatient. 'As you wish. This is the order: Marianne, Harriet, Georgiana, Everina, Alathea. Is that agreeable to everybody?'

They all nodded.

'Good. We'll leave it to "Monsieur" to suggest the number of lessons in a week. Now, what about clothes? Do you think pianoforte-playing requires a new type of garment, Elizabeth?'

44

Silence. 'Yes, I thought you might,' said Mrs Frogmorton, 'though I'm not sure you're right.'

This was how conversations with Mrs Brass were always conducted. Mrs Frogmorton and Mrs Drigg had long agreed between themselves that since Elizabeth seemed incapable of answering for herself, they would answer for her. It was a pact meant kindly and had become one of the bonds between the three mothers, bonds that were born of their husbands' close connections and that grew in strength when Grace Frogmorton, disregarding the danger, billowed into Stratton Street when Everina Drigg had the pox, kissed Mrs Drigg and held Everina's hand; when Elizabeth Brass sent a note, smudged, unsigned and saying only 'Weeping', to Grace Frogmorton after that first stillbirth; when Grace Frogmorton sent a tiny lace gown for Marianne Drigg when her own little girl (the second before Harriet) had, once again, needed only a shroud; when Elizabeth Brass turned up at Stratton Street, a weal across her face and her eyes glazed, and Agnes Drigg offered unquestioning shelter. Compared to the deep bonds of birthbed, marriage bed and deathbed, the mothers' daily mutual irritations were only a scab. That all three could remember each child the others had lost, however brief its flicker of life, was indissoluble glue. When particular anniversaries came round, something, perhaps a little cake, perhaps a posy, would arrive. Every year, each husband asked what for. The mothers felt wounded by their husbands on those days. Those wounds were bonding too.

'Tea mid-lesson?' queried Mrs Drigg. 'How big a fire should be made? Is an hour's tuition too long, do you think? Can the girls practise on their harpsichords?'

Mrs Frogmorton began to answer. Mrs Drigg begged to disagree, or agree, or both.

Alathea raised her voice. 'What are we to play?'

Cut off mid-stream, Mrs Drigg thought, Why does Alathea always sound so knowing? Why can't she chat and giggle like the others?

'I expect Monsieur Belladroit will decide,' Mrs Frogmorton said, thinking the same as Mrs Drigg.

'Let's ask him.' Alathea unfolded herself.

'Sit still.' Mrs Frogmorton felt proprietorial. This was her house and Monsieur Belladroit was, for the day, hers. She would introduce him. 'Are we ready?' she asked. They nodded. Mrs Frogmorton rang the bell.

Nobody heard his footsteps but Monsieur was among them at once, in grey breeches, dark stockings, short jacket and shoes with no buckle, his demeanour absurdly deferential – not at all the jaunty cove who had earlier left Mr Cantabile's. Only his hair was the same, although his ribbon today was black. Harriet, Marianne and Everina offered haughty greetings. Georgiana stared at her feet. Alathea's lips twitched: Well, well, what's this?

Monsieur's eyes darted. The variety of young womanhood pleased him: the soft, the elfin, the solid, the nervous, the – he could not quite categorise Alathea, which was unusually delicious. Cantabile was right. He had said the job he had for his dear Claude would be a pleasure, and it would be. Monsieur would steal the girls' virtue and be away before their new husbands discovered the cherry picked, the goods second-hand. Claude Belladroit quite envied these husbands. What a favour he was doing, enabling them to ditch the wife as sullied but keep the marriage settlement. Should he demand a cut? Unnecessary, if he took Cantabile's bonus for marrying one of the girls himself. An odd man, his old friend Cantabile. He was tight-fisted, yet he wanted to pay over and above the fee Monsieur was charging to the fathers for music lessons. But then, I'm an odd man myself, Monsieur thought.

This was nothing but the truth. With his penchant for varied personal histories and inability to settle in one place, Monsieur was not quite as others. He had welcomed the revolution in his native France, not for its ideas but because it made everybody as restless as himself, at least those not sent to their rest by Madame Guillotine. Monsieur had seen two executions: parents of pupils. It was not the blood that appalled him, or the mob. It was the tipping of the headless bodies into muddy holes of permanent dark. When he died, he wanted to be burned and scattered in the wind.

Vittorio Cantabile's invitation had come at just the right time. Monsieur stopped considering those dark and muddy holes and instead considered marriage – laughable, of course, since he could hardly bear either a landlady or a lover for more than a month.

If he were to marry one of these girls, though, which one would be the most profitable? His eyes flickered around the room, assessing the furniture, the drapes, the appalling clock. My goodness, he thought, fancy coming home to this every evening. Nevertheless, the house was solid. The fathers were City men. It would be possible to discover exact amounts. He stopped: one thing at a time. Marriage was for after, if at all. Seduction was first.

Seduction was important. Monsieur would deflower any girl from fifteen to fifty – well, perhaps not fifty. He had his standards, one of which was that, whatever the age and ugliness of the girl, he would never resort to rape. He disapproved of it. Even more, he feared a charge of it. Voluntary capitulation was the thing. That, so he had learned over many years, was what stopped girls tale-telling to parents – or at least stopped them telling before he had disappeared. He imagined they felt complicit; he encouraged them to do so. Not that it mattered if his conquests did tell. Wise parents covered up their daughters' indiscretions, as was only sensible, and in France, at least, many husbands did not care if their wives were shop-soiled. Englishmen must be ridiculously fastidious, Monsieur thought, otherwise Cantabile would not have cococted this plan. He felt flattered to be the plan's executor. He had never seduced an English girl before, let alone five. He rose on tiptoe then subsided. Getting these creatures to capitulate would be a charming exercise. He would, however, lace determination with caution.

'*Mesdemoiselles!*' He took each of the girls' hands in turn and peered at their faces. Why did portraitists depict women as flat-skinned with pearly teeth and red lips? Women were not flat, or pearly, or red. Women's skin was like the wood of a pianoforte frame: the little whorls, knots and faults gave or withheld beauty. And their lips were actually notched as a man's bedpost. Take this one (it was Harriet). Her lips were thin. Smooth, they would be nothing more than a gash. Notched, with perhaps five tiny bee-sting swellings, they offered all manner of treats. Portraitists should try harder. He was much amused when Harriet snapped her wrist away. He was not to know that she took his lingering on her lips to be a deliberate focus on what she considered her worst feature.

Monsieur moved on to Marianne. Oh dear. A coarse girl. Skin pitted like an orange; mole like a slug on her left cheek. Freckles. Miserable hair. No neck. Portraitists had a point. It would be foolhardy to tell the truth.

Everina submitted with little shrieks. Those teeth, thought Monsieur with well-hidden shock. A cartoon. A creature of puffs and pompoms. Still, her hands were plump, the fingernails clean, and she had plucked her eyebrows into the semi-circles of fixed surprise favoured for mannequins. It was unappealing but showed attention to detail.

Georgiana, trembling like a sinner before the priest, seemed too insubstantial to scrutinise. Gently, gently with her. She was a nervous dove. He would have to gain her confidence.

Alathea held out her right hand voluntarily. On her thumb was her mother's wedding ring. Sawneyford would have buried it with the corpse but Alathea had clung so hard to her mother's finger that Sawneyford had removed the ring and given it to the child. At that time, it had been too big even for her thumb. On Alathea's first visit to the V&B Mrs W had helped secure it with a bandage. As Alathea grew, the ring fitted better and she became so accustomed to it on her thumb that she never moved it to a finger. She had taken it off only twice, both times for a goldsmith to refit. Monsieur guessed none of this. The only lady he had seen wearing a thumb ring would not have been welcome in Mrs Frogmorton's drawing room. *Tiens!* he said to himself. He made to drop Alathea's hand and found his own held for inspection. He cocked his head. Well, well. Even without the ring, this girl was unusual: dark-skinned, dark-eyed, dark-haired – not black, if you really looked, more the tarry coppers and russets of the inside of a volcano. He withdrew his hand with a quick '*Mademoiselle.*' He would think of her later. Now for the mothers. 'You will want to know our programme,' he said, giving them also a quick once-over. Portly, dumpy, skinny. Mothers, but not enough of them. Two girls must be sisters, or perhaps one or two were without mothers? It did not matter. 'I shall teach these lovely girls some easy madrigal accompaniments and simple ditties,' Monsieur said. 'They can sing and play. It will be charming.'

Mrs Frogmorton jolted. 'Easy madrigals and simple ditties? The pianoforte up the stairs is not for trifles, sir. Attracting husbands for our girls is a serious business. Madrigals may do for bank clerks and milliners but they won't do for us, will they, Elizabeth?'

Monsieur waited for Mrs Brass to answer. When she did not,

he carried on. 'I see, I see. Well then. What are your thoughts, *mesdames*?'

Mrs Frogmorton made a magnanimous gesture. 'Marianne? You're something of an expert, I gather?'

'I believe the *cognoscenti* admire music by a man called Bach,' Marianne said, stressing the Italian with a smug nod at Mrs Frogmorton and a slight simper for Monsieur.

'They do,' Monsieur agreed.

'Does Mr Bach write for the pianoforte? Could he compose something specially for us?'

'I doubt that.' Monsieur Belladroit fanned his fingers.

'Is a commission from us not important enough?' Marianne was at her most superior. 'If that's so, I think Herr Bach over-estimates himself.'

'Herr Bach, good ladies, is dead, and has been for some time.'

Mrs Frogmorton hid a smile. Everina giggled. Alathea bit her lip.

'Herr Bach may be dead,' Marianne declared, flushing, 'but his music lives on. What about some preludes, some fugues or some' – she struggled only for a moment, then dug the phrase out and sent it swinging – 'some *suites de pièces*?'

Monsieur was delighted. 'Ah, my dear girl! I see now what you are after.' His tongue peeped from the corner of his lips. Alathea noted it. 'You want drama, you want thrill, you want arabesques, canons, *sarabandes*, the *adagio arioso*, the dotted *gigue*, the *rondo alla Turca*.' He flourished the terms like a box of treats.

'They want husbands,' Mrs Frogmorton said bluntly.

'You want to show your girls at their most delirious.'

'Desirable,' said Mrs Frogmorton and Mrs Drigg together.

'As I say, delirious,' agreed Monsieur. Mrs Frogmorton and Mrs Drigg clicked their tongues but let it pass.

'What to choose, what to choose.' Monsieur placed a finger

flat against his cheek. 'The pianoforte, you must understand, is an upstager. It upstages the little harpsichord as a river upstages a stream.'

'There's no such word as "upstager",' said Marianne, 'and rivers don't upstage streams. They're entirely different things.'

Monsieur narrowed his eyes. 'I bow before higher knowledge of waterways. You perhaps already know Mr Handel's *Water Music*?' He hummed and waved for her to join in.

Marianne looked sour. 'I don't hum.'

'Oh, but you must. I shall teach you. You just press your lips together – such pretty lips – press them together—'

'For goodness' sake!' Mrs Frogmorton glared at Marianne. 'Never mind this nonsense. What are they to play, *monsieur*?'

'*Madame*, you must understand several things. The pianoforte is a garden waiting for a gardener.'

'What?' All the mothers stared at him.

'It is an instrument waiting for music,' Monsieur explained.

'Monsieur Belladroit,' said Mrs Frogmorton, accentuating his name. 'Never mind about the pianoforte waiting. We are waiting. What music are the girls to play? It's a perfectly simple question.'

Monsieur seemed to be considering. 'I think I have it.' Eight female faces were expectant. A tingle of anticipation. Should he try his luck with the mothers too? Old meat could be tasty. He did not dismiss the thought. 'The girls can perform a sonata each by the lovely Mrs Barthélemon.' He laughed to himself. Cantabile would find this amusing.

Mrs Frogmorton sounded a ship's horn. 'Music by a woman?'

'Women also write music, *madame*.'

Her voice rose. 'I dare say they do, but we can't have a woman composer for our girls. It's hardly respectable. Music's a man's thing, *monsieur*, and a man's music is what we want. There must be something suitable.'

Monsieur pressed his fingers to his lips. Mrs Barthélemon was a nice idea. He dismissed her reluctantly. The matrons leaned forward. 'I have it,' Monsieur said at last. 'An aria with diverse variations.'

Silence, broken by Mrs Frogmorton. 'An aria, you say? We've already told you about ditties. Our girls are not simpletons.'

Monsieur fixed her with his eye. '*Madame*, the work to which I refer could not be played by simpletons. When played on the harpsichord for which it was written it is a work of the utmost difficulty. On the pianoforte, it is a work almost of impossibility.' A groan escaped Georgiana. Monsieur softened his voice. 'Do not worry, *mademoiselle*. Under my tuition and with a little rearrangement of the music, the difficulties will be overcome. That is *my* forte.'

'Does it have a name, this rearranged aria with variables?' Mrs Frogmorton asked. 'It would be easier if it had a name.'

'The name? It is called a *Clavier-Übung*,' Monsieur replied.

'*Clavier-Übung*?' Mrs Frogmorton was doubtful. 'Sounds French.'

'German,' said Mrs Brass unexpectedly.

Ah, she speaks, Monsieur thought, and she was once pretty. 'Quite right, German,' he said. 'In France we call what I shall teach your girls something different.' Mrs Brass looked up quickly. Monsieur checked. She was not so dozy, this silent one. He waited.

'And in English?' Mrs Drigg was anxious to relieve Mrs Brass of the pressure of saying anything more.

'Keyboard practice.'

'Oh dear! Not very romantic.'

'For goodness' sake, Agnes,' said Mrs Frogmorton. 'We're talking about marriage.'

'Of course, Grace, I just thought—'

'I dare say,' Mrs Frogmorton snapped. It was time for this

conversation to conclude. 'Now, *monsieur*, which man wrote this – this variable thing?'

'Herr Bach,' Monsieur told her, 'about whom we have just been speaking.'

'I think we'd all prefer a piece written by an Englishman. Doesn't have to be dead.'

'You find me a suitable piece by an Englishman, *madame*, and I will be happy to oblige.'

'Alathea?' said Mrs Frogmorton, conscious of trying to include her. 'Do you have any suggestions?'

Alathea shook her head.

'Marianne?'

Marianne, unable to think of any English composer, dead or alive, blustered, 'Will this aria attract husbands for us?'

Monsieur considered. 'Herr Bach himself described this work as "prepared for the soul's delight". What could be more apt? You girls, like the piece, are already delightful. Your delight will add to the delight of the music. The occasion will be delightful. Never will there have been such delight.'

'Are you mocking us?' Mrs Drigg could be tart when not fluttering.

Monsieur grew grave. 'I offer an important work, a serious work, a holy work. Matrimony is an important undertaking, a serious undertaking, a holy undertaking. When music and matrimony themselves are married, the marriage is the music and the music is the marriage. I have the only copy of this serious and holy work in London, perhaps the only copy anywhere. Who would dare to mock?'

He confounded them all, except Alathea, who blinked again. A bead of sweat trickled down Mrs Frogmorton's neck. Just above the gauze fichu, it veered to one side and started a new course. She felt Monsieur's eyes follow it into the chasm of embonpoint which, today, Frilly had abandoned in favour of causing havoc in the kitchen by growling and nipping at his replacement as turnspit.

'Now,' Monsieur said in more normal tones, 'do you wish your girls to play this music or not?'

Mrs Frogmorton felt another trickle of sweat and a surge of misgiving. This whole musical notion seemed suddenly foolish. Mr Frogmorton should have brought it up for discussion at breakfast, over a cup of tea, not at dinner, over wine. Two decanters that night. She had been too easily persuaded. Should she put a stop to it right now?

'Well, *mesdames*?' said Monsieur with some impatience.

Too late, Mrs Frogmorton thought, and anyway, what's the worst that can happen with a pianoforte? 'If it's suitable, the girls will play it. If it's not suitable, they won't,' she said, and added, to reassert her authority, 'I would have thought that obvious, *monsieur*.'

Monsieur clicked his heels. 'Very well. We have chosen the music and with my help, all the girls will ... ' He searched for the precise word he wanted. 'They will startle,' he said.

'Startle?' It was the first time this word had been used in Mrs Frogmorton's parlour. The Frogmortons were not people who 'startled'.

Monsieur did not offer a correction. 'We begin tomorrow,' he said. 'No time-wasting. Please ensure that the girls wear suitable garments. I will hear them each in turn. After that, they will each have a lesson twice a week and practise for three hours every day including lesson days. If they do not reach my standards by practising three hours, they will practise four.' He bowed and vanished.

Immediately, Marianne and Everina were clamouring. They did not want to 'startle'. Nor did they want to trail to Manchester Square twice a week for something as dreary as a lesson. They refused, refused, refused to practise for three hours a day. Half an hour had sufficed on the harpsichord at the Misses Lee's Academy for Young Ladies. 'I don't like this *monsieur*,' Marianne shouted with childish pique. 'None of us wants to play holy music. This is a nonsensical plan. There are other ways of catching husbands, surely.' Georgiana was teary, Harriet annoyed. Only Alathea appeared unmoved.

'Enough!' Mrs Frogmorton barked and sailed over to berth next to Mrs Brass. Mrs Drigg stood behind. Mrs Frogmorton spoke loudly. The girls would do as they were told. They would learn from Monsieur. They would play. They would startle, secure their husbands and be done with it. Harriet knew her mother in this voice: complaining was a waste of effort. She dug Marianne and Everina in the ribs. 'When we're married,' she hissed, 'our mammas will do as we say. When they knock, we'll not be at home.' Mothers and daughters glowered over the red Turkey carpet. Upstairs with the pianoforte, Monsieur's eyes were bright. He stretched and bent slowly to touch his toes, legs straight, an athlete limbering up. The morning would come soon enough. He was ready.

At the V&B, the fathers were easy, slurping from coffee bowls without ceremony, breaking wind without apology, stretching and mingling pipes and legs with their usual familiarity. Now that the die was cast, they could relax, though Brass had been stirring things, asking what would happen if Harriet married a duke and Marianne a baronet. Would one set of grandchildren have to bow to another? And what would happen if one girl was left unwed?

'We can't arrange for them all to be of the same rank,' Frogmorton said. 'We must take what we can get.' He, like the others, wanted a son-in-law of a certain kind, and certainly, he was willing to pay. However, the alderman's desire had nothing to do with snobbery. As practical as his daughter,

Frogmorton admired his social superiors because their fore-fathers had hacked, trampled and murdered their way to the top of England's tree, and stuck there. Strong blood, not blue blood, was what he desired for his grandchildren. Harriet's marriage constituted less a social aspiration and more a place of safety. To find such a place, Frogmorton thought, was every father's duty.

'And they'll make no distinctions in private, surely?' Drigg could not bear the thought.

Brass flexed a leg. 'It might do my Georgiana good to be top of the pile. Give her a bit of body.' Georgiana would be queen of this venture. Skinny and fey she might be, but she could bang the keys well enough.

Drigg seized the opportunity to snipe. 'She's certainly very thin.'

Brass turned on him. 'Are you suggesting I keep a mean house?'

'I'm simply saying she's very thin. If you want my opinion—'

'I don't.'

'—it's unnatural,' Drigg said.

Brass sneered. 'Like Everina's teeth?'

Drigg flushed. Everina's dentures, so expensively, glaringly white, were an uncomfortable running joke. 'At least we can get those fixed. You can't buy Georgiana a pair of hips.'

Brass pushed back his chair, veins bulging, fists clenched.

'Gentlemen, please!' Frogmorton raised his hands. 'Drigg, apologise. Brass, sit down.'

Frogmorton was fed up with Brass, a perennial exasperation because he had started out the luckiest of the four. His parents owned a brewery before being carried off by cholera. The chief brewer, sorry for the boy, offered home comforts, and even love, but Brass was a thankless charity. Sullen and thuggish, he fought and scowled his way out of the brewer's affections and was quickly apprenticed in a silk factory, where he encountered Sawneyford. The brewery was sold and with his inheritance Brass had bought a fighting dog. Sawneyford was useful because he knew how to sharpen its teeth.

'Tell me again how the pianoforte's different from the harpsichord,' Frogmorton said. 'I suppose we should know.'

'Well, you make the tone by, em, touch. It's very subtle,' Drigg replied.

Frogmorton frowned. 'You're sure it's quite decent?'

'More than decent,' Drigg reassured him. 'It's perfect for our daughters.' A vision of Annie briefly surfaced. With some effort, he obliterated it.

'Good. Now, Sawney. We haven't heard much from you. Are you happy with the plan?' The others paid attention. Sawneyford's utterances were rare enough to be over-valued.

'I suppose so.' Sawneyford picked at fraying cuffs.

'You suppose, Sawney? *Suppose?*' rapped Brass. He thought, Why does Sawneyford wear rags? He could buy a whole tailoring business. Or get that disturbing daughter to do some mending.

'I suppose so,' repeated Sawneyford, his tone neither agreement nor disagreement, a confusion he cultivated. Marriage talk unsettled him. The others saw silken grandchildren behind unassailable social ramparts; Sawneyford saw Alathea sweating under Tamworth-pink flesh. Was that worth a coronet? Was it worth a rampart? Was it worth a dead candle? Sharp against his buttocks were three diamonds he liked to keep secreted in the lining of his coat, tiny things, the first gems he ever touched. Diamonds suited Alathea. Where was she now? The man set to tail her would be waiting to report. Sawneyford hoped she hadn't given this one the slip. He felt a rush of anxiety. What was he doing here? He didn't want Alathea to marry at all.

Outside the light was beginning to fade, and the coffeepots

arranged on the hearthstone in strict height order (Mrs W's little foible) cast dwarfish shadows. The cat had slid from the urn's lid and gone hunting. The long table was empty save for the tide calendars and old bills of lading which Mrs W was piling up before the evening rush.

Brass picked up his coffee bowl and raised it for a toast. 'Here's to the concert, and since you suggested it, Drigg, I'll hold you responsible if Georgiana ends up an old maid.' He drank the dregs and grimaced. Ottoman beans. Looked like tar, tasted like tar. Frogmorton and Drigg drank too. Sawneyford picked up his bowl, half raised it to his lips and put it down again.

Mrs W, seeing movement, came over with a note of each man's dues. Each signed his own. Mr W accepted few credit notes but he trusted these men to pay at the end of each quarter and so far had never had to prompt. The men shrugged on their coats. Frogmorton waited for his gig in the doorway between Gadhill the barber and the old gunpowder office, now used to store, roast and grind the V&B's beans. The distance to his office was scarcely worth the horse, but the alderman had a horror of stepping in shit. Drigg had his usual problems hailing a chair, though there were plenty for hire. Brass sidled off on foot to sniff out a cockfight.

Sawney Sawneyford was last to step back into London's sticky spread. If he trod in shit, he did not care. He was the City's child, as well as the city's. Indeed, he was much more the child of the City than the child of the jostling, poking brother and crying sister who physically brought him into being. The City was the womb through which his world reverberated. How he arrived at the silk factory in which he had met Brass was of no interest to him, just as he had no interest in an uncle/father press-ganged and drowned at sea, or an aunt/mother still crying, or the whore who had cut the cord after servicing a customer –

'You're in a hurry, sir, extra for that, sir, threepence and a pint of ale to wash out the taste, sir' – and who, on a whim, had decided not to dash his head against the cobbles but to push him through the pavement boards, where he was found by a human rat living underneath. The rat, drunk, mistook Sawneyford for her own. At four, the mistake for ever unrealised, she sold him: agile fingers were valuable to the factory loom. Sawneyford was quick: he kept his fingers and his place. At ten, he met Brass. At twelve, Frogmorton and Drigg. At thirteen, he made his first bet of over a penny. At fourteen, three successful betting scams; at fifteen, a deal; at eighteen, a banking account; at twenty, a house. At twenty-one, a wife; at twenty-six, a dead wife and Alathea. A-la-*thee*-a. She had offered Sawneyford something quite unexpected and he had taken it. He headed towards a tannery for sale in Bermondsey and considered the pianoforte without enthusiasm. He reassured himself: Alathea might be no good at it. He kicked a broken lantern lying in his way. She would, though, damn her. She would.

At Tyburn, Annie and her father observed an uneasy truce. The gap left by the pianoforte remained unfilled, and every time Cantabile passed he shed a tear for Annie's benefit. Annie took no notice. Her mother was bad. Spring was the most dangerous time: nature softened, and its softening suffocated the weak. Annie never knew whether to close the curtains round her mother's box bed for warmth, or leave them open for air. The concert girls were pushed aside for the moment, as was Monsieur. Annie had seen his coat and heard his voice but they had not met.

Now Annie was anxious for the doctor, expected imminently. It was a relief that Drigg's money made the man more willing. It was also a relief that her father refused to have anything to do with the stacks of coins Annie collected from the bank and

59

stored where she alone would look for them. The coins would last for months. Their clink was a kind of music, and she did not underestimate its value.

For hours she had been laying cloths on her mother's forehead and tripping to and fro with pans of boiling water. Steam helped her mother breathe more easily. Francesca Cantabile murmured thanks and stroked Annie's hand. Enough steam. Time drifted. Only when her mother's breathing eased did Annie's mind turn back to Manchester Square. At first, she imagined the pianoforte. The image changed. She imagined the girls' rosebud mouths. She imagined them crushed against Monsieur's, their white teeth nipping his tongue. She dabbed her mouth. Bile had sprung upwards, stinging her lip.

A shout from below. At last! She ran to let the doctor in. He had seen too many deformities even to notice Annie's. He pushed past her up the stairs to listen and poke, advise and ruminate, turning Mrs Cantabile over as though she were a rag-doll. The news was not good, but not the worst either. He took his money and left. Annie straightened her mother's night-clothes, smoothed the pillows and sat quietly, holding her mother's hand again until they both dozed off. Annie woke an hour later, cold and stiff. She checked her mother's pulse, then closed the bed-curtains as the doctor had advised. Mrs Cantabile's eyelids flickered. 'Thank you, my Annie,' she whispered. 'You're a blessing to me.'

'Sssh, mother,' said Annie. 'You're a blessing to me.'

'We're blessings to each other.' Mrs Cantabile smiled the sweet smile Annie should have inherited. Annnie pressed her cheek against her mother's as she had done since she was a little girl. It was an accommodation they had come to: an acceptable kiss. It made Annie want to howl.

4

AT half-past eight, Mrs Frogmorton was already a cumbersome presence in her drawing room. She kept the drapes shut through some notion of secrecy, though the room was too high for peeping Toms. The lamps hissed. She stood on a chair to turn them down: no need for waste. The fire, stacked high, shed light enough and there were four three-armed candelabras on the pianoforte itself. Monsieur arrived, in brown again, workaday. He gazed with renewed disgust at the room, whose furniture, all depressingly resistant to woodworm, cast shadows as bulky as his employer's. An old suit of armour hanging between two of the three long windows hinted at a baronial past, the effect rendered comic by the greaves, not a matching pair, and the helmet stolen from a dressing-up box. A screen embroidered with Chinese dragons nodded to the privacy of the lesson, though Mrs Frogmorton had ensured it did not completely obstruct her view. The floor was highly polished – no carpet. Monsieur was, for a moment, tempted to skate across it as he had skated on the river when a boy. Instead he padded over to the pianoforte, removed two of the candelabra and murmured his condolences to the keyboard.

Mrs Frogmorton stared at the instrument. Four-square and square-tailed, pedals angled like a bow-legged girl, it seemed unlikely that such a thing could attract a husband for Harriet. Monsieur Belladroit was soon busy under the pianoforte lid, twisting, tightening, prodding, dusting, stroking. Mrs Frogmorton sighed. As chaperone, she was stuck here. She nodded to Monsieur, gathered Frilly to herself, rang for more coal and plunged her needle into a small piece of tapestry. She would be bored. She was used to that.

Marianne arrived. Monsieur set to work. Had Marianne any skill at the keys? Of course, she replied. Well, then she should play something to him, so he could judge how best to progress. Marianne stopped after two bars of Couperin. 'This thing doesn't make what I call music,' she declared. 'It's all uneven, and so dull. My harpsichord's much better.'

'The pianoforte does not make music for you, *mademoiselle*,' Monsieur agreed. 'That we must acknowledge.'

'Why can't I just play my harpsichord – or Harriet's? It's over there.'

'With a harpsichord everything you say is the same. With a pianoforte, you may say many different things.'

'I don't want to say different things. I'm supposed to say "Marry me." Isn't that the whole point?' She bashed out the *Barricades Mystérieuses*.

Monsieur considered the unmysterious noise she was making. This girl was, and would always be, no more a musician than Mrs Frogmorton's dog was an orator. If she played in time, that would have to be enough. As for seduction, yesterday's anticipation had been optimistic. There could be no pleasure here. Marianne did not only lack delicacy in feature and limb, she lacked any vestige of girlish charm, and her breath was still fuzzy from breakfast. Still, he told himself firmly, she had swellings in the correct places and, assisted by silk, lace and some decent brocade, a clever dressmaker was keeping her just short of impossible. When the time came, he could always close his eyes and hold his nose. He nudged the pianoforte with a sympathetic knee. With luck, Marianne would be the worst. She ground out the final chord.

'B flat major is a pleasant key, yes?' said Monsieur.

Marianne snorted. 'You music masters! It's just a key, like the others. Now, let's get on. Where shall we start? I don't want to be here for ever.'

'Indeed not, *mademoiselle*. That would be intolerable.' He gave her exercises. She copied them badly. He could not bring himself to care.

Harriet was next, in high-waisted, short-sleeved pale blue – rather too smart for a pianoforte lesson, Harriet well knew – with a long cherry-coloured sash. She greeted Marianne at the door and dawdled without greeting her mother. 'It's very dark,' she said, picking up one of the discarded candelabra and placing it back on the pianoforte so that it shone directly on her. 'That's better.' She sat with learned grace, hands carefully in her lap. She studied the keyboard.

'This concert has been dreamed up by our parents,' she said, *sotto voce*. 'I'm not against it, but . . . ' She shrugged prettily.

'Dreamed up or not, we must make the best of the hour and the instrument your parents are so generously providing.'

Harriet poked middle C with her index finger. The note responded softly. She frowned. She rolled a chord. A different frown. She rolled the chord again, more carefully. 'It sounds peculiar.' She bumped a toe against the pedals.

'The notes are struck, not plucked,' Monsieur explained. 'It makes the sound a little cloudier than you are used to. And you have bumped your toe on the pedals.'

She regarded the pedals. 'What are they for?'

'The right-hand pedal sustains the notes, the left-hand hushes them. It is the modern way.'

Harriet looked faintly disbelieving. 'Monsieur Belladroit, can we be frank?'

'Of course.'

'I know I must be married,' Harriet said, 'and indeed, I want to be married. I will be married. I've decided to marry Mr Thomas Buller. He lives next door and he'll marry me without any piano-playing. I know he will.'

'You are already engaged?' Monsieur cocked his head.

'Not exactly, and please keep your voice down. He was kind to me when we first moved here, so I know he likes me, and he's rich. I really don't have to bother with any of this. The servants tell me his father's considering buying an earldom.'

Monsieur was amazed. 'People still buy such things? Do you not see what goes on across the sea?'

Harriet laughed. 'Oh, *monsieur*, they're all foreigners across the sea! We're *English*.'

'Well,' Monsieur said, collecting himself, 'even the English cannot buy the soul of Herr Bach.'

'Oh, come now!' Harriet faced him. 'Of course they can. Isn't that just what we are doing? We're buying his aria, or whatever it's called, and using it to attract customers. It's no different from buying and selling cheese.'

Monsieur was taken aback. He had no real liking for Harriet's type: too neat, self-conscious, pale; too contrived; too English. Yet a prickle of whip and leash. If she had made up her mind to grab this Thomas, the boy would not escape her. 'You speak nothing but the truth,' Monsieur said. 'Perhaps you will be wasted as a wife. You should rather be a husband.'

'Are you saying I'm bossy?'

Monsieur was humble. 'I beg your pardon, no. I simply observe that you would be a good lady of business.'

She considered. 'I think that's a compliment?'

'Indeed.'

'I like it.'

Monsieur laughed. 'Let's to the music, *mademoiselle*.' He rearranged the exercises on the stand. 'To play Herr Bach properly, the fingers must be dextrous. Do you have dextrous fingers?'

'My father says I play perfectly.'

'Is your father always right?'

She tilted her head and flashed him a look, then leaned in to the music. First finger, third finger, second then fourth. Up the keyboard she went. Her father was not right in this case, as Monsieur and Harriet could both see. She began again. 'Careful of your wrist, *mademoiselle*. Don't let it drop. Listen.' He played with wrist raised and again with wrist sunk. 'Can you hear a difference?'

She looked surprised. 'Yes. That's extraordinary.'

'You try.'

She tried. 'Goodness.' The lesson progressed. After a while, the future Mrs Thomas Buller worked with some pleasure, and when she gave up her seat to Georgiana, she and Monsieur were humming.

Georgiana was late. Dressed by a well-meaning servant, she was so tied up in stiff damask and whalebone that she hobbled like a trussed goose.

'Suitable clothes, *mademoiselle*,' Monsieur said reprovingly.

Georgiana had seen her mistake before he spoke. 'I'm sorry,' she stammered, her speech as impeded as her movement. 'I didn't know what that meant.' Her tears dripped as she attempted to sit down. Behind the screen, Mrs Frogmorton was whispering to Frilly. Georgiana, certain the whisper was criticism, crumpled further.

Monsieur Belladroit hastily mopped her tears with a silk handkerchief Annie had given him years ago. He settled the whalebones. When Georgiana stopped crying, he perched beside her. 'Dear *mademoiselle*. What can I do? Your papa does not wish you to be miserable.'

'I don't know what he wishes, *monsieur*.'

'He wishes for you to marry well and be happy. We shall do our best to oblige.'

'Yes. Our best.' The notion of 'best' nearly set her off again.

Monsieur tutted. '*Mademoiselle*, please do not cry. It is bad for your skin. It is bad for the pianoforte. It is bad for my nerves. What I say to you during our hours together will not be to criticise. It will be to help towards your concert performance.' He paused until she had control of herself. 'So. We have already established that it is impossible to play music in such clothes as you are wearing. To play the pianoforte you must be able to move freely. Let me advise. Tomorrow, wear muslin; wear gauze; wear silk; wear satin; wear ribbons; wear pearls; wear flowers. These will suit you and our lessons very well.' He raised the handkerchief to her cheek, to mop up the last of the damp, as a father might. He spoke about the pianoforte, explaining the touch, pointing to the pedals. He played a little Mozart. Her eyes were grey pools. Monsieur had never seen anything so grey. Even the pupils were grey, as though constant tears had washed all the colour out. 'This instrument sings,' he told her, 'and tomorrow, little dove, when you are dressed more softly, it will sing for you.'

He bent down, as if to check the pedals. Yes, she had satisfactory ankles, and her feet, encased in blue leather with tiny buttons, were enchanting.

The hour with Everina dragged the most. She blasted her

way through the *Barricades*, stamping on the pedals as though crushing beetles. She never enquired about their use. The only thing in Everina's favour was greater accuracy than Marianne's. Once she had finished the piece, she hammered through a Giustini sonata more *prestissimo* than Giustini ever intended, snorted, then hammered through another, Frilly yapping his disapproval half a beat behind the time.

'Stop! Enough!' Monsieur Belladroit waggled his hands as though warding off hornets. Pert as her ruching, Everina giggled. Monsieur closed the lid over the keyboard. 'Very illuminating, Mademoiselle Everina. I feel for your harpsichord.'

'Feel for it?'

'Feel for how busy you must keep it,' he said. 'Can you hear a difference between it and this pianoforte?'

She giggled again. 'You can go just as fast on either.'

'That's not what I asked. Can you hear a difference?'

'What does it matter, *monsieur*? Once you've finished playing, the sound's over.'

Monsieur wondered what Cantabile would do if he were suddenly in the room. He might chop Everina's fingers off. At this moment, Monsieur would be happy to help him. He tried a different tack. 'Do you read books, *mademoiselle*?'

'Of course,' Everina said. 'Every parlour boarder at the Misses Lee's Academy reads books.'

'And do you like them?'

'I found Mr Richardson's *Virtue Rewarded* very instructive,' she recited, as she had been taught.

'And is Mr Richardson's story the same as every other story?'

'Of course not.'

'But all stories are made of words, so why are they not all the same?'

She wagged a coquettish finger. 'I see what you're doing. You're saying words are like notes. They're not. Words aren't

67

notes. Books aren't music. Now, how am I go to on with the lid closed?'

Monsieur gave her a look that was not benign. 'I shall reopen the lid if you promise to do as I ask.'

'And what will you ask, *monsieur*?'

Her tone was so arch that it flashed across Monsieur's mind that this pudding had already been tasted. He did not have to wait until the end of the lesson to know this would be a relief.

Luncheon arrived: three lamb patties, a hunk of bread and some weak ale. He picked with distaste.

Alathea's lesson did not start well. The lamb patty repeated on Monsieur, and in this dismal room she seemed completely ordinary, her skin dull, her hair lustreless. A quick glance revealed thick stockings. He was disappointed. This girl was not intriguing at all.

'Good afternoon,' he said as she settled herself at the keyboard. 'Please accustom yourself to the pianoforte and then play something. I hope it will not be Giustini.' The fire had been banked up again. Mrs Frogmorton was reinstalled. Monsieur stifled a yawn.

Alathea did not look at the pianoforte. She looked at him. A twitch in her cheek – Monsieur could not tell how it was done – splintered any sense of ordinariness. 'I think Herr Bach is a very good choice,' Alathea said. 'The *Clavier-Übung* will challenge us all. You'll have to give us a great deal of help.'

'You know this work?'

'Prepared for the soul's delight of music lovers,' she said. 'You told us yourself.'

'And you count yourself amongst their number?'

'Music lovers?' She stressed the 'music'.

'*Music* lovers,' he repeated without taking his eyes from her. 'Would you?'

'Count you or myself?'

'Whichever you like.'

He relaxed. She was playing a game. He could play too. 'How do you know the work? It is not printed in London.'

'Sir John Hawkins has some of it in his *History of Music*. The rest was not hard to find. My father has Leipzig contacts and it's not a secret work, only a work containing secrets.'

A peppercorn scorch in his throat. 'And you know these secrets?'

'*Monsieur*, we waste time.'

His brows flattened and he resisted an urge to loosen his collar. 'You have played a pianoforte before, *mademoiselle*?'

'I have a pianoforte at home,' she said.

'You never said so.'

'You didn't ask me.'

I'll test this girl, he thought. He reached into his case and pulled out the aria and variations. 'Very well,' he said crisply. 'Begin.'

'We'll play together,' she said, moving along the pianoforte stool. He was aware of a scent – musk, he thought, yes, musk, smokily beguiling. Unusual choice for a young girl. He was not sure he liked it. From behind the screen Mrs Frogmorton cursed as she pricked her finger, and Frilly yapped commiseration. Monsieur curled his lip. The dog needed drowning. He caught Alathea's eye. It was clear she was thinking the same – an unexpectedly murderous connection. Alathea pointed to the music.

And now Mrs Frogmorton and Frilly were left behind. Monsieur and Alathea sat completely still, completely silent, and from the silence something marvellous emerged: G, G, A-trill to B, A, grace-note to F sharp, grace-note to D. So sure was each note, so confident of its place, the ornaments so neat and the sequence so clean that Mrs Frogmorton was hardly aware the silence had been broken.

Monsieur played with questioning delicacy. Musically, he was prepared for anything. Alathea played with complete belief. She knew this music. She did not flirt or tinker with it. It was a beam she drew directly from the instrument. Monsieur's top lip fluttered. *Quelle merveille.* He and this girl were perfectly in time, sympathetically phrased, drawing the beam together. Though a music master from an early age, Monsieur did not reckon to feel like a musician when he taught. His pupils sometimes had talent, yet never this kind of intelligence. Usually he wondered why his lessons were called 'music lessons' at all. 'Lessons in mechanical reproduction' would have been more apt. Naturally he corrected and instructed, but his mind always strayed, and the years had blunted his sensibility. He knew this and regretted it. Yet here, now, in this unlikely room, was a taste of what might have been had circumstances allowed him to be discriminating. Melancholy threatened to overwhelm him.

Taking the aria as a duet, Monsieur's unused right hand and Alathea's left rested on their respective knees. They both kept their feet from the pedals. Occasionally their hands touched, a touching of music, not flesh. They repeated, then moved over the repeat marks to the second section. They repeated this. Grace-note, crotchet, the aria ended, the beam broke.

As if to ask a question, Alathea turned to face Monsieur. He wanted to thank her. He wanted to confide his melancholy. However, before he could say a word and with no change of expression, her unoccupied hand was no longer on her own knee, it was on his. It was above his knee. It was halfway up his thigh. It did not rest there. Melancholy vanished. Flesh was very quickly flesh again. Monsieur's gasp made Frilly stir and growl. Mrs Frogmorton rose and peeped round the screen, where she observed Monsieur's eyes fixed glassily on the score and Alathea looking much as Alathea always did: irritatingly amused, as though enjoying a private joke.

Alathea smiled at Mrs Frogmorton. Such a strange thing, a smile. Alathea knew as much about smiles as she knew about tongues. She knew how the pull of the cheek, one or both, and the releasing of the lips to expose just this or that amount of tooth, or no teeth at all, or no teeth to start with, could alter the thing entirely. She knew how to keep Mrs Frogmorton looking at her smile (at the moment, both cheeks drawn back, lips just beginning to open) so that she did not look elsewhere. This was essential, since things with Monsieur were warming up considerably. When she was ready, Alathea dissolved her smile slowly, first relaxing her cheek muscles, then allowing her lips naturally to resume their resting position. The whole affair took nearly half a minute.

Mrs Frogmorton's irritation subsided. The girl was only smiling. She couldn't help being the way she was. Mrs Frogmorton returned to her seat. Half an hour to go. Another leaf to embroider.

Alathea turned her attention back to Monsieur. Things were nearly over. Monsieur, not wanting Mrs Frogmorton to appear again, swallowed a small gasp, then nearly choked on a bigger one. The luncheon lamb fat refluxed. He turned a gasp into a burp. *Mon Dieu!* When he could breathe again, he smelled like Marianne. Alathea rose, leaving Monsieur Belladroit gripping the pianoforte stool. 'Goodbye,' she said. 'I shall see you next week.' She nodded at Mrs Frogmorton as she passed. Mrs Frogmorton caught a whiff of musk, and of something else that she couldn't quite place. She did not give it another thought. Her chaperoning was finished for the day. With a sigh of relief, she put away her needlework and followed Alathea down the stairs.

A full five minutes passed before Monsieur put the music away, and ten before he was fit for the street. His shirt stuck unpleasantly to his stomach. He closed the door of no. 23 behind him and walked swiftly in the direction of Tyburn. He had forgotten his surprise at Alathea's music-making. He had forgotten his melancholia. All he remembered was that hand. He was both in awe of and revolted by its expertise. Alathea was so young. How had she dared? Never mind the daring; where could she have learned such arts? He checked his breeches as he walked. He did not feel in control of his legs. He slowed, stopped and leaned against a wall.

It was the dead hour between three and four. Few people were about. Behind curtains, women drooped. Behind desks, men rubbed inky thumbs and counted the hours still to be worked. Whores inspected themselves frankly in the glass before applying their paint. Even the sewers were still. Monsieur tried to breathe in some of the deadness. He did not want to blurt out what had just happened to Cantabile or anybody else. In his own time, he walked on, trying to notice ordinary things: the way you heard carriage wheels before carriage-horses' hooves. The same with Mrs Frogmorton: the rustle of hoops before the stamp of shoes. A corpse was being manhandled out of a doorway. A little girl was crying. He breathed the breath of ordinary life. Brushing himself down again, he walked more quickly, searching the mud for a lucky coin, as he sometimes did in Paris. Just outside Cantabile's he did find a penny, though it was so dirty he did not pick it up.

The shop was, as usual, closed against the world. Monsieur fumbled for his key and pulled his pistol against a gang threatening to fleece him. The weight of the stock restored him fully to himself. He stopped fumbling. After locking the door behind him, he paused, not because it was dark – he knew his way – but because somebody was playing. Mozart. The second movement of the Sonata in C. He leaned against Cantabile's desk. It must be Annie: her father could not play like this. My, he thought, she must have come on in the – how many years since I saw her last? Five? Six? The movement's little dramas, so often syrup, were individual droplets: simple, understated, with every regard for timing. Monsieur felt the droplets gather and rinse Alathea away. He made his way into the warehouse. Annie had her back to him.

'Annie?'

Annie had been waiting. She dreaded Monsieur's first view of her after so many years. She was no longer a child, the sweetness of an innocent, trusting face reducing the calamity of her lip. He would see her as she really was. She needed all the courage Mozart could give her. She hesitated just long enough to say '*Monsieur*,' then she grasped the lamp, sparing herself his first reaction by turning so she was entirely lit and he was still in the dark. 'I knew it must be you,' Monsieur exclaimed before the light spilled over her. Then a pause. Annie held the lamp closer so he would know for certain that what he saw was not a trick of the candle. She gave him time. She played Mozart in her head.

When she was twelve, Monsieur had found Annie's lip bad. He had thought it might improve as she grew older. Now she was seventeen, his shock was greater because of the permanence: this was how Annie would always be, and the malformation of her lip contrasted so starkly with the rest of her face. The pity of it! She could have been lovely. 'It is, er, it is very good to see you.' He knew his reaction was more marked by his attempt to hide it. 'It has been a long time. Too long,' he finished lamely.

Annie lowered the lamp. The introduction was done. Nothing untoward said. Everything untoward said. 'You're welcome, *monsieur*.' Her voice betrayed nothing. 'I'm sorry I missed your arrival. I have been taken up with my mother. Come, please. You must be hungry.'

73

She led the way to the stairs, and took him up into what her mother had once called the dining room, though it was really the kitchen, its furnishings three hard chairs, a small doorless cupboard containing plates and glasses (the doors were burned for heat last winter), a meshed box they used as a larder, and a table. She poured a glass of the fine port Monsieur used to like and searched for signs of seduction. Blotches of lip paint? A smudge of powder? A band of perspiration? Monsieur flipped his coat-tails as he sat. A waft of musk. Annie smelled it at once.

Monsieur took a large swig of the port and tried to make conversation. Annie's lip glowed. Never, Monsieur thought, had a man experienced quite such a day as this. 'How long since I stayed here last?' He looked in Annie's direction.

'Five years, *monsieur*,' she replied.

'Five years! And how is your mother?'

'Better tonight.' She refilled his glass. Now that he was actually in front of her and looking at her just as she was, against her will Annie's dream revived. Certainly, it underwent rapid moderations. Monsieur did not need to kiss her, and there was no question of marriage. She would be his friend. He could take her into his confidence. In due course, he could share details of the girls' tumblings and he and she could laugh at them together. That would make both the seductions, and even any marriage, easier to bear. She made a great effort to put him at his ease. 'People are flocking to hear Herr Haydn,' she said, sitting squarely in the light. The more he saw of her, the more he would get used to her. 'Have you heard him?'

'No. Have you?' Monsieur picked up the poker and put it down.

'No.'

'I would like to, Annie. Perhaps you and I—'

Her heart leapt. She could not stop it.

Mr Cantabile thrust open the door. 'Ah, Claude . . .'

Monsieur did not finish his invitation and it was never repeated. Annie wondered if her father had chosen his moment deliberately. She got up, fixed the lamps, closed the curtains and produced the dinner. Monsieur was aware of being good to her in the way men are good to a dog of whom they are fond but wish to keep at arm's length.

When the evening drew to a close, Annie checked on her mother before going to her own room. She undressed, got into bed and tugged the blankets under her nose. Then, despising herself, she got up and opened the door. Monsieur's room was beyond hers. She heard his footsteps. They were quite slow. She pulled up her knees. Was that a hesitation? She pushed her knees down only when it was clear that Monsieur was not going to put his head round the door to wish her good-night. She had known he would not. Nevertheless, it was bitter. Annie decided that Monsieur's girls would pay for his omission. The girl with the musk scent would be her first target. She would learn her name and her address, and when she struck, her aim would be deadly.

5

A FORTNIGHT passed before Alathea knew for certain that she was being followed by a new and rather different stalker. March was now April and although winter seemed to have returned for a last blast, she took to walking more slowly, just to be sure. She had fun with most of those set on her trail, walking for miles, sometimes south towards the river's wharves, sometimes east to the lanes around the law courts, sometimes west to Piccadilly to hover outside the offices of the London Corresponding Society where she had once, by chance, managed to get her tail taken into custody by pointing to him when arrests for treason were being made. Today she was simply squelching her way home from Newgate Street. She knew these two miles well. Three times in the last three years she had required an abortionist, and her father had recommended Newgate's Salutation & Cat as where everybody went – everybody, that is, who could afford more than a slurp of poison and a knitting needle.

On her first visit, Alathea thought her father mistaken in the place. Instead of a huddle of miserable women, she found a man standing on a chair and extolling the virtues of some utopia to a group of more or less interested drinkers. A pamphlet was pressed on her. She would have left had her arm not been taken by a respectable lady arising from a makeshift office in the corner. Alathea was sent up two sets of narrow stairs. The pamphlet had provided at least some distraction from the heap of instruments to be employed should the administered potion fail. Twice the potion had worked and Alathea had stumbled home an hour later. Once, there had to be poking, plucking, stretching, sucking, scraping, clamping. On that occasion, she remained in that room for two days, at first unconscious, then, when her eyes could focus, reading steadfastly, turning the pamphlet phrases 'strong tyrannise weak; government of all for all' into bulwarks against everything else. Odd words caught at her particularly: 'pantisocracy', 'Susquehanna', the former some kind of society of incorruptibles, the second the name of a river. Even in her distress, she was struck by the irony of the abortionist above and the incorruptibles below, and when the pain was bad, she clung to the name of the river as to a talisman. After she understood that she would never need the abortionist again (nor a midwife, for that matter) she returned to the Salutation & Cat to hear more about utopia and the river. Today she had been expecting a new speaker – a poet, no less – but he had not turned up and his replacement, wretched with cold, had abandoned utopia in favour of complaints about too little sugar and nutmeg in his egg-hot. Alathea had left after half an hour, emerging into the street at quite the wrong time. The Thursday market was drawing to a close and it was hard to move for carts parked back to back. From an open cage, six angry geese hissed and nipped at her. She hissed back and glanced behind. Yes, she was right. Up to now, her stalkers had always been men, which was why, this time, she had taken so long to be sure. A girl.

She pushed through the crowd. The shadow pushed after her. She stopped to haggle over a knuckle of ham. The shadow stopped. She paused to give the ham to a beggar. The shadow paused. When the crush thinned and grand houses gave way to shacks, Alathea whipped round. Even then she caught only a glimpse, what with the rain and the umbrellas. Certainly a woman. This made the shadow much more interesting. She rejected her usual practices. She would draw this stalker home and take her into custody herself.

Once the road was clear, Alathea set her course and kept steady until she could smell the pickle factory that made all new Soho Square residents sneeze. She looked behind. The stalker was sneezing: her first time here. At the corner of Charles Street, Alathea glanced back again. The shadow had recovered. Alathea walked briskly past Trotter's warehouses, the academy, the surgeon's house, and avoided four gentlemen just finished with the whores at no. 12. The stalker avoided them too.

Alathea made for her front door. The house was imposing, though Alathea felt no pride in it. It had not been chosen; her father had acquired it in lieu of a debt. The number plate had fallen off and they had not bothered to learn what the number was, referring to the house only as 'Soho Square', as though it had no individual identity at all. It was too big for the two of them, but neither wanted to be cosy. Neighbours often con-jectured about the inside – they had never been invited in – and in truth, Alathea and her father knew little more about the inside than a stranger, since few covers had been removed from the furniture and the other household goods left in their entirety by Sawneyford's debtors. To all intents and purposes, the house was uninhabited.

On the doorstep, Alathea bent to scrape the mud from her overshoes, rain trickling down her neck. Now the shadow hung back, and Alathea was nervous of a quick disappearance. The stalker was too far away to grab. Alathea needed her to come nearer. She took a gamble. She stood straight, got out her key and let herself in (they had one servant only and he was never attending the door). She kicked off her overshoes so that she could run, then jerked the door open again, preparing to dive out in pursuit. She stopped short. The shadow was standing directly in front of her, face hidden behind a veil of unusual thickness, right hand half raised as though to ring the bell. No tail had ever rung the bell before.

Annie was fumbling. Under the loose cuff draping her right hand, she held a small jar of acid. With the other hand, she was trying to pull off the stopper. She must do this instantly. Any kind of conversation and she might lose courage. Come off! Come off! The stopper stuck. Her hands were shaking, her thumbs and fingers slimy from the wet. She should have brought a knife. A quick slash across the face would have been more certain. The moment was passing. Her veil was sticking to her nose. She panicked. She would run away and return another time. She spun round. Alathea darted forward and seized her arm. The acid bottle dropped and smashed, white vapour hissing through the rain like the geese. Both girls jumped and Annie cried out. She was still held. After a brief tussle, she was propelled by Alathea's knee over the doorstep and into the hall, with the door slammed and locked behind her.

The two girls stood, panting slightly, water puddling from soaked hems. Alathea could sense that the person beneath the soggy veil was young. She wondered, Is this girl my father's mistress? She let Annie go. 'Are you looking for my father?'

'I'm looking for nobody,' Annie said. 'I've made a mistake.' How she regretted the lack of a knife.

'I don't believe you,' Alathea said. 'You followed me from Newgate Street, and you must have followed me there from Manchester Square. If you want my father, you should have waited for him at your home.'

'I'm not looking for your father,' Annie said. 'I don't know him. As I say, I've made a mistake.' She contemplated rushing the door.

'Did my father set you to spy on me?'

'Let me leave, please.'

Alathea had another thought. 'Perhaps you're a stooge of Mrs Frogmorton's? She likes to know others' business.'

'I don't know Mrs Frogmorton,' Annie said.

'You don't seem to know anybody.' Alathea shook off her cloak. 'Yet you were following me most particularly. I know you were.' She threw the cloak over a chair.

Annie seized her chance, slid past and turned the door handle. Alathea held up the key. 'Are you a thief?' she asked. 'Did you want my jewels?'

'I don't want anything.'

'Why were you going to ring the bell then?'

Annie shook her head. She was shivering, and in the sepulchral chill of the hall, Alathea began to shiver herself. 'Come,' she said, and when Annie did not move, pulled her away from the door, past the stairs and shrouded statues into what had been a card room. Beneath the mugginess of wet garments lurked the smell of musk. Annie's gorge rose. She could imagine Monsieur with this girl. If only she still had the acid! As it was, her nails were not long enough even to scratch. Alathea kicked the card-room door shut and tried to flick back Annie's veil. Annie resisted strongly. There was just enough light from the windows for Alathea to see her lip, and this Annie could not allow. Scorn would be tolerable; pity outrageous. Annie caught her veil with both hands and pulled it tight. Alathea abandoned

80

the veil, locked the door and closed the two sets of window shutters to prevent her prisoner breaking through the glass – she seemed desperate enough. Alathea struck a flint and lit a small lantern. Annie was a shadow again. 'Take off your cloak and remove that veil,' Alathea commanded.

Annie did nothing.

'I want to know what you look like,' Alathea said. Annie clung to the veil more tightly. Alathea held up the lamp. 'I'll let you go when I know who you are. Take off the veil.'

'I can't. I won't.'

'You can. You will.' Alathea put the lamp down. Annie ran to the door and rattled it. Alathea was after her at once, forcing her back round, struggling for the veil. She pulled it right off. Annie reeled back into the room, seized the lamp and waved it at the sheets covering everything except one sofa, one table, one upright chair and one oval miniature, a portrait, hanging on the wall.

Alathea sucked her lips. If the girl fired the house, she would have to unlock the door. She dropped the veil. They tussled for the lamp, splashing oil. Flames guttered. Alathea stamped them out. A sheet smouldered. Alathea yanked it to the side of the hearth. Finally she wrested the lamp from Annie and raised it high.

At once, Annie began to curl up. Alathea was quick. She caught Annie's hair, yanked her head back and spilled light all over her face. Annie stopped struggling at once. Her humiliation was complete. Alathea blinked. 'Who are you?'

'This is who I am,' Annie said.

Alathea tugged her hair. 'What is who you are?'

Annie gritted her teeth. 'You can see.'

Alathea let go of Annie's hair. 'I see your face but I don't know who you are.'

Annie contemplated lying. Yet lying would be another form

of humiliation. She would tell the truth and let the girl make of it what she would. 'I'm Annie Cantabile,' she said. 'I'm the daughter of the man who made the pianoforte you're playing.'

'The pianoforte in Manchester Square?'

'Do you have another?'

Alathea ignored that. 'What on earth do you want with me?'

Annie backed into the sofa and sat down. Her skirt was flabby, her feet soaking, her veil a rag. Alathea kept hold of the lamp and sat in the stiff-backed chair she thought of as her father's. A considerable pause. 'I know Monsieur Belladroit,' Annie said. 'You're his pupil.'

'Are you a pupil too?'

'No,' Annie said. 'I've no need of lessons.' Alathea's ignoring of her lip was as insupportable as if she were gloating over it. She felt like a circus bear waiting for the dogs.

Alathea considered Annie, the whole of her, sitting bolt upright. 'You may not need lessons at the pianoforte, but you've something to learn about following people. I've known for a fortnight, and today I knew you were behind me before I got to the end of Newgate Street.' She got up. 'I'm going to ring for some tea and ask for the fire to be lit. If I unlock the door, will you run away?'

'You have the front-door key,' Annie said. Her lip twitched. She could not stop it. She half bent her head, then decided against it. She would stay upright and hold on to her dignity.

Alathea unlocked the card-room door without looking back. 'Crouch,' she called. From somewhere footsteps echoed, and an old man appeared in a frock coat dirty beyond cleaning and shabby beyond mending. He too had been bequeathed by the house's previous occupants, glad to be rid of him since he was never where expected or doing what was required. 'A fire, and tea. Two cups. I have a visitor,' Alathea said. She had never before uttered those last four words. She stood for a second.

She returned. Annie had not moved, not even to replace her veil. The girls sat without speaking as Crouch shuffled to light the fire, shrugging at Alathea and with no interest in Annie, at whom he did not glance. Crouch was interested in only one person and that person was not here, nor ever likely to be. Every day since God had carried off his wife and child, Crouch dreamed of turning assassin and going to Rome to kill the Pope, whom, for reasons he explained to nobody, not even himself, he held directly responsible. But life had kept him a footman. Alathea and her father suited him well: their demands were small and they never checked the bills. He had a tidy sum stashed away. He returned with tea, hoping visitors were not going to become a habit. He saw Annie's lip as he deposited the tray, started, faltered badly and shuffled swiftly out, slamming the door as though the lip were alive and might escape.

Alathea poured the tea. She set a cup on the floor beside Annie and drank her own standing. The fire sulked. Alathea kicked it several times. Her shoes steamed. 'So, you're Annie Cantabile, daughter of the pianoforte maker, and you've no need for pianoforte lessons.'

'No,' said Annie. She was determined to force Alathea to acknowledge her lip. She must get that over with.

Alathea's face still registered nothing. 'Monsieur Belladroit taught you until you reached this happy stage?'

'No. He has never taught me.' Annie kept her face raised high. Say something, she willed. Then we can fight.

'I see.'

Silence. Alathea looked as though she could remain silent for ever. Annie could hardly bear it. She had achieved nothing. She tried something else. She picked up the teacup and sipped, and when a drop dripped from her lip, didn't dab it. Now, surely, with the lip glistening and the tea dripping, Alathea would at least blench. After people blenched, so Annie had learned, they usually felt the need to say something. Alathea neither blenched nor spoke. Instead, Annie found herself speaking. 'Monsieur's living with us while he teaches at Manchester Square. I believe there's to be a concert.'

'Monsieur Belladroit told you about the concert?'

'Your father told us when he came to buy the pianoforte.' Annie made an assumption.

Alathea shook her head violently. 'Drigg! That oaf! Not my father.' She put her teacup on the table. 'We're indebted to your father, though. The pianoforte is remarkable.'

Annie's feet were so cold that it was hard to be still. 'It's just a pianoforte.'

Alathea frowned. 'Is that what you think?'

Annie did not want to have a conversation about the pianoforte. She huddled into herself. She needed the fire. Suddenly the world moved – or at least the sofa. Alathea was pushing it forward towards the blaze and was now kneeling, her hands untying the laces of Annie's boots. 'No,' Annie said. Without her boots she could never escape. Alathea was determined and deft. The laces were undone, the boots were off and Annie's stockinged feet were set on the hearthstone. The flames were more lively now. The heat was wonderful.

Alathea shifted to one side, still kneeling. 'You'll ruin your boots without overshoes,' she observed. 'What neat feet you have. I've neat feet too. Sometimes I look at women with large feet and feel sorry for them, don't you?'

'Sorry for them?' Annie was astounded. She should feel sorry for women with large feet!

'Yes, sorry for them. You can't do anything about large feet. They're there, like dinner plates, sticking out. I always look at feet. It's how I judge people. Yours are fine feet, the feet of a lady.' Alathea chose what she said with care. She was not sure, at the moment, how she wished things to continue or end.

'I can't bear this!' Annie burst out, pulling her feet away. 'Let me go home.'

'Can't bear your feet to be judged? Why not? You came to judge me on behalf of your father, didn't you? He knows what his pianoforte is. He can't have wanted to let it go to people like the Frogmortons.'

'I didn't come for my father.'

'For whom, then?'

'You know why I came. You saw.'

'Oh, the acid. Were you really going to throw it at me?'

'Why else would I have brought it?'

'Well, I'm glad you didn't throw it, and I'm glad you came. I've never met anybody else who had no need of pianoforte lessons.'

Annie raised her eyes. Before she could snatch them away, a tiny spark. Alathea smiled. Annie stayed very still.

'There are five of us learning with Monsieur,' Alathea said conversationally. Conversation was certainly not her usual custom, but then having a visitor to tea was not her custom either. 'The others have barely an ounce of talent between them.'

'I'm sure they've nice feet.' Annie meant her voice to sting.

Alathea laughed. 'Everina and Marianne's feet are not hopeless, which is just as well. They certainly can't rely on their faces.'

Now, Annie thought. Now she'll say something about my lip. The poker was within reach. She could seize it. She would seize it. She prepared herself. 'We're all to be married, you know,' Alathea said. 'Our concert is supposed to increase our value – not monetary, you understand. Our fathers are rich. It's to make up for our parentage. You've played our pianoforte?'

'Of course.' Annie was still contemplating the poker.

'Does Monsieur Belladroit speak of us?'

Annie's voice was clipped. 'I do not speak to Monsieur about you.'

'But you'd like to know what he feels about us, I think.'

Annie fixed her eyes on the portrait. It was too small to see any detail except that it was a child. Her gaoler-hostess?

Alathea's own eyes flicked briefly to the portrait, then back. 'Monsieur's the reason you followed me.' She wondered why she had been so slow to guess.

'Of what interest could Monsieur possibly be to me?' Annie made herself stand up.

'The same as for any other girl,' Alathea replied. 'Monsieur may not be young but his charms are undiminished.'

'Monsieur's a friend,' Annie said tightly.

'A man like Monsieur can only be a friend to old women, or women possessed of no beauty – and that, Annie Cantabile, is a category to which neither of us belongs.' Alathea's response was not remotely thoughtless. She waited for Annie to break.

Annie broke. She collapsed back on to the sofa. 'Are you blind? Do you see nothing?'

'I see everything,' Alathea said.

'Well, then!' Annie cried.

'I think we may be quite similar, you and I.'

Annie pointed to Alathea's perfect lips and then her own. Not content with that, she pulled her lips wide and thrust them in front of Alathea's. The musk scent was overpowering and Annie's lip pulsed hard enough to hurt. She thought it might burst. She hoped it would drench Alathea in blood.

Alathea grabbed Annie's hands and locked them together, forcing the girl backwards. Furious, resistant, despairing, powerless, Annie tried to imagine she had the acid, that she had thrown it, that Alathea's purple pupils, so dense, so cool, were shrinking and shrivelling instead of softening and spreading. Annie shook her head. A quirk of Alathea's cheek. A certain

86

unconscious pleading in those lips, those lips whose perfection should, if there had been any justice in the world, have been matched by Annie's. Pleading? Alathea was making fun of her. Annie punched against the spell being cast about her. And now something worse. Perhaps it was the warmth, perhaps it was the desperation, perhaps it was even something in the tea, but tears arose. Annie bit them back, wrenched Alathea's hands from her shoulders and crouched down facing the fire. Alathea crouched too. 'I've always had a strange taste in beauty,' Alathea said. Annie exhaled. At last, the acknowledgement. The relief was unusually intense. She remained crouched. From the corner of her eye she saw Alathea pick up one of her boots. 'Is your lip painful?'

Annie contemplated not answering. In the end, she said, 'No.'

'I'm glad.' Alathea put the boot where it would dry more efficiently.

'Are you an idiot?' Annie began to rock. 'It pains me every minute of every day.'

Alathea picked up the other boot, then dropped it. The singed sheet toasting on the hearthstone had begun to smoke. With a sudden swoop, Alathea bundled it over the logs. The blaze thundered, enormous, threatening the chimney, pouring warmth into the room and making the other sheets billow. Annie threw up her head. Alathea's own head was thrown back, her throat entirely exposed. Annie could reach for the poker unhindered. She wanted to. She even made a small movement. Alathea turned. She put her hands on Annie's shoulders, the pressure intense as the heat. Annie wondered if they were both about to go up in flames. She felt half drugged. She wondered again about the tea.

'I think you have two lips,' Alathea said softly, 'this one' – she ran a finger first over Annie's bottom lip – 'and this one'. She ran a finger over the top lip, which took a little longer. She took Annie's index finger. 'And I think that I have this one,' she ran Annie's finger over her own top lip, 'and this one.' She kept hold of Annie's hand. 'Come,' she said. 'I've something to show you.'

She drew Annie to her feet. Annie made to put her boots on, but Alathea would not wait. She picked up the lamp. When they reached the door, she indicated her pocket. Annie pulled out the key. She could smash the lamp, unlock the door and be free. She should do it now. She unlocked the door. She could refuse to climb the stairs. She climbed the stairs. She and Alathea walked together past the dead rooms. Outside a large set of double doors Alathea let go of Annie's hand and reached for a bronze key hidden behind a draped madonna. She unlocked one door and swung it open. She walked in. Annie walked in behind her. Alathea closed the door and locked it.

The room had been a small ballroom. Alathea still called it that, though nobody had ever danced in it. Sheets covered three of the four consoles in the four alcoves on the right-hand side, with more sheeting covering the sitting-out sofas between each console. A large fireplace, clearly in frequent use, divided the four alcoves. The console nearest the door was uncovered and on it was an assortment of lamps, candles and flintboxes. On the left-hand wall of the room hung a complete set of gilt-framed mirrors. These were uncovered. To save space, a musicians' balcony had been built above the mirrors. At the far end, the two long windows were heavily shuttered and above the girls' heads six chandeliers shivered. Annie saw none of this. She saw only that in the middle of the room, in lonely polished splendour, stood a pianoforte, a harpsichord set to its right, nose to tail. Two long stools waited. Alathea lit a second lamp and gave it to Annie. 'Shall we play?'

Both girls moved forward. Annie could feel the dust under her stockinged feet and in her nostrils. It mingled with Alathea's musk, thickening the air. Alathea set down her lamp and went to light the fire. Annie ignored the harpsichord and sat at the pianoforte. Alathea returned and sat on Annie's right. There was music on the stand. Alathea set it aside and chose some sheets from a pile on the floor. Mozart duets? An imperceptible nod from Annie. Alathea counted them in. Two sets of hands on the keyboard; two sets of eyes reading the script; two investigatory glances and listenings. No need of pianoforte lessons. True? False? Two intellects phrasing the music, probing, coaxing. Two sets of shoulders sinking, loosening. Four hands obedient, powerful, practised. Occasionally one girl would stumble and correct. Occasionally the other would tap a bar in the text for a repeat. Occasionally Alathea would stop and make a suggestion.

At first, Annie was content to follow Alathea. Then, as the room warmed and the music took hold, Annie made suggestions of her own. This was her skill and her language. She was equal here. Together they filled the room. The last motif. The last recapitulation. The last chord. They turned to each other. Alathea raised her hands, palms out. Annie raised her hands in response. Their fingers gently beat together: one, two, three, four; one, two, three, four. Alathea drew back. Annie was left poised. Alathea opened her arms and from her, like a draught, blew exhilaration, triumph and joy. It was the joy that swept Annie in. With a long sigh, she tipped forward and clung to Alathea. Without hesitation, Alathea clung to Annie.

It might have been an hour after the embrace before the girls returned to the card room. The tea things were as they had left them. The fire was almost out, the sheet reduced to ash. What had happened in the ballroom after the music puzzled them both, and it was in neither girl's nature to speak about what they did not know. They could recount their movements chronologically. They had clung. They had clung very close. Their clinging had moved them from pianoforte stool to the rug in front of the fireplace. There had been movements of hands under clothes. There had been skin and hair, strokes of various urgencies, intrusions and exclamations. There had been no kiss. None had been proffered by either girl and none had been taken. When movement ceased, they had lain still until, without a word, both got up and made ready to come downstairs.

They had not returned to the pianoforte before they left the ballroom, though Annie had touched it as she passed, like an explorer touching a marker flag. She had been here. She might not come again. In the card room both girls could see they were extremely grimy. Still nothing said. Annie wiped her hands before bending to put on her boots. She stood and they moved to the hall. Alathea was ready with the veil and Annie was glad of its cover, not to hide her lip – how could she care about that now? – but to hide her expression. She had no idea what it revealed to Alathea, or what it might reveal to passers-by or to her father.

There was no sentimental parting. Annie secured her veil. Alathea ran upstairs. Annie waited. Alathea returned in moments with a score. This was the invitation to return. Annie tucked the score under her arm and prepared for the street.

When the door shut between them, Alathea leaned on it. She had an unfamiliar feeling in her stomach. It was happiness, though she assessed it as one might assess pain. Good? Bad? Dangerous? It was good, and it was dangerous, she decided. She also knew she could not, and did not want to, get rid of it.

She dined with her father in the card room, Crouch in reluctant attendance as both cook and waiter. Alathea was ravenous.

She was not concerned that Crouch might speak of her visitor. Crouch said nothing to anybody, not even when asked. As usual, Alathea went upstairs directly after supper. Unusually, she did not look in at the pianoforte. Instead, she lit the fire in her bedroom and sat in front of one of the many mirrors, brushing her hair. A sense of shock was part of the happiness. Though Alathea had had no previous encounter such as this afternoon's, the shock was not sexual. What shocked her as she stared at herself, unsmiling, was something new she saw in those elastic eyes of hers, something unlooked-for, uncultivated, unarmoured. Ridiculous. Annie was a stranger, and a malignant one at that. She had brought acid, to destroy. Alathea did not know Annie well enough to be her enemy, let alone her – her what? Alathea stopped brushing. How could they not know each other? The music they had made! She pulled a guard in front of the fire, got into bed and waited.

In the most secret hour of the night, her father came to her, as was his habit. As was hers, she accommodated him, tonight very careful that he should sense no difference. As always, he was furtive, scarcely moved. As always, she chose the form, directed proceedings, did the work. She kept her eyes open. His were closed. Neither spoke. This was the way it had always been, only varied if Sawneyford brought jewels. Then, before the other business, she would light a candle and he would place the stones where he liked to place them, admire them, play with them, then slip them back into their soft bag or into a box he had given her and which she kept under her bed. Tonight, no jewels. She was quick and efficient. He arrived as the clocks struck three and was in his own bed before they struck the quarter. When Alathea had washed and changed her nightdress, she re-read her pamphlet, lay back and gazed at the ceiling. The foolishness of men. How strong they seemed; how authoritative. They owned their wives and children. They could start a war with a nod. Yet all the while they were powerless against a reflexive judder which made them ludicrous. No wonder men preferred to rut in the dark. Her smile hardened and broadened. She and Annie would not rut in the dark. In utopia there would always be candles.

Once in the street, Annie was sorry the rain had stopped since with every step she expected shame to engulf her and rain might help wash the shame away. She wondered if shame would leap out of the whorehouse, out of the academy, out of Trotter's warehouses, even out of the pickle factory, whose hot vinegar made her sneeze again. Nothing. She wondered if shame was waiting on the corner of Charles Street or as she turned into Oxford Street, splashing her way westward among the wheelbarrows, dung, livestock and people, always people, all confronting or avoiding, threatening or persuading, hiding or revealing, meeting or parting. Hats on. Hats off. Deference, contempt, derision, admiration, the lucky, the unlucky and the shameful, to whose ranks she now belonged. Shame would surely stalk her more efficiently than she had stalked Alathea. But it had not caught her yet.

She hurried into Tyburn's muddle of lanes. Shame might grab her as she picked up some fish from the fishmonger for supper, or insinuate itself as she flung a coin at the local amputee. Nothing. Surely it would stamp on her as she opened the workshop door. She halted in front of her father's desk, all ready to be engulfed. Her father was filing ivory. Annie removed her veil. Nothing. Perhaps when she went to tell her mother she was back. Nothing. She went to her own room, hid Alathea's music under her mattress, washed her face, brushed down her skirt and tidied her hair. For the first time, she wanted a mirror: she needed to be sure of her expression. She went to the kitchen and did what she always did: rinsed the fish, peeled the potatoes, unwrapped the bread she had made earlier. She felt she was looking at herself from the outside. She glanced about. Monsieur would be back soon. Perhaps he was already here, in his room, resting. Yes, see: his coat was slung across a chair. She breathed in, out. Steady.

When Monsieur appeared for supper, she kept herself away from him, nervous that he might smell Alathea's musk on her as she had smelled it on him. She did not allow herself to revisit the afternoon, not one second of it, until she was in her bed. Then, to her horror, it was in the dark that shame and ridicule flooded through. She could no longer hear the music in the ballroom. She heard Alathea laughing – and Alathea was not alone. Annie saw her in Manchester Square with the other girls, and they were all laughing and chanting her name. Annie Cantabile! Annie Cantabile! As they chanted, they stuck fingers in their mouths in rude approximation of her deformity, Alathea pulling her mouth widest, turning her lips inside-out. Alathea was telling the girls what she had said; she was showing the girls what they had done; she was turning it into a freakshow. 'Sixpence to see the lip lady!' The girls were loving it, their mouths slashes of derision. Annie lay rigid. Was that how Alathea had spent her evening?

She heard St Mary's chime three o'clock. The images of the other girls dissolved. Alathea's alone remained, and she no longer had her fingers in her mouth, she had them quite elsewhere, and Annie was again lying in the music-studded dust with Alathea's pulse beating through flesh, nerve and sinew. Annie gave herself up to the beat until it was not a beat in her life but the beat *of* her life, her heart's song, her soul's music. She and Alathea were composers together, conductors together, instruments together. She clenched her fists. This was the way to madness. To Alathea, Annie would be a passing fancy. So many other girls – all perfect. Yet those few short hours had been the crown of Annie's life. How could she live if those hours, already over, were all there was?

She got out of bed, pulled the music from under her mattress and pressed it against her stomach. The flatness of the paper calmed her. The clefs calmed her. The black printed notes calmed her. She would not have only those hours. Alathea would be expecting her tomorrow. The door was open. The music said so.

She returned to Soho Square late the following afternoon. She had the music with her. Crouch was standing by the door like a sentinel. Annie lost courage. The day after, she saw Alathea going out. In a deep-blue cloak and a hat with feathers, supremely confident and self-possessed, Alathea looked right and left. She might have been looking for Annie, she might not. Whatever the truth, her confidence depleted Annie's. She dared not approach Alathea in the street, not in full sunlight, not even in her veil. She could not risk Alathea uttering that telling 'Oh, hello' that really meant 'Oh, what a nuisance.' Annie watched Alathea pause, walk and pause again. If she looks my way, I'll go to her, Annie thought. Alathea walked swiftly the other way and Annie returned to Tyburn in agony, half revolted at her memories, half longing to relive them.

6

ON Alathea's lesson days, Monsieur wore a long coat, a garment appropriate for the chilly early-morning walk from Tyburn but far too hot in the stale air of no. 23. It came down to his knees, all round. There must be no possibility of embarrassment. He did not always need the coat. Alathea chose what she did and when. He wore it, though, in hope. On the days he was not teaching, he wandered through the shrill clamour of the streets, quite contented, a man who had made more of himself than anticipated by the grey childhood, dull schoolmaster father, stolid mother and dreary provincial town known for nothing at all.

Monsieur did not believe in God, but had he done so, he would have thanked him for the musical talent that had taken him to Paris at an early age. A dutiful son, he had sent some of his first pay back to his parents, who had returned it with a kindly letter; they had no need of it. That, Claude had taken some time to admit to himself, had been a curious blow. He had wanted them to need it, just as all these years later he had wanted them to be concerned about him living in Paris, with its streets aflame. However, his father had no knowledge, or desire for knowledge, of flaming streets. His little school was still well attended; Claude's brother was taking classes for younger children; one sister was married to a butcher, the other to a baker. There were grandchildren in the offing. When Claude had returned to tell them he was off to London, he found the only shadow cast by the revolution was his mother asking if the door to Claude's lodgings possessed a good lock and, in an oblique reference to the state of his shirt, if all the laundries had closed down. In the end Claude had not bothered to say he was leaving the country. Nor did he say he was resolved never to revisit his childhood home as long as he lived. Paris was awful, Paris was dangerous, but at least Paris was alive.

On Manchester Square days, he was fully occupied. The girls' technique and the learning of the *Clavier-Übung* progressed in line with his seductions – in other words, slowly. Marianne had taken to wearing a sprigged *faux*-shepherdess dress and ringlets. Was this an English joke at the dead French Queen's rural affectations? If so, it was a failure. Marianne looked like a sheep decked out for a May holiday. Fat fingers, fat arms, fat brain. 'Brace yourself, *mon petit*,' he took to murmuring before Marianne attacked the pianoforte.

His scoldings over the music were careful. Everina and Marianne might not know the difference between making music and making a din, but – and apologies to poor Herr Bach's celestial variations – what did it really matter? When the time came, the girls would be deflowered after the manner of their playing: coarsely and without compunction. All the composers they had traduced would have their revenge. Sometimes he could not help lecturing. 'My father, who has been *Kapellmeister* to emperors, told me when I was still a baby that instruments must be coaxed like shy choirboys, not slapped about,' he barked at Marianne when her thumping hit him directly behind the eyes. He wanted to beat her like a carpet. He would enjoy it.

He worked them all hard and, to his relief, found as much to amuse as annoy. Harriet, for instance, now often wore an expensively simple rose-coloured muslin sack-dress, no whalebone, no stiffening, no decoration, her hair loosely bound up. The effect should have been pleasing, but Harriet, nervously unconstricted, moved as though caught in the street in her nightdress. Still, as Monsieur coached her through the crossing hands, the arpeggio patterns and finger-swapping needed for the concert piece, her garments made appreciation of her lovely neck, downy below the hairline, very easy. 'Duckling hair,' he murmured to himself. 'How did la Frog produce such a creature? Nature performs miracles.'

He thought about Mrs Frogmorton more than that lady could have imagined. Principally, he thought how to get rid of her. No seduction could reach its grand finale with a chaperone hovering. But sometimes, when she came over to exchange a word, he found himself amazed that there was one word for both her flesh and Alathea's. Not that he had experienced Alathea's flesh as yet. A hand is not flesh. Yet Madame Frogmorton's hand would not do. Had la Frog once been like Alathea, he wondered? Take away a chin or two, thin the cheeks, cut away the belt of neck fat and rake off twenty years, he thought, and yes, la Frog could have passed muster. She had good round eyes and her one eyebrow had presumably once been two.

Harriet practised well. Monsieur was pleased with her. 'Feel every finger as a cog in a weaving machine,' he told her. 'Each part has its own job, and together all the parts weave the cloth.' He encouraged her to think of their relationship as a contract. 'Partners,' he suggested after Harriet had told him rather wistfully that had she been a boy she would have been in her father's office. 'You will be my little businesslady and I your office manager, your chief clerk, your steward.' It had been a good conceit. Harriet had shaken his hand with a twinkle and swished out leaving him appreciating, through her gown, the slight overflow of flesh from the top of her stockings.

Then there was the day when Everina turned up sporting frizzed hair with some kind of nest atop, and an absurd dress of slashes and frills. From whom did she take fashion advice, a turkey cock? 'And what book have you been reading today, young lady?' he asked as she tripped towards him.

'Classical mythology,' Everina told him.

'Are the stories moving?'

'They're silly. I like flesh-and-blood heroes. Who wants to be loved by a god dressed up as some horrible bird? And I'd be furious if any husband of mine flapped off leaving me with a scrawny baby who was going to grow up to kill me.'

Monsieur Belladroit's laughter was quite genuine. Everina began to drill out some preludes he had given her: small works, easy on the fingers, of no musical importance. She paid no attention to Monsieur's instructions so he seated himself on her right and began, with malice, to copy exactly what she did, two octaves above. The faster and louder Everina played, the faster and louder he played. Everina began to giggle, her tongue protruding, a flash of greyish pink, thin as a hen's. Faster and faster she played. Faster and faster Monsieur played. More and more percussive grew the sound, with Everina working the pedals like treadles on a sewing machine. Monsieur felt the pianoforte cry out for mercy. 'Not yet, *mon petit*,' he muttered. When the final chord rolled, Everina was sweating like the Stratton Street step scrubber. She mopped her brow with her sleeve. Mrs Frogmorton clapped. Monsieur tilted. Everina braced, anticipating a scolding. Monsieur surprised her. 'Again!' he whispered, his breath like sulphur on her cheek.

The volume increased. Frilly began to whine, and then to howl. Monsieur grinned. This might be the way to get rid of la Frog. '*Continuez*,' he ordered Everina, and poked his head round the screen. Mrs Frogmorton's sewing was abandoned. She was half out of her seat. Monsieur waved and shouted above the din. 'Apologies! Mademoiselle Drigg does play a little loudly, dear *madame*. That is her style. My ears are of no consequence, but I worry for you. It cannot be good to sit so close.'

Mrs Frogmorton resented a charge of weakness. 'My ears will manage perfectly well,' she said and sank down again. Frilly whimpered.

'But the little dog suffers, no?'

Mrs Frogmorton eyed Monsieur, picked up her embroidery and stabbed it. 'You leave the dog to me.' Monsieur bowed and returned to the pianoforte. A different approach must be taken, and taken soon.

Of the girls themselves, Georgiana troubled him most, floating tremulously towards him, a wisp of pale foam amid folds of indeterminate colour and texture. At least, after that first lesson, she remained untrammelled by hoops or stays, her hair usually down, a lick of honey loosely gathered by a gauze ribbon. Unlike Harriet, Georgiana was more comfortable in this ethereal state, imagining that floating clothes rendered her almost invisible. To Monsieur's delight, she had no idea that the almost invisible is also the almost visible, and the almost visible shouts 'Look at me' very loudly. When he sat beside her on the pianoforte stool, Monsieur made the happy discovery that there was more flesh than he imagined within the foam.

He won her confidence with a pretty untruth. 'We are both perchers, if I am not mistaken,' he said at their third lesson,

Georgiana still too paralysed with shyness to play more than simple scales.

'Perchers?'

'Yes, perchers. Birds for whom no position is ever comfortable. I do not know about you, *mademoiselle*, but perching came to me early. My father died when I was a baby, you see. I never knew him. It was always just my mother and myself, perching together, never sure enough of anywhere to make a home. During our early perchings, I had no instrument on which to play and barely a stool on which to sit. In the end, my mother gave up struggling for a perch. She died when I was ten, with nothing.'

Georgiana, wide-eyed: 'She had you.'

'I was not enough, *mademoiselle*.'

Georgiana's eyes filled. 'It's not nice, not to be enough.'

'Not nice, no, *mademoiselle*.' Monsieur let her droop a moment. 'I was enough for another, though, a girl of great talent whom I taught as I teach you.' He sighed. 'She was taken from me by a fever. Mine was the last name on her lips.' He bowed his head. Georgiana's tears sparkled. Monsieur waited until one or two had dropped on to the keys. 'I fear my confidences make you sad.'

'We're sad together,' she said.

After that, he got her to play her initials, G and B, in various combinations, then his own, C and B, then put the two sets of initials together. Georgiana was unable to resist. Soon she was playing music carefully chosen by Monsieur not to frighten, and she proved to have more natural musicality than Harriet, though it was a pity, Monsieur thought, that she would never play like Annie. Annie. What a terrible shame to be a musical prodigy afflicted with deformity. If only she could offer the world her music out of sight. Monsieur supposed it would be possible, but it would take some arrangement and he did not have the inclination. Georgiana had no need to play out of sight and she would at least do Herr Bach more justice than Marianne and Everina. When he told her that the instrument liked her, he was speaking sincerely.

He remembered little of the verbal exchanges he had with Alathea. However he remembered very clearly the purple satin open robe with a paler underdress, a crossover handkerchief covering her shoulders and caught at the neck with a nondescript brooch, all individual constituents demure, yet the girl emerging through the green gloom like a ripe plum. Her hair, too wiry for conventional beauty and uncovered by any cap, was a nimbus of Muscovy sugar. Monsieur breathed her in like brandy.

Alathea never offered any greeting, or acknowledgement of what happened between them – or, more accurately, what she did to him. Usually, she filled the hour uttering almost no words at all. But oh! Oh! One day she played Bach's gentle aria again, this time making it peep like a courtesan through a grille. When she spread the chord of the eleventh measure, Monsieur's mouth was dry. Then it was wet. Then it was dry again. The fingers and the beringed thumb now feathering those notes absorbed all his attention, as though he had taken some drug. He could not help imagining them feathering a different place entirely. Only Mrs Frogmorton's infernal presence prevented him from grabbing those hands. At the final Gs, he was reduced to quiet panting. He would never forget what happened next. She turned to him, then turned back to the keys and played Variation 1. He hissed. Then Variation 2. This time, no repeats. She did not begin Variation 3. Instead, 'Play,' she ordered.

'What shall I play?' he asked in a husky voice.

'Whatever you please.'

He began immediately, though he could not have said what

he began. (It was Bach's Prelude and Figure No. 2 in C Minor – Alathea recognised it at once.) Without blinking, she undid two buttons of his trousers. His hands shook. He could not think how he kept on playing. She pushed back his coat and undid a third button. He was released. Relief and terror on his part. There he was, Monsieur Belladroit, playing Bach while fully exposed. He thought, If that dog barks now, I'll have to kill it. Was it the fugue he reached before Alathea bent over? He recalled no sound. He recalled only hair, hand, lips, then lips, hand, hair. At the crucial moment, the fire crackling, the heat rising, his face contorting, she gave him her thumb and he bit down on the ring. As soon as practicable, she withdrew her thumb, thanked him for the lesson, nodded to Mrs Frogmorton and left him winded and speechless, his heart hammering, a host of nameless sensations rampaging, and sweat crackling in unexpected places – the back of his knees, the crook of his elbows, behind his ears.

After that, she took to missing lessons, and after her fourth absence, though Harriet suggested she was probably unwell, he wondered if she was waiting for him to shift the great mass of Mrs Frogmorton before she returned. Surely she must return? He must get rid of la Frog.

One sunny Friday in May, as Mrs Frogmorton was leaving for her lunch, Monsieur seized a candelabra and spilled wax on to the floor. He shouted aloud at his clumsiness. 'Oh no! Oh *mon Dieu*!'

Mrs Frogmorton, alarmed, appeared around the screen.

'So sorry, *madame*. What a clot. Is that what you say, a clot? Yes? No?'

'For goodness' sake, *monsieur*, don't dab at the wax like that. If you leave it to dry, it'll peel off and the servants can polish over the mark.'

'Indeed, but I'm sorry. Your beautiful floor in this beautiful room.' He got up slowly, picking wax out of his nails.

Mrs Frogmorton frowned. She thought he was making fun of her. Then she thought he seemed downcast. 'The girls are getting on well,' she said, since it was hard simply to turn her back. He nodded. 'And I hope your pay has been left for you every Friday on the table in the hall? The servants are honest, I believe, but I trust you still count it.'

Monsieur made no comment. The reminder that he was hired displeased him.

Mrs Frogmorton blew out the candles. She thought Monsieur looked a little overcome. She felt kindly, and kindliness led to confidentiality. 'It's a great worry, having daughters to marry,' she said. 'Do you have daughters yourself?'

'I have—' A heartbeat as he considered whether a daughter might be useful. 'I have not,' he amended. He made a motion of regret. 'The fact is . . . ' he looked up, as though gauging her trustworthiness.

'Yes?' said Mrs Frogmorton. She hoped this was not going to take long.

Monsieur took a deep breath. 'The fact is, *madame*, I am not as other men.' Frilly growled. Monsieur narrowed his eyes.

Mrs Frogmorton caressed her pet. 'Of course you're not as other men, *monsieur*. You're French.'

Monsieur stared at her. What did the old fool mean? Did she seriously think Frenchmen were constituted differently to Englishmen? *Mon Dieu*, but he could show her. He clenched and unclenched a fist. Back to the task in hand. 'Not just because I am French, I am sorry to say.'

'Oh? Why then?'

You could always rely on women's curiosity. He dangled. 'I cannot tell you, *madame*. The story is too horrible.'

Mrs Frogmorton took the bait. 'Horrible?'

Monsieur did not waste his chance. 'I was orphaned as a baby, and at just five years old was taken in by a choirmaster on account of my beautiful soprano voice.'

From Monsieur's emphasis on the final words, Mrs Frogmorton gathered she was supposed to learn something, although what, she had no idea. 'You never knew your parents?'

'No. Had they lived, they would never have allowed what occurred to occur.'

'And what did occur, Monsieur Belladroit?'

Monsieur's lips pursed. 'That is what I cannot tell you.'

She spread her feet. 'Monsieur, you've begun so you must finish. I doubt you can tell me anything I haven't heard before.'

Monsieur shuffled his music. 'I think I can.'

'Let me be the judge of that.' She cast a huge shadow over the pianoforte.

'Very well. Perhaps you are right. Perhaps you will not find it so shocking, being a lady of experience. Perhaps it is even common practice amongst you English. Many odd things are.' He coughed. 'My beautiful soprano voice made money for the choirmaster. When I reached a certain age, he did not wish to lose his income. Do you follow?'

'He sounds a very practical man.'

Monsieur bit his lip. This woman! 'He was frightened of my voice, how do you say?, cracking.'

'Breaking,' Mrs Frogmorton corrected.

'Thank you. Breaking. Do you know how he made sure my voice would not break?'

'I cannot ...'

A pause as Mrs Frogmorton's imagination began to grind and her jaw to drop. 'Monsieur ...'

'Butchery, Madame Frogmorton, nothing less than butchery. One night, during the dark hours, he rendered me deliberately insensible through drugged wine. Then he and a medical man

104

crept into my bedchamber, uncovered me and used abominable tools against my—'

'Oh, glory!' said Mrs Frogmorton and clapped her hand hard on Frilly's head.

'Against my—'

'Enough, *monsieur*!' Mrs Frogmorton trumpeted.

'I hope I have not caused offence.'

Mrs Frogmorton was not sure what Monsieur Belladroit had caused. There was a name for such men. *Castrati*. It sounded absurd. It was absurd. Nevertheless, she must respond. 'I am sorry for you, *monsieur*,' she said. 'A man without—' She stopped and searched about. 'A man without, er, without – without *parents* is unhappy indeed.' She backed away.

'Please say nothing,' Monsieur begged. 'It is a hideous embarrassment to me. As you may imagine, I am in a constant state of . . . ' He looked to her for help.

'Mortification,' said Mrs Frogmorton.

'Exactly as you say.'

'I'm sorry for you,' Mrs Frogmorton said again. 'Now, I think your lunch is about to arrive.' She rustled smartly off. Foreigners. What dreadful things they did. Poor Monsieur Belladroit. She wondered if the same practice went on with those Spaniards over the road. She must watch out for her younger servants.

Monsieur brushed his lapels and congratulated himself. That had been quicker than expected. He worried a little that Mrs Frogmorton had not waited for him to explain in more detail, since it was common knowledge that *castrati* were not always incapable of the act of sex, even if incapable of fathering children. He had wanted to stress that his butchery had been very complete indeed. No matter. He doubted she would discuss the finer points. To her, with luck, he would be 'unfortunate Monsieur Belladroit', a man but not a man and certainly not necessitating a chaperone. He did not care whether or not she respected his confidence. Indeed, it might be helpful if the girls believed him incapable. Alathea would not be fooled, of course. She would laugh out loud. Mrs Frogmorton might tell the servants. That bothered him more. Still, Cantabile's money would make the humiliation tolerable.

He was pleased with himself as he packed away his music and let himself out. (Spencer the footman did not consider Monsieur's comings and goings any business of his.) In Oxford Street, a crocodile of schoolboys tossed dung at their teacher. Boys were very unpleasant, Monsieur thought. He had never taught one to play the pianoforte and never would. He headed straight back to Tyburn.

'These girls,' he said much later, and after Cantabile had been suitably entertained by the recounting of the ruse.

Cantabile poured more wine. 'What's the matter with them?'

'Oh, everything with two of them. But there is more to the others than you might think.'

'So?'

'At least one is worthy of your pianoforte.'

Cantabile banged down the bottle, no longer entertained. 'Don't speak of that instrument.'

Monsieur raised his hand. 'Come now, Vittorio.'

Cantabile growled. 'I don't want details. Just do what has to be done. Bed the girls and leave them. That's what I'm paying you for.'

'What about the one Monsieur is to marry? Isn't that part of the plot?' Annie's voice was cool from the corner. She was mending a nightcap.

Both men jumped. 'What are you doing skulking in the dark?' snarled her father.

'Hardly skulking. I've been sitting here for an hour or more and I have a candle.'

'You know what I mean. Your clothes are always dark. You might as well be a nun. But she's got a point, Claude. What about marriage?' He drank his glass in one gulp and poured another while Annie took the cover off a veal pie she had left warming on the hearth.

Monsieur sniffed. In the absence of a daughter, he thought about the attractions of a wife. Marianne? *Mon Dieu*. Harriet? Too prim. Georgiana? Too exhausting. Everina? He shuddered. Alathea? He blinked. What would that be like? He tried to imagine her cooking a veal pie. 'I do not envy their husbands,' he said.

Cantabile snorted. 'No husband is to be envied. We don't marry to be envied. We marry because we can't see the future. If we could, well—'

Monsieur said quickly, without looking at Annie, 'Annie's pie makes me hungry.'

Without a word, Annie laid out plates and dished up for the men before taking a tray to her mother. She returned once the meal was finished, collected the plates and washed them in a bucket.

She was wiping her hands when Monsieur put down his wine and caught her arm, wanting to make up for her father's unpleasantness. 'Play for me,' he said. It was the only thing he could think of.

Annie paused. She thought about Alathea day and night. Yet despite her longings, her old fantasy (since her father's guessing of it, this was how she termed her concert dream) was still not completely dead. Monsieur had asked her to play. Perhaps she could at least give her concert. Indeed, she could give it right now. She picked up a lamp and went down the stairs. For the moment, she pushed Alathea away. She would have faith in the music. It would lead where it led.

She did not choose a perfect instrument. She chose the

carriage-horse, and, after flexing her fingers, began with Mozart because Mozart said so much with so little. This evening, Mozart did not satisfy. The sonata she chose was too symmetrical, the player's movements too restricted. Mozart could also be trite. He felt trite tonight so she took a deep breath and played something of her own. This music was nothing like the music heard in a drawing room, or in the promenade gardens, or at a court amusement. It recognised the sol-fa but would not settle in one key. Transitions were not orderly; form was not followed. Annie's music was neither sonata nor rondo, prelude or bagatelle. It was a kind of spillage, in that it spilled out and retreated and spilled again. But it was not uncontrolled. Every note, every unnatural (to Monsieur's ear) cadence, every surge and eddy was choreographed to bear witness to some truth that Monsieur could barely grasp. He did not care for the harmony: it was the control and choreography that touched his heart. Annie's music was an uncomfortable wave, but it never crashed. Whether he liked it or not, it drew Monsieur into its swell. Had Herr Haydn heard the music, he would have shaken his head. Herr Haydn would have had a point; but so did Annie.

Cantabile stamped his disapproval on the floor above. Annie ignored him. This music was not for her father, it was for Monsieur and for herself. And it was working on Monsieur. He came to her, his face alight, just as she dreamed. She had made him forget the girls. Perhaps he was even insensible of her lip. Her faith had won the day. The music was all. She turned to him. This was her moment.

Monsieur ran five quick fingers over the keys. He did not know what to say about Annie's music. He could say that it challenged his notions of construction and execution. He could say that it agitated. He could say that he both wanted to hear more and wished he had heard none. He rejected all these things in the face of the most important thing, which was to say something that would make Annie feel she was of value.

He began by asking practical questions. Annie showed him the score, explained the counterpoint and harmonies, the balance and the underpinning, and how she had not rejected form, just overturned it. He exclaimed in wonder at her insights. He nodded his head. More questions, more answers. Annie was voluble. The sparkle extinguished by her father was relit. Eventually, long before the music was exhausted, Monsieur was exhausted himself. He threw up his hands. 'You have a talent, Annie. More than a talent. You play better than anybody I have ever heard, better than the late Herr Christian Schubart. Better, perhaps, even than I—' He could not quite allow that. 'At least your use of both the sustaining and *una corda* pedal is remarkable. As for your composing – remarkable too, truly remarkable. Only I am not sure. It is very odd. That is not always an advantage.' He dropped his hands. He looked at her directly. He did not want his smile to alter. He could not stop it doing so.

Annie saw the alteration. She knew instantly that her moment had gone. The sparkle in her eyes flattened and went out. 'Herr Mozart wrote oddly sometimes,' she said, chasing the moment and despising herself for it.

'Herr Mozart wrote like a man. You write like a woman. Listen.' He sat beside her and began to play. 'Here is what Mozart does.' He bent his head. 'Here is what you do.' Annie did not disagree. She simply thought, And is what I do so much less? She did not voice her question because she knew she would not care for Monsieur's answer.

When at last Monsieur stood up, Annie set him a final test. She lifted her face to him. She waited. Could he muster the courage? Monsieur could not pretend to misunderstand what she wanted, not for a second. Yet not for a second could he contemplate those lips after Alathea's. Annie, face still lifted, watched him spin round. His 'Good-night' was inaudible. She slowly lowered her chin and closed the carriage-horse. Entering her own room, having looked in on her mother, Annie thought how strange life was. She should have been devastated by the renewed loss of her dream, but instead found herself wondering if the loss was not Monsieur's.

7

ANNIE went to Soho Square the next afternoon, Alathea's music hugged against her. She would see Alathea today or she would die. She found her sitting on the step. When Alathea saw Annie, she got up and without a word pulled Annie inside, shut the door and headed upstairs to the ballroom. The fire was already burning. Annie removed her veil. 'I came—'

'Yes. But you went.'

'How did you know I'd come today?'

'How did you know I'd be waiting?'

Other girls would have smiled, but since Annie never smiled Alathea did not either. Annie set out the music. Alathea lit candles, came to Annie and put up her hand. Annie put up hers, their fingers brushed, then they sat down to play together at the pianoforte. They played Clementi, Couperin and Haydn's Sonata in C before turning to Bach. They played for two hours without ceasing.

'I must go,' said Annie. 'My mother needs me.'

'Go,' said Alathea. 'But if you don't come back tomorrow, I'll come and find you.'

Thereafter, there was no hesitation on Annie's part. She calculated when she could safely be away from Tyburn without causing her mother discomfort or her father or Monsieur to comment. She prepared food early. She cleaned late. She left things out in the workshop so that her father would believe her still there.

Soho Square was always the girls' meeting place, but it was Bach – demanding, thrilling, unforgiving – who joined them, stretching them and sometimes parting them in disagreements over, say, the phrasing of repeats or the best way to transfer music from harpsichord to pianoforte. They argued fiercely about dynamics, ornamentation and fingering, and most fiercely of all about whether the copyist had made an error with an A flat or an F sharp or whether it was the composer's intention. In a fortnight they had progressed far beyond duets. They still played together, but no longer four hands on one instrument. They played on separate instruments, and since both preferred the pianoforte, they took turn and turn about. Some days they did not play at all, only transcribed for the keyboard quartets, cantatas and the orchestral parts of concertos, or indeed any music that Alathea bought from printers, stole from churches or removed from publishers' windows. Annie did not yet dare reveal her own compositions, but she turned her hand to all manner of arrangements, distortions, inversions, perversions, reversions. The sounds the girls made playing in unison, in harmony, playing things never intended for the pianoforte, empowered them. Their bodily unions, when they happened, which was not every visit, were splendid. It was music, though, that brought the world to light and made them sharp and unafraid. They did not need God, in whom neither placed any trust.

They did not need family. The keyboard was enough to feel fresh, salty and utterly free.

Annie could not see how she had lived before this. She did not resent her former life, as she labelled it. In the hours back at Tyburn tending her mother and cooking for her father and Monsieur – and this was still most of her day – Annie recognised that her solitary existence, her father's insults and her mother's infirmities had been necessary. That life, enclosed in the workshop and burnishing her musicianship, had been preparation for this one. It had made her Alathea's match. She could not regret that, not ever.

On a fine day in mid-June, Annie suggested opening the ballroom shutters. To Annie's surprise, Alathea demurred, and for the first time since that rainy day in March, non-musical tension arose between the girls. Annie's tension was fuelled by the sudden realisation that Alathea had never seen her uncovered in natural light. Annie in candlelight was not the same as Annie in sunlight. Despite their intimacy, it was possible that Alathea did not know Annie as she really was. It was possible she did not want to.

Alathea was not thinking of Annie. She rejected daylight for herself: it deadened her. If her father was a creature of the City of London, she was a creature of the city, and, like the city, shone best in the man-made: the watchman's flare, the burst of the brazier, the flash of a flint, the blaze in the hearth. Sun, moon, glare of summer and crisp winter dawn diminished her and were to be avoided.

Had Annie pressed her, Alathea might have explained, but Annie's own fears stopped her from pressing. She simply acquiesced and sat down to play. It was the slight hunch of her shoulders, a hunch of which Annie herself was unaware, that alerted Alathea and tempted her to allow considerations other than her own to dictate how things would be.

Annie, at the harpsichord, was listening with the exaggerated care of one whose mind is somewhere else when Alathea got up, took a candle and, before she could change her mind, tore back a curtain. In a shower of green dust, a deluge of dead spiders rattled to the floor, live ones scuttled crazily and a canopy of bats surged up. Annie screamed and leapt on to the harpsichord stool, hauling her skirt over her head. Alathea screamed too and waved the candle. The bats swirled in a ragged cloud of twitters and chirps, punching out droppings. Floor and ceiling were alive. Clamping her mouth shut, Alathea dropped the candle and with both hands yanked at the shutter bolts, praying they would not be rusted shut. Eventually they gave way and she wrenched the shutter back, grabbed the candle and smashed the window with the base of the stick. Sunlight flooded in; the bats did not flood out. Alathea ran to the pianoforte, trying not hear the crunch of spiders dead and alive. 'Make a noise,' she cried, and began to bang the pianoforte's lid. Annie stamped on the harpsichord keys.

The vibrations confused the bats. They did not want to go out. They could not stay here. Finally they seethed through the broken glass, whirled around the square's lime trees and settled unhappily among the new leaves as nurses seized their charges, shrieked and fled. When the room was empty, Alathea jumped from the pianoforte and slammed the shutter shut. All the candles had blown out in the stramash and the fire was very low. Everything was obscured. Alathea made her way back to the harpsichord and touched Annie, who screamed again. 'They're gone,' Alathea said.

Annie crouched, her skirt still over her head. Alathea climbed on to the stool beside her, out of reach of scurrying spiders. Annie shuddered. 'I should never have suggested it. I didn't realise. I didn't think.'

'Shhh.' Alathea shuddered too. 'I didn't think either.'

'Do you suppose they're in every room?'

'I suppose so,' Alathea said, folding her skirts round her legs.

'How can you bear to live here?' Annie asked.

'We don't live here,' Alathea said. Her arms were sticky with torn cobweb. 'Ugh. Horrible.'

Annie slowly let her skirt down. 'You have another house?' She tried not to peer into the darkness above or below.

'I mean we don't live anywhere. This place is just a shelter. You have to have some protection from the weather.' Alathea began to recover. 'I live inside my skin. It suits me very well, unless it's invaded by bats or spiders. I suppose my father does the same. Now, I'm going to relight some candles from the fire. You stay here.'

'We have a house,' said Annie, peering after Alathea's shadow. She did not want, even for a second, to feel alone in here. 'It's my father's home, and my mother's, so I suppose mine too, but I feel more at home here than I ever feel at Tyburn.'

'Even with the bats and spiders?'

Annie said, in a burst, 'It's not the place. It's you.'

It was the first explicit declaration. It hung in the air. Alathea lit five candles. Treading carefully, she placed them on the instruments. 'We need brushes, cloths and water,' she said. 'All the keys will be filthy. We'll have to swill the floor.' Annie was left alone. She did not move a muscle. What if Alathea did not acknowledge her declaration? She wanted to take it back yet she was glad she couldn't.

Alathea returned with buckets, and vanished again to bring more lamps.

'Should we pull down the dust sheets?' Annie asked.

'No,' Alathea answered. 'We'll just do what's necessary. I'm not going to touch the curtains again. That one can stay open.'

Annie took a brush and the girls cleaned in silence, sweeping and swilling the floor, dusting down the instruments and stools and shaking out the music. Occasionally there was a flutter from above: not all the bats had taken to the skies. The girls shrank down. The fire was damped enough for occasional bats to scud up the chimney. 'Let's hope they stay there,' said Alathea.

When the cleaning was over, and with Annie's declaration still hanging, the girls settled themselves with Handel. They needed to stud the room with music again. They played loudly. The unexpected flurries had disturbed the cornicework. Before the sonata was finished – they only played the quick movements – the girls were white with flakes. 'I believe this house will fall down,' Alathea said as she wiped Annie's face.

'Then we'll find shelter elsewhere.' Annie wiped Alathea's. She jumped when Alathea clutched her arm.

'Listen to me, Annie.' An edge in Alathea's voice. A warning. Annie shrank, filled with foreboding. She should have said nothing. It hadn't been necessary. She was about to lose everything.

Alathea gave her a little shake. 'The thing is, we mustn't become dependent,' she said swiftly and without preamble. 'Never, ever, dependent. Not on each other. Not on anybody. We can depend on music, but that's all. Do you see? Being dependent on other people, on any other person, it gives them a way in, a way right inside you, like a worm. Have you ever tried to kill a worm?'

Annie shook her head.

'It's very hard. One becomes two and they wriggle in different directions. Being dependent's like that. It wriggles right into your core, and when you try and kill it, you never kill quite all of it. Or at least killing all of it nearly kills you. If you depend only on yourself, there's no worm. You are intact, completely whole. You do see, don't you?'

Annie did not see. To her, Alathea's sense of being intact

sounded much like being alone, and being alone was not powerfulness or wormlessness, it was loneliness. When Annie thought of being intact, she thought of herself and Alathea attached together, dependent on each other in an unassailable circle. How could she think otherwise? She was not Alathea. She knew nothing of the treacheries of Alathea's life, the what should be and was not, the what was and should not be. Alathea had not told her – withholding was part of her power, part of her independence – so the result of Alathea's warning was that Annie's heart sank beyond her boots. What a fool she was. This ballroom life was, in truth, another fantasy. It had come quickly; it would vanish as quickly. Alathea did not want her, or need her, so this could all stop in the same way it started: on Alathea's whim. Annie felt she must leave while her legs would still carry her. She tried to get up.

Alathea pinned her down. 'You must see.' Alathea knew her voice sounded different from normal. It pleaded, almost begged. She did not like it, but she had to go on. 'Dependence makes you weak. If you don't depend, all your strength is your own.' She hesitated. She was not used to making long speeches. 'And there's something else. If you don't depend and aren't depended on, you can never disappoint. How could you? You can't disappoint somebody if you're not attached to them and they're not attached to you.' Her voice strengthened. 'Detachment's a shield – it should be our shield. If we can be detached, we can never disappoint each other.'

'But what about—' Annie couldn't bring herself to cry 'love'.

'What about love?' Alathea let go of Annie's shoulders. 'Love's perfectly possible. We can be together but still apart; we can be in love, just not dependent. That's how to be happy. I know it.' Alathea pressed her palms on Annie's cheeks, as if her convictions were stamps. 'Most people don't understand, so they're never happy, not really. Once you're hooked by someone, you're always frightened of being lost or betrayed or hurt in some way. Let's not be frightened, or lost or betrayed or hurt. Let's not even entertain the possibility. We can be truly happy. Do you know why?' She did not wait for an answer. 'Because we're rare, Annie, rare.'

'I don't know!' This burst from Annie despite herself. 'I don't feel rare. How can I?'

'How can you not? We're bound together by music but we can play separately just as well. What use would we be if we couldn't? Think about it. Attached yet detached. It's what everybody would be if only they could. Most can't and we can. You and I. We can.'

Alathea was almost crushing Annie's jaw. Annie's lip was halfway up her nose. She caught Alathea's wrists and pulled them away. She did not want life to be the same as music, but there was something worse: the threatened loss of this ballroom existence in this shrouded house of bats and spiders. She could not lose it. She laced her hands behind Alathea's neck. She imagined a core forming and a slow tongue of molten silver folding round this core, encasing it. The tongue met round the middle, its soft edges soldering and hardening into a silver shell with no seam, no wrinkle, no escape hatch. She imagined the same in Alathea, in gold. She drew their faces together. Alathea bared her teeth. Annie bared hers. Their teeth clashed, enamel on enamel. Their hands were at each other. There was tearing of cloth and, in this moment of supreme untenderness, with a few baffled bats above and homeless spiders below, detachment bound them together.

Annie remained in Soho Square very late. When finally she left, her silver armour moulded and bolted, welded and polished, she stalked through the night streets like a queen. Had her father remained up to ask where on earth she had been, she might have killed him.

8

OUT of respect for Monsieur, Mrs Frogmorton had kept his secret. Nevertheless, as summer bloomed, she quietly abandoned her chaperoning for her closet and warming-stove – it was always chilly in Manchester Square. There came a day when, with the cook negotiating for a new store cupboard and an upstairs maid to chide, she openly left Monsieur to it. Nobody remarked. Everybody was used to him; he was no more than furniture. Mrs Frogmorton thought she would tell the alderman of Monsieur's mishap soon, and Mrs Drigg and Mrs Brass. She did not wish to be thought careless of her chaperoning duties but there was no particular hurry and she did not wish Monsieur to think her a blabbermouth.

Monsieur had used the time it took for Mrs Frogmorton to loosen her grip to good effect, warming his seductions every day – a touch here, a flirtatious remark there, no pushing or shoving. When not in the room, Mrs Frogmorton usually left the door open. In due course, he would close it and she would not notice.

There were irritations. At the beginning of July, Mrs Frogmorton told him that the concert would not take place until late in the year. The delay was something to do with the room they wanted, some reluctant duke, some squeamish earl – whatever it was, it irked Monsieur. Why not have the concert in Manchester Square? La Frog was implacable about that. Manchester Square had no saloon and the dining room was too small for the supper. (In fact, Mrs Frogmorton was nervous of the quality of her furniture and plate.) There was a row. Mrs Frogmorton told Monsieur that he could leave if he wanted: there would be other teachers. Monsieur replied that Mrs Frogmorton must understand that he had other calls on his time.

The row was pointless and Monsieur knew it. He did not want to leave. What, after all, awaited him in Paris? Blood; shouting; flag-waving. And he would never rescind his decision to cut himself off from his childhood home. Anyway, the weather in London was lovely. The plantings in the middle of Manchester Square had flourished into syringa and roses, with jessamine following on and the promise of peaches and cherries. London seemed generous, happy even. His berth at Cantabile's was tolerable enough. And there was Alathea. Or sometimes Alathea. She seemed to be playing a different game now. Nevertheless, she could still surprise, and the surprises were worth the wait. The row blew away. Mrs Frogmorton was pleased to note that Monsieur was very gracious when they next met.

Now that he had an accurate idea of the girls' capabilities, Monsieur divided up Herr Bach's variations. For Marianne and Everina's sake, two pianofortes would be required for the concert so that he or one of the other girls could play the left hand and they only had to manage the right. For certain variations, this would be needed for Georgiana and Harriet too. Not that his insistence on exercises wasn't bearing some fruit. Techniques really had strengthened, fingers grown more dextrous, touch more secure, pedalling less arbitrary. Last week, after giving each girl her allocation of the *Clavier-Übung* score, he had prevailed on Cantabile to send an inferior pianoforte to the Driggs at Stratton Street for the girls to practise together. Already they were reasonably familiar with the form of the work, though the variations' difficulty was a matter of constant exclamation and complaint from Everina and Marianne. Despite improvements, for all except Alathea Monsieur regretted the music he had suggested. It had been no part of the plan for the girls to make musical fools of themselves, or of Herr Bach. Rather the opposite. So there was one good thing about the delay: musically speaking, particularly for Marianne and Everina, it was helpful.

In Manchester Square, the Frogmortons were delighted with the blooming Harriet. In Stratton Street, the Driggs endured either furious sulks or giggling good humour from Marianne and Everina, but whatever the girls' moods, Mrs Drigg's daily headaches and the complaints of the neighbours were testament to the dreadful drumming of practice. In Covent Garden, Georgiana Brass began to speak, occasionally, at dinner. At the Sunday tea held in mid-July to celebrate the start of a three-week holiday (Mrs Frogmorton's proposal, not Monsieur's), she had even eaten a tiny cake. The following morning she asked for new clothes, which caused Mr Brass to remark to his mistress (his long-standing French *belle amie* had been thrown over for a sulky Russian Jewess) that his daughter might make a decent wife after all. The Jewess shrugged: she had no interest in Georgiana. Mrs Brass, on the other hand, wondered if she should take up the pianoforte herself.

On the morning of that Sunday tea, Monsieur met with the mothers in the Manchester Square drawing room to report officially on progress. No refreshments were served: Monsieur should not imagine this was a social occasion. Mrs Frogmorton had the drapes thrown back to give the room an airing. If she hoped the room would be transformed by the sun, she was disappointed. The green was still too green, the brown too brown and the armour, once unshadowed, too ridiculous.

Mrs Drigg was reminded of a funeral parlour. 'What a good room this is, Grace, so bright and cheerful. I've always thought so,' she said, tiptoeing to the pianoforte and inspecting it as she might have inspected an incendiary device. Mrs Brass sat on the stool and touched four notes: A, B, C sharp, A. Was that the start of a nursery rhyme?

'Elizabeth?'

Mrs Brass drifted up and sat where directed. Monsieur appeared from behind a curtain. Frilly yapped, making the women jump. 'Goodness, *monsieur*!' said Mrs Frogmorton.

'Madame Frogmorton? *Mesdames?*' Monsieur tried to catch the women's expressions before they had time to adjust their faces, to see if la Frog had revealed his secret to her friends. What woman could resist? He searched for a tightening of lips, just a hint of teeth set in sympathetic disgust. Nothing. He was surprised, then annoyed. He meant nothing to these women at all, not even gossip. A rage took hold of him.

Mrs Frogmorton quieted Frilly. Mrs Drigg sat down. 'Now,' Mrs Frogmorton said.

'The girls make progress,' Monsieur began with a snap.

'Come now,' Mrs Drigg urged. 'You'll have to do better than that.'

'The girls improve.'

'*Monsieur!*' Mrs Frogmorton was hurt. She had kept this man's secret. Her husband paid him on time. He had decent dinners and was never kept late. Just when she had forgotten about it, he suddenly seemed disagreeably French, tilting his head and glaring. An English music master would have stood hat in hand and praised his charges, as mothers had every right to expect. 'We wish to know *how* they improve,' she said. 'We wish for details.'

Monsieur's voice was sharp as a needle. 'The *mesdemoiselles* capture the *capriccio* and the *cavatina*, the *gigue* and the fugue, the overture and the canon. They master the *appoggiatura*, the *acciaccatura*, the inverted mordent, the trill with inversions and subversions and occasional perversions – oh, and the shake.'

'The what?' Mrs Frogmorton really was trying to follow.

'The shake,' repeated Monsieur. 'The shake, *madame*. The shake. Of course they learn the shake.' He walked back and forth. 'They also know of *portar la voce, accento, tremolo, esclamazione*' – he threw his fingers up like knives – 'and all manner of cadences, deceptive, receptive, unfinished – no, no – I beg pardon, not unfinished, nearly finished. Then there is the staccato, the legato, the *bragato*, the *ragato*' – he saw a twitch of the lip from Mrs Brass. He paused. Ah, that one. His second finger tapped his thumb.

'Perversions? Deceptions? Exclamations? Ragatos? I'm warning you, Monsieur Belladroit,' said Mrs Frogmorton with rising anger.

'Really!' echoed Mrs Drigg. 'It's too bad!'

Monsieur jerked his head. 'What is too bad?'

'All this – all this—'

A weightless voice interrupted. 'All this is as it should be,' said Mrs Brass. Six eyes swivelled towards her.

'As it should be? Are you sure, Elizabeth?' said Mrs Frogmorton, astonished and pleased that Mrs Brass had spoken, yet feeling sorely tried.

A nod.

'Well then,' said Mrs Frogmorton to Monsieur, her voice still testy. 'I suppose that will have to do.' She wished him a pleasant rest. They would see him in three weeks.

*

Monsieur did not have a pleasant rest. He spent the time unhappily cooped up at Tyburn with a summer cold and failing to persuade Cantabile to offer him cash in advance. He had his salary, which continued to be paid, but he wanted to spend money, lots of it. He wanted to feel, for once, like a rich man. Annie was a ghost in the house. She kept the place clean, served up the dinners and tended to her mother, yet even as she went about her work in full sight, she was somehow absent. When Monsieur asked her to play with him, she always agreed, though these days this seemed more of an indulgence on her part than a desire. She never again played her own compositions, only what he suggested, and there was something new in the sound she created, which Monsieur took some while to identify as joy. Why she was joyful, he could not imagine.

Over this long visit, Monsieur had become used to Annie's lip and grew tired of her father's constant references to it. He said so. He and Vittorio argued, and the disagreeable atmosphere was worsened by a stuffed nose and the weather: outside objectionably hot, inside chilled. Monsieur either sweated or shivered. Never, he thought, had he lived in a city with houses so badly arranged.

At Soho Square there was also an atmosphere, though this had nothing to do with the weather. Sawney Sawneyford had never had cause for complaint about his daughter before, and though he had no discernible cause now, he felt that something was not as it used to be.

Alathea had been a half-blossomed child of twelve when she first crept to him in the night. They were living at Blackfriars, renting two rooms from an actress whose admirers often fought for her attention. Alathea had been frightened by the midnight din erupting on the stairs. She had knocked at his door. He had allowed her in. The next night, for the same reason, she crept to him again, all round and warm, with a scent like her mamma's. Of course he knew it was his daughter not his wife who was pressing against his side. Nevertheless, if he did not open his eyes, he could pretend. It could do no harm. An innocent comfort. He kept his eyes closed. He shifted. She shifted. That scent. He turned towards her. He had expected stillness, but after a moment's confusion, she was actively accommodating. It was over in seconds. The following night, with no din on the stairs, she returned. He never asked why; she never said. After that, though she did not creep in every night, and he never ordered her, he was always waiting. They never referred to it except when Alathea needed the abortionist, and even then, after her first alarmed request for help, only obliquely until the abortionist was needed no more. Nor did Sawneyford ask his daughter to remove his wife's wedding ring from her thumb. He hoped she would, then ceased to notice it. The actress's admirers called Alathea 'beguiling'. The actress herself, catching the tilt of Alathea's eyes, called her 'unnatural'. The lady began to harbour suspicions. Before her suspicions could be aired, the Soho Square house turned up. Overnight, Sawneyford and Alathea were gone, with no forwarding address.

It was in Soho Square that Sawneyford first visited Alathea's own bed. He had not been sure of his reception, but need not have worried. Alathea was accommodating as always. In her own domain – she had chosen top-floor rooms originally designed for servants – she appeared more adult. That was when he began to bring jewels. Some men might, by this time, have been pretending their daughter was a changeling, not their daughter at all. Sawneyford did not bother. There was no need for make-believe since the arrangement suited them both. Sawneyford had never thought it would last for ever. He did, however, believe – more than that, he *knew* – that until she left him for a husband, Alathea would be exclusively his.

Sawneyford prided himself on what he knew. He knew, for example, all the sharp practices of the trading floor and the sharpest practitioners. He knew the name of every member of the Society of the Friends of the People. He knew that Brass's hairdresser had not paid the powder tax. He knew that Mrs Frogmorton hid Frilly's butcher's bill. He also knew, although it was of no interest to him, that Everina Drigg's new teeth had cost £20 and were, in fact, second-hand. It was troublesome to realise that there was something about Alathea he both knew and did not know. Whilst outwardly nothing had changed, Sawneyford discerned a presence. When he dripped his diamonds, he felt another's eyes. When he touched her hidden folds, he felt another's fingers. Her lips were darkened by another's shadow, her scent edged with something unfamiliar. He feared a trespasser. In his own bed, in this state of knowing unknowing, he lay unmoving and uneasy. Alathea, Alathea, Alathea. Daughter, lover, the only person in the world about whom he cared. How to discover what he wanted to without breaking the silences they both observed? He tried several times. He scuffed over words, never sure which ones to use. He grew angry with himself, and then with her. She waited patiently, whatever his mood, never interrupting. They ate meals together. They sat together. He knew they were no longer together. Somehow, without any visible sign of departure, she was leaving him and he could not bear it.

9

LESSONS resumed and Monsieur rejoiced, at first, when his mornings were busy again. But he, too, had a problem. It was not Mrs Frogmorton: she never came to the drawing room now. Monsieur could have stripped quite naked and danced a jig without fear of interruption. It was not even that if he wished for Alathea's services, he must now instigate proceedings. Her lips, hair and hands were willing, only he must ask. His problem was unexpected, namely that when he thought of tumbling Marianne, everything wilted. Marianne was not a girl. She was not even an animal. She was a vegetable, and he could muster no desire for a vegetable. Yet he could not leave her out. Once one girl had fallen, all must quickly follow. Any day now, Mrs Frogmorton would give him the actual concert date and then he must set his own date for the deflowerings.

With some exasperation, he also found himself at a loss with Georgiana, though for different reasons. Georgiana touched him. Apart from Alathea's lessons, which were hardly lessons, the hour with Mademoiselle Brass was the one to which he looked forward the most. It amused him that the perfection of her nose occasionally stopped him mid-sentence. The blue veins tracing her wrists delighted him. The small dip at the base of her neck moved him. And that tiny mole behind her left ear. He had only recently noticed it himself and thought she was quite unaware.

Monsieur had chosen Georgiana's particular *Clavier-Übung* variations with care. 'Variation 2, my dear dove. The tune is so wistful if taken slowly, and the left hand – my hand to start with, I will play with you until you are sure of it – so steady and dependable. You will imbue it with magic. Then Variation 3, the first canon, no less. Not the best of canons – even Herr Bach nods from time to time – but my arrangement of it and your playing will remedy its deficiencies.' He could hear himself now, and could see her rapt attention. It was very flattering. This was what disconcerted the most: he was not a man easily flattered.

Worse, her innocence dampened his lust. It would be like defiling a child. True, when her skin flushed with effort and the milk-white top of a breast blossomed through the stitching of a gown, if he concentrated hard, he felt reassuring stirrings. But a man needed more than stirrings.

Today, with September well established, he had decided to try stiffening the stirrings. He wondered if laughter would help. He could remember instances when it had.

Georgiana arrived wearing green, the end of her nose still charmingly tanned from her week by the sea. Before she sat down, he played Variation 30. 'Now, *mademoiselle*, Herr Bach called this a *quodlibet*, or "what pleases". And do you know what pleased him?' He was smiling so broadly, she had to smile too. 'Folk dances, and comic songs,' Monsieur said. 'He would gather his family together and they would mix up all manner of songs' – he twinkled like a galaxy – 'some rather naughty, Mademoiselle Georgiana! And how they would laugh, Herr Bach and his family, at those naughty concoctions. And Herr Bach wanted to share his fun. So here, at the end of this work for the soul's delight, is Herr Bach laughing.' He played the *quodlibet* again, with mock-solemnity, then again, taking liberties with the time that might not have pleased Herr Bach quite so much.

Georgiana obligingly laughed out loud. She was still laughing as she and Monsieur left the *quodlibet* and practised the third canon's semi-quavers, his fingers playing the bass, hers the treble, their shoulders brushing. 'Curve, curve, curve, *mademoiselle*!' She curved, her semi-quavers grew lighter and there she was, flying and laughing as their hands collided. 'My dear Georgiana,' Monsieur murmured. He directed his eyes to her bosom, to those thighs, separated for the pedals. A slight flicker. He concentrated on it.

As the variation ended, Georgiana leaned in to look at some fingering, then turned, her face open to his. 'When we both play, it's like cat's-cradle,' she told him with her shy smile.

'A cat with a cradle? What strange habits you English have!'

'Don't you know it?'

'I know nothing of cats.'

'It's a game, *monsieur*!' She pulled out a ribbon from her hair, tied it and spread it taut over her fingers. 'See! You must take it from me by catching these two strands between finger and thumb and passing them under.' Since both hands were occupied, she touched the ribbon with her nose.

'Like this?' He followed her instructions.

'Up and over, *monsieur*, and then spread your fingers and thumbs.' He spread – the ribbon collapsed.

'No, no, Monsieur Belladroit,' Georgiana shook her head. 'Let's try again.'

They tried again, Georgiana the sweetest of tutors, Monsieur the humblest of pupils, and there, amid the collapse of the cradle, Monsieur reckoned that with Georgiana all would be well. The deflowering would be managed. He would treat her with the care she deserved.

Mrs Frogmorton caught him as he was leaving. 'The concert day,' she said, beaming. 'The second Saturday in December.'

'The girls will be ready,' he said, looking her straight in the eye. 'Quite ready.' On his way back to Cantabile's, he lectured himself about Marianne and set a date of his own.

In early October, everything damp, summer's light and heat vanished as though never intending to return (the Manchester Square winter drapes went up smartish), Harriet was the first to spot a change in Monsieur. She noticed it in his mouth. 'Are you quite well?' she asked. 'Is it the drizzle? It doesn't always rain in October. Sometimes we can have a nice week. Sometimes.' She did not wish to raise his hopes.

'It is my father, *mademoiselle*,' Monsieur said.

She stopped playing. 'Bad news?'

'Yes.' He sighed. Harriet was encouraging. Monsieur feigned unwillingness, then capitulated. 'He is dead.'

'Oh! I am sorry!' Harriet removed her hands entirely from the keys – she had been just about to start, almost at full speed, Variation 17, which she was to play with Georgiana, and with which she still had many difficulties. 'Is your mother alone?'

Monsieur considered. 'My mother has been alone for some time,' he told her. It was useful, a pianoforte stool, for this kind of story. You could turn to face or look ahead at the music. Both seemed natural. 'She and my father married for love, but love did not last. Since I was a tiny child they have lived separately.'

'That is sad,' said Harriet.

'The sadness, *mademoiselle*, lies in the fact that my father was a wastrel and cared neither for me nor for my mother. He has now been executed as a Jacobin. He was not a Jacobin. It matters little. My father has always been on the wrong side of everything.'

'Executed?' Harriet's round eyes grew rounder. She was wearing her bloody shoes today. The stain had never quite come out. She rubbed the toe on the underside of the sustaining pedal. 'Oh, *monsieur*. That's horrible.'

'Horrible? Oh no. Very quick, I think. And my mother did not mind. She has always depended on me, not on him. It is why I give lessons. I do not resent it. Though the sea currently parts us, my mother and I are very close.'

'The reward you get from teaching us can't be more than shillings,' Harriet said, glad to move on from the blood, 'and you've no time to teach anybody else. Your mother must survive on very little.'

'I send everything I can, and it is sent with love, *mademoiselle*.' He did not hide the fact that his heart was stirred by Harriet's practicality. His expression had precisely the right effect.

'Of course,' said Harriet, and touched his arm. 'We can't supply love but I'm sure we can supply more money. I'll tell my father.'

'Indeed no,' said Monsieur, slightly caught out. 'I am paid most satisfactorily, and I would be grateful also if you would not tell the others.' He could not remember precisely what he had said to Marianne or Georgiana about his parentage. 'I do not wish for pity. Let us continue. Your respective papas do not pay me to talk of my troubles. We need to work on your staccato, and I would like to hear Variations 11 and 20 before we finish. You are doing well, Mademoiselle Harriet, but both are difficult, and I think, even at the concert, I must help you out. If you are ready, let us arrange ourselves carefully.'

Harriet was still concerned. 'Don't you want to go home for the funeral?'

'The funeral has been already. So many funerals in Paris over the past years. It is a city of funerals. Grave diggers are richer than aristocrats. My mother could not afford privacy and writes that my father shares a grave with at least three others, two of them without heads.' He gave a little shrug. 'Grave diggers give no discounted charge for that. Everybody wants to make quick money, even out of the dead.'

Harriet did not know how to answer, so she played Variation 11 slowly and carefully as the best way to please. The three semi-quavers against dotted quavers were tricky. Monsieur chose to play the left-hand notes with his right hand. As was inevitable, given the music, their hands glanced, crossed and were muddled together. Disconcerted, Harriet withdrew hers. Monsieur carried on without blinking. After a while, Harriet resumed the treble. When they reached the end of the first section, Monsieur gave a small smile. 'Mademoiselle Harriet, you have cheered me,' he said. She only then noticed that their legs were touching all the way down.

'I'm glad, *monsieur*,' she said, moving her leg away.

'Again,' he said. 'If you play more quickly, you may find the timing easier. Remember, though, delicate fingers. Do no press the notes. Drop your wrist. Persuade the notes down. Light, light, light.'

Harriet nodded. They began again. The pace was quick. Harriet, her tongue slightly protruding, rose to the challenge. 'Excellent, *mademoiselle*,' Monsieur murmured into her ear, making the drops in her lobes swing. He put up one finger for quiet. Nobody could have sworn, in a court of law, that he brushed the earlobe on purpose. Harriet gave a shiver and

Monsieur smiled to himself. He imagined it the first of those kinds of shivers, an indication of being ripe and ready. He was wrong. Harriet had shivered in just such a way several times over the summer, when she saw Mr Buller, shirtless, helping to saw up a fallen branch in Manchester Square's central gardens. She had not yet spoken to her intended. Like Monsieur, she was biding her time. As Monsieur delved deep into the intricacies of Variation 11, Harriet's earlobe pulsed. She thought she might not wear earrings again. She thought she would never forget to put them on. To stop Harriet's left wrist sinking too low, Monsieur placed two fingers lightly beneath her cotton cuff. Harriet continued to play, but the shiver from her earlobe now tingled down her arm. She wondered at herself. She wondered if Monsieur had noticed. She thought not: he seemed absorbed by the music, frowning, nodding in time and humming. Occasionally he removed his fingers. Harriet felt their loss and was aware, for the first time, that Monsieur carried the faintest hint of rosemary on his breath.

The end of the hour came unexpectedly quickly and she gave up her place without a word. At dinner that night, when her father asked how the lessons were going now that the concert was getting nearer, she nodded, yes, yes, they were going well. Monsieur was an excellent teacher. She hoped he was being properly recompensed. Her parents exchanged glances. How fortunate to have produced Harriet, so thoughtful, so beautiful, so talented, so unlike Marianne or Everina.

Next day, Friday, Monsieur eased forward with Georgiana. 'Sadness becomes you,' he told her as though continuing a conversation started earlier, 'yet I think happiness becomes you better and I believe that I, through Herr Bach, am teaching you something of happiness, no?' She was tripping through Variation 19 with gentle melancholy, nostalgic for she didn't quite know what. She continued playing. The music gave her courage. 'Are

133

you happy, *monsieur*?' Her fingers drew out, not without feeling, the music's pretty tunefulness.

'I am happy at this moment, *mademoiselle*.'

'Yet you must miss your family: your loving mother and the father you never knew,' she said.

'Ah,' Monsieur murmured. 'Yes, yes. Naturally.'

'And your homeland. Do you miss France?'

'Ah, France! What is it now? It is your enemy, and I am now a poor *émigré*, which is a pretty word for a lonely state.'

A wrinkle appeared in her brow. She reached the repeat marks and began again. 'You could never be an enemy, *monsieur*,' she said, then stopped playing and burst out, 'It's terrible to be lonely.' Monsieur seized the moment, leaned over and kissed her. It was a light kiss on the mouth, and he had his excuses all ready: her sympathy, the remembrance of his parents, his home-sickness for the home he never had. In the event, and rather to his surprise, no excuse was necessary. Georgiana did exclaim loudly, but when he withdrew, her face was alight with an expression he could only describe as gratitude.

On Monday, on the pretext of demonstrating the best posture to master the considerable difficulties of Variation 14, he stroked her neck. Her semi-quavers grew no faster, only more delicate, until they matched his fingers on her skin. He moved his fingers into her hair. She sighed. She slowed. Monsieur removed his fingers. 'Until tomorrow,' he said, closing the text. On her way out, Georgiana unfurled the beatific smile of a Renaissance angel and Monsieur, his conscience not entirely easy, nevertheless judged his own performance masterly.

The deflowering of Everina was his most methodical undertaking. She continued to batter the pianoforte with whatever music Monsieur produced, and Monsieur, eyes glinting with fury, contempt or amusement depending on his mood, continued to chase her up and down the keyboard. On some days their chase became a wild game of musical tag. Today, the chosen day, Monsieur removed Herr Bach's music – he sometimes felt a sense of shame, allowing its massacre – and sacrificed Clementi, telling Everina she needed to exercise her fingers. Everina, panting hard, finished her third sonata with banging triumph. As usual, Monsieur allowed her no rest. 'Now you chase me!' he shouted, balanced on one buttock as though the stool was steeply cambered, and thundering away in the bass. Shrieking, Everina flung her hands at the keys and caught him up. 'How quick you are, *mademoiselle*,' Monsieur trilled. He played faster. She played faster. Oh, the clashing semi-tones! Oh, the thrashing melodies! Oh, the lusty muddle of pedalling legs! When Everina eventually bawled, 'Enough,' Monsieur seized her plump shoulders. 'Everina Drigg,' he gasped, 'you are right to reject the mythical gods of your books. Quite right! You are fully flesh and blood. Happy the hero who gets you!' He was already sliding his hands downwards.

Everina caught them and grew coy. 'I know I'm flesh and blood, but I'm also a pianist, *monsieur*, wouldn't you say? Much better than Marianne. Wouldn't composers die to get me to play their works? So many girls are water. Am I not wine, *monsieur*? Am I not?' She held him at a distance, apple-cheeks quivering.

She had spoiled a spontaneous seizing of her virtue. All he could see were those terrible shining teeth. He could never kiss her. Yet she was so unintentionally droll. 'Die for you, my dear! Indeed! You are quite the kind of pianist to make a composer die.'

Everina let go of him and began Clementi all over again. Monsieur was obliged to follow. By the time she had finished, he heard footsteps outside. He could go no further with Everina today. Alathea was going to grace him with her presence.

*

At Everina's next lesson, Monsieur made her play hunt-the-tune, and midst the hunt removed one hand from the keyboard and slipped it determinedly where it should not have been. Everina roared. Monsieur's fingers began a cavernous game. She commanded him to stop. Monsieur carried on, confident that pleasure would trump astonished offence. He was right. Everina gasped, gasped again, and now bleated when he threatened to stop. Her movements were not subtle. It was clear she wanted to scream and shout, to smack him, to see him shot, to cling to him, to open herself wider, to arch, to writhe, to hang round his neck, to chop his neck in half. An odour arose that reminded Monsieur of the country nurse who had first taken him in hand.

Everina balked only at the final act. He would not force her, even though this reticence posed a danger: wholly undone, her silence would be guaranteed unless she wanted to ruin herself as well as him; half undone, she must be drawn into a conspiracy of pleasure. Accordingly, he began to whisper gothic nonsense about kindling love and overwhelming passion, scattering mythical references and ardent sighs of the kind he imagined littered the favourite pages of her books. When she tried to speak, he raised one of her fingers to his lips and one of his to hers. It was an old trick, always effective. She kept her finger on his lips for a long minute and removed it with a mispronounced stage-whisper of 'À demain.'

On the next lesson day, he hurried the other girls through. Nothing must distract him from Everina now. He heard her greet Georgiana on the stairs. He stood up. What were they saying? He could only hear Everina's interminable giggle and the clack-clack-clack of her teeth. Then she made her entrance. Today she had dressed from a fashion plate, with a large white chip bonnet tied under her chin with red ribbons. The hat sported a large red ostrich feather, and on either side of the feather her brown hair had been teased into corkscrew curls. Her red gown, almost indecently high-waisted and low-cut, had sleeves designed especially to display milk-white arms, though Everina's incipient underhang rather spoiled the effect. Jet pendants dangled from her ears and, sneaking into Marianne's room, she had stolen rouge for her lips. It was as well Marianne had not seen her leave Stratton Street. It was as well Mrs Drigg had not either. Monsieur would have laughed had he not been relieved. Mademoiselle Everina could not have given him a clearer signal that she was open for business.

He greeted her with a bow and a very personal purr then took her hand and led her to the pianoforte stool. Without removing her hat, she subsided, a giggle in her throat, and arranged herself. Monsieur did some preliminary work, as expected, before once again offering something more substantial than his hand. This time, no rebuff. Everina's giggling turned to a hiccup and she opened her eyes very wide. 'Monsieur! Oh my goodness!'

Monsieur viewed Everina as an excavation. He prepared the ground, levered in, dug about, then withdrew with the least amount of disturbance. He was more delicate than her music-making deserved and he was very careful. Consequences must be avoided. He was pleased by Everina's giggle, and even more pleased when for one minute during and one minute after, her haunches upended and her fists clenched, she stopped giggling entirely.

Everina was not a dissembler. She was not displeased. She had been ready, had dressed for the part, and now it was over felt she might take to this new activity, given a few more goes. Yet all was not comfortable. Bits of her were hot with ache and she longed, more than for any caress or loving mumble, to run outside, take down her drawers and squat in the cool mud. This was not what she expected to feel and it was certainly not the response written about in any book. In books, the heroine was always either affronted, angry or distressed – always the last if she were duped or doped by a villain. Monsieur was not a villain, so distress was unnecessary, doubly so because he loved her. He had said so, hadn't he?, and she was eminently lovable, much more lovable than Marianne. Moreover, last night she had decided she loved him too, which was why she had let him have his way today. And she must be right about their loving each other, otherwise she would have felt nothing, and she had felt far from nothing. Still, what *was* the right response? She shifted from buttock to buttock. Failing mud, an ice-block would be nice.

Monsieur helped her to sit. She grimaced. Her teeth felt glued together. Monsieur moved to consolidate his advantage. 'Ah, *mademoiselle*,' he said, stroking her as he might stroke a sheep, palm flat, mechanical pace. 'You and I – do you see? – Do you feel?'

'I do, *monsieur*, I do.'

Monsieur was very solicitous as he resumed his role as pianoforte master. He had brought a small bottle of water and a handkerchief. The pianoforte must not become sticky. He was finishing wiping his fingers when he found his head pressed against Everina's bosom. 'Say you love me,' she commanded.

He tried to remove his head but she held it in a vice. '*Mademoiselle*, love,' he muttered.

It was not enough. 'Say "I love you",' she insisted. 'All the words. Say it now.'

She was hurting his ears. 'Release me, please, Mademoiselle Everina,' he said.

'Not until I hear you say you love me.'

'I'll hear myself damned first,' he muttered, not quietly enough.

She let go. Her lower lip was trembling. 'You'll tell me you love me or I'll tell my father and mother what you've just done.'

He brushed down his hair, checked his ears and clicked his tongue. 'Come now, *mademoiselle*, you will not, because if you do they will punish me, and then everybody will know and you will never get a husband.'

'That's blackmail. You could go to Newgate! You could hang!'

'And you would be alone for the rest of your life.'

'Perhaps it's worth it.' She was certainly affronted now.

'Really, *mademoiselle*? I think not. You were not meant to be alone.'

Her affront evaporated. She began to snivel, then suddenly looked genuinely panic-stricken. 'What if I have a child, *monsieur*?'

It cost Monsieur nothing to be kind. 'Dear Mademoiselle Everina,' he said, 'what we have done does not make babies.'

'Are you sure?'

'Making babies is an entirely different process,' he said, thinking that not altogether an untruth. 'Come now. You are a young and delightful girl and we had fun, did we not? Only do not mistake things. What I give to you is not love and what you give to me is not love.'

'What is it then?' She wiped her nose on her sleeve. 'All those things you did. All those things you said. They're what lovers do and say.'

'Sometimes, *mademoiselle*. But they can also be said simply for the pleasure of saying them, and you are a woman who deserves a lot of pleasure. You have a gift for it, which makes you precious. Do you realise how precious you are?'

Her ostrich feather drooped over her face. 'But you do love me?'

'Dear *mademoiselle*! Have you been listening at all?' His patience was running out. 'You know nothing of love just as

139

you know nothing of music. In matters of love you are like a goat—' She drew a stinging breath. 'My little goat,' he reassured her hastily. 'We are goats together.' (Goats, he thought with a silent groan. That was her smell. Why did it have to be goat?)

Everina tilted backwards and forwards. 'I don't want to be a goat. I want to be a lover, like Ethelinda and Celestina.'

'I do not know these ladies.'

'They're in my books.'

Monsieur controlled his temper. 'My dear little goat,' he said, taking her hand and deciding there and then that, if he were ever to have a daughter, he would forbid her to read novels. 'You want love, yes, but not from me. I am giving you something much more useful than love.'

'What could be—'

He talked over her. 'Your parents asked Mr Cantabile very particularly to send a teacher to make their daughters fit for marriage. First I have taught you incomparable music.'

She wiped her nose again. 'You can't claim credit for the music. Somebody else wrote it and I play what's written.'

'You do not,' Monsieur told her. 'You play what is on the page, which is not the same thing. It is I who have turned what you play into music.' She threatened to be querulous. He must placate. He patted her hand. 'Listen to me, *mademoiselle*. When you step out of your wedding dress and into your wedding bed, you will play a better tune than ever you could play on a pianoforte. Hush!' He gave her chin a teasing tap. 'I have taught you something very important. You will surprise your husband – he may even be shocked – but these skills we have just exercised, *mademoiselle*, if you use them artfully, will marry you and your lucky spouse together far better than God, priest or even Herr Bach. What is more, these skills will remain long after the *Clavier-Übung* is forgotten. Do you understand?'

'But I don't feel I've learned much yet,' she complained, though more cheerfully. 'I'll need more lessons.'

He blew out his lips. Artful indeed. Still, a few more tumbles; a few tricks of the trade. He nodded. 'And you shall have them.'

Everina was flattered. She straightened her feather and wiped her mouth, nose and eyes on her skirt. 'And you do love me.'

Monsieur resisted the urge to slap her. He smiled cleverly. 'I chose you, did I not, to be my little goat?'

She regarded him, still uncertain. Being a goat did not appeal. Nevertheless, he had said she was precious. He had said she was his. She sought one last reassurance. 'And you won't tell the others, particularly not Marianne?'

Monsieur pitched his reply perfectly. He had used it several times before. 'Does one ever speak of matters of the heart?' He gave her a brilliant, conspiratorial smile then pointed to the page. 'Come now. Even little goats must play their Bach. Let us try the right hand of Variation 26 before your *maman* comes for you.'

Everina looked at the music. Apart from Herr Bach, nothing today was as she had imagined it would be. Was it nicer or nastier? Better or worse? She never answered that question satisfactorily. In years to come, all she remembered of this particular day was that while playing the right hand of Variation 26, she had longed to sit in the mud.

Monsieur remembered something different. He remembered wishing, not on that day but very soon after, that Everina might die. She was not a girl given to suppressing her appetites, and being Monsieur's little goat meant, she made very clear, that the pleasures of his hand, and on occasion other parts of his person, were hers whenever required. How else might she learn all he could teach her? Within days, his wrists ached at the very thought of her. He cursed himself for not leaving her until last –

or at least until he had conquered Harriet, who put up unexpected opposition.

After the first priming, Monsieur had stored Mademoiselle Frogmorton for, as he thought, an easy uncorking. A week after Everina's first tumble, he set Harriet more practice of Variation 20, the crossing of hands offering an excellent opportunity to brush against her breasts. At every brush, she flushed and her mouth opened. But then, despite the pulse he saw beating in her neck, she snapped her mouth shut again and crossed her hands with such speed and determination that she might have injured him had he not ducked. He was at something of a loss. He paused, considering. Harriet pre-empted him. 'I know what you're trying to do, *monsieur*,' she said, quite candid, 'and I'm not shocked. You're a music master, I'm an heiress. You're a man, I'm a girl. This kind of business goes on. But even if I hadn't decided to be Mrs Thomas Buller, we couldn't do what I think you're suggesting. You see, I can't pretend not to know that Georgiana is in love with you. It would feel disloyal.'

'No, no, you are mistaken, *mademoiselle*,' he said. 'Mademoiselle Georgiana likes me, I think, but I am not of the class that excites the love of young ladies like her.'

'That's as may be,' said Harriet, resuming her triplets. 'I really think she is. I know she is. She told me the other day.'

Monsieur took down the music and wrote in unnecessary instructions. 'Continue,' he said.

'With the music,' said Harriet firmly. 'I shall continue with the music.'

'With the music,' said Monsieur. Damnation.

He now viewed Georgiana with some trepidation. Mild infatuation was all very well, but love was no part of his plan. Unfortunately for him, it was part of hers, as he soon discovered. Boosted by mastery of variations she thought beyond her, by

142

Harriet's down-to-earth advice and by Monsieur's artful and solicitous care, Georgiana took matters into her own hands. In the afterwash of Variation 10's *fughetta*, open-eyed and full of trusting hope, she shyly declared her love to Monsieur and, with another of those beatific smiles, clearly expected him to respond. Monsieur's heart thumped, though not with love. It was true that Georgiana touched him, moved him, and that he cared for her – but if this was love, it was the kind of love a man feels for a kitten. And she must certainly not even think of loving him, not with real love. Real love brought all kinds of difficulties. He had no time for it, so when Georgiana raised her face to him, he shook his head and scowled. This had no effect. Georgiana understood head-shaking and scowling only as the despair of a man who imagined their love impossible. 'Oh, *monsieur*,' she said. 'Don't be concerned. Anything is possible between us.' He saw his mistake, stopped scowling and spoke very seriously. '*Mademoiselle*, dear *mademoiselle*, I am flattered, very flattered indeed, but love is not yours to give nor mine to take.'

Georgiana just smiled again. 'If my love's not mine, then whose is it?'

'Your future husband's.'

'Yes, *monsieur*,' said Georgiana, her smile deepening.

'Ah, *mademoiselle*.' Monsieur's voice was far calmer than his nerves. 'I mean that your love belongs to the man your papa will approve as the best person to care for you.'

'How kind you are!' she exclaimed.

'Kind?'

'Yes, to try and be good to my papa. But how can he judge who's best to care for me since he doesn't care for me himself? You care for me, and I care for you.'

'You must care for your papa. You must obey him.'

She kept smiling her smile. 'Oh, I do care for him. I think he'll be pleased.'

'Your mamma will be horrified.'

She was still smiling. Monsieur wondered if, after all, she was simple. 'Not at all, *monsieur*,' Georgiana said. 'If Mamma ever spoke, I think she'd say she wants me to be happy, as she perhaps has never been happy, and I've been so much happier these past months. Everybody's noticed – the other girls, I mean. Harriet asked me about it directly, and I was very glad to answer.'

'Mademoiselle Georgiana,' Monsieur said, much more firmly. He did not want a return to her previous fearful state, but he could not allow this to continue. 'Enough. We shall forget this conversation has taken place. We will continue our work. The *fughetta* again, please. Left hand only.'

'*Monsieur*,' Georgiana said, taking his hands instead. Why, Claude scolded himself, had he not removed them out of reach? 'I'm not just offering my love. I don't even need marriage. I want you to have everything I can give because you have given me everything.'

He had to look at her. Her eyes were beautifully clear when not filled with tears – hazy and green, not grey as he had first thought – and they boasted a narrow flinty rim that could not be new, though he thought it was. There were no tears today. Her eyes were open, trusting, and offering, just as she said and without flirtation, the whole of herself. Alathea, offering just as much – indeed, offering more – never looked like this. Though Alathea must once have been as innocent as Georgiana, he would never have called her a dove. And really, Monsieur was not a dove man, not when it came to love, and if ever a girl was a dove it was Georgiana. He coughed so that he could, without offence, reclaim his hands to cover his mouth. 'Mademoiselle Georgiana. Little dove. I am honoured. But you must keep all that kind of thing for the husband who will love you and whose home you will grace. Please understand. That husband will not be me; it could never be me. I am not a husband.'

'And I don't need to be a wife!' She clasped her own hands together. 'With you, *monsieur*, I could be anything.'

This was too much. His temper began to rise and this, exasperatingly, precipitated the rise of something else. Hell and damnation. Just when he did not want her, he wanted her. He knew he had to have her sometime. But not now. Not now.

'I thought, perhaps, I – I ...' She was beginning to disintegrate. Monsieur felt a brute. He made a final attempt. 'What man would not want you? You are a pearl, mademoiselle, a pearl. But pearls must not be sullied by baser stones, and I am such a stone. Please, *mademoiselle*, think of me as such. Now let us go back to work. This passage. Variation 17. Sixths against thirds. Left hand, please. It is difficult. I think – yes – shall we try fourth instead of third finger here? It might be easier for the staccato.'

She did not move. 'You're in love with Harriet.'

He was stung into quick denial. 'No, *mademoiselle*, indeed I am not. Come. Variation 17 is waiting.'

'But you would have taken her. She told me.'

'She told you? When?'

'Last Saturday, when she asked me why I seemed so happy – before I told her I loved you.'

'What did she say, exactly?'

'That you had touched her earring.'

Monsieur shifted on his seat. 'Oh, that. Earrings get in the way.'

'You're being kind again,' Georgiana said, tears smudging those flinty rims. 'You can't help it. I know she's more perfect, more ... more ...'

'Little dove,' said Monsieur, rather frantic, 'please do not cry.

You are perfect. Too perfect. You are like a daughter to me, not a lover. I am twice your age.'

'You're twice Harriet's age!'

'*Mademoiselle!*'

'I thought when you touched my neck, my hair, I thought that meant ... ' She sat for a moment, fighting with herself. With an effort, she clipped her own wings. 'I'm sorry, *monsieur*. I've misunderstood. I've embarrassed you. I've embarrassed myself.'

'You have embarrassed nobody,' Monsieur said with some relief, 'nobody at all.'

There was a pause. Georgiana twisted her hands. 'So you don't love Harriet?'

'No, *mademoiselle*.'

'Or any of the others?'

'No,' he said.

Georgiana wiped her eyes. She looked straight ahead. 'I'll always love you, *monsieur*, and I see that you can't love me. If I've spoiled everything, I apologise. I'm ready for work.'

It was her tone that undid him. She was not self-pitying or manipulative, not whining or depressed; she was Georgiana. Perhaps he should have her now and put a smile back on her face for the weeks they had left. His hand found hers. At first, she thought he was correcting the angle of her wrist. When his hand remained, she murmured – tenderly, no triumph – turned and drew him to herself. Still, there was time to withdraw. He should withdraw. The danger was so clear, so obvious. Yet somehow they were kneeling behind the pianoforte stool, then lying, that dear little mole behind her ear, Georgiana raising her skirt, neat leather ankle boots, a golden sheen of hair beneath the stocking, the shocking whiteness between top of stocking and frill of drawers. Rather unexpectedly, her garters were mismatching. She had clearly not noticed; a child's mistake. Now he could not help himself. She wanted him. He wanted her. He made ready. He made her ready. He took her. Three thrusts, one groan and it was over.

The experience was a disappointment. The blond flesh had not been solid; Georgiana was only foam after all. The peculiar rush he always got from being the first vanished in seconds. He had not even squeezed a breast. With a surgeon's detachment, he wiped her clean of blood and hoped, with alarmed and chilly hope, that he had been careful enough. Closing her legs, he could not imagine his desire of only three minutes before. When he murmured her name, 'Sweet Georgiana, sweet, sweet Georgiana,' fulfilling, as he imagined, a post-coital womanly need, he might have been reciting a luncheon menu. Still, he had done his duty for Cantabile. He never need take her again.

Georgiana had anticipated exaltation. When all she got was pain, she blamed herself. She had expected too much. She was a fool. Careful to show no sign of her own disappointment, she comforted herself that Monsieur's animal spasm was ecstasy enough for both of them. She heard no alteration in tone as he muttered her name. For all his selfless denials, she felt certain that Monsieur did love her. This was what a man's love was like. She was a most fortunate girl. When righted on to the pianoforte stool, without a word she began Variation 17. Her rendition was ecstatic, her ornaments bird-like chirrups. At the end of the hour, when she had taken her radiance down into the Brass carriage, Monsieur leaned against the drawing-room door. What an idiot he was. Idiot, idiot, idiot. He slammed the lid of the pianoforte, shouted that he was taken ill and returned to Cantabile's, where he shut himself in his room for the rest of the day.

He emerged at dinner. Rested and away from Manchester Square, he convinced himself that the experience, being so underwhelming, would pale for Georgiana and that when they next met, if he made no mention of it, things would be as they ever were. He must believe it, because this was how things must be. Annie poured him a third glass of wine. As she raised her arm, he caught a distinct and powerful scent of musk. He was puzzled. The scent must have come from himself, although Georgiana did not smell of musk and he had not seen Alathea either this day or the day before. He felt Annie looking at him. He looked at her. A drip coursed down the neck of the wine bottle. She allowed it to roll over her fingers, then raised her hand and slid her fingers into her mouth. Monsieur winced. Horribly, he was reminded of Cantabile's shellfish taunt. Equally horribly, he could not look away. Finger in mouth. A childish habit. It was still childish in Annie; yet nothing of the child was here. He momentarily forgot Georgiana and swallowed and swallowed and swallowed.

Annie removed her fingers, wiped both them and the wine bottle and fetched the bread. She unrolled the cloth in which it was wrapped. The smell of musk turned yeasty. Monsieur gazed anywhere but at Annie. She did not, could not, know Alathea. And she certainly could not know her like that. Yet the fingers in the mouth. The unmistakable scent. He followed it with his nose, like a hound.

Cantabile shuffled upstairs. 'Give me wine, Annie.' He pulled out a chair. 'All done, Claude?'

Monsieur twitched. 'Not quite done.'

'How many have you taken?'

'Three,' Monsieur answered. He would not say that Alathea had taken him.

'Only three?' Cantabile stopped tearing at the bread. 'The year marches on. Don't let me down.'

'It takes half a minute, Vittorio. Less. What difference does it make if I take the last girl now or the day before the concert?'

'No difference,' Cantabile said. 'But don't dally, it doesn't become you.'

148

Annie served the dinner and, as always, left the room. The musk scent lingered. Monsieur hardly ate. He felt the scuff of Everina beneath his nails. Georgiana would not forget. Alathea was playing tricks. Monsieur was suddenly weary. He was an instrument as much played-upon as playing. It was a novel experience. He could not recommend it.

10

ANNIE'S pleasure at teasing Monsieur was matched by the pleasure of her days. There was always music, but there had been three outings too, three sunny afternoons when she and Alathea, wearing matching veils, had walked together. It mattered little to Annie where they went or what they did. With Alathea beside her, she was happy to stroll around markets, to shiver outside Newgate as Alathea described how the stone arches punctuating the condemned man's final walk got narrower as he approached the drop – how did she know these things? – or to sit for an hour or two in the Salutation & Cat, up the street from the prison, listening to men she did not know using words she did not recognise to describe a world that could never be. Over this last, Alathea disagreed. 'If a world is possible to describe, it must be possible to organise. What's so difficult? Everybody equal, everybody free, everybody owning everything in common.'

'If it's so easy, why isn't it done already?' Annie posed the question gently, more for the delight of conversation than for an answer.

Alathea had an answer anyway. 'Men. It doesn't suit them.'

'It's men who are suggesting it,' Annie pointed out. They had left the Salutation & Cat. She stopped and uncrumpled her leaflet. '"Pantisocracy and aspheterism",' she quoted, '"will minimise greed amongst men. They are antidotes to the corruption of power and the problems of property." It's written by a man.'

'A poet,' said Alathea, curling her lip and walking on. 'Can't you tell? What woman would talk of "pantisocracy" and "aspheterism" when all they mean is equality and the abolition of property rights? Would you?'

Annie, catching up, had to agree that she would not. 'So women could organise such a world?' she said. 'It could happen?'

Alathea nodded emphatically. 'It will happen.'

'Here?'

'No,' said Alathea. 'In the New World. Anything's possible there.'

A chill in the sun. 'You're going to join them,' Annie said.

'I might.'

Annie waited for an invitation. None came. Alathea talked easily of other things. Annie did not mention the New World again. When they arrived at Soho Square, she expected to go straight to the ballroom. Instead, Alathea led her past the waiting pianoforte, upstairs to her eyrie bedroom. Annie prepared herself for something awful: trunks filled and labelled; a travelling cloak laid out. What she got was her first full-on-the-mouth kiss. It was a huge affair of lips, tongues, spittle, suckings, blowings, leakings, nippings, subtle and unsubtle tilts, forces, pressings and pressures. Taken by surprise, Annie's lip exploded in spasms over which she had no control. This frightened her. She did not know such sensations existed, the biggest sensation of all being that Annie of the hare lip was being kissed, kissed, kissed as she had never, ever expected to be. She wanted to cleave to Alathea, to shout her love aloud. She did not say a word, for even as they struggled for breath she read the warning in Alathea's eyes: together but apart; love but no attachment. This was why there had been no invitation. There would never be one. Were Annie to complain, the door of Soho Square would be closed to her.

On her way home she purchased a pocket looking-glass and that night burned two candles right down to the stumps as she scrutinised herself. Surely the kiss had transformed her. Yet there was her lip, obscene as ever. Then she was seized by a horrible thought: perhaps the transformation was the other way round. Perhaps her lip had rendered the kiss obscene. And there was another question. Could she have kissed lips like hers if they were on Alathea's face? The answer did not really matter, but the question nagged.

The kiss changed the pattern of the afternoons. They never went out again, and after they finished making music in the ballroom Alathea always took Annie up to her bedroom. There were never travelling cases. Annie's alarm about Alathea leaving for the New World subsided to an occasional gnawing worry.

From the dust and dirt in the upstairs passages, it was clear that no servant, let alone Crouch, had been up here for years. Annie relished the sense of complete privacy, yet noticed that Alathea always locked the door. Annie wondered if this was because up here the girls undressed each other fully, as they never did downstairs. Perhaps Alathea's father, about whom Alathea never spoke and whom Annie had never seen, had been away and was expected home. Perhaps, when he arrived, he might come up the stairs to find his daughter. As the weeks drew on, she began to look out for signs of Sawneyford and saw none that were new. Eventually, her curiosity got the better of her. 'Does your father really exist?' she asked. The girls were wrapped in negligées. Alathea was lighting the first fire of autumn.

'He does exist,' Alathea said. She came to brush Annie's hair. 'There's nothing of him in the rooms we use.'

Alathea swept Annie's hair up, silent for a while. 'There's something of him in here,' she said.

Annie glanced about. The room was a plain box, its sole decoration being Alathea's clothes. Dresses were strung on a rope between the window hook and a nail in the wall. Undergarments were set about in piles, some on a chest, some on the floor. The bedstead was wooden and piled high with thick blankets retrieved from one of the house's grander bedrooms. A table with a ewer and jug stood against a wall, and Alathea had brought up a dressing table, two chairs and a night-stand from the same room as the blankets. The fireplace was set opposite the door. There were no pictures or ornaments, only Alathea's mirrors, dozens of them, of all sizes, everywhere. It was a room of reflections from which Annie could never escape. This was the only thing about the room Annie disliked, but she never complained. 'I can't see anything,' she said.

'There's me.' Alathea let Annie's hair slip through her fingers.

Annie crinkled her eyes. Despite the kiss, she still would not smile, and certainly not here, with these mirrors. 'That's not quite what I meant.'

There was a pause. 'I don't mean I'm my father's daughter.' Alathea strained Annie's hair again through her fingers. 'I'm his in another way.' She stopped straining Annie's hair. The girls regarded one another. Annie frowned and turned to face Alathea. 'No,' she said. She turned again to the mirror. 'No.'

'Yes.' Alathea put the brush down.

Annie focused on Alathea's reflected clothes so as not to see either Alathea or herself. She wished she could hide her face. She remained flat-voiced. 'Is that why you lock the door? To keep him out?'

'No,' said Alathea. 'I don't keep him out.'

'Are you frightened of him punishing you if you do?'

'Not at all,' said Alathea.

'Then why?'

'I don't wish to keep him out. I lock the door because I lock the door.'

'But—'

Alathea picked up the brush. 'But what?'

Annie had to pinch her voice to stop it disgracing her. 'Don't you mind?'

Alathea shrugged.

Annie could not stop herself. She faced Alathea directly again. 'I mind for you. It's wicked.'

Alathea observed her. 'It's given me my freedom,' she said.

'Your father does that and you call it freedom?'

'Why not? I could ask anything of my father now.'

'But it's not right! It's—'

'Rape?'

Annie nodded.

'No, it's not rape. It never was. I made the choice. What harm has it done me?'

'He's your father!'

Alathea seemed amused. 'Fathers,' she said. 'They're just men like any other.'

'But fathers are supposed to—'

'Supposed to what? Protect you? Provide for you? Love you? Mine does, in his way. Does yours?'

Now Annie stared back into the mirror. 'My father would never think of doing to me what your father does to you.'

'Because he cares for you?'

'No,' said Annie, her voice hard. 'Because he would vomit.'

'There then.' Alathea began to brush Annie's hair again. 'It's your father who should be ashamed.'

'Should your father have no shame at all?'

'Some might think so. I don't. I look on him as practice.'

'Practice?'

'Yes. I hone my skills on him, just as I hone them on the harpsichord or pianoforte. It works well, I think. Don't you?'

'And Monsieur?' Annie could not help herself. She tried to look away from the reflections but there was nowhere else to look. 'Do you hone yourself on him as well?'

'Monsieur has been useful,' said Alathea, her voice tighter. 'I've tested out what I've learned. I thought musicians and poets might be different. Not so.'

Annie tried to feel as Alathea spoke: passionless, matter-of-fact. She could not. She was raw, not with revulsion but with sickening jealousy. 'I don't like to think of you with any man,' she said.

'Detachment, Annie, remember.'

Jealousy swept detachment aside. 'It can't please you, what your father does.'

Alathea left off brushing and began to plait. 'It neither pleases nor displeases me. What happens happens. Then it's over. I don't think of the act, only the use I can make of it.'

Annie persisted. 'I'm thinking of the act and I hate it.'

Alathea stopped plaiting. For one dreadful moment Annie thought she was going to be ordered out of the room, out of the house, out of Alathea's life, and perhaps she would have been had she been dressed, but Annie was not dressed. Moreover, her eyes were not craven, which Alathea would have despised, or pitying, which Alathea would never have tolerated. Instead, Annie's eyes were filled with venom. It was like having a tiger in the room. Alathea slowly began to plait again. Annie licked her lower lip and sought safety on more practical ground. 'Don't you fear a child?'

An easing. The practical didn't bother Alathea. Her voice was warm again. 'There's a widow-hag. She's vile. It's a vile trade. If you can stand the' – a hesitation – 'if you can stand it, she takes care of everything. She advertises quite respectably in the Salutation & Cat – that's the reason I went there first. Father found her. He always pays. I never say anything. He leaves the money in my bonnet. I'm never short of money.' Alathea was still plaiting. 'You see ...' She seemed uncertain whether or not to continue. Annie barely breathed. Don't let a clock chime. Don't let a dog bark.

'My mother died when I was very young,' Alathea said. 'I don't remember her.' She raised her thumb. 'This ring was her wedding ring. It's why I always wear it. My father could have drowned me, or dumped me, but he kept me. Mrs Frogmorton and the other mothers helped, I suppose, and my father and I stuck together – except for once.' She picked up a ribbon. 'I was about ten. We were staying at the Frogmortons', in the house they had before Manchester Square. I forget where it was. When I woke – I must have been in Harriet's bed as the house wasn't big ... anyhow, when I woke I went to find him and he'd gone.' She finished the plait. 'There.'

Annie didn't move. 'Where was he?'

'Oh, abroad somewhere.' Alathea began to make short plaits in her own hair. 'I never asked Mrs Frogmorton where he was. I never asked if he was coming back. I never asked anything.'

'But you must have been so distressed – more than distressed, much more, you must have been beside yourself! Without a mother, and then your father leaving without a word?'

Alathea moved away from Annie and sat on the bed, plaiting, unplaiting, replaiting. 'When I saw his bag had gone, I ran downstairs without getting dressed. Mrs Frogmorton was standing at the front door. She saw me running. She saw my face. She

156

saw it and she waited. The power of that wait. I could see the satisfaction of it in her eyes. She had something I wanted and she was going to make me beg for it, so as she waited, I turned away, walked back up the stairs, dressed and carried on. She's waiting still.' Alathea secured three plaits and began on three more. 'The first day was the hardest. I kept listening for the door. But Mrs Frogmorton made it easy for me because every time I saw her, that eyebrow of hers jibed, "Aren't you going to ask me now?" and I never would. When my father returned, I didn't ask where he'd been. I didn't need to know because I knew something much more useful. I knew the power of not asking. Some people go their whole lives not knowing that.'

'Did he ever leave you again?'

'No.' Alathea ceased plaiting and sat on her hands. 'There was a time at Blackfriars when a woman – an actress – thought to marry him. It was in her lodgings that I first climbed into his bed. There'd be no point in him marrying anybody if I could provide what he needed. He's never left me since. He depends on me.'

'But you don't like dependence.'

Alathea's dark eyes were reflected everywhere. 'I don't like it with equal people.' She paused. 'My father and I aren't equal. I'm indispensable to him but he's not indispensable to me. I survived his leaving me without a word, letter or message. He couldn't survive if I left him, even if I told him where I was going. I know it. I've made it so.'

'What will happen when you marry?'

'I may choose not to, but if I do marry I'll feel quite sorry for him. It will torment him.'

It will torment me! Annie cried inside, but she said only, 'I suppose that will be his punishment.'

'Yes,' said Alathea, the multitude of mirrored eyes growing darker. 'Punishment's interesting, don't you think?'

Annie suppressed a quiver, half fear and half something else. Alathea stood up and traced all Annie's features with the handle of the hairbrush. 'Those condemned men at Newgate. That death walk is far worse than the execution.'

'Don't criminals deserve it all?' Annie said.

'And your father?' Alathea kept up her tracing with the hairbrush. 'Isn't he a criminal of sorts, the way he treats you? Doesn't he deserve the same?' She ran the hairbrush downward from Annie's chin. 'And Monsieur? What about it?' Her voice dropped. 'Punishment might be fun.'

Annie's eyes never left Alathea's face. She took the brush herself and ran the bone handle from the point of Alathea's chin, down her neck, downward, downward, downward over the contours loosely covered in silk, then suddenly inward, taking a roll of silk with it. Alathea bit her lip. Her eyes were violet diamonds. The mirrors reflected all. Annie could see a dozen Annies, a dozen Alatheas, a dozen hairbrushes. The hairbrush handle remained where it was. She controlled it. Alathea lay back, lips apart.

'I've punished my father already,' Annie said, mesmerised by their reflections. 'He never wanted to sell the pianoforte you play at Manchester Square. I sold it. It was to punish me for that that my father sent Monsieur to you. When I first came, you guessed I cared for Monsieur. You were right.'

'And you came here to punish me for having him.'

Annie twisted the hairbrush handle.

'Ah!' Alathea's face melted. 'I'm punished.'

'I smelled your musk on him,' Annie said. At some angles, the mirrors spread her lip over her whole face. At others, it was an artist's blot. Occasionally it vanished altogether and she was just a normal girl, with hair and a nose and a slightly oddly shaped mouth. She moved her head. New angles. Her lip was now a bruise. Now it was – God help her – a flat line.

How had she ever dreaded the mirrors? They painted things that weren't with what there was. She watched herself. She watched Alathea. 'Do you want Monsieur now?' She tapped the hairbrush handle lightly with her index finger. 'Or now?' She heard Alathea hiss. 'Or now?' Annie circled the handle like a conductor's baton. 'Tell me.' Alathea arched and Annie lost her reflection as the girls clashed together, Alathea grasping Annie's plait and slowly pulling her head backward. Annie remained in charge of the brush handle. She would not give it up.

'Who needs Monsieur?' Alathea said.

'Not me,' Annie answered. She twisted the handle and opened her mouth.

'Not *us*,' said Alathea, flushing russet up her neck and into her cheeks. She rolled Annie over. She still held her by the hair, their noses almost touching. 'Poor Annie,' she gently mocked. 'Monsieur was to teach us girls to get husbands and you weren't to have one.'

Annie's mouth quivered. 'Poor me. And you poor girls, with Monsieur's lessons not stopping at music.'

'I rather think *I* taught *him*.' Alathea flicked her tongue at Annie's chin.

'And he taught the others,' said Annie, catching Alathea's tongue with her lips.

After a muddle of tongues, Alathea paused. 'What do you mean?'

'Monsieur's taught the others some of what you taught him.' Annie rolled them both right over. 'That was his job. He was to pick all the cherries before your husbands got a chance. My punishment, for selling the pianoforte, is that Monsieur should take all you beauties and not take me. *Your* punishment, for having the pianoforte, is to be ruined by Monsieur.'

Alathea let go of Annie's hair and laughed with delight. 'Well

I never! Harriet, Marianne, Everina and Georgiana! The old goat! And to think I never guessed.'

'It gives my father a thrill.'

'Yes, I see that.' Alathea was still laughing. 'Why didn't you tell me before?'

Annie shrugged and removed the brush. Alathea rolled back. 'What a triumph for your father!'

Annie was quite still. She thought of her father's past triumphs. Her throat silted up. 'Why should he triumph?'

'Because it's a perfect plan.'

'That's not what I mean. I mean why *should* he triumph?'

Alathea smoothed her legs and untangled her robe. 'You don't want the girls to be ruined? You want them to collect husbands and live happily ever after?'

'No. I just don't want my father to win. I want—' Annie sat up. 'I want to show him he counts for nothing.'

Alathea finished the untangling. 'So you do want to punish him.' She paused. 'And the girls?'

'I don't care about the girls.'

'And Monsieur?'

'I don't know. I'd like him to feel something ... '

Alathea searched Annie's face. 'You'd like him to feel trumped,' she said.

'Trumped?'

'Out-manoeuvred.' Alathea sprang up and stood by the window, strong as a sapling. Annie remained on the bed and pulled her legs under her chin.

'Your father is your business, Annie,' said Alathea, 'but Monsieur ... ' She rubbed her lips with finger and thumb. 'We could do it. If, somehow, we could show that Monsieur is the puppet, not the puppet master, that would be a real trumping.'

Annie hugged her knees. 'The turning of the tables,' she murmured. 'Could we do it in public, so that everybody could see?'

Alathea, walking about, hovered mid-tread. 'The concert. That's public,' she said.

'The music?' Annie could follow Alathea in all the mirrors. She didn't need to move.

'Yes, the music. It could tell a different story from the story Monsieur expects.'

'Not the *Clavier-Übung*.' Annie found a ribbon to secure her plait. 'It's so precise and the audience will be stupid. Any story would have to be clear as speech.'

'Well,' said Alathea, 'the pianoforte speaks a looser language than the harpsichord, so will be on our side. Still, you're right. Making everything clear through the music will be hard. We'd have to break a great many rules.' She began to dress. 'We could see if it's possible.'

Annie, still doubtful, peeled herself off the bed. She dressed more quickly as the idea took hold. By the time she pulled on her shift, she was already experimenting in her mind, her fingers itching for the keyboard as, most of the day, they itched for Alathea. 'I think we could tell a different story at the keyboard,' she said, tugging the strings of her chemise, 'only would the girls agree to join in and tell it too? I mean, could they? It would require some skill. And what would happen to them afterwards?'

Alathea lowered the candle for Annie to find her shoes. 'I'm sure I can persuade them to join in,' she said. 'I can teach them the skills they need, and do you care what happens to them afterwards?'

Annie tied her laces. 'Don't you?'

Alathea considered. 'It will be good for them. Girls shouldn't be puppets, though I can't think of any other use for Everina and Marianne. But this plan might be the making of Georgiana. As for Harriet, she may even thank us. Are you ready?'

The girls' names and the familiarity of Alathea's judgements were a small sting, a reminder that Alathea inhabited worlds closed to Annie. Annie wanted to be rid of those worlds. There should be only one world for her and Alathea. She would never say so. She hardly dared even feel it, lest Alathea should guess. 'Ready,' she said.

Halfway down the stairs, Alathea stopped. She was gleaming in the dark. 'I know what will happen to us, though, and you know too.'

'I do?'

'We're going to the New World, you and I. We're going to make that world as we want it.'

Annie's heart leapt. Not an invitation, an order!

Alathea was lit with excitement. She gripped Annie's arm. 'We'll be free of everything! I can take money from my father, I have a box of diamonds, and we can make a living through music.'

Annie was swept away. She and Alathea at the dock. She and Alathea boarding a ship. She and Alathea in a cabin on the high seas, tossed towards a new shore. She and Alathea giving concerts. Annie and Alathea, bound together in a new life with music at its heart. She rocked. Then, a terrible thought. Her mother. How could she leave her? Detachment, that was what Alathea would say. But would Annie be detached enough for that? Could she be? She crunched her eyes tightly so as not to see what she knew she hoped for. Yet it couldn't be blocked out. Annie hoped with all her heart that her mother would die before the day came for the ship to sail.

Alathea was already opening the ballroom door. Annie hurried after her. They sat very close on the pianoforte stool, Herr Bach's variations open in front of them, and for the next two hours they played, planned, discussed and argued, tried things out, rejected, accepted, marked up and crossed out. Love would be their engine, detachment their creed and music their passport. When Annie got home, she went straight to her mother. She would tell her everything.

Her mother was asleep. Annie wanted to wake her. She didn't.

11

THE Virginia & Baltick, noon, the last day of October, the four fathers seated at the small table rather than the long trestle, Mr Spence's weekly still wedged under the leg. Three discussed their daughters' progress. Sawneyford, as usual, was silent. The day was the hot finale of a late week of Indian summer. The heat made little difference in the V&B, where the coffee required a constant fire. Wood swelled, legs ached, heads throbbed. Nowhere was comfortable. Everything was sticky.

Dinner had been ordered at the long table but a squabble over the wisdom or otherwise of French abolition of slavery had blown up, two shipmasters declaring money would be lost and three fur traders declaring money would be gained. Boiling coffee had been thrown in an abolitionist's face and there was general sneering at the fools more concerned with the rights and wrongs of slavery than the threat to profits of drawn-out war. Outside, the scalded abolitionist was splashing his face with water from the Threadneedle Street pump.

Inside, uneaten pies leaked gravy on to the *Morning Herald* and a coffee boy was trying to mop up the slop with a likeness of 'the late Queen of France taken from life in the year 1789'. Eventually she disintegrated and the boy used the tail of his shirt instead. The argument reflared. More coffee was thrown, though aimed to miss. The atmosphere was increasingly ill-tempered. Still, as Mr W remarked, a good rumpus livened the place up.

The fathers had not ordered pies. Nor had they got involved in debate. Small glasses of port had replaced their coffee cups, and Brass and Frogmorton had drunk more than one glass already. In a fit of sunny generosity, Mrs W had provided a wax candle. The generosity had one good effect and one bad: the men could see each other; but they could also see that their skin, despite the wash of blue sky outside, glowed without health, like London itself. They had pushed back their wigs. Only Gregory Brass still had a full head of hair, and it was glued to his scalp like paint.

The fathers prickled gently, palms sweating, feet swimming in their boots, fingers leaving tacky pads on the table. The concert was a month and a half away. They spoke with no direct knowledge of either the music or the arrangements. Since setting this venture in motion, Frogmorton and Drigg had confidently left everything to their wives. Brass knew that Mrs Frogmorton and Mrs Drigg would steer his own wife, and they could steer her to perdition for all he cared. Only Frogmorton had met Monsieur Belladroit. This caused no worry. Mrs Frogmorton had assured her husband, and he had assured the others, that Monsieur was doing just what they had employed him to do.

Drigg basked in Mrs Frogmorton's approval. The image of Annie Cantabile had faded. These days he never allowed his companions to forget that it was he who had suggested the whole idea of the pianoforte. The concert looming, the competitive spirit was hot as the room. 'Mrs Drigg tells me that when she gets home, even our Marianne rushes straightway to practise on the pianoforte just as the music master directs her,' Drigg boasted, 'although I don't believe there's any need. She plays naturally, you know.' He irritated even more by repeating, as though from the Book of Revelation, what Everina said about the movements of the *Clavier-Übung*.

Brass broke in, banging his fist. 'For the love of Christ, Drigg! Do cease your babbling.' Brass's mistress was cranky. Her acting skills had not gained her membership of a Drury Lane company and as a consequence she would not be gracing the new stage at the Theatre Royal. Brass had laughed at her. She had slapped him and cried. He had slapped her back. She had screamed for the neighbours. There had been a scene. 'What with this and those school prizes, your girls are turning into clever misses. Marriage to hell, they'll be writing pamphlets next.'

'Really, Gregory.' Drigg looked to Frogmorton.

The alderman was barely listening. For nearly five months he had been carrying around Monsieur's little secret. There were two reasons he had not shared it. First, it seemed faintly improper for Mrs Frogmorton to have been told such a thing about a person, in person, by a pianoforte tuner. He did not wish his friends to imagine his wife having such a conversation. The second reason he described to himself as 'delicate', although where Mrs Frogmorton was involved, it was hard to imagine delicacy.

The delicacy, none the less, was this. Mrs Frogmorton had told him of Monsieur Belladroit's mishap as they were lighting candles for their night-stands. She had actually blushed and that, combined with the thought of a eunuch in the house, reminded the alderman of parts of himself that routine worries and his wife's bulk had reduced to an occasional itch. He itched that night. He had assessed the itch. It was enough to need satisfaction so he abandoned the bed in his dressing chamber and, for the first time in several years, climbed under the marital canopy without an appointment. His intrusion was remarked on but not resisted. A eunuch, it seemed, was not just a male aphrodisiac. Heavy flesh met heavy flesh. He remembered his way. She remembered hers. Directly afterwards, the alderman removed back to his own bed, where he slept with astonished soundness. Dressing, he wondered what his reception at the breakfast table would be. It was more than pleasing. Mrs Frogmorton not only poured her husband's coffee with her own hand, she sent Frilly to the kitchen instead of feeding him at the table, a habit she knew the alderman disliked. An hour and a half later, on the stairs to his office, Frogmorton passed a spittoon boy he had recruited from the V&B. The boy winked at the roses in his employer's cheeks. The wink was insolent. Mr Frogmorton growled but his pleasure increased.

He did not push his luck. He took to visiting Mrs Frogmorton twice a week. She did not pour his coffee again; however she evinced no revulsion the alderman could sense. As a result, Frogmorton harboured a certain gratitude towards Monsieur Belladroit. He kept his secret, though it weighed on him. Such a secret to share. Should he? Shouldn't he? When Drigg pondered aloud, for a second time, whether the girls' concert gowns should be splendid, to show off their wealth, or simple, to show off their taste, Frogmorton only grunted.

With his chair drawn slightly back from the table, Sawneyford was also preoccupied. The suspicions raised in the summer over a trespasser in Alathea's garden had not abated, and he had come to suspect Monsieur. Suspicions bite harder than knowledge. Some days they bit hard indeed, yet the tails he set on Alathea reported no clandestine meetings. Alathea traversed, for the most part, only between Manchester Square and her home. A woman visitor was reported, nothing else, and the pianoforte lessons, so he assumed, were chaperoned. Other days, after he had visited Alathea and she had willingly welcomed him, he scolded himself. Even if Mrs Frogmorton nodded at her chaperoning duties, his daughter knew her worth. She would not lower herself with a music master. Then there were days when business took over and he had scarcely time to think of it at all. Here in the V&B, though, with the daughters the subject of the meeting, the suspicions were biting harder than ever. Despite her willingness, was Alathea still his alone? She had to be. He had given her everything: money, freedom, and above all himself. He would never marry again and she was the reason. She must know he would never allow her to be usurped. The world might never understand fathers like him and daughters like her, but by some miracle she and he understood each other. And yet, and yet: bite, bite, bite went Sawneyford's suspicions. Bite, bite, bite.

Frogmorton cracked under the weight of his secret. 'I'll tell you something about Monsieur Belladroit that might surprise you,' he said, interrupting the squabblesome see-saw developing between Drigg and Brass. 'The man's a gelding.'

'What?' said Drigg.

'A gelding,' Frogmorton repeated. His companions stared at him.

'Who?'

'Monsieur Belladroit,' said Frogmorton impatiently. 'The music master.'

'You mean . . . ?' said Drigg, his eyes wide.

'I mean,' said Frogmorton, 'that he's castrated, de-balled, a eunuch. What else could "gelding" mean?'

'Well, blow the bridges,' whistled Brass. 'Our Monsieur not such a *monsieur*. How on earth do you know?'

Frogmorton blushed slightly. 'Grace told me.'

'Grace? Heavens, man! During what kind of conversation?'

'Oh, he thought she ought to know,' Frogmorton said airily, not wishing to dwell. Brass raised a thicket eyebrow. Frogmorton felt obliged to go on. 'For goodness' sake, Brass, they're alone together sometimes, and I expect he was thinking of Grace's reputation.' Brass snorted and grinned and Frogmorton found himself grinning too. 'Those Frenchies don't just chop off heads with that National Razor.'

All but Sawneyford sniggered. They shifted about, their imaginations in their breeches. Brass openly gave himself a stroke. 'All present and correct,' he said. The weight of the secret lifted, the alderman sent a coffee boy for champagne. When it arrived and was poured, he raised a glass. 'To the parts of a man that matter,' he said. They laughed so loudly that the men at the long table, assuming some great financial bonanza, raised glasses and coffee bowls too.

Sawneyford drank without tasting, his face blank with shock. What fools his companions were! What dolts! No man who had really been cut would volunteer such information about himself. His suspicions roared at him, scoffed at him and jeered that they had tried to warn him. Monsieur Whatshisname was a fox, his suspicions bellowed, and the girls, including Alathea, unprotected chickens. Sawneyford gripped his glass, unable to suppress the image of the music master's papery skin scratching against skin that was his own since, God help him, he had created it, he nurtured it, he owned it. A husband for Alathea, he could barely accept. A music master's fumblings were an abomination. 'How long?' he said, trying to keep his voice steady.

'How long have I known?' Frogmorton was caught a little on the hop. 'I can't say for certain. A few months—'

'A few months?' Sawneyford could not disguise the outrage.

Frogmorton bristled. What was wrong with Sawneyford? 'What does it matter?' he said. 'You know now.' The others drowned Sawneyford's silence with jests.

Sawneyford sat perfectly still. From long habit, his face still registered nothing, but his rage was wild. He cursed himself. He had known. He had *known*. He should have acted. And he knew his daughter. She was no victim. Did she think she could share her favours? Did she think that, once having chosen her father as the keeper of her body – chosen, mind: he had never forced himself and he had accepted the guardianship in good faith – she could just open and close her legs like the lock-gates on a canal? They had had a bargain and she could hardly accuse him of not fulfilling it. He had forbidden her nothing, not even a husband. He was doing his duty. She needed reminding of hers.

He smacked down his glass, shoved back his chair and made no apologies for leaving. Since he was adding nothing to the gaiety of the gathering, nobody tried to stop him. He ran down the stairs and slammed the street door behind him. There was not enough air, even outside. He leaned heavily on a beggar and was conscious of having his pocket picked. That made him stand upright. He sliced at the thief, retrieved a few coins and pushed into a crowd bidding for sheep. He thought he could smell Alathea on all these men, and all the sheep too. He struck out and, once the street cleared, strode blindly down it, down any street, picturing himself in Manchester Square grasping Monsieur's scrawny neck and wrenching down his breeches to reveal his scrawny balls. 'Here,' he would shout to Mrs Frogmorton and the others. 'Here's your damned eunuch. Look! Look!' He pictured what he might do next to Monsieur. Fists curled like a boxer's, he strode and strode.

He strode for an hour or more and found himself right out of the city, on a path flanked by uncultivated fields. Two cows were wandering slowly, tended by a ragged grasshopper of a boy. A platoon of cavalry in half-uniform was drilling half a mile away. Thin plumes of smoke rose from the squat chimneys of squatter cottages set higgledy-piggledy around a pen. The sun, hanging low, seemed balanced on the bare bones of a chestnut tree. He could hear birdsong and a stream. His forehead puckered. The blindness of anger cleared. He shielded his eyes from the sun, turning slowly, the City man, always the City man, jostling the injured father.

'Christ,' the City man said aloud, 'what a waste.' The idleness of the land disgusted him. There was London, barely – what? – three miles away, its mouth agape for food, and here was this, this – he wrinkled his lip – this desert. This land with its desultory cottages, tethered goats and three pigs was an affront, that grasshopper boy chewing weeds like his charges worse than an affront. The boy would be better off being press-ganged. In Sawneyford's view, the press-gang wasn't slavery, as he'd heard argued. Far from it. Sawneyford disapproved of slavery, since it deprived men of aspiration and any desire to work. The press-gang, on the other hand, if you could survive a couple of voyages, offered prospects, and what prospects were there here, in these acres of nothingness, for a boy enslaved to cows? The shouts of the cavalry drifted over, the swearing, sweating men, the steam from flanks, the thump of hooves. War was escalating. Sawneyford screwed up his eyes. The City man took over completely.

War was tricky. It forced restrictions and opened doors, taking with one hand and giving with the other. It gave particularly generously to fathers with no sons to lose. Damn his daughter, but thank God he had no son. He needed to make a list. Leather, cloth, buttons, swords, sabres, belts, muskets, gunpowder, bridles, saddles, bits, horseshoes – millions of horseshoes – timber and fodder. His eyes quartered the land. How much of it was there? To whom did it belong? How much ready cash had he? He'd need money to invest in ploughs, rakes, men, horses, barns, workers' dwellings. Cattle enclosures. A sawmill. A proper road into town. He saw the acres transformed, the carts rolling in. He saw the grasshopper boy up the rigging, learning a trade. He smelled the smell of production and as he breathed opportunity in, he assigned it to 'business in the making' and 'business yet to be made'. He inspected the stream for the possibility of a navigable channel. Not until the City man was fully satisfied did he turn and retrace his steps.

Sawneyford's domestic problem did not fully revive until he was once again negotiating the outlying sprawl of the city, and then it revived more coolly. His contemplation of Alathea became more clinical, only a twitch in his cheek and a tightening of the lips betraying the occasional lurch of his stomach. The creature, as he called Monsieur, would have realised that Alathea was no virgin. Might Alathea have confided in him? If so, how would the Frenchman use the confidence? Would he try some kind of blackmail on Sawneyford? Alathea. Monsieur. This unconscionable concert. Himself. What to do. What to do. What to do.

There was no heat in the sun now. Sawneyford shivered and dodged the mail coach. The road broadened. Wooden shacks gave way to sturdier timber. Timber gave way to stone. He padded towards the City: Hackney, Stepney, Whitechapel. The bells rang four, or was it five o'clock? He would confront Alathea. They would have it out. He should have done it earlier. Monsieur could be dealt with. All could be made well. By the time he padded down Leadenhall Street into Bishopsgate and along Threadneedle Street, his blood was calm. He did not pause at the V&B. He needed his daughter, he needed a land agent and, above all, he needed a piece of paper on which to write his list.

As soon as the champagne was finished, Brass left the V&B and made for his mistress's house. Scarcely even bothering to close the door, he tumbled her with a straightforward boyish enthusiasm that surprised her, since Brass usually favoured diversions. Afterwards, he told her of Monsieur's physical infirmities, then tumbled her again. For a moment she forgot her Drury Lane disappointment and was happy. When Brass lay snoring, she rose, fetched a pair of embroidery scissors and set to work. Brass snored on. When he woke, he pulled on his breeches, slapped her behind and left. It was some hours before he urinated and noticed that the hair of his nether regions was now tufted into a heart. He guffawed. He'd get her on to that Drury Lane stage yet.

After draining a second bottle, which Frogmorton also paid for, Drigg and he stumbled down the stairs and into the street. Frogmorton hailed a cab. Drigg waved him off and wandered slowly west. The sheep were gone, the crowd too. With a cloak pulled about you, walking was quite pleasant. It was even more pleasant when you thought of what you had and another man did not. Music! What a world it was.

Alderman Frogmorton headed straight home to inform his wife that Monsieur's affliction was now known to Brass, Drigg and Sawneyford. Mrs Frogmorton frowned. Though she had been tempted many times – sorely tempted, after the insolent delivery of the progress report – she had still not told the wives. What with one thing (the alderman's visitations) and another (the embarrassment of anybody sniffing out the alderman's visitations) and the fact that whenever she thought she might venture it a servant or a daughter threatened interruption, it had never happened. Oh well. 'I expect Agnes and Elizabeth know by now,' she said. 'Archibald, I wonder.'

'What, Grace?'

'I wonder how the operation is done.'

The alderman did not pursue this. Mrs Frogmorton was wonderful in many ways but she never knew where to draw the line.

12

AT Tyburn, sitting at the capricious pianoforte with which she had entertained Mr Drigg, Annie toyed with the score of Maria Barthélemon's sonatas, signed *To my very dear Vittorio, whose instrument has given me such pleasure.* Annie did not need the score: the sonatas were firmly lodged in her mind and muscle memory. She traced the words with her right index finger and contemplated murdering Mrs B's music. She had not been to Soho Square today or yesterday. She had been with her mother. Her father had refused the doctor entry, not because of the money but because on the previous visit the medic had tried to prepare them for the worst and her father feared the doctor would, if allowed to come again, pronounce there was no more hope.

It was impossible for Annie not to feel relief at the diagnosis, though she had hidden her relief from herself as well as her mother. Her father, on the other hand, did not hide his futile and despairing rage. According to Cantabile, the doctor was both a Jewish poisoner and a murderous Jacobin, an incompetent, a corpse botherer, a grave defiler, a quack and a misanthrope. When the poor man fled, Vittorio Cantabile declared his wife better. She would soon be up and about. The last twelve years of infirmity were just a passing malady. Nobody had given the infirmity a name, therefore it did not exist. Then he turned on Annie. Had she nursed her mother better, Mrs Cantabile would have been up years ago. It was Annie's fault – she was always out these days. Did she think he hadn't noticed? Had her deformity deprived her of a heart? What kind of a daughter was she? Her mother needed her day and night. She was forbidden to go out again.

Annie had seen the sonatas' dedication many times but with her father's tirade ringing in her ears, his admiration for Maria Barthélemon riled as never before. She stopped tracing the letters and tore the score carefully into shreds. This shredding however was not the murder Annie contemplated. That murder came through her playing of these sonatas, one by one, in her own particular way. It was only what her father and Mrs Barthélemon deserved. The sonatas were not great works. Nevertheless, they had been carefully composed, so where the articulation was precise, Annie smudged. Tight runs were spread. She pedalled over phrase-endings, slurred through pauses, expanded or reduced the rests and overdid the syncopation. The murders delighted her. She stopped only to open the pianoforte's lid for a more public execution.

As she killed Mrs Barthélemon she sensed her father pausing, lever in one hand, wedge in another. She sensed him breathing. Her playing dripped whimsy. How her father hated whimsy! She rejoiced in every note she extended, every pause she milked, every barline she strained. Her enjoyment decreased when she became conscious of something else: she was not an efficient music murderer. Whatever she did, the music failed to die of shame. Instead, Maria Barthélemon's sonatas began to speak a different language. Annie frowned. What language was it? She realised only slowly that it was the language of revelation and that she was not murdering Mrs Barthélemon's music: Mrs Barthélemon's music was exposing her. Disconcerted, she raised her hands, lowered them slowly, resumed her playing and listened. She could hear it now. She was telling the story of herself. She played on. She did not hold back. She gathered the remains of Mrs Barthélemon and allowed the music free rein.

Then, to her surprise and dismay, she found herself entertaining an unwanted hope. Might music of itself open her father's heart to her, just a crack? She scoffed. Music never had and never would dissolve his scorn, his derision, his implacable ill-will. There could never be a change. Yet as the music cleaned itself of whimsy and resumed its proper shape, she found herself reminded that his life had not flowed easily. Blighted by a wife who was no wife and a daughter with a deformity, would she have acted differently? Alathea would condemn these thoughts as weakness. But Alathea was, at this moment, in Manchester Square, in the world that would never include Annie. This was Annie's world: her sick mother, Maria Barthélemon, her father and herself.

Cantabile was as familiar with the music as Annie. His skin tingled and his nerves grated as he heard Maria's sonata pulled, squeezed, elongated and squashed. It was sacrilege. How dare Annie? Then came the transformation, the whimsy left behind. This was worse. Amid the tingling and grating, he saw his wife, a dimpled girl behind the counter in her father's pastry shop, and in her wedding dress, her hair coming loose on that windy Milanese day when his own mother had danced and his father had sung. He recalled the hopes. He recalled their dashing. His throat knotted. Annie was manipulating her own father. It was an outrage.

The allegro ended; now a largo. Cantabile pressed his lever into his palm as the melody floated towards him, an echo of another's work – Maria had never been very original.

Why his wife had been drawn to him, Vittorio had no idea. All he knew was that her smile had once warmed him and here was smileless Annie, daring to tease him with the memory. He knew what Annie wanted; he could hear it. She wanted love, and her need of it was a rope pulling at his insides. Why couldn't she stop? He dropped the lever on to his toe. The pain was acute and triggered some upsurge in his windpipe. His breathing grew loud; he could feel his throat blocking, his mouth filling, his nostrils widening, his whole face swelling, and all accompanied by a heaving of his heart fit to burst his whole frame open. He knew what was happening. He was going to weep. He, Vittorio Cantabile, who only wept for his pianofortes, was going to weep for himself, for his wife and for his daughter. Well, he would not weep. He staggered to his desk and clung to his stool. He would never weep for himself. He would never weep for his wife and he would never weep for the daughter who sold his pianoforte. He unpeeled his hand, stumbled to pick up his lever and hurried into the back workshop. He found his voice. 'You're a wicked creature. That's not how music is. That's not what it's for.'

Annie heard the choke and carried on playing. 'What do you mean, Father? What is music not for?'

'Not for this!' he gargled, hitting his own face to bat the tears away.

Annie stopped playing. Hope had not quite vanished. 'Music can be for anything, can't it? We who know music know that.'

'You know nothing,' he roared. 'You're no musician, Annie. Not musician, not daughter, not wife, not anything.' Annie began to play again, this time something of her own. 'Stop that!' shrieked Cantabile.

'Why?' Annie raised her voice. 'Herr Mozart wrote things like this. He knew what music was, and what it was for.'

Cantabile crashed the main lid over the strings. 'How dare you speak of Herr Mozart? He would have spat at your playing today.'

Annie played more loudly. 'He would have spat at your Maria Barthélemon. He would never have spat at me.'

'Enough!' Her father raised the tuning lever. Annie did not blench. Hope of any paternal warmth or even a glimmer of understanding was ridiculous. She felt completely detached. Whatever Cantabile did to her, it would not hurt. He had not the power any more. Cantabile dropped the lever and made for the keyboard lid. Her fingers would pay, those menacing, wheedling, treacherous fingers. Annie played on. His breath came in rasps. There were no tears now. He reached for the lid. She never stopped playing. He fumbled and looked down. The lid was not there: Annie had removed it. It was lying on the floor amid the sonata scraps. Cantabile roared again and crouched, scrabbling to get his lever back. Annie spread a chord. Cantabile found the lever and raised it again, his thin arm quaking.

'Do you know, Father?' Annie said, as he tensed to make the blow.

'Do I know what?' His voice was high as fever; there was thunder in his ears.

'Do you know that I am happy?' she said, and left him, lever still above his head, with nobody to strike.

179

13

SAWNEYFORD got home well after eight o'clock and let himself in. He had had no dinner and did not want any. Crouch gave no proper response to his enquiry about visitors. Sawneyford picked up the lamp. He had prepared a speech. Alathea was not in the card room so he climbed the stairs. No light in the ballroom so he climbed again. Her door was closed but not locked. He went in without knocking. She was sitting by the window, an amber smudge in a loose green gown, reading, her book slightly tilted. The place was awash with candles. Sawneyford hesitated. He had never before seen this room in complete light. He had no idea it was filled with mirrors. They caught him every which way, like set-builders testing different aspects for a bedroom scene. Musk, strong as beef gravy in a cooking pot, rose from the bed's rumpled linens. Sawneyford swallowed. Crouch was a liar: Monsieur had been here.

'Downstairs,' he rapped, his reflection caught amidst ribbons, silk scarves and stockings. Alathea was reflected too, her toes peeping from the bottom of her gown. She was regarding him

180

over the top of her book. The piece might have been labelled 'A man and His Mistress'. Sawneyford stumbled out.

He collected himself, at least physically, in the card room, leaning on the mantelpiece. His legs were tired, his hands sticky, his palms rough with dust, and he wanted to wash. There was, however, no time. He wiped his hands on his breeches as Alathea glided in. Over her nightgown she had a brocade jacket, all the buttons secured, tight as a breastplate. Christ in heaven, Sawneyford thought. What on earth is she expecting? Faced with her, he found he could remember only random phrases of the speech he thought he had prepared. He should have written it down. Failing his speech, he waited, hoping she might ask about his day as she usually did if they met downstairs. Perhaps, once she had spoken, his speech would return to him. She sat down demurely on the sofa. Tucking her feet underneath her, she raised her eyes to him as though she would answer any question in the world, just as a good daughter, on an ordinary evening – fire lit, supper eaten – should, and Sawneyford knew at once that if the silence were to be broken, he would have to break it. His nerves jangled. How had he let City business intervene? This was far more important. If he was not careful, he could crack their whole world in two. He rubbed his hands on his coat and reconsidered. He should not speak. It was too dangerous. He should send her back upstairs and they should just carry on. He would have to learn to share her soon enough. He was a fool to work himself up over a music master. Yet he could not bear it. He clasped his hands. 'Alathea.'

'Father?'

'Alathea, I need—' Now he had spoken her name, he knew what he needed: he needed to revive his earlier anger. A return of that red-throated blindness would see him through. Yet no. Anger would confuse. Think, Sawney, think. What did he know? What did he want? He clenched his teeth. It's just business. Yes, business. Treat it as business. Identify the problem. Identify the outcome. Identify the risk. Identify the plan of action. A few phrases of his speech floated past. He opened his mouth. 'Frogmorton tells me the music master's a eunuch,' he said before he could stop himself. 'I don't believe him.' This was not a part of his speech. He could not take it back.

'He's not a eunuch, Father.'

Sawneyford heard himself breathe. Steady, steady. 'How can you know that?'

'In the same way as I know you're not a eunuch, Father.'

Her candour almost knocked him over. He abandoned any attempt to formulate a plan of action. Speech came now, but he could barely open his lips. 'Alathea. If you're that man's whore, well and good. But just you remember: what happens in this house remains in this house. If you ever speak of it, I'll deny it and throw you into the gutter.' He was appalled at his words. Where had they come from? They were nothing like what he meant to say. He did not want to beg forgiveness. What for? He could not speak of love. He could, though, have spoken about the duty a daughter owes to a father. Yet here she was, with her suit of armour, and now her face was armour-plated too. Too late he knew what he really wanted. How simple it was! He wanted her to acknowledge that she was his, just as he was hers. That was what he desired more than anything, and he had botched it.

Alathea twisted her thumb ring. 'It's not long since we were out of the gutter, so it'll not be far to fall,' she remarked.

Her tone was so normal it helped him. This was still just business. Business could be rethought and plans of action rearranged. The botched could be unbotched. 'A music master, Alathea!'

'He doesn't have your diamonds, it's true,' she said, twisting and twisting her mother's wedding ring. 'He plays well, though – at the pianoforte too.'

Sawneyford grimaced. She still sat, twisting and watching. She seemed amused.

'Don't you have any pride?' he said, slumping into his usual chair.

'I suppose I don't,' she said. 'Pride's not useful, you see, Father, not like power. Now *that* is useful.'

'You have no power, Alathea. I own you entirely.'

'No, Father, you don't. It's not your fault – I'm just not an ownable kind of daughter.' She never raised her voice. They might have been speaking about the weather.

He had to ask her. 'Do you speak of—' He could not go on.

'Do I speak of you to him? Do I speak of what we do?' She stopped. He knew why. She was going to force him explicitly to acknowledge what had never been openly acknowledged before. He nodded. He felt too tired to do anything else.

'You're not a subject he's raised,' she said.

His heart fluttered. 'Have you spoken of me to anybody?'

She glanced from beneath her lashes. 'I speak of you often.'

'In your prayers?' Christ Almighty! What was he saying?

Alathea stopped twisting for a second. 'In my prayers? Of course not! I say no prayers because there is no God. You know that as well as I know it. You must, or you wouldn't do what you do. Even I can't be worth eternal damnation.'

Ah, that tongue. Proficient in all its purposes. He was not too tired to clench his fists. 'You're the devil, Alathea! Who do you speak to?'

She resumed her twisting. He wanted to grind that ring into dust.

'I have another lover,' she said. 'I speak to her.'

'*Her?*' That brought him up short.

'Yes. Her.'

Her? Her? What was she saying? 'Are you talking about Monsieur – but we both know he's not been—'

'Why should I speak about Monsieur? I have another lover. She is a woman.'

Sawneyford paled. He wondered if he was losing his mind. A girl. *A girl!* She must be one of the others' daughters. He could not guess which one because he had never bothered to look at them.

Alathea stopped twisting for a second. 'She has a father too, you know. She's not close to him in the way that we're close, although she may confide, I suppose. That's what daughters do, I think. Indeed, that is what we do, isn't it? The deepest kind of confiding?' Her tone was pleasant, her demeanour cool, but her eyes were like powder pans. She flashed them up and they lit a charge in his. Overwrought and overcome, mad with weariness, with frustration, with fear, with love even, Sawneyford rushed at her, all control collapsing. 'Alathea!'

She caught him, held, him, soothed him, goaded him. 'I do what I want, I am what I want and I take what I want. You've taught me how.' She tried to stand, to ease from under him and glide out of the room as she had glided in. She was strong but he was stronger. They struggled. He floored her. She cried out. She hammered at him with her fists. Sawneyford heard nothing but his own snarl. His fingers ripped. Damn that breastplate. Off with it. Off. He had diamonds but there would be no scattering tonight. She thought she could play him like she played that damned pianoforte? He would show her that he had her absolutely. He pulled and he pushed. She was spreadeagled. He was blind. If there were any boundaries left to breach, there were none now.

Immediately after her father had left, Alathea got up, adjusted her clothes and picked up a candle. She walked slowly, clenching her legs together. She stopped to look at the portrait of herself. The child in the picture stared out, almost smiling. Had that ever been her? She put her candle down, took the picture off the wall, threw it into the fire and watched it burn, then made her way to the stairs and felt for the banister. She leaned on it. She did not feel sorry for herself; she did not feel anything. She decided something, though. Her father would never have her again. Her choice had been everything in the matter. He had removed the choice, so she would remove herself.

A week passed. She did not tell Annie what had happened. The act itself could have been admitted – Alathea could have spun that any way she wanted. It was Alathea's urgent longing to be consoled that was inadmissible. Consolation was a crumbling brick in the wall of detachment. It rendered the impermeable permeable. It must never be sought. Yet the desire to be held, to be comforted, to be reassured, would not subside. She ached with it, and it was at its most potent when she and Annie were making music.

Alathea had never seen music as the enemy before; but it became the enemy now. When she played, the intensity of her longing shocked her. More shockingly, it was not just longing, it was need. More shockingly still, it was just the kind of need Alathea despised.

Two weeks passed. She and Annie were working on their own variations of Herr Bach's variations – the variations with which the other girls would, if Alathea could persuade them, surprise the concert audience. Today they were studying the cavernous sonorities of Variation 25. Annie was frowning, brown head bent to study, fingers of the right hand absent-mindedly testing the keys, left-hand forefinger tapping the paper. She was humming. The circle of absorption, so self-contained, so focused, melted something in Alathea. She felt her core warm and soften and the next thing she knew, jabbing its way into the warmth, was that need, and the need was ordering, begging and compelling her to wriggle her way into Annie's core and seal it up with both the girls inside. Alathea could not be without Annie. Annie was mother, father, sister, lover. I need her! Alathea who never wept, could have wept then. Her father's physical assault was nothing. His real crime was to have fatally undermined her.

Annie, unaware, continued to work. The *Clavier-Übung* was a series of small seas and she was a diver mining with fierce intensity. She counted. She calculated. Occasionally she made a silent suggestion. Surely, a quicker resolution. No, no, said Herr Bach to Annie. You have not understood. Mine deeper. Count again. Calculate again. Work it out. Annie counted, calculated and worked it out. Yes, you're right. If we lose a finger here, we can use it here. But how to make it smooth? Both hands flitted over the keys, crossing, testing. Herr Bach held up his own hand – a strong hand, capable of good business. Even if you are using my music for your own purpose, you must observe the rests, he said. Observe them to the end. Silence is a note. Annie worked on, her fingers understanding, her muscles flexed, her intelligence grasping the destination and only faltering occasionally on the journey. Every sequence, every cadence, every modulation, every nuance was scrutinised, dissected, executed again and again until perfected. Everything must fit together.

Alathea, holed beneath the water, joined her on the pianoforte stool. Annie moved along. Usually when the girls touched at the keyboard it was entirely professional, but now Alathea pressed against her, her whole length shaking. Annie felt the shaking, its strength betraying Alathea's weakness, though Annie had no idea what had brought this weakness about. For a moment, she allowed the pressure. For another moment she returned it. This was what she had longed for.

Alathea was not detached at all. She needed a prop, and Annie was that prop, offering everything (though Alathea had everything already). But an inner voice whispered, Beware. Alathea was changeable. Before Annie's arms had opened, she might be withdrawing, detaching, and then Annie would be left exposed. And there was something else. Annie could still see her father's hand raised to strike her. Her detachment had beaten him, left him standing with the lever raised, helpless as a baby. She understood detachment's power now and she understood more clearly than ever before that she would be a fool to give such power up. Neither she nor Alathea was a fool. She moved away. 'The *gigue*,' she said. 'Variation 7. I'll play, you dance.' She gave Alathea a small push.

Alathea got off the stool. Not knowing what else to do, she danced.

14

THE girls were surprised to receive an invitation from Marianne to come to Stratton Street. It was Sunday – the second Sunday in November – so there were no pianoforte lessons. The weather had deteriorated and the day was miserable. The Frogmorton carriage called for Georgiana, and Harriet and she arrived together. Georgiana was cheerful – just like a real friend, thought Harriet with pleasure as Georgiana showed her some dolls' clothes she had brought in a bag. 'Mamma helped me make them,' Georgiana said. 'Aren't the dolls going to look just the thing? We should never have let them get so dowdy. Will you help me dress them?' Harriet, feeling guilty that she had forgotten all about their promise to the dolls, said that she would.

Alathea arrived on foot, the bottom of her skirt clodded with mud. She had debated, right to the door, whether she would go. She could tell Annie had not wanted her to. They had agreed, though, that Alathea might discover how far Monsieur had got in his seductions, and it was a good opportunity to introduce the

188

idea of turning the tables. If the girls liked the idea, they would have to get practising. Nevertheless, Alathea wished the invitation had not come. She did not feel up to it. Worse, she no longer quite trusted herself. She might give something of her weakness away. She walked fast to try to drum up some energy, and was at the front door more quickly than anticipated. 'Goodness me, you never walked!' admonished Marianne as Alathea dragged dirt over chequered marble. Marianne was bristling. She had hardly been able to wait for today. She had something very important to say.

The previous Wednesday, after dressmakers' fittings (all conducted separately, even Marianne's and Everina's since sisters as well as mothers wished to surprise, or possibly outdo, each other on the concert night), she and Everina had been practising Variation 8, which they were to share. Everina could not keep up with Marianne. Marianne refused to slow down. They never ended together. Frustrated by the music and fed up with being queened over, Everina had blurted out that she didn't care about the music: she was doing other things with Monsieur.

'What sort of other things?' Marianne had immediately asked.

'Things, which are usually very – well, very nice,' Everina said. She could not think of the best word. She tried again. '*Lover-like*. You know. Special things, just for us.' She wanted Marianne to feel left out.

Marianne's long jaw dropped. 'Are you saying he treats you like a wife?'

'Oh no!' said Everina. 'Not like a *wife*. Like a lover.'

Marianne closed her jaw. 'That's disgusting.'

'Not at all. It's to help with my marriage.'

'Is that what he's told you?'

'It's true.'

'For goodness' sake! Have you told Mamma?'

Everina stopped crowing. 'Of course not, Marianne, and you mustn't say anything either.' She back-tracked slightly. 'The thing is, I'm not absolutely sure what he does. It's certainly not disgusting. In any case, please don't tell Mamma.'

Marianne demanded details. Everina refused. Marianne insisted. She almost begged, and in the end, Everina, unable to resist, embroidered and fantasised her way through a panoply of euphemisms.

Marianne was a perfect audience. By the time Everina had finished, she was speechless, and Everina for once felt superior.

At nine o'clock on Thursday morning, Marianne had accosted Monsieur. Why was she being done out of these special things, these lover-like delights, these throes of ecstasy, these fields of bliss? Was she not as pretty as Everina? She certainly had better teeth. It was too bad, and unless he showed her these things straight away she would tell their mother and father.

Monsieur expressed shock. What had Mademoiselle Everina been saying? What could she mean? He became coy. Had Mademoiselle not heard of his, his – er, his affliction? She looked blank. He tried to explain. She laughed. What nonsense. Monsieur regarded her. He swallowed. Well, now was as good a time as any. '*Mademoiselle*,' he said. 'Can I be frank with you?'

'Frank as you please.'

He picked his words. 'You wish me to—'

She had the grace to blush slightly. 'I just want what Everina had – is having.'

'You wish that from me?'

'Look, Monsieur Belladroit. I know what's to be done when I marry. Mamma has told me about the making of babies. But Everina says what you do is different. She says it's not about making a child. She says it's French.'

'The French are your enemies.'

'Not in everything,' said Marianne. 'We drink French wine.

Harriet has some French shoes. And you're not our enemy or you wouldn't be here.'

'*Mademoiselle*—'

'I know I'm to marry an Englishman. I just want to feel this French feeling first and I don't see why I shouldn't have what Everina's having. After all, I am the elder.' She stood, a lumpy shadow amongst the lumpy furnishings, hands on lumpy hips. 'I'm waiting, *monsieur*.'

Monsieur sighed. Never again would he agree to seduce a gaggle of girls. He did not want to take Marianne now, with some weeks still to go, in case, like Everina, she demanded repeat performances. That would be torture, so he had planned to do her on the Thursday before the concert, once only. But here she was, immovable. Nothing for it. He got up, faced her to the wall to avoid her breath, planted each of her palms against the green flock and raised her skirt. 'Brace yourself,' he said. He undid himself. His fingers performed a perfunctory exploration. There? Or there? There. Serve her right. A manoeuvre. A jerk. Another. Over.

It was not as her mother had described, it was not as Everina had described and it was certainly not as she had expected. She gave a shriek and turned round, her jaw clenched. 'That was horrible.'

'I'm sorry. That's how it is.'

'Are you sure?'

'Quite sure. Maybe marriage will not suit you, *mademoiselle*, for I am sure your husband, particularly if he is a wise man, will do exactly the same as I.'

She began to cry. Everina must be deranged to enjoy such a thing. She could not resume her lesson as she could not sit down. She hobbled down the stairs. Once home again, she brooded. On Friday, she wrote to summon Harriet, Georgiana and Alathea, and here they were.

Ordering a maid to clean the marble and fearful for the carpet, Marianne nevertheless hurried Alathea up the stairs and into the sitting room. The room had been turned into a wedding store. Two trousseaus of dresses, chemises, undergarments, nightgowns, jackets, gloves, hats, shawls, feathers, shoes and stockings were laid out. On a table under the window, silk-threaded needles were ready to embroider whatever initials might be required – an abundance of scarlet, in case of coronets. Two empty chests had already been marked SMALL WEDDING PRESENTS.

Georgiana, in yellow velvet, and Harriet, in a high-waisted cotton dress she liked though it was really more suited to summer, had pulled low stools to the dolls' house and sat together stripping the dolls of their unfashionable clothes and redressing them. Neither girl was enjoying it as much as expected: the dolls seemed particularly lifeless. Harriet continued for Georgiana's sake; Georgiana for the sake of her promise. Everina, in maroon, had plumped herself on top of a travelling hatbox near the fire. Alathea, brushing the last of the mud from her plain black skirt, settled on a chair strung about with stockings. Marianne eyed Alathea's skirt anxiously and removed the new stockings. She rang the bell. Georgiana surprised herself by observing to Harriet, only half joking, that the laundry aspect improved the room.

As they waited for tea and fancies, Harriet, fiddling with diminutive buttons, remarked on the trousseaus, surmising that Marianne wanted to talk about the dresses they would wear for the concert. The girls respected their mothers' secrecy but their dresses, still in the early stages of construction, were a source of anxiety. What their mothers thought suitable and what the girls thought attractive might not coincide, and the dressmaker would always side with the mother.

'I'm set on gold, though Mamma says no,' Harriet confided,

giving up with the buttons and setting the doll back into the chest with the buttons hidden. 'She thinks gold is too old but I think it suits me.'

'I don't know,' said Everina, envious of the bridal nightwear their mother had ordered for Marianne and determined hers would be a match. 'Gold can be fetching.' It would not hurt Everina if Harriet looked older than her years.

Marianne did not join in; nor, when the tray arrived, did she serve the tea. Instead, she motioned the servants away, stood before the fireplace and prepared to scandalise. 'I've asked you here to discuss Monsieur Belladroit's behaviour,' she said.

'What?' said Harriet, leaving the dolls and finding a seat on a sofa whose arms were draped with petticoats.

Everina giggled. Marianne glowered. 'It's not funny.'

'Tea?' Alathea rose and busied herself. She would take charge of spirit stove and kettle. It would settle her.

'I didn't ask you to do that,' said Marianne sharply.

'Cake?' Alathea said, pressing a plate on her.

'Can't you sit down?' Marianne barked. 'And Georgiana, do put those dolls away. Who on earth is going to see their clothes anyway?' Georgiana wrapped the last doll in a travelling cloak. 'I'll dress you another day,' she whispered, and added as an afterthought to preserve the truth, 'or somebody will.' She closed the chest and found a space next to Harriet.

'Alathea!' Marianne almost stamped her foot.

'In a moment.' Alathea made the tea and handed it round. She then handed round the cakes, offering another one to Marianne, who refused with a violent shake of her head. Finally, Alathea set her cup and plate on a table.

'At last,' Marianne said. 'Monsieur Belladroit ...' She wanted to gesticulate but her hands were full of cup, saucer and plate.

'What of him?' asked Harriet.

Marianne dumped her cup, saucer and plate on the floor. She could not think of eating. 'Monsieur Belladroit has been giving Everina more than pianoforte lessons.'

Everina half choked. She, too, had thought Marianne wanted to talk about dresses. That's what Marianne had told her. Georgiana, whose decision to eat cake had been hard enough, froze, mouth open. Crumbling cake between index finger and thumb, Alathea watched.

Harriet felt Georgiana's shock. Georgiana was aware, of course, that Monsieur had propositioned Harriet, but Everina? Harriet was quite shocked herself. When Harriet had turned Monsieur down, it was for Georgiana's sake. She did not realise all the girls were in his sights. He plummeted in her estimation.

Marianne moved away from the fire. 'I see you all know what I mean.'

Harriet made a vague gesture. '"More than pianoforte lessons"?' It was hard to think of anything proper to say.

'Don't pretend, Harriet.' Marianne glared around. 'And it's not only Everina, is it? I mean ...' She breathed and flushed slightly, remembering Wednesday. 'He's been at—'

Everina was still choking. Alathea got up and patted her on the back. 'He's been at all of us. Is that what you're trying to say?' she put in.

'You too?' Marianne asked.

Alathea hardly moved her head. Like her father's gestures, it could have been yes or no. She felt more herself as she took command. Monsieur had clearly had Marianne and Everina. Had he actually had Georgiana? Alathea calculated from the stunned expression on Georgiana's face that he had. Harriet? Harriet didn't move her legs. Her mouth didn't quirk. No. Harriet was so far untouched. Surprising. Alathea's estimation of Harriet went up.

Everina recovered herself. 'I don't believe Monsieur's touched anybody but me. He loves me. He said so.'

At the word 'love', Georgiana wilted. Harriet squeezed her hand. 'Love? What are you talking about?' Marianne filled the room with her noisy complaint. 'What Monsieur did wasn't anything to do with love. It wasn't even nice, and not remotely what you said, Everina. Nothing like fireworks, and you never told me you had to face the wall. If that's really what the French like, Harriet's mamma's right to hate them.'

'You traitor!' Everina was on her feet. 'What I told you was private. How dare you! And . . . and' – she was choking again – 'all I can say is that if he did things with you, you must have bribed or blackmailed him. He would never have betrayed me otherwise.'

'Betrayed? You think he's in love with you? You must be stupider than I thought.' Marianne planted her feet wide.

Everina squared up to her. 'Did he say "I love you?" to you? Did he use those words?'

'What does it matter what he said? *I'm* saying he's defiled us all.'

'Do stop shouting,' begged Harriet.

Everina ignored her and glared at Marianne. 'Even if he has "defiled" us all, you said what he did to you was horrible, which means he doesn't love you. I enjoy myself every time, which means he does love me.' Entirely persuaded by her own argument, she sat back on the hatbox. 'And if he doesn't love you, Marianne, you've cheapened yourself.'

'Cheapened myself?' Marianne could hardly get the words out. 'How cheap does this affair make *you*?'

'Please,' begged Harriet again, but was interrupted by Georgiana, jolted into unexpected life. 'Every time?' Georgiana said, her voice high. 'You enjoy yourself every time, Everina? You mean you've done it often?'

Both Marianne and Everina turned towards her. 'Every time I have a lesson,' said Everina with some triumph. Marianne snorted.

Georgiana clung to Harriet's hand. 'Every lesson! Monsieur and Everina do it every lesson!'

'Really every lesson, Everina?' Harriet said, patting Georgiana's arm.

'Yes.'

'When did it start?'

'Oh, I don't remember exactly. Weeks ago.'

Georgiana raised her head. 'After the holiday?'

'Yes. It was September time, so you can see that Monsieur does love me, can't you, Georgiana?'

Harriet kept a firm hold of Georgiana's hand. 'I think Marianne may be right that love doesn't have much to do with it,' she said.

'Obviously not with Marianne,' agreed Everina. 'I mean, he can't love a person if he makes them face the wall. I never do that. He's never even suggested it.'

'Perhaps that's because he wants to laugh at your teeth,' cried Marianne, scarlet with fury.

'Don't be so cruel! Why do you always spoil things?' Everina cried back. 'He's just using you for practice.'

'That's outrageous!'

'Girls!' interrupted Alathea, raising her hand. 'Why are we squabbling?' She launched a comforting smile, first at the pale lake of sorrow that was Georgiana's face, then at all the others. 'Don't you know that men love different girls in different ways?'

Harriet, grateful to Alathea, quickly nodded. 'Yes,' she said, wanting to stop Georgiana's happiness evaporating completely. 'Alathea's right. That's how love is. It comes in lots of different forms, so it's possible that Monsieur loves us all in different ways, and each way is just as true as any other, although some ways of love will be stronger.' She looked rather helplessly at Alathea while continuing to pat Georgiana's hand. 'Isn't that how it is?' She herself doubted that this could be true. Nevertheless, it would be good for Georgiana to believe it.

'Well, as far as I'm concerned, Monsieur loves me in an exclusive way as well as a different way,' piped up Everina, determined to lay a particular claim on the music master. 'I'm the special one.' She turned again to Marianne. 'I can't think what it must feel like, to do it the wrong way round. I didn't know it was possible.' She took another cake. 'Come on, Marianne. Tell us. After all, we may marry Frenchmen whether our mammas like it or no, and it's best to be prepared.'

Marianne opened her mouth to snarl.

'Don't be like that,' Everina said. 'We all want to know, don't we?' She nodded at the others, to make them nod back. 'And if you don't like talking about it, that's your fault. You asked everybody here. You started it.'

Harriet staved off another row with a solicitous 'Was it dreadful, Marianne? He shouldn't have hurt you, he really shouldn't.'

Marianne, finding herself the centre of sympathetic attention, was encouraged to answer the question directly. 'It was a most extraordinary as well as an unpleasant – more than unpleasant – feeling, what Monsieur did,' she said.

'You poor thing,' said Harriet, still encouraging.

'The best way to describe it is like sitting on a tree root – you know, as happens sometimes on a picnic if you don't choose your place carefully,' Marianne continued. 'A kind of bump, and then if you can get past the pain' – she pursed her lips – 'a bit ... well, a bit fizzy, if you know what I mean.'

'Fizzy!' Everina exploded. Marianne looked daggers. 'No,' hooted Everina, 'I'm not scoffing. That's it exactly, Marianne, exactly, except when it's done the other way there's no pain, or at least only to start with, and then after the pain there's a lot of fizziness.' In her excitement, Everina spilled half her tea in her saucer. 'Fizziness.' She wanted to be friends with Marianne, to make sure she said nothing to their mother. 'That's excellent.'

Harriet was concerned. 'But don't you worry about consequences?' she asked. 'I mean, I would worry if – if I'd—'

'Poor Harriet!' Everina interrupted. 'I don't believe Monsieur has done anything with you.'

Harriet shook her head.

'Oh dear,' said Everina, delightedly winking at Marianne. It was rare that these two were one up on Harriet. It was at least some kind of a bond between them. 'I wonder why not. What do you think, Marianne? Do you think Harriet's too bony? I think he likes to be comfortable, and for your information, Harriet, fizziness isn't the same as making a baby. At least Monsieur says not, and it really can't be,' she added a little uncertainly, 'because Monsieur wouldn't want that. What he does with me can't ever have any – you know, consequences. It's not that kind of thing.'

'Now I understand.' Georgiana let go of Harriet's hand and sighed with relief. 'You see, I didn't feel this fizziness either, just like Marianne, but then with me Monsieur didn't do fizzy things. He actually made love to me, which is obviously a little different, and if there are consequences, he'll look after me.' Harriet tried to interrupt, but Georgiana's brightening radiance silenced her. 'No, Harriet, for once I know I'm right. The difference between Monsieur's love for the others and his love for me is that he knows you're all to be married to titled people, whereas I' – she grew rather shy – 'I'm just for him.'

There was an incredulous pause. Everina decided to be blunt. 'I don't think so, Georgiana.'

Georgiana turned on her with some passion. 'Monsieur needs somebody just for him. He's so lonely. He's got nobody.'

'He has his mother,' Harriet said a little tartly.

'His mother died when he was ten,' Georgiana said, 'and his father when he was born. And he had a love, but lost her too.'

Harriet's forehead furrowed. 'His father died the other day. He was executed as a Jacobin.'

'No,' insisted Georgiana. 'His father's been dead for years.'

'His father's seventy and *Kapellmeister* to emperors. That's what he told me,' said Marianne. 'He never said anything about his mother.'

'He told me both his parents died when he was born,' said Everina. Monsieur had told her the previous week, trying, with an elongated tale of woe, to save his wrist from her demands for endless 'lovers' intimacies', as she called them.

Those still holding teacups put them down. 'What did he tell you?' Harriet demanded of Alathea.

'Nothing,' said Alathea, fingering her hair. 'We don't speak much.'

Everina took a deep breath and asked what they all wanted to know. 'Did you get the fizziness too?' Alathea seemed hesitant. Everina leaned so far forward she almost fell off her hatbox. 'Come on, Alathea. Tell us.'

'I'll tell you something more interesting and useful,' she said, lowering her voice, 'if you want to listen.'

'Of course we want to listen!' cried Everina.

'Make sure nobody can overhear,' said Alathea.

'Mamma is out.'

'Check for the servants.'

Marianne went to the door, flung it open, then closed and locked it. Alathea slid off the chair and sank down in front of the fire. 'I'll tell you then,' she began with no further delay, drawing the girls into a circle. 'There are worlds out there, some of which we know and some of which we have to discover for ourselves. There's the world of men, the City world where our fathers do their business. Women don't go there. Why would we want to? It's a dull world of deals and ledgers and men rattling antlers at each other.' Even Harriet smiled. The alderman with antlers!

Alathea held out her hands to the fire. 'Then there's the women's world – the world of your mothers and the one for which we're destined. And then ...' She paused.

'Oh, do go on!' urged Everina.

Alathea dropped her hands and licked her lips. 'There's the world neither your mothers nor fathers are going to tell you about. Perhaps they don't know much about it themselves. It's a world where men and women don't just live for business or domestic things. It's a world of pleasure given and pleasure taken. It's a private world, but it's the best world there is.'

'When you say "pleasure", are you talking about the fizziness?' asked Everina.

'I am.'

'But isn't the fizziness what a man gives to us?'

Alathea blinked. 'Don't men want the feeling too?'

'Of course, but don't they get it themselves?' Everina was genuinely puzzled. 'What's *their* fizziness got to do with *us*?'

Alathea drew up her knees. 'Why do you think men go to whores?'

The girls were taken aback. They had never thought about it.

'They don't want to,' explained Alathea, 'but what's the choice if their wedded wives just lie back, spread their legs and screw up their faces? If there's no fun – fizziness – at home, they'll go out looking for it.' She looked at the girls each in turn. 'Don't you see how kind Monsieur is being?'

'Kind?' Marianne echoed. '*Kind?*'

'Yes, kind,' said Alathea. 'Our fathers want to marry us into good positions in society. That's commendable. Monsieur wants that and more. He's introduced us to the world of pleasure so that we can be happy and know how to make our husbands happy too.'

'That's just what he told me,' said Everina in triumph.

'Our parents want us to be happy,' said Harriet, ignoring Everina.

'Of course,' said Alathea, 'but can you imagine your father talking to you about how to keep your husband from the whore-house?'

Harriet blushed.

'Exactly,' said Alathea.

'I only feel happy when I'm with Monsieur,' whispered Georgiana. 'I could never be happy with anybody else.'

Harriet hugged her. 'I'm sure you'll be happy.'

'We'll all be happy,' said Alathea, 'but only if ...'

'Only if what?' Everina's eyes were round. 'Only if what, Alathea?'

'Only if we marry men who appreciate what Monsieur has taught us about pleasure.'

'I thought you said all husbands would appreciate it,' said Marianne quickly.

'Not all,' said Alathea mildly. 'That's why we must make sure we marry those who will. If we make sure to do that, then we'll be happy for ever.'

'But how can we make sure? We won't see any future husband until the concert,' Everina said, 'and we can hardly send out a letter telling them what we want them to know.'

'And we're playing music at the concert, not making speeches, even if we could find the right words, which we couldn't,' added Harriet.

They looked to Alathea for an answer and she was ready.

'Music can be more than music,' she said. 'Herr Bach's variations can show off everything we've learned, including our knowledge of pleasure.'

'How?' said Marianne, disbelieving.

'If you like, I could teach you.'

Marianne looked scornful. 'You may be an accomplished player, Alathea, but I don't believe you're much better than the rest of us, and Herr Bach doesn't seem very fizzy. Indeed, he's not fizzy at all.'

'I've been practising already, just to be sure,' Alathea said smoothly, 'and I've found Herr Bach to be perfectly fizzy. That's his genius. If we try, we can play him any way we want.' She was shining brightly enough to burn away any misgivings. 'Believe me, we can play Herr Bach so that any man worthy of us recognises *all* our talents.'

She sat back. The girls sat back too, their heads – even Everina's – full of doubts that spilled out and that Alathea deftly mopped up and swept away. It still wasn't right, what Monsieur had done. Perhaps not strictly right, agreed Alathea, but he only wanted what was best for them. And what about their virginity? (This from Everina, on whose mind the question had been preying, since virginity was so prized in the books she read.) Virginity, Alathea explained, much to Everina's relief, was old-fashioned. The men they would marry would care not a jot for it. At length there was only one puzzle left. How could it work at the concert? 'We can hardly hitch up our skirts in front of the audience,' Harriet observed.

'Oh, there is no need for anything like that,' Alathea replied. 'There'll be no impropriety, no exposing of flesh, nothing at all shocking. As I said, we'll reveal our magic through our playing. The pianoforte will speak for us.'

'But we don't play how we speak. Monsieur insists on strict time,' Marianne still persisted.

'That's true,' Alathea agreed. 'But honestly, Marianne, it can work. Let's see. The concert is five weeks away yesterday. There's time for me to show you everything I know about making the pianoforte say what each of us wants it to say. We can meet after our ordinary lessons. There would be just one thing: if we decide to make ourselves and our husbands happy in this way, I think we should keep it secret from Monsieur, so that the concert is a marvellous finale for him – a kind of thank-you.' She put a finger to her lips and met their eyes, pair by pair. The girls' hearts beat quickly. There is always something delicious about a conspiracy. Even Georgiana was cheered. Her face lit up again. 'My playing could speak to Monsieur himself!'

Alathea nodded. 'Through Herr Bach you can shout of love and Monsieur may hear you.'

Georgiana rose, tall and full of joy. 'Oh, he will,' she said. 'I know he will. I'll make him understand that he needs me and loves me. Thank you, Alathea. You've shown us what we were too blind to see.' She leaned down and kissed her. Alathea did not want to be kissed by Georgiana, but she did not move.

Harriet stood up next. What if Mr Thomas Buller, seeing she was deficient in any knowledge of the fizziness, chose one of the others? She took a deep breath. 'I've not yet been taken by Monsieur,' she reminded them.

'Don't concern yourself, Harriet,' Alathea reassured. 'There's time. Be determined. He'll not resist. What's more,' she added, 'all of you must get Monsieur to teach you everything he knows. Now he's begun, he can't deny you.'

'We must practise hard, at everything,' said Georgiana, ready to start at once.

The girls agreed, even Marianne.

'The invitations go out on Monday,' Harriet said.

'Yes, so we should meet every day from now on. Our

mammas will be pleased we're doing extra practice. Nobody will suspect,' said Everina.

'Only we'll have to fit practice in with the dressmaker and shopping,' Marianne reminded them, gesturing round the room. The girls' eyes flitted over the trousseaus. Something struck Harriet. 'Who's going to get your trousseau ready, Alathea? You can't do it on your own.'

Alathea's smile was fixed. 'Thank you. I'll manage very well.' She got up and moved to find paper and ink to draw up a schedule of work to be done. She wanted to go home, yet it was another hour including copious goodbyes laced with whispered plans and arrangements before she could, without rudeness, take her leave. She walked to Soho Square exhausted as from some great challenge, though duping the girls had hardly been that. Her skirt dragged and was soon muddy again. The distance seemed great. At Holborn, she bought a sprig of berries – to reassure? To cheer? Just to hold? Men might be fools, but girls were fools too, she thought as she turned into the square. Once she would have excepted herself, but since the day of the incident – she never called it rape, since that would make her a victim – the only person she excepted was Annie.

In the Stratton Street parlour, the scent of musk lingered. Mrs Drigg smelled it when she returned from Mrs Brass's, and, despite the chill, opened the window to let it out.

15

IN music, there are repeats. This is a misnomer. The notes are repeated, but music is not a parade of notes. A repeat offers subtle or not-so-subtle differences in phrasing, and in tone – a fourth finger instead of a thumb can change a mood entirely, and a wrist carried higher or lower shifts the hand's balance. Such non-repetitious repetition is observed in a court of law, where two witnesses observing the same phenomenon never tell the same story.

FIRST PRESENTATION

Sawney Sawneyford was in the card room, lamps and fire lit, opened wine untouched and two glasses on the table. He was waiting for Alathea. They had seen each other every day since the disagreement – Sawneyford never called it 'rape', since that would make him a rapist. They had passed on the stairs. They had sat at dinner. They had not, however, spoken, not a word.

Sawneyford had spent the first part of the night after the disagreement in turmoil. What had she done? What had he done? She had been insolent. He had been angry. She had come towards him. He had taken her. He did not shy away from that, only the manner of it. It was not a good manner. For some hours he wondered if the manner had been bad enough for Alathea to run away. He should stop her. He should post Crouch at the front door. He did nothing. If she wanted to go, she should go. By dawn, when the front door remained closed and there was no sound from above, he was reconfiguring. What had she really said? What had he really done? She had purposely annoyed him. He had taken her, and certainly his manner had been hasty, which was not their usual manner. But nothing really untoward, he thought. After all, she had not screamed. Had she screamed, he would have stopped. The best thing would be to draw a line, as he had learned to do over bad deals, and move along. He would not speak of it.

This had seemed enough at breakfast the following morning. It had seemed enough at dinner that evening. However, as the days had gone by, it was not enough. Silence had long been a feature of Soho Square, but silence was now hard where once it had been soft. Despite all his rationalisations, Sawneyford could not stand it. His temper shortened. What he wanted, he told himself, was entirely reasonable. It would suit them both very well for things to be as they were before – not just before the disagreement, but before the marriage talk at the V&B. Alathea should return to being as she was on the first night she had come to him. He would accept her and be as he had always been. After all, that arrangment had contented them both. Had Alathea not been content, she would have spoken out, and had he not been content, he would have spoken out. It was fair to say that in the absence of any speaking out, they had been content together, and in her contentment he had been happy, and in his contentment, presumably, she had been happy also. He was willing to turn the clock back. She should be willing too.

He heard the front-door latch. Alathea would see, from the lamps, where he was. He heard her remove her overshoes and brush down her skirt. He heard her foot on the stair. He spurred himself out of the card room. 'Alathea.' She stopped. She was holding berries, a spray of red. Who were they for? He swallowed and made a gesture. 'There's a fire and wine.' She did not argue, just glided before him, bringing her musk scent with her. 'You've been quite a time at the Driggs',' he said. It sounded accusatory. He had not meant it to.

'We took tea and spoke of the concert,' Alathea said. She sat down.

Some of the dust sheets billowed. The room was warm. Sawneyford breathed a little more easily. Alathea sounded the same as always. He had been worrying about nothing. Perhaps she had already forgotten. His anger abated. 'And are preparations going well?' It was what any father might ask.

'Yes.' She began picking off the berries and throwing them into the fire. They hissed.

'Wine?' Sawneyford poured two glasses and went to give her one. Both her hands were occupied with the spray so he put the glass on the floor beside her. Raindrops sparkled in her hair and dripped on to her shoulders. The diamonds in the lining of his coat scraped against each other.

'Did you walk all the way home?' he asked. She nodded. 'Well, I suppose it's not far.' He was like an actor practising a part. How could silence still hum when they were speaking? He coughed and moved about. 'I've been thinking,' he said. Alathea kept on picking the berries. 'I've been thinking,' he said, more loudly. 'I don't see why you should marry.' She stopped picking. Good. He drank. It only took a moment for the silence to hum again. He kicked at the fire, for the noise. 'That's a better blaze.' He kicked it again. 'Drigg, Brass and Frogmorton need their daughters to marry. I don't need you to marry. You can stay with me.' Humming silence. 'What do you say to that?'

Alathea put the shorn spray down and picked up the wine. She was in shadow, hard to read. Still, she was drinking.

'Would you like that, Alathea?'

She did not answer at once and anxiety rose in him again. She had not forgotten. He drank some more.

Alathea put her glass down. 'I don't want to marry,' she said.

'Well then,' said Sawneyford with forced cheeriness, 'you won't. We'll carry on here together.' He paused. 'Just as we were before.' He wanted Alathea to nod. If she would just nod, the slate would be clean.

She did more than that. She rose and came to him, just as she used to before the disagreement, except things were quite different. Before the disagreement, all her movements fuelled his desire. In his present relief, he felt no desire at all, at least not that kind of desire. What he felt, as he stepped towards her, was an ache for the world as it might have been, the world, indeed, as it had been before that night of the din in those lodgings, the world where she had been only his daughter and he had been only her father. And she understood. Here she was, coming to him and standing before him, just a girl in front of her father. He greeted her as a father. She gave a half-smile. She raised her hand and touched his cheeks. A considerate daughter, apologising for a disagreement, comforting a father after a hard time and a long day. She ran her fingers over his face. He dropped his wineglass and heard it smash on the hearth. Now her fingers probed and soothed the knots in his forehead, the knots in his neck, probed and soothed, probed and soothed. Her hands were cool and clean. How did she keep them so clean? He stood quite still and allowed his relief to flood upwards, right from his toes. He closed his eyes. Probing, soothing, her fingers asked his eyes to open. He obliged. Her face was turned up to his, so close that her hair, some rain diamonds still persisting, brushed his nose. Her eyes, black tonight, drew him in, offering entrance to the core of her being. This was new, and the novelty, combined with relief, was so great that it turned into something else – love, Sawneyford thought with thankful recognition. Love has survived. I love my daughter. It's love that welds us together. Everything over these past months has been leading to this, not a parting but a tighter binding. So what if Monsieur has had her? He is nothing to her, whereas she and I are one flesh. I've always known it and she's always known it too.

The silence still hummed, but the hum no longer threatened and he did not want it broken. He wrapped his arms around her. Her musk scent caught in his throat. She was smiling. The fire spat and blazed and he saw her in flashes. Her hands moved from his face, those expert hands with that wedding ring glinting. She licked his lips with her tongue. Ah, now he was moved beyond words. She was forgiving and giving. He could see it. He could feel it. He had no fear of her. There was no need, nor ever had been. His ache for the world of only-father-and-daughter evaporated. This was the world he wanted, the familiar world where she both was and was not his child, both was and was not his wife, was more than either, was Alathea, just Alathea, that was all, and what an all it was. He was conscious that the door was not entirely closed. She slipped from his arms and ran to close and lock it. She could read his mind! She was a miracle.

Then she was back, undoing buttons, hers and his, sinking

him to the floor, unrolling her stockings, removing her skirt. He was breathing with difficulty. This was not as it had been. This was in the light, where before it had always been dark. This was gloriously abandoned, where before it had been clandestine. This was two lovers, equal in passion, where before it had been ... not quite that. He was lying flat. She was above him. She paused. Every part of him reached up for her. He could smell her. He could feel her. She leaned down. 'Now?' she asked. He groaned. He didn't want her to speak. He was powerless to stop her.

'Now?' she asked again.

'Now,' he said. 'Yes, now.'

She crouched over him, then, quick as a fish, her hands were on the hearth, then behind her, and a burning pain shot from his groin along his legs and up into his throat. At first he mistook the pain for pleasure. His hands thrust upwards to her shoulders, pressing her down. But something was amiss. The pain seared. Alathea was no longer crouching. She was standing above him. She was still half naked but she was watching him, just watching. His hands flew to his groin. His fingers were soaked. Everything was soaked. He felt himself. Nothing was as it should be. 'Oh Jesus!' he cried. 'What have you done?'

'I've turned you into a father,' she said and, pulling on her skirt, she walked to the door, opened it and shouted for Crouch to get the doctor.

REPEAT

Alathea closed the door behind her and removed her overshoes. She saw, from the lamps, that her father was in the card room. She brushed down her skirt and headed for the stairs. Her father's speed was unexpected, as was his calling of her name.

She stopped and turned before she thought. Her father was eyeing her spray of berries. He couldn't possibly imagine they were for him? She saw him gesture. 'There's a fire and wine.' She could still have gone straight up the stairs. She chose not to: he could come after her, and she did not want to run. She went to the card room.

'You've been quite a time at the Driggs',' Sawneyford said.

She felt it an accusation. 'We took tea and spoke of the concert,' she said warily. She sat down because she did not want to admit to herself that she was frightened. Some of the dust sheets billowed. She thought, This room's like a warm mausoleum. These sheets could be my winding-sheets.

'And are preparations going well?' It was what any father might ask.

'Yes.' She wished for Annie. She began pulling berries from the spray and throwing them into the fire. The hiss brought Annie nearer.

'Wine?'

She said nothing, and when her father came over, kept pulling berries from the spray. The glass was put beside her. As Sawneyford turned back to the fire, she could see the outline of the diamonds in the lining of his coat. The coat-tails swung.

'Did you walk all the way home?' Sawneyford asked. She nodded. 'Well, I suppose it's not far.'

Her father seemed unusually uncomfortable. She wondered if he was going to beg her to forgive him. What would she say? He coughed and moved about. 'I've been thinking,' he said. Alathea kept on picking the berries. 'I've been thinking,' he said, more loudly. 'I don't see why you should marry.'

The surprise made her stop picking. Was this supposed to be an apology? Or a reward for her silence? Or, to make her sweet again, tacit approval of her taking a woman as a lover, since he didn't see a woman as any threat? She watched him knock back his wine and kick at the fire. Was that a warning? Since she didn't know what to say, she said nothing.

'That's a better blaze,' he said. She watched him kick the fire again. Yes, a warning, she thought. 'Drigg, Brass and Frogmorton need their daughters to marry. I don't need you to marry. You can stay with me. What do you say to that?'

Alathea put the shorn spray down. She picked up her wine. She needed it.

'Would you like that, Alathea?'

It did not seem a question so much as a statement. Her father drank more. She did not know how much he had consumed. She had better answer now. She put her glass down. 'I don't want to marry,' she said.

'Well then,' said Sawneyford, 'you won't. We'll carry on here together.' He paused. 'Just as we were before.'

'As we were before'. That was when she looked at him properly. Of course there was no possibility of an apology. Sawneyford had already put the incident behind him. He had drawn a line, just as he did under soured business deals. He had no idea what he had done to her, no idea what he had shattered. He had already recalibrated what had taken place, yet he still needed an acknowledgement of 'Just as we were before,' an explicit willingness to wipe the slate clean. Now she knew this, a little power returned to her, a little confidence. Her edges hardened. She could wipe the slate clean or she could not.

She told Annie afterwards, and it was true, that she had no idea what she intended to do. She only knew that, despite the incident, her best power over him was always going to be physical. She went to him and when she reached him, she ran her fingers over his cheeks, his neck, his forehead, wondering whether to gouge out his eyes. When he dropped his glass, the musical tinkle made her think of Monsieur's tinkling laugh. That was when it came to her. She would not gouge his eyes out, she would make him keep them open. This time, he would see her so close that he would never forget the face she turned up to his. Two more strokes down his cheeks, and then to begin. When she turned up her face, she saw the relief in his eyes. All was as it was before! Her eyes said as much to him and she made them say more, opening them wide to draw him in. She saw desire melt him, felt it as he wrapped his arms around her. Men. When they weren't destroying you, you could do what you liked with them.

Her hands moved from his face, those expert hands with that glinting wedding ring. She licked his lips with her tongue. She would give him the full works. She would be and not be his child. She would be and not be his wife. She would be more than either. She was conscious that the door was not entirely closed. She needed to close and lock it. She was quick, turning the key and then coming back, undoing buttons, hers and his, sinking down with him to the floor, unrolling her stockings, removing her skirt. She heard his breathing thicken. It was the first time he had actually seen her at work. It restored her power completely. He was hers. She almost laughed. Indeed, she could have laughed: he would not have heard her, she knew all he could hear was the din of his own desire. He was lying flat. She was above him. She paused until every part of him reached up for her. She knew he could smell her, could feel her. She leaned down. 'Now?' she asked. He groaned. She knew he didn't want her to speak. She knew he was powerless to stop her.

'Now?' she asked again.

'Now,' he said. 'Yes, now.'

She crouched over him, then, quick as a fish, her hands were on the hearth. There were shards everywhere. Any one would do. Her hands were behind her. She had no wish to kill him – far from it – but she must get this right. His desire made everything easier, and all those years of practice had made her more than familiar with the external geography. Shaft, hair, two pimpled, wrinkled sacks, the weight, the dampish underside. Despite her study of anatomy books, she wasn't so certain of the internal layout but she didn't fumble, only calculated. It must work like this. Wasn't that what the book suggested? Lift, hold, two deep slashes, easy as slicing cloth. His hands were on her shoulders, pressing her down. What was he doing? Had she made a mistake? Couldn't he feel? She pulled herself up. A quick look behind reassured. No mistake. He was no longer pressing her down. His hands were at his groin, his fingers soaked. Everything was soaked. He was feeling himself. 'Oh Jesus!' he cried. 'What have you done?'

He was helpless between her legs. An inspiration came to her. 'I've turned you into a father,' she said and, pulling on her skirt, she walked to the door, opened it and shouted for Crouch to get the doctor.

CODA

Annie came to Soho Square as soon as she could. Alathea's message had been cryptic, suggesting a development of some kind, nothing more. Annie thought Alathea wanted to tell her about the tea party at Stratton Street, so when she arrived at Soho Square she was surprised to find the place unusually busy – that is to say, the door was open and a boy was helping an elderly man whose bag proclaimed him a doctor into a trap drawn by a lop-eared cob. Crouch was standing in the street. Neighbours were peering.

Annie clutched the railings. Alathea was ill. She was dying. She was dead. She didn't care who saw her run to the front door. When Alathea's arms drew her inside, Annie kicked the door closed, leaving Crouch on the outside. 'Alathea! Are you ill? Why was the doctor here?' Annie tore off her veil.

'It's my father.' In some agitation, Alathea hurried Annie up the stairs to her bedroom. She did not lock the door and now they were here, in the forest of reflections, she turned preternaturally calm.

Annie scrutinised her, still very nervous. 'What's the matter with him?'

'Here,' Alathea said, 'this is for you.' She presented the almost naked spray. Annie took it and was baffled. 'Tell me. What's the matter with him?' So many pairs of reflected eyes, all burning. 'What is it? Is it catching?'

Alathea laughed harshly. 'Why? Are you frightened?'

Annie had never seen this mood before. She suspected something dreadful. 'Not for myself,' she said. 'I'm frightened for you. What is it? Please tell me.'

'Nothing to tell,' said Alathea. 'It's an injury, not an illness.' Her eyes flashed. 'He'll recover.'

'Oh.' Annie did not bother to hide her disappointment about his recovery. 'What kind of injury? Will he need nursing?' Her heart sank. She had nursed her own mother long enough to know what this might mean.

Alathea shone in all the mirrors. 'He will need nursing,' she said.

'And you'll have to do it?' Annie could not read Alathea at all. The mirrors made her dizzy. 'Did he fall?'

Alathea laughed gaily. 'I suppose he did, but not down the stairs or from his horse. It was a different kind of fall.' She stopped laughing. 'Didn't I tell you detachment was the most useful thing in the world?' Annie nodded. 'That's what I used, that and a broken wineglass.' She was looking at one of Annie's many reflections. 'I thought of Monsieur.'

Annie turned Alathea so that they were face to face, no

reflection. Her hands were on Alathea's shoulders. 'You're making no sense at all. Tell me. What did you do?'

'I cut him, Annie.'

'On his face? On his arms? Was he hurting you?'

'No. I cut him as you cut a horse.'

'What?' Annie was quite still. 'You mean, you ...'

'I mean that I have catapulted him into the ranks of the *castrati*.' All the blood drained from Annie's face. 'That's what I did. I did it yesterday evening after getting home from Marianne and Everina's.'

The tea party! That other world. And now this world, which was beginning to spin. Annie kept her hands on Alathea's shoulders. 'Are you telling the truth?'

'Do you doubt me?'

'No, it's just – why now? I thought—'

'You thought I didn't mind?' Alathea tossed her head in case a spasm should reveal what she would rather keep hidden. Even now, she wouldn't tell Annie about the incident. Nobody would ever know except herself and her father.

'You said it gave you all the power in the world.'

'It did,' said Alathea. 'Then I decided it should come to an end.' She shrugged. 'That's all.'

'And your father?' Annie did not know what to ask.

'He lost blood. The card-room floor looks like a butcher's shop. I don't expect Crouch will clean it up. The doctor patched him and – oh, Annie, his words when he explained to my father what he must expect when he's recovered. So blunt.'

'Didn't he ask how it happened?'

'That was the funniest thing. Crouch blamed you.'

'Me?' Annie let go of Alathea's shoulders. '*Me?*'

'Yes. I sent him for the doctor directly after I'd' – a momentary shiver at the memory of glass on skin – 'directly after I'd done it. My father fainted, so I staunched the blood with his shirt. The doctor found me and was quite horrified, fussing about the unsuitability of a girl of my class tending a man, even a father, in such an intimate way. He never looked at me. He assumed I was in a state of silent hysteria, I suppose. He spoke only to Crouch, and Crouch didn't care at all about my father. He wanted the doctor out of the house. But when the doctor asked him directly who might have done such a thing, Crouch said he had seen a veiled woman come and go who, he assumed, was my father's mistress. He thought my father had probably thrown you over and you'd taken your revenge. When the doctor asked your identity, Crouch just said, "A Catholic, I'll be bound," and the doctor couldn't get any more from him.'

'Crouch saw me come in just now,' said Annie, highly alarmed.

'There's no need to worry. Crouch is probably on your side. A funnier thing is that this morning, in his fever, my father kept shouting my name and the poor doctor kept exclaiming, "Don't call for your daughter! It's not right, Mr Sawneyford, that she should see this." He kept patting my shoulder.' She took Annie's hands. 'Forget all this. My father will recover perfectly well, and quickly. He'll be back in the City in no time. It makes no difference to us. As for the girls, they were easy to persuade about the concert. The evening will certainly be startling. The moment it's over, we'll fly.'

Had her eyes been completely frank and sparkling, Annie might have worried about Alathea's sanity, but there was a strain, a continuous tic, a suspicion of panic that reassured her. Alathea was trying to make things normal when they were not normal at all. Annie would help her, but she still worried. 'When your father's fever has abated, you're sure he still won't say anything about you? Shouldn't we go now, just in case?' Too late did Annie think of her mother. Whatever the circumstances, Annie could not just walk out and leave her.

Alathea's shake of the head was, for this reason only, a relief. 'I'm as sure as I can be that my father will say nothing. Admit to being a gelding? He'd rather die.'

They remained on the bed, neither sure what to do next. Gradually they sank down and Alathea drew the covers over them. They held each other. Alathea pushed against Annie. They pressed together when repulsive images of Sawneyford intruded. Eventually, Annie sat up and asked about the tea party. So they sat, still pressed together, with Alathea describing her afternoon with the girls – even laughing sometimes – for all the world like any two young innocents on the dizzy brink of womanhood. Only, Alathea could not quite let go of Annie's hand, and Annie kept seeing that shard of glass.

16

PREPARATIONS for the concert were far advanced. It was the Earl of Allemonde who, owing Brass money and Sawneyford gratitude for discretion, (the earl still kept a slave or two in the country), had agreed to lend his house for the performance. To the Countess of Allemonde's fury, Mrs Frogmorton, Mrs Drigg and Mrs Brass had already been to the Pall Mall saloon several times to plan winter flowers, supper tables and where exactly the pianofortes should be placed to show off the girls to best advantage. After Mrs Frogmorton complained that the kitchens were dirty and the vases inferior, the countess took herself and her children out of town. They would not grace this concert. The Allemonde heir, however, would be parted from his horses for the duration of the aria and variations. When he objected, he was shown the stable bills. He, sensibly, asked how much money each girl had. The four fathers, sensibly, supplied the answer.

The guest list had been easy to draw up. It included all peers, down to baronets, secure in their title (wealth was not required) who had an eldest son (or second son, if the elder was sickly) of marriageable age. Any peer not fulfilling the criteria was excluded. Sworn to secrecy, the printer responsible for the invitations quickly alerted Pall Mall, Westminster and St James's. The aristocracy laughed.

'Why bother with thick card?' the Marquess of Poderum remarked, having heard of the concert from his tailor. 'Why not parade the creatures at Smithfield, after the cows?'

'With the wedding settlement tied round their necks in bags,' chortled his son. 'I'd rather go to Smithfield than endure some poxy concert.'

'You'll go to that concert,' his father said sharply, 'and we'll make an offer. Choose the one who takes your fancy. I hear the fortunes are more or less the same.'

Similar conversations were heard in similar establishments, though not in all. Some fathers looked at their own children and wondered what kind of City men these were, who sold their daughters for a title. They did it themselves, of course, but that was old blood trading with old. New trading with old was different – necessary, sometimes, if old blood had run out of old money, but that was for old blood to decide. This concert was crude. What was more, City girls were ugly girls, everybody knew that. Still, they reassured their sons that, duty done, husbands were free to roam.

At the V&B, Frogmorton, Brass and Drigg also laughed. The printer had blabbed, just as they expected. The aristocracy had laughed, just as they expected. When the invitations were delivered, nobody refused, just as they expected.

The mothers took to meeting at ten o'clock every morning so that Mrs Frogmorton could update them on the guests. So far, they were pleased with the list. They were less pleased with their daughters' new practice arrangements. 'Do you think it healthy, Elizabeth?' Mrs Frogmorton asked, seated in the Drigg parlour, legs splayed to the fire in the hearth, cup of chocolate at her side. She sat between stockings and handkerchiefs, the room being still decked out with marriage clothes a fortnight or so after Marianne's tea party. 'I mean to say, do you think it healthy that our daughters spend quite so much time at their music?'

Mrs Brass did not reply.

'Whatever can you mean? What's health got to do with it?' Mrs Drigg shifted, to toast her other side.

Mrs Frogmorton clicked her tongue. Agnes could be obtuse. 'The point was not to turn them into pianoforte players, just into girls who can play the pianoforte. I'm happy enough with their lessons from Monsieur. He doesn't tax them too much. Indeed, sometimes there are long gaps when, I gather, they just speak about the music without playing, so that they shouldn't tire themselves. But I don't know why they need to practise so much when they're not with him. Harriet spends more time here than she does at home. It's not at all convenient for the dressmaker.'

Mrs Drigg tried not to blench when she heard Monsieur mentioned. Since her husband had revealed what he had learned from Frogmorton about Monsieur's unfortunate history, this was hard. The knife. *Down there*. She twitched. 'Do we really need to worry? Marianne says this air and variations are so spectacular they need the extra time.'

'That's as maybe,' said Mrs Frogmorton 'But why does Alathea always have to be with them? I saw her when I left here last week. She had that smile. You know the one.'

Mrs Drigg and Mrs Frogmorton grimaced in unison. Mrs Brass made a small *moue* with her lips.

'I agree, Elizabeth,' said Mrs Drigg. 'I wish she would keep away too, but Marianne says that Monsieur has suggested she practises with them. For all her faults, she's a fine musician and the concert's so soon now. Can it harm?'

'I suppose not.' Mrs Frogmorton picked up a pair of brand-new stockings and began absent-mindedly to roll them as if for a journey. Her hands were slightly chocolate-stained but Mrs Drigg did not like to stop her. 'And perhaps you're right. I expect they spend most of the time talking nonsense and comparing clothes. You know what girls are like.'

'Indeed we do, don't we, Elizabeth?' Mrs Drigg nodded for herself and Mrs Brass. Mrs Frogmorton finished rolling. Mrs Drigg quickly took the stockings from her and removed all others within reach.

Mrs Frogmorton hardly noticed. She sighed. 'Why can't Alathea be like our daughters?' She sat musing for a moment, then blinked back into the present. 'Don't you think she's been worse lately?'

'In what way worse?' asked Mrs Drigg, setting both knees to the blaze. There was guilty enjoyment in gossiping about Alathea.

'There's a sort of excitement about her,' Mrs Frogmorton said. 'I saw her after her lesson the other day. She seemed ... I want to say sly, only Alathea isn't sly, not like' – she was about to say 'Everina', and halted only just in time – 'not like some others, none of ours, of course. Anyway, not sly. She was ...' Mrs Frogmorton sought the word she needed, 'I'd say, fizzing. Yes. Fizzing.'

Mrs Drigg looked blank. 'Could it be because her father's ill?' she suggested after a moment. 'Drigg told me this morning that Sawneyford hasn't set foot in the City for over a week. Perhaps this "fizzing" of Alathea's is something to do with that?'

'Oh?' said Mrs Frogmorton, startled. 'I hope it isn't serious with Sawneyford?' The awful possibility of Alathea, if unmarried, being left an orphan under her charge made her grip her knees together.

'I thought you might know?'

'I know nothing,' said Mrs Frogmorton.

'I did make enquiries as soon as Drigg had gone,' said Mrs Drigg, pleased to be the imparter of news but disappointed that she was going to learn nothing further from Mrs Frogmorton. 'According to the servants, the doctor's been at least four times, only he's saying nothing, not even for half a crown.'

Mrs Frogmorton became agitated. 'What can it be? Could it be catching?'

'I don't think so,' Mrs Drigg said quickly. She did not like it when Mrs Frogmorton was agitated. 'I mean, if it was catching, wouldn't Alathea have been sent away?'

'You never know with Sawneyford,' said Mrs Frogmorton, half rising now. 'He's a queer fish, and—'

'But he's fond of his daughter,' Mrs Drigg interjected. 'He wouldn't wish her ill.'

'I suppose not.' Mrs Frogmorton subsided. Her motherly instincts surfaced. 'I wonder if he's got somebody to help with her concert dress? I do wish we knew what was wrong.'

'I'll send Sam again this afternoon,' said Mrs Drigg. 'He's a great one for prying. Now, we were going to decide about flowers, and we've never discovered if the Allemondes will allow our guests to use their water closets. I can't see any reason why not, can you, Elizabeth?' She and Mrs Frogmorton both turned to Mrs Brass and answered for her, 'No reason at all.'

At Manchester Square, Harriet was sitting in the footman's chair, huddled in a cloak and gazing through the window into the communal garden. Severely hampered by fat winter outer garments, children were attempting to play hoop. Harriet fought an urge to join them. She could, she thought. After all, there must be some advantages to being still a child, by which she meant still untouched. Though she had swung her earrings every day at Monsieur, he kept his hands firmly on his lap and now Harriet was faced with having to force his hands, a concept she found insulting. Nevertheless, it must be done and, she had already decided, it must be done today. She would not return to her bedroom in the same state as she left it.

She swung her legs. Why didn't he want her? Marianne said she was learning new techniques from him almost every day and even facing the wall had become quite enjoyable. Yet she, Harriet, was far prettier than Marianne. Harriet decided that despite her best efforts she was being too coy. Monsieur must think she was still concerned about Georgiana's feelings. She would have to be less coy. She tweaked her cloak. Underneath, she was wearing the loose pink tea-gown she had worn to Marianne's the previous Sunday, only today, after the dressing-maid had gone, she had removed all its underpinnings. Between dress and specially scented skin was only a gossamer shift, pale stockings and a pair of silk slippers with bows. She shivered. The fire was some distance away. Her feet were cold. She pulled them under her and admired her ankles. From upstairs she could hear the same phrase being played again and again, left hand only, right hand only, hands together. Marianne might be good at the fizziness; she was no good at the pianoforte.

A noise in the street. Mr Thomas Buller emerged from next door, evidently waiting for his horse to be brought round. On impulse, Harriet jumped up. She had been waiting for an opportunity to see Thomas. How infuriating that she was not more suitably dressed. Could she really go out in these shoes? She knocked on the window. Mr Thomas Buller, fresh-faced, round-faced, red-faced, of little brain and endless good humour, gave a *faux*-salute and grinned cheerfully. Not being the son of a peer, he had not been asked to the concert. Not *yet*, Harriet thought.

Harriet and Thomas were not well acquainted and Harriet suspected that the Buller parents had aspirations for their son beyond marrying a Frogmorton. It was true, however, that

Thomas liked her – at least he always seemed pleased to see her – and she calculated that he would be more than obliging if she could persuade him that the feeling was mutual. Commendably self-deprecatory, she did not think her charms her best weapon; she thought her best weapon would be surprise. The Bullers, like the rest of Manchester Square, must know that the Frogmortons had a peer in mind for Harriet, so Thomas must believe that Harriet was not for him. Now might be a good moment to shock him into imagining how nice it would be if she were. She knocked on the window, then smiled and waved.

Thomas waved back without embarrassment. Harriet was right: since he thought she was not for him, he was perfectly at ease. Even if he had to speak to her, he thought, it mattered little that he was neither interesting nor clever. Harriet was destined for another.

Harriet pulled her cloak about her and opened the door. The shoes would have to be sacrificed. She went into the street, her warm breath wafts of steam. At once, Thomas was full of concern. 'You'll get cold, Miss Frogmorton,' he exclaimed, 'and your feet'll get all wet in those slippers.' He bundled his own cloak over hers, exuding heat. He's like a large dog, Harriet thought. Once they were married, she would pet him and stroke him and give him plenty of treats. She looked forward to it. 'I've something for you, Mr Buller.'

'Thomas, please.'

'Thomas.' She twinkled at him. 'I've something for you, Thomas. I'm inviting you to a concert. It's on Saturday next in the evening, at the Duke of Allemonde's saloon in Pall Mall.'

Thomas fidgeted with his gloves. 'I think he's an earl,' he said.

'Earl, duke, what does it matter? I want you to come to the concert.'

'That's very kind of you, Miss Frogmorton,' Thomas said, 'but I've heard it's only for those with titles.'

'Ah,' she said, twinkling more, 'you've heard that.'

He blushed. 'Everybody's heard. Well, obviously not everybody. I mean, lion-tamers in India won't have heard.'

Harriet laughed kindly. 'You mean everybody who matters has heard.'

'Yes, that's it. Everybody who matters.'

'Your father could buy a title, you know,' said Harriet, hoping her nose was not turning red. It really was cold.

'Even if he did, Miss Frogmorton—'

'Harriet, please.'

He flushed beetroot. 'Even if he did – Harriet – I'm not – well, you know, I'm not – I'm never going to be ...'

'Never going to be the type of person my parents want at the concert – a bit like the lion-tamer?'

'Yes, that's it. I like the way you say just what I mean.'

Thomas's horse arrived. It was a pleasant creature, large, solid and dependable, much like its owner. Harriet formed an enchanting 'o' with her lips and blew on its muzzle. It blew back in a friendly fashion and lipped a stray oat from a whisker. 'But Tom – can I call you Tom?'

He nodded. 'Please do. It's what my friends call me.'

'Well, Tom, it's me who has to play at the concert' – she turned from his horse to himself – 'just as it's me who'll have to get married after it.' Would that be direct enough?

It wasn't. Thomas kept fiddling with his gloves. 'Yes, indeed. But you want what your parents want.'

Harriet gave a feathery sigh. 'Do I, Tom? Do I?' She looked him straight in the eye.

A slow computation. 'You mean you don't want what your parents want?' Harriet didn't blink. 'You mean—' Thomas said, his Adam's apple shooting first up, then down into his stock.

There, Harriet thought. Now he's getting it. The horse stamped a back foot. Harriet blew on its muzzle again. 'Come to the concert, Tom,' she said. 'That's what I want. Will you promise?'

He looked stunned. 'Really?' he said.

'Please promise.' She twinkled. She purred. She folded herself more neatly into his cloak. 'I want to see a friendly face, somebody who might care for – well, you know, more than my father's stock of gold in the bank.'

'Only a fool wouldn't care for more than that,' Thomas said.

Harriet touched his arm. 'Then you'll come?'

He stood to attention. 'I promise.'

'Excellent,' said Harriet. Her task accomplished, she began to take off the cloak. 'That's all arranged. Now you'd better get on before – what is the horse's name?'

'Gallant.'

She smiled. 'Gallant. Like you, Tom. Better mount up before Gallant turns into an icicle, or I do. Have a pleasant ride.' She returned his cloak and skipped back through her own front door.

Thomas Buller was transfixed. Had the groom not broken the spell, he might have spent the rest of his life gazing at the place where Harriet had stood. As it was, the groom nudged him with a word and the horse nudged him with a shoulder. He put on his cloak, found his stirrup, mounted and with a loud 'I will have a pleasant ride, Miss Frogmorton, I certainly will,' headed out into Oxford Street.

Harriet tossed off her shoes – Yes, ruined, she thought – and looked out of the window. For all that his heavy cloak accentuated his roundness and dogginess, Thomas looked quite fine on a horse; martial, even, with his spurs shining. Harriet was glad. It was good to marry somebody who looked nice. More important, though, was her certainty that with Thomas she would have a life of her own choosing, and, once they got over their annoyance, her parents would be content. After all, her parents were happy together. Why shouldn't she and Thomas be equally happy? It was only after Gallant clattered off that Harriet realised she was herself being looked at – more than looked at. Harriet was being inspected.

Annie was well wrapped against the weather, her whole face, except for her eyes, covered. She had come through the square on her way to buy iron wire for strings, though Manchester Square was not a direct route and she did not even really want to be here. She came because she had seen Alathea only rarely since the day when Alathea told her what she had done to her father, and she missed her. Annie knew she was not being deliberately ignored. She knew that time must be spent at Manchester Square or at Stratton Street practising with the girls if the concert was to go as she and Alathea had planned. Nevertheless, on the rare occasions Alathea was with Annie, she now spoke of the girls, imitated the girls, was always so full of the girls that Annie could not help wanting to see the girls in the flesh. Alathea told Annie she despised them, and Annie believed her, certainly from her descriptions of the Drigg sisters. She was not so sure about Harriet and Georgiana. Alathea had some regard for their dedication; she had even commended their playing. This last had shaken Annie. It was why she needed to see the girls for herself.

At first, to Harriet, Annie was a black distortion through the glass. Then, when Annie was clearly a person, a female person at that, and not just looking at the window but studying it, Harriet wondered what business a woman could possibly have at Manchester Square. Perhaps, under the veil, she was one of those old crones who pestered for money. Yet she seemed disinclined to ring the bell. Harriet called for the footman. 'There's someone hovering at the railings, Spencer. See what she wants.'

Spencer went outside and addressed Annie without deference. He saw from her cloak that she was not a lady. 'Madam?'

Annie backed away.

'Wait.' Harriet was hopping in her stocking feet on the cold doorstep. 'Who are you looking for?' she called.

Annie instantly focused on Harriet's pretty cheeks, her pretty hair, her perfect mouth. Alathea had never described these. On impulse Annie said, 'I've come from Mr Cantabile's.'

'Mr Who?'

Annie raised her voice. 'Cantabile.'

'Who's he?'

'The pianoforte maker. He sent me to ask if you're happy with your instrument and the teacher he sent with it.'

'Happy?' echoed Harriet, puzzled. 'Yes, of course we're happy with the pianoforte and with Monsieur Belladroit. If we weren't, we'd have complained long ago.' It seemed to Annie that Harriet's lips involuntarily twitched into a small kiss.

Annie moved forward. She couldn't look away from that mouth. How slim it was! How elegant! How could Alathea resist it? Here in Manchester Square, with Harriet alive in front of her, Annie felt as though a cataract had been removed. In the space of a second, the past months took on a different aspect and all Alathea's talk of America struck a false note. Until she saw the reality of Harriet, Annie had accepted without question that Alathea's lessons, the lessons that were going to show the girls as tainted goods, were being learned by the girls only through music. But of course Alathea had never said so explicitly. She had never said, in terms, that music was her only connection with Harriet or the others, and knowing what she did of Alathea's appetites, knowing what she did of Alathea's impulses, it occurred to Annie that she had been too trusting. Alathea could have been doing anything all these long afternoons when Annie was at Tyburn with her sick mother and surly father. After all, Alathea never suggested that Annie join her to help with the practice. Why not? If she chose, Alathea could make the girls see beyond Annie's ruined face. It must be that she did not want to do so. Annie thought of that shard of glass. Once Alathea no longer wanted her father, look what she had done to him. Once she no longer wanted Annie, what might she do to her?

Harriet was still on the doorstep. 'Would you like to come and inspect it?' She peered at Annie, who, almost unknowingly, had moved closer. The veil disconcerted Harriet, who wanted to see beneath it. She lifted her arm as though to touch it. A hint of musk. It cut up Annie's nose as the glass shard had cut into Sawneyford. She imagined Harriet and Alathea sitting together, playing together, the pale and the dark lit up for the world to admire. She could feel Alathea's hands on the warm porcelain of Harriet's flesh. And those lips. Those lips. Harriet touched her veil and Annie whizzed round and fled, slipping in the frost, sliding into children, prams, dogs and all the domestic clamjamfry of Manchester Square families, seeing nothing except that her own lips, those very things about which poets wrote and lovers dreamed, were absurd and always would be. Alathea could kiss them and set each nerve athrob, but they were still absurd. Alathea knew that. Monsieur, though he spoke kindly to Annie and admired her playing, knew that. Her mother knew that. Her father was the only person brave enough to tell Annie the truth, and the truth was this, that Annie was a joke, somebody to be toyed with or played with, but certainly not somebody to flee with to America. There would be no new life. Annie had been dreaming, just as this time last year she dreamed of her concert and Monsieur. She rushed into Oxford Street and back to Tyburn. When she arrived, fumbling for her key and crashing through the door, her father could have destroyed her completely with a word. Luckily, he was out.

Harriet shut the front door and told Spencer to lock it. There seemed something ominous about the veiled girl, and Harriet did not like ominous things. Marianne tripped down the stairs, humming. She winked at Harriet, the first of the leery winks for which she eventually became known. Harriet murmured something, then made her way slowly up the two flights of stairs to her own room, collected some new shoes, came down and quite forgot to make the beguiling entrance into the drawing room that she had planned.

It hardly mattered. Monsieur was not looking. 'Good morning, Mademoiselle Harriet,' he said from the depths of the pianoforte when he heard the door click shut. He was fiddling with one of the dampers, to calm his temper. What was the matter with Marianne, that she wouldn't rest until he had her again and again? She could not enjoy it, for he took no trouble, not even to enjoy it himself. And the questions she asked, as though his person was some new kind of musket. How did it fire? How did it recharge? English girls of her sort were vulgar, vulgar, vulgar. He finished his work. 'Are you ready to play?'

Harriet pulled herself together and wafted over. 'A girl was here,' she said. 'She came from the pianoforte workshop and needed to know if we were satisfied with our instrument.'

Monsieur started. 'What did she look like?'

'I don't know,' Harriet said. 'She was heavily veiled. I wanted to see her face but she ran away.'

'I expect that was Annie.' Monsieur wondered if he should tell Harriet about Annie's lip. He decided against it. 'She is the daughter of Vittorio Cantabile, the pianoforte maker.' He opened the music. What was Annie doing here? Cantabile most certainly hadn't sent her. 'She is a fine player herself,' he explained, as Harriet seemed to be waiting. He tapped the music. 'Variation 27. Begin.'

'Annie,' said Harriet, not beginning.

Monsieur tapped the music again. Annie should not have come. What could she want here? 'Annie. That is her name. Now come along, *mademoiselle*. We have not long until the concert and you are not yet ready.'

Harriet opened her mouth, nearly saying, 'Oh, but I am, *monsieur*, you've no idea how hard we all practise when we're not here,' but quickly shut it again. Alathea had been very insistent on the pact of secrecy over the extra hours they put in. Harriet stopped thinking about Annie and thought instead about Thomas, then about Monsieur. She must concentrate on what must happen within her allotted hour. She began Variation 27, the ninth canon, proficiently enough to set the semi-quavers tripping and the ornaments adding intricate vivacity. She shifted her knees so that her dress fell between. Everina had suggested that. She raised her chin to expose her smooth neck. Georgiana had suggested that. Her hair was already bound up. Her earrings danced. Come on, *monsieur*, she thought. Come on. I've already caught Thomas today. What's the delay with you?

Monsieur could tell that Harriet was not concentrating on the music. He himself was finding concentration hard. He was slightly sore from Marianne, and it was not just her who irritated and alarmed. All the girls' behaviour had altered. Like Marianne, Everina had turned questioner, always asking how she might improve her technique, by which she did not mean at the pianoforte. He preferred her giggle to her questions. Then there was Georgiana. No matter what he said or did, she still worshipped him, and when he took her, which he found himself obliged to do just often enough to spare her the indignity of begging, the whole operation moved him less than washing his hands. Harriet was still untaken, though he could see from her dress today that for some reason she was no longer unwilling. And Alathea ... His brow furrowed more. She was

232

still irresistible. She was still sensational. Monsieur wondered if she was also some kind of a witch, since sex with her sucked the pleasure out of sex with any other. His frown turned into a sigh. Perhaps he would never tumble Harriet. Perhaps he would hand back a fifth of Cantabile's money and leave her untouched. Perhaps, for his next assignment, he would go to the East, where girls were kept in harems and never let loose on music masters.

'*Monsieur?*'

He had not noticed that Harriet had finished. 'That was good, Mademoiselle Harriet, very good.'

'I'd like to practise Variations 4 and 5 now,' she said.

'Ah, your great entry.'

'Yes, and my hands get in such a muddle in 5. You must help me.'

'You must try on your own.' Monsieur edged away.

'Very well.' She began. Her left-hand G was confident enough, but she faltered over the right-hand run, and put the wrong finger of her left hand on the treble B. She stopped to correct, but to no avail. Everything collided in the last six bars.

'Try again,' Monsieur encouraged her.

She tried again. The same. 'Can you show me, *monsieur*?'

He did not want to. There was a small battle of wills, which Harriet, by easing along the pianoforte stool and sitting determinedly expectant, won. Monsieur touched the keys. Harriet at once set to work trying to drum up the pulses she had felt at least once before in his presence. That she felt no such pulse today did not alter her determination. Business was business. Tightening her lips, she leaned down, straightened the pink bows on her shoes and made her move. She went first for Monsieur's ear, into which she breathed, as Alathea had suggested. No response. She breathed harder and placed a hand on his knee. Still nothing. She tried a more direct approach. She

233

seized his left hand and placed it on her breast. Monsieur snapped it away and continued playing. Harriet took a deep breath and plunged both hands into his lap. At that, Monsieur leapt up and flung her hands back, knocking his knees against the pianoforte frame. She expected him to shout, and was perfectly prepared for that. She could shout too. She deserved his attention, just as the others did. He said nothing. Harriet stood. They were about three feet apart.

'*Monsieur*, is there something the matter with me, or is there something the matter with you?'

'What can you mean, *mademoiselle*?'

'Come now, *monsieur*. You know just what I mean.' Harriet knew she sounded like her mother.

Monsieur folded his arms. 'Mademoiselle Harriet. Do you want to be married to Mr Thomas Buller?'

'Of course.'

'Then let us concentrate on the pianoforte.'

'But, *monsieur*, that's exactly the point. Thomas won't care about the pianoforte, not now, not ever. He will care about other things, though, and I know you've been teaching these things to the other girls. Don't I deserve to know them too?' She blazed a little. 'You wanted me badly enough before, and I hardly think it boasting to say that I'm more of a beauty than Everina or Marianne. What's the matter with me? Do you hate the colour of my hair?' She loosed it to drift over her shoulders. 'Isn't my skin soft enough?' She seized his hand again and pressed it against her cheek. 'Am I too thin or too fat?' She ran his hands down her body.

Monsieur pushed away. Those stupid, blabbing girls. He must think quickly. 'You are very pretty, *mademoiselle*,' he said, 'every part of you. Teaching you these – these things, would be a pleasure. But it is for Mr Buller to be the master. I am sure he will be an excellent guide.' He was astounded at this statement, which he had never imagined himself making. Harriet grew cross. 'Thomas Buller only knows about horses.'

'I only know about pianofortes.'

'*Monsieur*, you're a liar.' Harriet's colour was high, and she had never looked more delicious, with her dander up and her defences down, and all barely enclosed in that rose-pink dress. Yet he must put an end to this. '*Mademoiselle*,' he said, 'please. Please. We are business partners, are we not?'

'Business partners must be honest with each other. Trust, *monsieur*, is at the heart of business.'

He sat down and, for safety, took both her hands in his.

'Mademoiselle Harriet. My dear business partner. Listen to me. I do not deny that my lessons with the others have not been restricted to the pianoforte, but those lessons are over.'

Harriet removed her hands from his. 'Oh, *monsieur*,' she said, a little world-weary. 'You think it's as easy as that? You think just because we're young and a few of us are silly that you can give lessons, withdraw lessons, teach some and not others, just as you choose?' She shook her head. 'You can't. What you give to one you must give to all.'

'Mademoiselle Harriet.'

'Stop repeating my name. Why should you lie with the others and not me? Lord above, I've made it easy. Look at me!'

He looked at the floor. 'And what will you do if I refuse? Call your mamma?'

'Of course not.' Harriet was effortlessly equal to this. 'I'll tell Georgiana you laugh at her and that all your kind words, all your cooing and my-little-doveing, have been false. It would finish her.'

A flash. 'You would not do such a thing, *mademoiselle*. You are too kind.'

'I am kind,' Harriet said, 'but I also like to get what I want.

Now come along.' She gripped his left hand and ran it between her legs. 'Is this a good way to start?'

'*Mademoiselle*,' said Monsieur rather pitifully. 'I am tired. I have just had Mademoiselle Marianne.' He regretted the words as soon as he said them.

'You see!' cried Harriet. 'Those lessons aren't finished at all. You can rest afterwards. From what I gather from Alathea, it doesn't take long.'

Ah, Alathea, Monsieur thought. She knew how to hurt a man. 'It entirely depends,' he said, trying not to sound injured.

'Well, it can't take long today,' Harriet said, 'because we've wasted so much time already. I suppose the time it takes is something to do with age?'

'Is that what Mademoiselle Alathea says?'

'I think she said something about age, and you're no longer young.'

Monsieur was now nettled. Harriet thought this a lively sign. She moved her hands. 'Is this right?' she asked. 'Or this?'

It was extraordinary, to Monsieur, to be taken by an untouched girl, as though he were the virgin. Extraordinary and, he could not deny it, arousing. He shifted slightly to allow Harriet to place his hands and hers where she would. He mumbled answers to her questions in a tone as polite as her own. 'A little to the right, *mademoiselle*.' 'Perhaps a little softer.' 'Yes, undoing the buttons would be a good idea now.' 'No, this is quite usual' (this last after the buttons were undone and Harriet gave a gulp of surprise).

'What next?' she asked.

'This,' he said, guiding her fingers.

'And for me?'

'This,' he said, guiding his own.

'Oh,' Harriet said. 'Oh. Oh. Oh. I see.'

For the finale, he carried her to the sofa – though she, in

effect, was carrying him, since she was far from passive. Concentrating hard, she followed his movements with her own. Occasionally, her murmurs gave way to brief groans or yelps, once an 'Ouch.' She persevered. When Monsieur felt the oncoming full cadence, he withdrew into his handkerchief, and when all was over he stood, did up his breeches and tossed the handkerchief into the fire, where it spat and smelled unpleasant. Despite the previous chafing from Marianne, he had enjoyed this.

Harriet tidied herself more slowly. 'Thank you, *monsieur*,' she said, as though they had just signed a contract.

'*Mademoiselle*,' he replied.

Harriet went straight to her room. The whole affair was messier than she had imagined, and more peculiar. She was worried about stains on her dress. She supposed she could tell her mother it was her monthly courses. She had had two shudders (she had counted) and suspected these were not the fizziness Everina had described. It would be very galling if Everina turned out better at this than she was. Still, even now, with a first session under her belt, she had something to show Thomas on their wedding night. She hoped he would appreciate it.

17

WITH all the girls now tumbled, and with their constant demands, Monsieur's days were exhausting. He returned to Cantabile's barely able to manage his supper. He forgot entirely that Annie had been to Manchester Square and even had he remembered, it was hardly important. December came. Only the short time left until the concert – a week – along with Cantabile's failure to pay the fee Monsieur felt he deserved twice over stopped the flagging music master feigning illness (hardly feigning – some days he really did feel quite sickly) and vanishing in the night. He had never gritted his teeth so often.

Dress-fittings for Harriet, Georgiana, Everina and Marianne took up the hours not spent at the pianoforte. Alathea kept their practice going with unremitting intensity. In Manchester Square, work began directly after Monsieur left. In Stratton Street, there was a strict timetable which Alathea ran with the precision of a Bach cantata, angry if the girls were late or said they must leave early. She left it to them to placate, confuse and

238

mislead the parents. It was she who must be accommodated, not them.

Very occasionally, if they could snatch an hour in the early evening, she and Annie sat sewing Alathea's concert dress in the latter's bedroom. After so much practice with the girls, Alathea declared herself too tired to play so they came straight up to the top floor and remained there, door locked. Annie never saw Sawneyford. She never said she had been to Manchester Square and spoken to Harriet. She did listen very carefully when Alathea spoke of America: how they would get there (Alathea assured Annie that passages were cheap and plentiful); how they would live (Alathea gave Annie the Pantisocratic Society pamphlet); how life would be. Alathea spoke of this new life with a passion Annie had not seen before. Alathea gripped her needle, but Annie did not grip hers because above all Alathea's grand protestations and plans hovered Harriet's perfect face, and this face was a question mark. 'You really think Alathea will stay with you? You really think she loves you?' Alathea's new lack of reserve, far from reassuring Annie, fuelled her doubts further. This chattiness did not seem genuine. As she sewed, Annie began to strengthen and reinforce her own armour. Her silvered core would protect her when the American dream came to nothing. With her armour on, even with Alathea hammering at the door, Annie could be queen of her own castle, drawbridge up.

It took Sawneyford ten days to recover physically from Alathea's assault. The doctor assured him nobody would know what had happened to him. After all, there was nothing to see. Sawneyford believed him. It was that or kill himself. A fortnight later he was back in the City, yet not quite. Perhaps nobody could see his deficit, but Sawneyford knew, he knew and he could not forget. So clerks, stewards, office boys, tradesmen, journeymen, jaggermen, naval spies, military spies, agricultural spies, builders, speculators, banking men, Lloyd's men, opportunists and hangers-on, crooks and enthusiasts – all his usual acquaintance – were avoided. He did not visit the barber to be shaved. He went nowhere near his office, with its flicking thumbs and clicking abacus. He went nowhere near the V&B. Instead, he hunched in alleys and crouched in corners, scuttling like a rat amid the City's jingling heave and ho. Scuttling was his distraction from the horror. More than a distraction: it was his lifeline. He had to scuttle in the City, for the City was his place of safety.

In his bed, he lay awake. It was not true that nobody knew of his gelding apart from himself and Alathea. The doctor knew. Crouch knew. He contemplated killing the doctor, and Crouch. He did not, however, contemplate killing Alathea. An irrationality gradually took hold of him. What Alathea had taken away, she could return. With her, he would still function as a man: her arts, her lips, her fingers would restore him. Alathea could stop this scuttling. He waited until she was practising at Manchester Square, then made a wax impression of the lock on her door. On his way out to get a key made, he left a folder of money for Crouch, enough for a one-way ticket to Rome. He left a note for the doctor. If Sawneyford found he had gossiped, he would know where to find him.

After the shard, Alathea avoided the card room. Since she had not planned her assault, she had not thought how things would be afterwards. And now she was frightened, for she thought her father as capable of murder as she was herself. It was fear that made her garrulous with Annie, both fear of her father and fear of seeming fearful, because fearful people were just the kind of people for whom she had no respect. She scolded herself. Her fear was needless, just a reaction. It would pass. After all, her father would surely be frail for some time yet, and the concert was so close. She and Annie would be gone in a week.

She did take precautions, though. Whether Annie was with her or not, she was doubly careful to lock her door, and kept the key with her, sleeping with it under her pillow. Several times in the night she thought she heard the pianoforte twang. She imagined Sawneyford cutting the strings. It was not the exhaustion of practice with the girls that made her avoid playing with Annie, it was fear of what they might find in the ballroom.

Sawneyford's missing coat told her he was up and out again. Trays of half-eaten pies from street vendors, left in the hall, told her that Crouch had abandoned the house and they were now without a servant. She left the trays where they were.

On the Thursday night before the concert, she woke from a half-sleep. At first she thought her room ablaze and started up. It was ablaze, though with light, not a conflagration. Candles were reflected in every mirror. Next to the bed, leaning over her, stood Sawneyford, hair awry, dry skin powdering hollowed cheeks. He was wearing a dressing gown loosely knotted and it was clear he wore nothing beneath. Alathea lay perfectly still. She could feel her key under her head. What a numskull. She should have changed the lock. She hardly breathed. She kept her eyes almost closed. The lamp beside her bed was heavy. She could hit him with that. But he was above her, and gazing at her. He would hit her first. Be still. Be still.

Sawneyford unknotted his dressing gown and climbed on to the bed. Alathea would not look at the scene of her destruction. She closed her eyes fully. Sawneyford lowered himself until he was resting on her thighs, and then pulled down the covers. Be still, Alathea, be still. His stubbled cheek scraped against her nose as he tilted forward, then up again. His breath rasped. He felt in his pocket for seven diamonds of different sizes, all cut and polished, drew up her nightgown and dripped the jewels on to her belly. One rolled into her belly button, the rest he slowly rolled downwards until they were half lost. He took her hand in his, her fingers so soft and unresponsive that he himself had to fold them round where they were needed. All the while he kept his eyes fixed on her face. She was beautiful, his daughter. She would see that after what she had done to destroy him she must help restore him. It was her duty, and she had always been dutiful. His lips were working. He moved her hand. It was smooth and cool. A nice feeling. That was all. His breathing hardened. He clenched her hand and winced. He clenched it again and rejoiced in his wince. Pain might help. His pain. Her pain. Clench, wince, clench, wince.

Nothing worked. He abandoned her hand and pulled her arms above her head, pressing both down with one of his. He shuffled the rest of himself up the bed and loomed above her, his knees at her shoulders. He raised himself. He lowered himself. Alathea, still as the dead, felt wetness on her eyelids, on her cheeks, on her lips. No, she begged silently, though her face never changed. No. It can't be possible. Not that. I've finished him for that. She heard her father groan. Her arms were no longer trapped. The bed creaked as Sawneyford clambered off, leaving the diamonds where they were. He was at the door, fumbling for the key. He was gone.

The second he was out, Alathea tipped her head sideways. She sat up and touched one cheek with a finger. She could have cried with relief. The wetness was light, not heavy; salty, not sticky; clear, not cloudy. She had done her work properly. Making both hands into fists, she used her knuckles to wipe away her father's tears.

On Friday morning, Cantabile went with Monsieur Belladroit to supervise the removal of the pianofortes from Manchester Square and Stratton Street to Pall Mall, where the final practice would take place. When Monsieur had made this request, Cantabile had at first refused even to listen, then declared point-blank that he would be happy to help remove the inferior pianoforte sent to the Driggs, but his own pianoforte, his one-time darling, was irrecoverably tainted, infected inside and out with the girls' mediocrity and inanity, and nothing would make him break his vow to have nothing to do with it again. Monsieur sighed, and spoke of what would happen to this pianoforte after the concert. Once the girls were exposed by their husbands and returned, disgraced, to their homes, the instrument would be a scandal. 'It will be passed from house to house like a blighted child,' Monsieur said. 'Only its value will prevent its destruction.' Could Cantabile not hear it call out to him? Did he want to abandon it in its distress? 'It is not a blighted child, it is your child, Vittorio,' Monsieur said, hard-eyed for all his sighs, 'and whatever the faults of the girls, it is the finest pianoforte I am ever likely to play. Come, do. Come where you can regulate it, comfort and save it. Must I go down on my knees on its behalf?'

It was not pleasant for Monsieur when Cantabile shrieked and shouted, flying first into a rage and then into a frenzy. Yet Monsieur persisted, not for the sake of the pianoforte, fine as it was, but for the sake of Annie, the blighted child Cantabile would never comfort. She who had so little should have the best pianoforte in London. It was the only thing he, Claude Belladroit, could offer her. Once he had gone, whatever erupted in that awful workshop, there would be beautiful music.

Monsieur's persistence was rewarded. Having been determined not to think about his pianoforte, Cantabile now heard it calling, and not just calling: he heard it pleading. He did want it back. He wanted it back so badly he could not sleep. He said nothing directly to Monsieur, giving his answer only through hiring the undertaker's cart again and sending an inflated bill for transportation to Mr Frogmorton. The pianoforte would go from Manchester Square to Pall Mall, and shortly afterwards to Tyburn. Cantabile underlined 'Tyburn' twice.

The two men walked to Manchester Square dressed against the weather.

'You're very quiet, Claude,' observed Cantabile, swinging his bag of tuning and regulating tools.

'I have the aria and variations going through my head,' Monsieur said untruthfully, for going through his head was the joy of the end. There would be no more girls, no more unwanted advances, no more sex. All that was over because at Pall Mall, thank all the gods in all the heavens, he and the girls would never be alone. Servants would already be busy in the saloon preparing tables and flowers. The doors would always be open. There would be no privacy, not for a second. He recollected with a wry shake of the head his desire to get rid of Mrs Frogmorton in the spring. Truly, there had been times in the last fortnight when he would have given ready money to have her back in her chair with that odious dog barking. Fancy, he thought. Claude Belladroit in need of a chaperone. *Mon Dieu.*

The cart was already outside no. 23, people gathering round waiting for a body. Neither the undertaker nor the hired muscle had corrected them. Cantabile rang the bell. It never crossed his mind to use the servants' entrance. Mrs Frogmorton was already in the hall, Frilly tucked in. She had been waiting for Monsieur and berated him at once. 'Do you still have no understanding of English taste, *monsieur*? An undertaker's cart again? You should have consulted with me. And who is that?' Mr Cantabile was already on the stairs.

'It is Vittorio Cantabile, the pianoforte maker.' Monsieur gave a quick apologetic bow.

'What is he doing in my house?'

'He is necessary for the removals, *madame*. Come now.' He smiled his most charming smile. 'Soon we will be out of your house and the undertakers' cart will be turned into a marriage wagon, yes?'

'Wagon?' Mrs Frogmorton was puffed up with vexation. 'You think Harriet will leave this house in a wagon? Really, Monsieur, you don't—'

'No, *madame*,' said Monsieur Belladroit sorrowfully. 'I expect I don't, but what matter now? After today I will trouble you no more.' He smiled again, ruefully this time, then made for the stairs.

Mrs Frogmorton deflated slowly. 'I've been charmed again, Frilly,' she said to the dog. 'Charmed by a foreigner. Music is awash with them. That's its tragedy, I suppose.' She followed Monsieur up the stairs.

Monsieur found Cantabile greeting his instrument as a mother greets a child released from a kidnapper. When his greeting was over, he methodically wiped down every inch of its frame, every key. 'Fetch the men,' he ordered Monsieur. 'Let's get my precious out of here.'

The hired muscle found the instrument an awkward corpse and were duly cursed and bawled at as they detached the body from the legs. It was an odd procession down the stairs: three men manoeuvring the bulk; two men manhandling the frame; one man clutching the pedal mechanism. The removal left a considerable gap and several stains on the floorboards that only poor light and the quick shifting of the harpsichord kept from Mrs Frogmorton's notice. She closed the door on the room's green gloom, patted Frilly on the head and remarked with some satisfaction that it was nice to have things back to normal.

At Stratton Street, Mrs Drigg was glad to see the borrowed pianoforte go to Pall Mall, since this meant that Alathea would no longer be a constant visitor. The concert could not come soon enough, Mrs Drigg thought as the instrument was trundled away, nor the moment when Alathea would be married, saddled with a dozen wailing children and holed up in the country, preferably with a husband too poor to have any decent carriage-horses. Mrs Drigg felt guilty at the unChristian quality of this thought, though guilt was quickly overtaken by relief at being able to dedicate herself completely to the subject of Everina's concert corset.

The fathers, minus Sawneyford, were also in good heart. They did not watch the pianoforte removals from their homes but Frogmorton, Drigg and Brass arrived at Pall Mall at noon to see the instruments installed at the far end of the Allemonde saloon. The earl had graciously provided two long stools from the servants' hall, and carpenters had been summoned to make certain they were the correct height. Drigg was not pleased to see Cantabile, and avoided him. They all ignored the under-taker's cart, at which the Allemonde servants sniggered.

This was the first time Brass and Drigg had seen Monsieur Belladroit, the *castrato*. Drigg glanced surreptitiously. Brass smirked openly, until Frogmorton reminded him that Monsieur was French and Frenchmen were notoriously huffy. If Monsieur walked out now, where would they all be? Brass growled and stopped smirking. Anyway, there was not much to smirk at. Monsieur was exactly as their wives had described. He did not, on the face of it, look like a eunuch. But what did a eunuch look like? Brass found it more useful to inspect the saloon furnishings, and wandered around calculating and assessing. The marble and gold consoles he considered French and without merit. None the less, though he had never seen the Allemonde son, he could imagine Georgiana mistress of both this house and the one fifty miles to the north, which he had had independently valued. He would tell Georgiana what he expected of her.

Mr Cantabile and Monsieur Belladroit cared nothing for the fathers and took no notice when Brass, having finished his inspection of the room, came over to examine the pianofortes at close quarters. Frogmorton was similarly engaged. 'It's a pity they don't match,' Frogmorton said.

'And a pity that they seem to insist on the brown one being in the front,' said Brass. 'It's an ugly piece.'

'Oh well,' said Frogmorton. 'The Frenchman knows best, and once the girls are playing, nobody will look at the instruments.' Something struck him. 'You,' he said to Cantabile, 'Mr . . .'

'Cantabile,' said Monsieur, when Cantabile did not reply.

'Mr Cantabile,' said Frogmorton. 'You'll be on hand during the concert to keep the pianofortes well tuned?' He turned and called Drigg over. 'Didn't you say tuning was necessary, Drigg?'

Drigg approached unwillingly. 'Well, I suppose—'

'Let's not suppose,' Frogmorton said. 'If tuning is important and we've two pianofortes, we'll need two pianoforte tuners. There must be no delays while the girls are playing. What do you say, Cantabile?'

Cantabile, lever in hand, grinned at Drigg. Drigg looked at his boots. 'I'd say two tuners would help the smooth running of your show. I'll send my daughter.' He spoke to Frogmorton but never took his eyes off Drigg. 'Would that be acceptable?'

Drigg paled.

'I don't care if you send your mother,' said Frogmorton, 'so long as she can tune properly.'

'Oh, my Annie can tune properly,' said Cantabile, 'and I'll have my pianoforte back after.'

Brass snorted at him. 'Have it back? We paid good money for that instrument.'

'Is that what he told you?' Cantabile jabbed a finger at Drigg.

Frogmorton was immediately suspicious, not of Drigg but of Cantabile. 'We paid what we paid,' he said, narrowing his eyes.

'What you paid was rent,' Cantabile said. 'No money in the world could come close to my pianoforte's true value, even after your children have – have – have . . .'

'Drigg?' said Frogmorton.

247

'Oh, er, I don't . . . '

Cantabile snarled his lips in fearsome imitation of Annie. 'Don't you remember, sir? Wasn't that our agreement, sir? I didn't want to sell. You must remember, sir.'

'Of course I remember,' snapped Drigg. He had nothing, really, to be ashamed of, or to hide. He had not told any lies. Not really. Why did he feel like a criminal?

Cantabile kept going. 'And I wanted to send Annie as teacher. Do you remember that?' Much to Frogmorton's surprise, the snarled lip was snarled up some more. 'You'd have done well with Annie,' Cantabile said. 'Really very well.'

'We've done very well with Monsieur Belladroit.' Drigg moved to block Cantabile off. 'I think, Archibald, that perhaps there was some equivocation. The quality of the instrument may have been – the day may have been – the arrangement may have been—'

'Oh, for goodness' sake, Tobias! It hardly matters. If the man wants his instrument back, let him have it. What else are we going to do with it? You should just have made it clear at the start. You can return some of our money if that makes you feel better. Add it to the money you owe for the Frenchman's lessons.'

Cantabile was already back at the pianoforte. After twenty minutes, with pressing business in the City, the fathers left.

The mothers arrived soon after, Mrs Frogmorton and Mrs Drigg bickering gently over the number and setting of the candles, Mrs Frogmorton wanting more light, Mrs Drigg rather less. With the pianofortes in place, they were nervous. The concert, so long spoken of, now lived and breathed on its own. The sale of their daughters was about to begin.

As they fussed, Mrs Drigg knew with depressing certainty that, one candle or a hundred, Marianne and Everina would be outshone by Harriet and Georgiana. Mrs Brass wished everything was over: concert, marriage, life. Mrs Frogmorton, confident of Harriet, worried about details. The hothouse flowers had arrived. She sent them back. 'Midday tomorrow,' she scolded. 'They must be perfect.' She made sure to inspect the kitchens, cleaned at her own expense. She had hired the cooks herself. For the fifth time, she counted out the plate bought specially for the occasion. It was bad enough that they had to borrow a room; their china must not be found wanting. Mrs Drigg's father provided the fish free of charge. It was in the larder, packed in ice. Mrs Frogmorton smelled it. Good fish. Excellent fish. It had been kind of him.

In the later afternoon, Cantabile returned to Tyburn, his heart filled equally with disgust and delight. The City men were frightful. Their daughters would be frightful. The concert would be torture. But the concert would soon be over and his pianoforte returned to him.

He pushed open the shop door and pricked his ears. Was Annie here? Was she not here? He could never be sure, these days. He heard the click of a lever in the back and smelled something bubbling on the stove upstairs. She was here. He moved warily. Since Annie had tried to murder Maria Barthélemon, she and he had padded around each other, alert to the possibility of bloodshed. 'Those City people,' he said aloud, going through to the back to find her. 'Hyenas.'

Annie did not look at him. 'I expect the girls are pretty.'

'The girls weren't there. If they're anything like their mothers, I should have paid Claude more. He'd have been better off with you.'

Cantabile knew that these days his jibes were wasted, his barbs blunt. He was unclear exactly how Annie had rendered him impotent, and he no longer cared. From now on, he would think solely of his pianoforte. How that pianoforte loved him.

It never had and never would disobey or challenge. It bent willingly to his will. It would never leave here again. He went further into the warehouse. From a tall cupboard he collected an axe, took it to the front, removed his coat and there, in the workshop, set about destroying his current project. Like his daughter, it was unworthy of him.

Monsieur Belladroit returned to the workshop directly after collecting his last pay pouch from Manchester Square. He had considered not collecting it: it always made him feel cheap. However, money was money. He weighed the bag – he never counted it – and put it in his pocket. For the first and last time, and only because he was ordered to do so by Mrs Frogmorton, Spencer opened and closed the front door for him. The footman and the music master exchanged glances containing not an ounce of camaraderie.

The evening sky was cloudless, the stars bright pinheads. It had already begun to freeze. Nevertheless, Monsieur stopped to look back at the house in which he had spent so many hours. How tightly the windows were shuttered, or curtained, or both, to keep the winter out. All that fuss about dangerous air, when real danger was warmly wrapped and came through the front door. His skin tingled. He wrapped his scarf closer round his throat. A wig would be good tonight; he did not like a cold head. He thrust his hands into gloves. Where next? Where had he not yet been? The possibilities should have excited him: he could go anywhere, but 'anywhere' suddenly seemed very bleak.

He was almost out of the square when, through clouds of steam and showers of sparks more suited to a return from the battlefield than a canter in the park, Thomas Buller clattered by on his horse. Monsieur nodded. Thomas did not nod back. He was already searching the upper windows of no. 23. The shutters meant there was nothing to see, yet his cheeks still reddened with more than the chill. Ah, thought Monsieur, Mademoiselle Harriet has made her move. Poor Thomas Buller. He will not escape now.

Banging his hands together, Monsieur made his way on to Oxford Street. In the gloaming, stone cutters were still at work. Buildings going up, buildings coming down. Shouting boys had tipped bricks out of a cart to make an ice-slide. The bricklayers, half annoyed and half indulgent, pelted the boys with mortar from above. Clamouring, belligerent and constantly battering the ears and nose, London was never so lovely as when one was about to leave it.

18

SATURDAY, 13 DECEMBER 1794

MONSIEUR returned to St James's early. In anticipation of the concert, the Allemonde servants had lit fires at either end of the saloon. The shutters were still closed, also the curtains, and despite its size, with six lamps and twenty candles blazing the room was warm. Monsieur ran his hand over the brown pianoforte. The sound, in here, would be rich as plum-cake, as anybody discerning would appreciate. Of course, the audience would not be discerning. He tested each note again. When he was satisfied with the brown instrument, he moved to the other. Again, he sounded the notes carefully, occasionally two notes together, A, A sharp, B, C, A and C together, C sharp and on, methodical as a workman testing the rungs of a ladder. Two young servants hoping for a dance returned to their duties disappointed.

Monsieur wiped his hands and appreciated the room. The major furniture had been cleared and it was still free from the larger elements of concert clutter. The walls, predominantly sand-coloured, were lightened by white-stucco cornice cherubs of unusual daintiness which Monsieur found graceful and pleasing. He bowed to an imaginary audience and sat down at the brown pianoforte. First, a scale. The scale became an arpeggio, then back to a scale in thirds and sixths, then finally scales and arpeggios decorated, ornamented, syncopated. He checked the clock. There was time. He took off his coat and played as he had not played for months: for himself. The toccatas, sonatas, fugues and inventions of Bach, Handel and Haydn stretched his fingers, wrists, wit, intellect and technique. Oh, he had forgotten! In teaching the girls, even Alathea, he had been denied the joy of music *toute seule*. It was glorious here, just himself and Cantabile's miraculous instrument. After two hours, he was as refreshed and reinvigorated as a man starved of books let loose in a library. He put his coat back on and relaxed. The girls would arrive soon, with no danger of even the mildest flirtation. He was in charge again. It would be quite like old times.

Mrs Frogmorton and Mrs Drigg arrived at Pall Mall before their daughters, each preceded by a cart bearing flowers, fruits and large silk balloons containing the girls' concert dresses. During the course of the morning, the graceful saloon was transformed into what Monsieur could only describe as an overblown village market. *Tant pis*. He tinkered happily with the instruments, checking the pitch for the sheer pleasure of it. A little later the girls themselves arrived, ready for their final practice. They would not go home afterwards, hence the concert dresses in their travelling covers. Alathea arrived last. She brought her own dress, also covered.

Monsieur set out the scores. The girls, apart from Alathea, studied them with alarm, all the familiar variations seeming, on this morning of mornings, as unfamiliar as something entirely new.

'I can't remember anything,' moaned Everina. 'I'm sure to go wrong.'

'Why did we have to play something so complicated?' whined Marianne.

Harriet and Georgiana were white and silent. They would forget. Their fingers would freeze or grow clumsy. The concert would be a disaster. They kept looking at Alathea.

Alathea was calm, though her heart beat faster than usual. She had not seen her father since Thursday night. On Friday morning, taking the diamonds he had left behind on that last dreadful visitation, she had sped out of the house, first to a jeweller, who had given her ready money for one of the diamonds and agreed to cut the others; then to the Salutation & Cat; and from there to the Pool of London, armed with the name of the captain of a merchant ship. The Pool had been chaotic. It was almost impossible to see the water, so closely were the ships crowded together. She had been determined, and not left until she had solicited a paper guaranteeing herself and Annie a berth on the *Maidenhead*, due to edge out at first tide tomorrow. Alathea had given a wry smile at the name. From the Pool straight to Stratton Street, where the girls had gathered at Marianne's harpsichord, the pianofortes already removed. She would have preferred to go to Tyburn to show Annie the passage papers, but she had promised the girls this final practice, so entrusted the papers and a letter to a courier. She would collect Annie from Tyburn directly after the concert. By Sunday noon, they would be on the high seas. Before she sealed the letter, she took her mother's ring from her thumb, kissed it and slid it inside. It was still a wedding ring. It would always be a wedding ring.

After finishing at Stratton Street, she had returned to the jeweller. Once back in Soho Square, she spent most of the night working on her dress. This morning, she was tired but exultant. She smiled confidently and confidentially at the girls. Everina and Marianne stopped wailing. Harriet and Georgiana hugged themselves. 'This is our day,' Alathea's smile said to them each in turn. 'Enjoy it.'

Monsieur rattled the score to get their attention. 'Now, *mesdemoiselles*. To work. This is how the morning will go.' He would hear each girl's particular variations first. Afterwards, they would run through the whole performance. During those variations where he was to help out, the girl should always play the brown pianoforte. The five chairs behind the pianoforte stools were where the girls should sit when not playing. Did they understand? They nodded. Practice began, and after a while Everina and Marianne were hammering away as always, Harriet and Georgiana offering something more sonorous. Alathea's sound was rich and – what else? Safe? Yes! For the first time since that first lesson Monsieur was not wondering what was going to happen next.

The room filled with servants, tradesmen, concert chairs. Occasionally the instructions of Mrs Frogmorton and the twitterings of Mrs Drigg, both resplendent in aprons and working caps, drowned out the music. There was still tension over the lighting. Mrs Drigg moved candles away. Mrs Frogmorton moved them back. Mrs Brass arrived. She whispered. Monsieur barked. The noise – human, musical, mechanical, domestic, congratulatory, admonitory – surged, until by one o'clock all was prepared.

Even Monsieur was content. He shut the pianofortes' lids. The girls made to leave the room. 'Wait!' Monsieur said. 'Sit.' The girls sat obediently in the front row of the seats arranged in two banks, six on each side of a centre aisle, not pressed together since the skirts of the lady guests' dresses were expected to be full.

Monsieur walked up and down. He had not intended to give the girls a lecture, but his morning's playing urged him to remind them of their duty to Herr Bach. He cleared his throat.

'As you know, *mesdemoiselles*, the *Clavier-Übung* is a serious piece,' he said. 'To be able to play it at all marks you out as young women of distinction, and it is, of course, this distinction that will attract the future husbands sitting in these rows. I have one last instruction.' He sought their eyes. All were wide, wide, wide. 'You must perform the music exactly as Herr Bach wrote it,' he said, 'exactly as we have practised. Do not allow yourselves to be distracted. Place yourselves in Herr Bach's hands. He will be your guide. That is all.' There was no hint, as he spoke, of the man who had taken and tumbled them. At this moment, Monsieur Belladroit was musician and music master only. Mrs Frogmorton and Mrs Drigg, grappling with ferns and oranges, nodded their approval. How silly their misgivings had been. The *castrato* was a serious man who had done a serious job. Mrs Frogmorton thought she would tell the alderman to tip him.

Four of the girls tripped out of the room. Georgiana remained seated. Monsieur went to her. 'You must go and have a little food, and then submit yourself to the hairsetter with the others,' he said. She did not move. 'Mademoiselle Georgiana, do not fear. You are well rehearsed,' Monsieur reassured her, 'and I will be here, playing my part, just as we have arranged. You will not be alone, little dove. The concert will be a success, and afterwards, you will never be alone again.' Georgiana squeezed his hand with ferocious intensity. Monsieur had not called her 'little dove' since their real intimacy began. Monsieur squeezed back and propelled her after the others.

Dressing the girls was a long affair, begun in the light and completed in the dark. An upstairs room had been made available, with fires lit and bathtubs provided. Troops of maids trudged to and fro with hot water and cinnamon oil, slicks of gentian cream and warmed towels. The girls did nothing for themselves. The mothers whisked soap and flannelled backs, patted shoulders and rubbed feet. Only Alathea demurred, asking for privacy. After some discussion, she was shown another room, in which a fire was hurriedly and rather resentfully lit and another tub brought. 'Call me when you're ready for the hairsetter,' said Mrs Frogmorton, 'and I'll help with your dress.'

Alathea was already shutting the door. 'I can manage myself.'

'Will your father be coming?' asked Mrs Drigg, wedging the door with her foot. 'Is he quite well? We heard—'

'He's quite well, thank you,' said Alathea. Mrs Drigg had to move her foot or have it crushed. Alathea called for hot water, but once her tub was filled, she locked the door and bathed herself slowly. She had no idea if her father would come. If he did, how would he be? Wrapped in a towel, she curled up in a chair and closed her eyes. She did not want either hairsetter or face painter. She must hear the music. That was the thing now. Just the music.

Marianne had ordered a low-cut, short-sleeved polonaise-style dress of midnight-blue velvet over a satin underdress, sky blue with silver spangles. Her arms were bare. The tight boning of the bodice made sitting difficult. Nevertheless, Marianne was firmly encased in the dress before she sat for the face painter and hairsetter, a sensible precaution given that she refused to wear a fichu, and the freckles on her neck, shoulders and cleavage required almost half a pound of powder to disguise. To ensure Marianne would be blue and white in the right places, it was best not to disturb the powder. A dust sheet provided the necessary protection. Mrs Drigg trimmed the hair in Marianne's armpits and hung small pomanders from her shoulders to nestle in the remaining tufts. Marianne would smell, as well as look, delicious. Mother and daughter were pleased with the dress, and it really was magnificent, its only disadvantage being to accentuate Marianne's miserable ringlets. No matter.

With the dress settled, the hairsetter tipped out the contents of his wig bags, and after some discussion Marianne chose a chalk-white, highly structured creation, creamed with pearls and silk lily-of-the-valley and topped with an ostrich feather. In moments the rats' tails were in a knot, the wig bearing down. Marianne opened her mouth to whine that the wig was too tight, then saw her reflection and was silent. The long feather shortened her long jaw. The pearls obscured her open pores and cast a peachy lustre over her skin. For the only time in her life, from the top of the feather to the tips of her blue velvet slippers, Marianne could have passed for a lady of sophisticated distinction. Mrs Drigg almost wept. And this before the face painter had even begun.

Everina had wanted the natural look currently fashionable. As soon as she saw Marianne dressed up, she regretted it. Her frock, unboned light grey silk with embroidered roses in pastel colours and crimped up at the back, was certainly pretty, and its floating train added a touch of fairy dust. But against Marianne's midnight blue, Everina's dress seemed insipid – a dairy maid in the court of a queen. Everina's chin began to wobble. With the inspiration and bravery of panic, Mrs Drigg quickly reassured her that although Marianne looked fine at the moment, everybody knew that wigs came off, and that Everina's unpowdered arms, spotted with fresh-scented petals, contrasted favourably, very favourably, with Marianne's, which required quantities of powder if they were to be left uncovered. Also, so Everina comforted herself, Marianne's décolletage was too low, as though she were a married woman already, and there was nothing even the powderer could do about that incipient moustache.

Georgiana emerged as a goddess, sprays of white buds peeping from a long, loose cascade of golden, newly washed hair – all her own. She had chosen the polonaise style like Marianne, but hers was a milky waterfall of pure white silk, no ruching, no decoration, the long-sleeved underdress of equally pure white lace, delicately patterned with white pimpernels. When, the day before, she had described the dress, the other girls secretly thought it too simple. Now they saw what simplicity could do. Once ready, Georgiana sat by herself, studying her pure white slippers.

There was nothing simple about Harriet. She had won her battle for gold, and Mrs Frogmorton, having given in, chose gold upon gold upon gold: a high-waisted underdress of heavy gold silk; then lighter gold-speckled net; then, from just under the breasts, a flutter of floor-length gold ribbons with tiny gold stars, echoing similar stars on gold-brocade shoes. On her head a golden turban, its folds secured by a large emerald, all the more dramatic for the plain gold setting. The effect was imperially Eastern. With her lips painted to a pout, Harriet was magnificent.

Alathea did not appear. The mothers conferred. Mrs Frogmorton knocked on her door. There was a polite rejection.

It was nearly six. With the hairsetter and face painter gone, the girls' everyday clothes tidied, the mothers also in their concert attire and running out of conversation, they were all aware of the arriving guests. Mrs Drigg opened the door, the better to catch snippets. 'I'm only here because the duke insisted,' drifted one voice. 'And I because my son's interested in music,' drifted another. 'Let's hope it doesn't go on too long,' drifted a third voice. 'I've heard the girls are frights,' drifted a fourth, or it might have been the first again. 'Frights with fortunes,' the second voice declared – no drift needed. Mrs Frogmorton got up, drew Mrs Drigg away and closed the door.

Monsieur waited downstairs. The arriving guests glanced briefly at the pianofortes before searching for the supper tables. Mrs Frogmorton had foreseen this, and wisely instructed that the supper should be firmly locked away. No food until after the concert. Nobody should get a free dinner and then slip off. Only champagne was offered, and graciously accepted.

The Duchess of Oxford put her finger on it. Asked why she was here when her older son was already engaged, she replied, 'Because everybody else is.' And it was true: everybody was – everybody who was asked, that is, and one other. Thomas Buller arrived alone, refused champagne and chose an unobtrusive seat. Only the Frogmortons would have recognised him, and they were otherwise engaged.

Cantabile arrived promptly, pushing his way past the dresses, jewels, velvet coats and embroidered cloaks. Once he and Monsieur had opened up the pianofortes, he sat glaring from the stool of his treasure. Drigg was very relieved to see him and not Annie.

The fathers greeted aristocratic creditors and non-creditors equally, their tone polite, not obsequious; deferential, not toadying. This evening, the City was ascendant, the fathers running the market. Only Brass's badgerish leer threatened to lower the tone. He enjoyed setting some of the ladies simpering, and enjoyed it more when their husbands scowled. Frogmorton nudged Drigg. 'Remind Brass that he's looking for a son-in-law, not a mistress.' Drigg, however, was not listening: Mrs Drigg had emerged from upstairs, fussing away and wondering, even at this late stage, whether she should go home and get more jewels for Everina. What if people did not realise how expensive the grey satin and gauze had been, with each embroidered flower individually stitched and different in design? What if the Driggs were thought poorer than the Frogmortons or Brasses? Drigg was angry. 'That side of things was your domain,' he barked. 'I'll not forgive you, Mrs Drigg, if you've let me down.' Mrs Drigg vanished upstairs again. Frogmorton smugly went to have words with Brass. Mrs Frogmorton would have made no such mistake.

There was a kerfuffle as the final guests arrived and everybody took their seats. For people who despised this concert of nobodies, the guests seemed uncommonly anxious to get a good view. And indeed it was a fine show, with the candles, the flower and fruit arrangements, the two instruments, all overlaid with the scent of money. 'Almost as good as a fox hunt,' so a son obliged to give up a day in the field conceded to his father. 'Tally ho!' his father replied.

Mrs Frogmorton, Mrs Drigg and Mrs Brass appeared all together, bowing stiffly to their few acquaintances and making for their appointed places on the ends of the first three rows, Mrs Frogmorton and Mrs Drigg on the right, Mrs Brass on the left, the adjacent chairs reserved for their husbands. They had dressed with careful formality, and had dressed their husbands similarly. All gowns were unyielding, all coats new, all breeches spotless, all boots clean. Nothing ostentatious, everything obviously expensive.

'Is Sawneyford still not here?' Brass said to Frogmorton as the fathers gathered at the back. 'Surely he's not going to miss this?'

Frogmorton frowned. 'I've been trying to locate him for days. Where can he have got to? And Cantabile was going to send his daughter to help Monsieur with the tuning. Is she here?'

'Cantabile's here himself,' said Drigg. 'As for Sawney, none of us has seen him, and not for want of trying. Anyway, we can't wait for him. He knows the place. He knows the time. The concert must start.'

Monsieur rose. The guests turned from their neighbours to face the front. Monsieur raised his arms. There was a hush, as in a congregation expecting a bride. The fathers clapped each other lightly on the back and separated, Frogmorton and Drigg up the right-hand outside aisle and Brass up the left-hand. They could not worry about Sawneyford now. The footmen, primed by Mrs Frogmorton, blew out the candelabra on the consoles, leaving only dozens of tiny flames floating in waterbowls (Elizabeth Brass's suggestion) and the candelabra on the pianofortes. Cantabile vanished to a bench set behind both the instruments, out of sight.

There was a small commotion, a slight altercation. Sawneyford appeared, no wig on his head and his hair untied. The footmen would have ejected him had not Drigg turned and raised a hand in an admonitory though relieved greeting. Sawneyford did not return the greeting, did not see it in fact. Nor did he want the glass of champagne thrust into his hand. He wanted to feel only the stock of the pistol hidden in the top of his breeches.

The girls, minus Alathea, gathered outside the door. 'Do you think she's fallen asleep?' Marianne was whispering. The audience was waiting. The door was opening for their entrance. 'What can we do?'

'You,' said Harriet from under her turban to one of the footman. 'Go upstairs and knock on Miss Alathea's door.' They could hear the saloon's expectant hush. Harriet gripped hands with the others very briefly. 'We've got to go in. She'll be here.'

'But—'

'Go, Marianne. By the time we've all walked in, she'll be here. She will be. Go.'

The door was wide now. With a tiny push from Harriet, Marianne entered, head up, eyes down, just as they had discussed. Any concerns over Alathea vanished when she heard murmurs of surprised appreciation.

As she walked, the murmurs grew louder, the appreciation deeper. The blue was gorgeous. The richness and fine cut of the cloth, expert hair and clever powdering had successfully transformed Marianne from potato to full-blown hyacinth. She could, at that moment, have had her pick of the room. Harriet next, her pretty face rendered royally beautiful by the turban, the emerald and the gown glowing like golden coin. 'A living bank,' exclaimed Lord Rathbone. His son was speechless. The concert had not even begun and already the audience's expectations were far exceeded. Two dozen heirs wondered why their mothers had scoffed. A blue orchid! A golden bank! And more to come.

Thomas Buller, too, was agog, though his heart was sinking. This glowing girl could not have chosen him. She was mythical queen and he was fleshy mortal. She would never be his. It was cruel of her to suggest it. As his rivals moved to the edges of their seats, he slumped.

Georgiana walked fastest up the aisle, a smudge of untouched snow, the train of her silk overdress rippling behind her. Only she was not snow. Her face was warmly alight with girlish hope and joy. Her father's jaw dropped further than anybody else's. His daughter seemed barely his daughter. Against the white of her gown, her flesh was bright with love. Brass did not recognise this look. How could he? Love like Georgiana's was not something with which he was familiar.

Next, Everina. The panic had been justified. After the blue, gold and white, the grey was almost invisible, the pastel flowers unremarkable, and Everina's arms were just arms, even under their petals and bows. But the spell had been cast already. In this atmosphere of surprise and thrills the floating flames rendered her ghostly and mysterious, a gauzy enigma – not what was intended, but it worked. Moreover, the shadowy colour and smudged outline hid her clumsy gait. Far from looking underdressed, Everina looked tastefully understated. Nobody would ever have guessed that her mother had started life on a fish stall.

Mrs Frogmorton and Mrs Drigg sagged with relief, as far as their bolstering corsets would allow. What did it matter what the girls played? The job was done already. The audience was delighted. Frogmorton leaned forward. 'A triumph,' he whispered. Drigg nodded. Only Alathea to go.

There was a pause. Where was the girl? A dull clinking sound. The audience turned and a different silence fell, the strange vacuumed silence that precedes an earthquake. If Gregory Brass's jaw had dropped at his own daughter, it gaped now.

Alathea was studded from top to toe with diamonds. Sewn on to the thinnest flesh-coloured, limb-clinging, lucent silk flowing up to her neck, down her wrists, down to the floor, each stone exploded with brilliance against her rich skin. All the light in the room was sucked towards her, and she reflected it back in splinters and shards. Apart from the stones, she seemed quite naked. Harriet, Everina and Marianne gasped. No wonder Alathea had hung back. She had outshone them all. For one uncharitable moment, Harriet saw the diamonds as winks of malice. Should they clap or hiss? Only Georgiana was oblivious, her mind firmly fixed on something else.

Alathea began to walk. The diamonds rippled. None was strategically placed over any part of her, and it was obvious to everybody that she had been at work with the tweezers. Apart from the hair on her head, the sculpted eyebrows and eyelashes thick as pelts, she was completely shorn. Against those deep, suggestive shadows even the diamond fireworks played second fiddle. Her hands were bare of jewels. Round her neck she had a diamond-spiked choker, as a fighting dog might have, and this served to complete her nakedness. 'Ye gods,' said Brass. '*Ye gods.*'

A sixth sense made Alathea aware of her father. She did not acknowledge him. She was beyond him. She moved slowly up the centre aisle looking neither right nor left. When the fathers and sons breathed again, they did not meet each other's eyes, nor the eyes of their wives or mothers. Those hard stones; that yielding flesh; the submission and the arrogance of that choker; those dagger flashes and – throttled throats – the shadows in those secret places. Footman and duke were as one: they all wanted her. She was all they wanted.

Annie had found it hard to open Alathea's note, convinced it was the rejection she dreaded and expected. It stood to reason that Alathea's treasured detachment and the separation of the past weeks would have made the note easier to write. She had tended her mother with the letter still unopened, then sat on the chair beside her mother's bed and propped the letter against the candle. She comforted herself. She could never leave her mother, and rejection would mean she did not have to. In the circumstances, rejection was the best thing. She focused on that. She picked up the note. If she opened it here, her mother's presence would ensure detachment, or at least some self-control. She broke the seal. The ring fell out. She read the written words. She could not control herself. She folded over.

'Annie?' Her mother whispered. 'Annie?' Mrs Cantabile tried to sit up. Fear injected strength. Her waxy face grew waxier still. 'Annie? What is it? Tell me.'

Annie did not know how. She must go with Alathea. She must. She could not ask Alathea to wait until her mother died. It might be months or even years. Alathea would go alone, and if she did that, Annie would lose her.

'Annie?' her mother's voice was frailly insistent. 'You must tell me.'

Annie moved the candle and handed her mother the letter. Her mother tried and failed to read it. 'Read it to me.'

Annie obeyed. When she looked again, her mother was staring at the ceiling. For one wild moment, Annie thought the shock had killed her. Her mother's lips moved. Annie leaned over in a dreadful confusion of hope and despair.

'Go,' her mother said.

A great weight descended. Annie knew she could not go. 'We'll take you,' she said. How ridiculous.

Her mother's fingers found hers. 'Annie,' she croaked and fixed her daughter with eyes empty of everything but pain, rheum and broken veins. 'I can go with you,' she mouthed. 'But not like this. Release me, Annie, as I release you. Let my soul fly from here. God brings death, I know, but sometimes he needs a little help.'

'I can't!' whispered Annie.

'Don't lie to me, Annie. You can, and why not? You want it. I want it.'

'No,' Annie said out loud.

'Yes, my sweet girl. Wishing me dead and wishing I was dead – they're not the same. Not for us. You know that. Don't deny it. Don't. There is no need.'

Annie was silent.

Mrs Cantabile lay back on her pillow. 'Your father won't help me. Only you have the courage and the generosity.'

'Generosity?' Annie burst out. 'Ah, Mother! Not generosity.'

Mrs Cantabile's fingers curled round Annie's hands. She smiled. 'Generosity, Annie. Yes, generosity, because it won't be easy. The body struggles for life against the wishes of the soul. My struggle will haunt you. But you'll bear it for me. You'll do it.'

'I don't know how, Mother.'

'I would say laudanum,' Mrs Cantabile said. 'Drifting off while you were playing one of your own compositions would be like being in heaven already. But it must be quick.' Her breath was shallow. 'The pillow,' she said. She did not let go of Annie's hands until Annie repeated, 'The pillow,' and both knew the decision was made.

Now Mrs Cantabile looked directly at Annie and Annie looked directly at her. Both were afraid, but through their fear, the strength of purpose in both faces was striking. Mrs Cantabile placed her own hands over her breast. Annie kissed her mother's forehead – a real kiss, the first. She kissed her mother's hands – a real kiss, the second. Then she slid a pillow from under her mother's head and with all the force of love held the pillow down. Ten minutes later Annie left the house carrying her small bag with her. Alathea would not have to come and fetch her after the concert. In black travelling clothes, heavily veiled, with the wedding ring on a chain around her neck, Alathea's note and the *Maidenhead* guarantee tucked into her bodice, Annie arrived in the Pall Mall saloon just as the doors were closing.

Alathea reached the top of the aisle and sat in her allocated chair. Monsieur, blinking, got up from the stool of the second pianoforte. He coughed. He fiddled with his lapels. 'We are going . . .' His voice was high. These girls, they were wonderful. And Alathea. Alathea. He tried again. He must bring himself and the audience back to the music. He dispensed with the proper greeting for such a gathering. 'Ladies, gentlemen,' he said, his omission of title gaining the titles' immediate attention. 'We are going to play for you today the last part of Herr Bach's *Clavier-Übung*.' Uttering Herr Bach's name helped Monsieur, though what Herr Bach would have made of this spectacle, he had no idea. 'We shall play this work in its entirety for the first time ever in London. It is a very particular work. It is a work those of you with taste and discernment will not forget, and a work that only those of very particular accomplishment can offer. These young ladies have that accomplishment. It is rare. As you can see,' he gestured at the girls, 'they are rare. Please save your applause until the end.' He sat down.

Alathea moved to the brown pianoforte. She did not open the score. She did not need to. She sat until expectation tightened to suspense. Had this diamond vision forgotten the music? Was this near-as-dammit naked girl ever going to start?

Only when she was completely ready did Alathea pick up her hands and, into the silence, drop top G, G, A ornamented dotted quaver to B. The tender run. Then the lower G, ornamented twice, and the running semi- and demi-semi-quavers measured into the steady cadence of the bass. The aria was begun, so economical, so clean, so clear – so slow, Monsieur thought, at first with alarm, then with increasing and wondering admiration. His buttocks unclenched. Of course. Slow, slow, slow. It was quite right. Alathea made no fuss, no untoward movement, no pedal. The aria was played straight as a die, just as Herr Bach intended. That it could sustain such a deliberate pace was Alathea's miracle. Monsieur had tears in his eyes.

The astonishment of the audience was palpable. This sound, so rich! How could it be, coming from this brown thing that most had assumed, not having read their invitation properly, was a harpsichord? Plumcake indeed, even to the uninitiated.

Sawney Sawneyford heard as though through a cloud and saw as through grit. He was sweating. His daughter, his lover, as only he should see her, a blur of sparkles and skin, on public view displayed. Jesus Christ. How could silk cling so close? And then those fingers, those fingers that were his, creating this beautiful, truthful sound. Sawneyford pinched his forefinger nail into the mound of his thumb.

On the opposite side to Sawneyford, Annie waited through the aria's second section; the long lines, the gathering tension. Just before the resolution, Alathea turned her head. Through the heavy gauze of her veil, it should have been impossible for Annie to see. Indeed, what need had she to see? She felt that turn. She felt Alathea feeling her presence. This was the trumpet welcome Annie longed for. Why had she ever doubted? Her veil billowed in, out. Breathing was the only movement she made.

Behind the pianofortes, almost out of sight, Cantabile was sitting bolt upright, his hands gripped together in furious astonishment. His pianoforte had never sounded like this. How dare this naked girl confound him? It was impossible that she had talent. It was unforgivable. It was not what he had expected, and what he did not expect could not be. The aria came to an end. Alathea, shimmering, left the pianoforte stool to Marianne.

Marianne rustled the score and rushed into Variation 1 like a horse out of the stalls. Monsieur winced. Cantabile relaxed: this was more like it. Marianne fluffed the hand-crossing. Monsieur tutted. She had often missed the G. She was going far too fast. Marianne gulped and slowed for the second part, keeping her eyes glued to the music. This was utilitarian, a respectable marshalling of notes. Monsieur nodded his head. Good. However long he might have had with her, Mademoiselle Marianne could never play better than a tolerably efficient automaton. He glanced at the audience. The initial speed of the variation, such a contrast with Alathea, had impressed. Frogmorton, Drigg and others were tapping their feet. What idiots, thought Monsieur. Still, the variation did have something of a swing to it. Marianne banged to a halt, returned to her seat and patted her wig. Monsieur gave her an encouraging nod.

Now Georgiana. Variation 2, a duet of echoing melodies over a steady bass. She began with obvious nerves, her timing careful, the tune taking its turn in each register, a walk after Marianne's gallop. She remained at the pianoforte for Variation 3, the first canon, introducing it with the same care. Only when the bass quavers erupted into semi-quavers did she surprise both the audience and Monsieur by directing a light smile into the air, suggestive of girlish elation.

Harriet made the most of her great entry, playing Variation 4 like a businessman constructing a letter of serious import. Pay attention. No slacking. Hint of whip-crack. Yours sincerely. The audience liked it. This golden girl had spirit. Thomas Buller remembered just in time not to clap.

Taking a deep breath, and glancing briefly over her shoulder at Alathea, Harriet began Variation 5. Over the first three bars, a nervous metamorphosis took place. She was no longer the businessman. Now she was a tease. Her face registered only concentration – the variation was technically difficult – yet what was it about the set of her shoulders as her left and right hands crossed and recrossed that made every man in the room feel as though her hands might, if he was lucky, land in his lap? As she gained confidence, Harriet's mouth quirked up at one corner. The semi-quavers, that deliberate fingering, turned Variation 5 into something literally sensational. Monsieur sucked in his cheeks. He clicked his tongue at Harriet. In the audience, Frogmorton tensed, although Mrs Frogmorton was clearly enjoying herself. Harriet was marvellous. The alderman scolded himself: he had been upset by Alathea. She made everything seem peculiar. Anyway, this variation would end soon. It did. Harriet stood, imperial once more, turban intact, face slightly flushed.

Everina rose. The contrast with Harriet was appreciated, and the scent released by the arm petals wafted pleasingly towards those in the front row. Monsieur nodded to her. She emanated panic. Monsieur frowned. He gestured to the pianoforte stool. She sat down, adjusted the score but did not start. Monsieur was annoyed. Everina could play this variation alone. He had heard her. Yet if she was nervous, it was unjust to be angry with her. He slid on to the stool next to her. They could play this variation on one pianoforte without impeding each other. Everina, happy now, eased into the music, a picture of unspoiled, childlike maidenhood.

Mr and Mrs Drigg pressed together. Oh, this was lovely. Everina was lovely. The dress was lovely. Everything was lovely. Mrs Drigg knew, without even looking about, that every mother in the room wished her daughter was sitting up there at the pianoforte, just like Everina. Only Monsieur was annoyed as Everina mistimed the runs and forgot the accidentals. It was good, though, he thought, to reassert control.

Everina started Variation 7 so quickly after Variation 6 that Monsieur was trapped beside her. Under Alathea's instruction, she had learned this variation by heart, and how to make it naughtily provocative. She accentuated the *gigue*, and showed her teeth, touching Monsieur's shoulder with her own and smiling at the audience from under her lashes. Mr Drigg's stomach lurched. That was not so lovely. He felt his wife stiffen through the stiffness of her gown. Both were glad when Everina was back on her chair.

Marianne again. Everina was supposed to be with her, but she remained on her seat. Marianne patted the seat beside her. Unless he was to cause a scene, Monsieur had to join her. She played cat-and-mouse with the music master, shimmying a little as their hands muddled and crossed. Monsieur tried to pull her back to earth, moving down an octave so that their fingers did not touch. Marianne moved down an octave too. The audience had no idea if this was in the score or not, but the pantomime effect made the fathers and sons grin and the wives and mothers fan themselves disapprovingly. Funny it might be, but for all Marianne's velvet and powder, it was not ladylike. Mrs Drigg gripped Mr Drigg's knee.

Alathea next. It was difficult to pinpoint exactly how she turned a stately melody of dowager propriety into an erotic invitation. Yet this is what happened to Herr Bach's third canon. With clustering diamond dewdrops between breasts and legs and that tantalising, breath-throttling tan where there should

271

have been dark cover, she played the audience as she played the keyboard, painting a picture of slow pleasures in which she was clearly well versed. Come, join me, Alathea said, see how pleasure can be found in unexpected places. Cold diamonds challenged; warm lips enticed. Above, a halo of hair; below, smooth as a glove.

Mrs Frogmorton's palms had not yet begun to sweat, though she was no longer sitting easy. Harriet would have none of this, surely. Mrs Frogmorton remembered businesslike Variation 4 and pinned her hopes on that. She was only gradually aware of Georgiana's intense *fughetta*, during which this vision in white never once looked at the keyboard, but leaned with passionate and, so the mothers could see clearly from the gentle sway of her head, intimate intent at Monsieur. Brass refused to believe his eyes. Georgiana was just showing character! This was all to the good. He felt his wife sit up. He nudged her. She began to rock.

Harriet again. Mr and Mrs Frogmorton held their breath. Variation 11 began innocently enough, and it was difficult. That was the trouble. Through that painted pout, Harriet's tongue appeared, and those hands again seemed capable of playing more than ivory keys. Harriet kept her eyes on the keyboard, demure but, so that tongue suggested, hardly innocent. Her legs, outlined by the fall of the ribbons to the side and down the middle, seemed far apart. And then, at the end, her tongue still just poking through, she wrinkled her eyes at Monsieur and then at somebody in the audience.

Mrs Frogmorton whipped round. Who? She could not see. 'Archibald!' she whispered. Her palms were sweating now.

Onward. Everina was back at the keyboard, playing Variation 12 with gusto, shaking her shoulders at the little ornaments – not, so her mother realised with horror, to assist in their execution but to advertise her embonpoint; the dress seemed lower-cut than it had at the start. The embroidered flowers were rollicking as though drunk. Monsieur was again sitting next to her and Everina, working the pedals with all her might, manufactured a stage-wink. One or two of the sons in the audience gave low guffaws. They had seen such winks before, and not in places their mothers would take them. Everina nodded to Monsieur to pick up the left hand. For the sake of the music, he did. Now free, Everina's left hand ran up and down her own thigh, occasionally tipping towards somewhere more intimate. Those who could not see properly strained to look. Those who could see had to look away. Mr Drigg was one of them. Mrs Drigg, who could only manage tiny, shallow breaths, drummed Mrs Frogmorton's shoulder. Mrs Frogmorton could not turn round. She could not admit that something untoward was happening. It was not possible that it was. Their daughters were not in Paris, in the low quarter, playing banjos. They were in a saloon in Pall Mall playing Herr Bach's holy music.

For a moment, as Alathea unfolded Variation 13, all seemed normal. She played only for Annie, glowing through the *sarabande doublée* with no pretence of detachment. On this public platform, ignoring the other girls, ignoring the audience, ignoring her father, Alathea spoke openly of a pure love, a real love, a love that acknowledged, albeit wistfully, a dependence Alathea could not, and no longer wanted, to deny. Annie's silver core dissolved. It was no longer needed and she let it melt away without regret.

The audience, though, were disappointed. After Alathea's last performance, they had hoped for something with more spice. There was a bit of muttering. They felt cheated. Not Sawneyford, however. He was sickened. Like Annie, he heard Alathea clearly. The girl was parading her love to someone in this room who was not him. Had she no pity? Had she no love left for him, who had so much for her?

273

Georgiana beckoned to Monsieur. He was to help with Variation 14. He remained firmly on the black pianoforte stool. In a gesture so extraordinarily bold that her father exclaimed out loud, Georgiana abandoned her own stool, sat beside Monsieur, placed his hands on the keys and gently forced him to begin. He began. Their hands crossed and Georgiana ensured that they sat closer and closer together. Monsieur could not move down an octave, or the lowest notes would fall off the end of the keyboard. Yet Georgiana was practically sitting on his knee. Worse, she kept looking at him, and her look was not just a look, it was a proposal. And the truly dreadful thing was that at this moment, in her white gown, the little brown mole beneath her hair known to him and him alone, Georgiana was absolutely delectable again.

In the audience, Brass was actually choking. 'Hell and damnation, Elizabeth!' His wife was still rocking. These girls were, in a most uncanny way, running wild.

At the end of Variation 14, Monsieur pulled himself together and virtually shoved Georgiana from the pianoforte stool. He would play the fifth canon himself, on the brown pianoforte, and restore order. After that, Cantabile could retune the instruments while Monsieur had severe words with the girls. When they resumed, it would be like starting the concert again. Variation 16 was, after all, an overture. Everything before would be forgotten. He turned his face into a stone and played Variation 15 with utter sobriety. The audience did not enjoy it – not, that is, until the girls rose and began to process round the pianofortes, stately (as far as Everina and Marianne could manage) and mesmeric. Monsieur, doing his best to restore the music's more respectable wonders, pretended not to see them. The Driggs, Frogmortons and Mr Brass gripped their chairs. Surely this was the end. Mrs Brass never stopped rocking.

It was not the end. Variation 15 had barely floated away when

Marianne knocked Monsieur aside with a cheeky hip and rolled the overture's opening chord. There would be no respite, no opportunity for a lecture. The audience cheered. Everina, suddenly jealous of the cheer, rushed to sit beside Marianne. At first, Marianne was cross. She could manage this variation on her own. She began the overture again, trying to push Everina out. Everina gave her a sly nudge. The audience whooped. Marianne's mood altered. Sly met sly. The two girls pushed so close together that the buckles on their slippers clashed. Giggling, they slid their slippers off. Two pairs of silkily stockinged feet were exposed to public view. When Georgiana and Harriet, now seated at the black pianoforte, took over in perfect staccato for Variation 17, Everina and Marianne, still slipperless, danced and flirted. Marianne's wig came adrift. She righted it, but not quite.

And so it continued, Monsieur helpless as a baby. He could neither stop the girls nor control them. When he tried to shut the pianoforte lids, they flipped them open. When he silently implored Cantabile to help, he was met with a cackle. Cantabile thought the girls were monsters, but he did not want this travesty to stop. His pianoforte was making guys of them all, and in less than half an hour it would be his again.

Monsieur contemplated running away. All that prevented him was the knowledge that the girls would pursue and catch him and then the fathers would kill him. So he sat or stood, played or did not play, he hardly knew which.

During Variation 18, Marianne and Everina were conspirators with a secret so naughty they challenged the audience to guess it. There were more guffaws. Georgiana, coming next, did not care about the audience. Every note of the nineteenth variation was for Monsieur, every note declaring her the model wife, gentle but glorious, undemanding but dedicated, externally soft with a core of white ivory. Georgiana shared secrets with Monsieur, her music said, and she did not care who knew.

Monsieur was supposed to play Variation 20 with Harriet, for it was fiendishly complicated, but Harriet set off on her own. It was a most inaccurate performance, leaving the pianoforte vibrating. Marianne and Everina, not waiting for the vibrations to die down, transformed the lament of the seventh canon into alehouse sentimentality, picking up their skirts at the end and skipping back to their chairs. On the way, one of Marianne's underarm pomanders worked its way out, came adrift from its string, dropped to the floor and rolled away.

Variation 22, 23 and 24 turned into a game of tag, the girls pulling Monsieur down then pushing him up. They were all getting hot, except for Alathea. Even Georgiana was pink. Marianne's wig came off her head entirely and flapped down her back from a small rope. Her powder dissolved into a shoal of white pimples. Everina's underarms were dark with spreading sweat. One of her stockings was laddered. Harriet's lipstick was smudged to a bruise but, being more careful, she kept her turban intact and her shoes on. Monsieur, living a nightmare, pinned his hopes on the intense chromatic pathos of Variation 25. Nobody could pervert that. Nobody.

Variation 25 was Alathea's. She played it just as Herr Bach intended, except that the pathos was so sinuous and sensual the audience might have been watching a very slow, very melancholy and very indecent ballet. Cantabile did not know whether to laugh or scream. Sawneyford, a small lick of spittle on his lips, pulled out his pistol.

Momentarily bonded as sisters, Everina and Marianne had ideas beyond anything Alathea had suggested during practice. They whispered together, then set Monsieur between them for Variation 26. The stool proved too crowded for them to play. Perfect, though, to show off arms and calves as they leaned over him. Eventually they pushed him off the stool and treated the variation as a romp. Who cared about mistakes now? Marianne's wig bounced and with her tongue right out she was a perfect bawdy-house madame counting the evening's takings. This was when her marriage prospects vanished and her real career began. Most of the men who eventually became her clients were sitting in the Allemonde saloon that day.

The sight of Marianne sobered Harriet. There was a boundary that must not be crossed. She played the ninth canon alone and without fault. I am not like these others, Thomas Buller, she said. Hear my left hand. Hear my right hand. Hear how I marry everything together. That's what I will do for you.

Everina desperately wanted to steal Variation 28 from Alathea. All those patterned, synchronised demi-semi-quaver trills! She tried to play it. She failed. Alathea waited, then rose as arranged. Not as arranged, she caught Georgiana's arm. 'Come,' she said. Georgiana, reckless, obeyed, so they sat together, the swan goddess and the diamond dagger. Every now and again, Georgiana threw her head back in joyous abandon and her goddess's drapes shivered. When she got up from the stool, she flew to Monsieur, eyes shining, and stood beside him, the music she had made still ringing in both their ears.

It had been clear since Variation 7 that Monsieur had been more than a music master, but only now did Frogmorton turn on his wife. 'You said the music was holy. You said he was a eunuch.' He hurled both accusations through gritted teeth. 'You *said*.'

'*He* said.' Mrs Frogmorton found she could not stop blinking. It was the shock. She could think of nothing to say about the music, but as for the other, 'He told me how. He told me when. Of all the tricks, Archibald. *Of all the tricks!* And I fell for it.' She would have sagged had her clothes not made this impossible. Frogmorton, seeing that his uncowable wife was cowed, controlled himself. Recriminations were for later. They must decide immediately what to do. It was far too late to stop the

277

concert. They must let these ghastly variations run their course. Frogmorton clung to one hope: that the brilliance of the girls' arrival might wipe out everything that had followed. He clung to that hope so hard it was a moment before he was aware that silence had fallen. He looked up. Four of the girls were sitting on their chairs. Monsieur was standing alone. Cantabile had stopped cackling. Alathea was back at the pianoforte. What now? thought Mr Frogmorton. What new circus could there be?

Alathea raised her hands. Top G, G, A ornamented dotted quaver to B, then that falling, falling. The aria again, exactly as it had been to start with. This was Alathea's final miracle. After the mayhem, through sheer force of touch, desire and focus, she recaptured the clarity, dignity and purity of Herr Bach's holy creation. She did not need to recapture the truth, for the music, from Variation 1 to Variation 30, had never told anything but the truth. Through the music, the girls had presented themselves just as they were. Alathea raised her eyes to the back of the hall. Annie moved into the aisle. Under her veil, she was smiling.

Sawneyford clapped his left hand over his left ear. Why was everything so loud? He must speak to Alathea. She must listen. He knew she was going to leave him. Father and daughter. Lover and loved. Loved and lover. He saw Annie. He had no idea who she was. He moved out behind her and past her. She saw him and she saw the pistol.

Alathea also saw her father and the pistol. She played on. The men nearest the aisle began to rise, some expostulating and raising their arms, some pushing, some pulling their wives out of Sawneyford's way. Nobody dared tackle him, not with the hammer cocked. Sawneyford reached the front. Still Alathea played on, the tender aria unhurried and unflinching. Sawneyford stood in front of her. Did he love her? Did he hate her? He could hardly tell. He just wanted her to stop playing. She played on. She had no fear of Sawneyford at all. Herr Bach's aria would protect her. She knew it would. Her father would not shoot her. Despite what she had done to him, he had come to her and he had cried. The pistol was not for her. She knew it and he did too. She watched him tilt the gun so that the barrel was under his chin, pointing up through his head. Their eyes met, hers steady, knowing, encouraging – It's the right thing, the decent thing, the best thing – his searching and clouded with despair. Still she played: G, G, A ornamented dotted quaver to B, then that falling, falling and rising to D, the perfect pattern again.

Annie was behind Sawneyford. She could not see much through her veil, but she saw him raise the pistol. She saw him wait. She saw his arm twitch. No! She flicked up her veil and launched herself at him. The pistol jerked, tilted, then went off with such a dull retort that at first Annie thought it had not gone off at all. The girls were screaming. Their parents were screaming. The room was an uproar of overturned chairs and screaming, fleeing titles. Cantabile crouched under the brown pianoforte. Alathea was no longer playing, she was tipping forward, and Monsieur was no longer sitting at the black piano; he was already out of the door.

The room emptied before the screaming stopped and in a very short time another sound was heard. It was laughter. Great peals of it, echoing down the street. The audience had come. They had been amazed. They had been amused. For a moment, they had even been alarmed. All in all, it had been a splendid evening. Now they were going home. There would be no supper. There would be no weddings. The concert was well and truly over. Thomas Buller alone stood quietly in the void. When he saw his opportunity, he took Harriet's hand and proposed.

19

O N a dank and chilly morning two weeks later – Boxing Day, as it happens – we find Alderman Frogmorton, Mr Brass and Mr Drigg walking solemnly behind a cart set for Kennington Common. Sawney Sawneyford is not with them. He is in Soho Square, nursing his daughter. That jerk, that tilt, propelled the pistol ball intended for his own brain forward and it is now lodged next to Alathea's heart. The damage is containable, the surgeon says, if the ball remains exactly where it settled. Any movement or attempt to remove it will most likely be fatal. If Alathea wishes to live, she must remain still. Alathea does not wish to live. Her father wishes the opposite, and he controls the laudanum with which she is made too drowsy to resist.

Alathea's astonishment as the ball embedded itself where it had not been aimed was obvious to everybody. Everybody heard Sawneyford's appalled 'No!' – the most unequivocal sound he had ever made. Only Annie saw Alathea's incredulity. This must be a dream, because how was this possible? The music was an unbreachable shield! Then wild disbelief, directed not at her father but at Annie. *Annie!* It was impossible, surely, that Annie, the girl who needed no lessons at the pianoforte, had not shared Alathea's faith in the pianoforte's power. Impossible that she had not trusted the aria's perfection. Impossible that she had not understood how Herr Bach would protect them both. Lord! Oh, Lord! *Annie!* Alathea's shattered incomprehension was a trauma beyond the wound's. It blistered Annie's soul long after Alathea's forehead hit the keys, creating discord after discord as she rolled sideways to the floor, blood flowing in streams over and through the diamonds.

Cantabile stepped over the blood, noting with distaste that the blot on Alathea's face came from Annie's lip, bitten when she fell to her knees. 'Why did you do that, Annie? Why did you destroy this girl? Were you jealous of her? Was that it?' He gazed without emotion at Alathea. 'Now *this* would have been a daughter.' He flicked Annie's veil back over her face and began shouting that if Frogmorton or any of his City friends touched the brown pianoforte, he, Vittorio Cantabile, would strangle them. He was seized from behind. The fathers threw him out and set an armed guard on the door.

Today, as they walk, Frogmorton, Brass and Drigg, thick-booted and thickly clothed, are still being threatened by Cantabile. He, in his thin working jacket, is hopping along behind, restrained by two of Brass's heavies. Cantabile has buried his wife. He is trying to forget his daughter. His only concern is his pianoforte.

The men take little notice. They dream they have Monsieur in the cart. In truth, Monsieur is in Paris. Worse, Georgiana has gone after him, flying from Covent Garden, still in her white gown, not even a cloak against the winter night, clutching a bag of jewels that Elizabeth Brass, with rare energy, bundled up for her. When Brass discovered Georgiana had fled, his fury had been loud and coarse, yet he did not send after her. Let the ruined daughter go, and the stinking jewels. Brass has another plan. Monsieur might have fooled their idiot wives about his nether regions but he will soon fool nobody. Brass has dispatched a very particular man for that job. (The man cheats him. The contract is never fulfilled. Monsieur is, though, found by Georgiana, and, dogged by a sense of irritated responsibility, he remains with her until her death, twenty-five years later. She bears him three children and sends for her mother to help look after them. Her father would be welcome but he never comes.)

In the cart is the brown pianoforte. With no Monsieur to lynch and Herr Bach already dead, the fathers turned on the instrument. Absurd, of course, but the pianoforte is the one thing on which they can take physical revenge. Drigg had been for breaking it up even before Alathea was carried away. Calmer counsel prevailed. In the event, it had taken only twenty-four hours to decide what to do and, with Christmas intervening, today is the designated day.

Like a criminal, the instrument is tied by the legs. The procession reaches the common, empty except for a group of boys supervising a cockfight. The carter asks, 'Where now?' Frogmorton gestures to the gallows in the middle. The wheels crunch over the half-soggy, half-frozen dew and the men stamp after it, breath steaming. They all help lever the instrument down. They take care. As with a traitor brought for hanging and evisceration, they want their prisoner intact. The strings twang gently as the frame is placed on the base just in front of the gallows platform. If the pianoforte had a stool, it would be ready to play. The stool, though, was judged not guilty, and the same judgement was made of the inferior pianoforte; both are still in the Allemonde saloon. The carter tosses out faggots and kindling. Drigg raises the pianoforte lid and places faggots inside the body, while Brass stacks faggots round the legs.

Cantabile is brought to a halt a little way off. He is crying like a baby, cursing Drigg, cursing his daughter, cursing Claude Belladroit. Drigg wants to shout, 'Curse yourself,' but since the other men are silent, he holds his peace.

The carter asks if he should light the kindling. 'Yes, light the thing,' Frogmorton snaps. For a moment, he can hear Harriet playing. Past pride heightens present humiliation. Burning the pianoforte, what a sign of impotence. If Cantabile would only stop his cursing, Frogmorton might halt the whole charade. But Cantabile curses on and Frogmorton stands, feet apart, recalling the forced calm of his wife in the carriage home, a calm that broke behind her closed bedroom door without even Frilly as witness. The tempest lasted ten minutes. Afterwards, Mrs Frogmorton emerged and carried on as usual, except she is deflated, diminished, unstitched. When Harriet announced she was marrying Thomas Buller, her mother registered neither pleasure nor displeasure. She would recover, the alderman thought. She would find some stuffing and stitch herself together. But it wasn't right that she should have to, not right at all. The carter strikes a light. Cantabile shrieks. Frogmorton wishes they could burn him.

Drigg suffers more acutely than Frogmorton. The sight of both his daughters flaunting themselves like tipsy heifers will never leave him. The servants knew even before the Drigg carriage brought them all home. Mrs Drigg has told him to put the house up for sale. Her first act the morning after the concert was to dispatch the girls' entire trousseaus to a City charity for unmarried mothers. (In the curious way things often turn out, Marianne herself became an unmarried mother, though her new career rendered charity unnecessary.) Mrs Drigg then drew the curtains, pulling one down as she blundered about. She could not face the neighbours. She could not face the girls. She could not face her own mirror. In the face of all this not facing, Drigg can do little. The girls, on the other hand, and for reasons unfathomable to their father, are in a state of high elation.

Everina decided early that Alathea had been right. After all, despite the concert's unhappy end, it had been followed by propositions pushed through the Stratton Street door on a daily basis. Men had seen what the Drigg sisters had to offer and wished to offer for it. She showed the propositions to Marianne and scoffed when Marianne wept at their crudity. True, these were not the offers their parents had hoped for, but look! The concert was barely over and already money, servants, houses were being paraded – all for them! 'We can do as we like,' Everina said. 'We just have to decide.'

'But there's nothing here about marriage,' Marianne sobbed. 'Propositions aren't proposals. Harriet's had a proper proposal.'

Everina made a face. 'Only from a plain "Mr".' She tossed her head. 'We don't need proposals. Look how much fun we had. I don't think our mother ever had fun like that. We're celebrated all over the newspapers, Marianne. We're more famous than anybody in a story, and we're real.' She giggled. 'The expressions on people's faces! They loved us!' She thrust out a handkerchief. 'Come on, wipe your nose. We should thank Alathea, and' – she gave Marianne a sly nudge – 'she's never going to upstage us again.'

This last cheered Marianne. The sisters did not have to disguise from each other that they went to see Alathea because they were sure she would not want to see them. Marianne made suitably pitying noises. They were both shocked by the house. On the way back to Stratton Street, they wondered what had happened to the diamond dress, and Marianne openly conjectured that Alathea was in a partnership with the underworld. 'It would be just like Alathea to have conjured up a demon,' she said, referring to Annie, whom she had briefly glimpsed unveiled.

Everina had hardly been conscious of Annie at all. They never spoke of her again.

The sisters grew closer. Instead of squabbling, they began to frequent taverns, playhouses, trinket shops and the house of a man offering tattoos – places to which they were guided by new friends. A world of novelty opened up, and it was productive. Offers continued to flow in abundance. The girls encouraged competition. When their mother returned to the comforting stink of her father's fish stall, Marianne and Everina opened the Stratton Street drawing room, in which, intoxicated by their new-found freedom, they held bawdy court until the house was sold and they moved, together, to lodgings paid for by the sons of three peers. Things progressed from there. Luckily for Drigg as he watches the execution of the pianoforte, he cannot see the future.

The kindling is smoking. The carter takes his guinea fee and leaves. The cockfighting boys truss their birds and wander over, highly entertained by the sight of four men rooted around a burning pianoforte, a skinny devil screeching in the background.

The men are silent. With flames licking its underbelly, the pianoforte tries to remain silent too, and also upright and dignified. It refuses to buckle, wishing to sink gracefully, not like a cow with foot-rot. It knows its worth, even if its murderers do not and never have. It has been sublime. The flames leap. The pianoforte cannot help itself. Its strings give voice as they melt: short high hums then snap-snap-snap with brave twang and stuttering cadence. The sounding-board's hisses are gentle, its cracks apologetic. The pianoforte would like to die to the strains of Herr Bach's aria, if only somebody would help. Where is Alathea? The keys begin to drop away. First the white, then the black. The pianoforte is being stripped. The lid, not yet alight, slips, to cover the nakedness. There is wood and soft iron, ivory and leather, brass and steel and a tarnished sound-board rose. There is nobody to comfort the instrument in its distress. Cantabile can only watch and grind his teeth. The end comes in a heap of charred fragments, blackened coils, brass screws and mangled, tangled strings pointing every which way, as though unsure from which direction help might come.

The boys are quickly amongst the smoking heap, scrabbling for loot. At this point, Brass's servants let Cantabile go. He rushes at the boys. They tease him and once they have nudged out anything of value, kick the remains of the pianoforte's guts in Cantabile's direction. He gathers up the pieces as a mother gathers up the bones of a child. The boys hold up their birds, beaks firmly tethered shut. 'Want to see some real sport, old man?' they shout, friendly enough. Cantabile does not answer. His hands are full. He cannot even shake a fist.

Frogmorton, Brass and Drigg make their way to Threadneedle Street and into the V&B, their first visit since the concert. They have been at home and in their offices. They have been in Pall Mall, trying to rectify matters with the Allemondes. They have met at Manchester Square, whose hall was the pianoforte's condemned cell. In the V&B, the familiar fug envelops them. Mr W, emptying coffee grounds into a measure, nods. Frogmorton nods back. Mrs W offers the comment 'Chilly day' and wipes the men's usual table. There is some whispering, but few City men have heard about the concert and fewer are interested. Trade is king, and trade is threatened by war, not by pianofortes or concerts or daughters' marriages. The tallow-dips splutter. The water urn, dirtier than it was this time last year, swings and gurgles. A new cat is warming its behind. The last copies of *Spence's Penny Weekly* have long since been thrown on the fire, except for the one still stuffed under the table leg.

Two noticeable changes. Mr W's lewd pictures have been

exchanged for patriotic songsheets, and there is a new awkwardness between the men. They remove their hats, push away the chair that might have been Sawneyford's and sit quietly until coffee arrives. Frogmorton shakes his head at the coffee boy. No, they don't want pipes.

'Well—' Brass says.

Drigg interrupts. He just needed somebody else to start. 'How did Grace not know?' he says quickly to Frogmorton. 'I mean, how could she not *know*?' This question has been asked before, many times, during these two weeks.

'Monsieur was convincing,' Frogmorton says wearily. This answer, too, has been given before, many times. 'I told you what he told her. You were convinced.'

'But she was acting chaperone!'

'She did what she thought was right.' Frogmorton puts down his coffee bowl with unaccustomed care. 'As I keep saying, nobody could be more sorry.'

'Agnes has collapsed,' says Drigg. 'Marianne and Everina are out of control.'

'I heard Everina say that the creature who jogged Sawneyford was a witch,' says Brass. 'I hardly saw her. Did you?'

Drigg takes a breath. 'She's Cantabile's daughter. She was there when I bought the pianoforte.'

'His daughter?' The notion seems to tickle Brass. 'Well, there's a thing. I'm glad she isn't mine.'

'Have you found Georgiana?' Drigg asks.

'No,' says Brass, 'and I don't intend to.' He wonders whether to keep his contract on Monsieur's offending parts to himself. He does not. There is strained laughter. It seems the only response. Brass stretches his legs. Drigg stops fidgeting. More coffee is poured.

'How's Sawneyford?' Frogmorton asks. 'Has anybody seen Alathea?'

287

A glance, flickering round. Alathea. Brass whistles. 'Wasn't that something.' They know he is not referring to the shooting.

'I reckon the diamonds in the choker alone were worth at least a thousand pounds,' Frogmorton says. They cannot talk of the other thing. They cannot even think about it. They must not. Even Brass must realise it is forbidden.

'More than a thousand,' Drigg declares.

'Did you count them?' asks Brass.

'Fifteen,' says Drigg. The laughter is more genuine.

'More valuable than that damnable music,' Brass says. 'Didn't Grace say Monsieur described it as holy?'

'Wholly unsuitable,' Drigg chips in. 'We could try and get it proscribed?'

Frogmorton shakes his head. 'No need. It'll go out of fashion soon enough.' The men nod.

'I think I will have a pipe,' Frogmorton says. 'You, Drigg?'

'Why not?'

Pipes are brought. An office clerk appears and produces an account that does not tally. Frogmorton and Drigg lean over it. Brass leans back and thinks of his new squeeze – a perky London miss. He has had enough of foreigners.

'So Harriet's to be Mrs Thomas Buller?' Drigg says when the account has been dissected and the miscalculation identified.

'She is,' says Frogmorton, and shrugs. 'His father has interests in India: indigo, salt, cotton, that kind of thing.' He sucks at his pipe. He starts to say, 'It won't be a bad match,' but realises the tactlessness just in time. There will be no matches at all for the others. He says, 'We should help Sawney out. I don't know what got into him. It's hardly his fault everything went wrong.'

Mr Drigg and Mr Brass agree. They will set up a fund. They may not like Sawneyford, but he is one of them. The fund will be generous. (It does not need to be. Sawneyford nurses

Alathea assiduously and with all due propriety but her wish to die is too strong, even for the laudanum. In a month, she is gone. Sawneyford sells his City businesses and leaves without a word, vanishing into the fog of revolution and war to re-emerge or sink, as fate decrees.)

Even as the men discuss the fund for Sawneyford and his daughter, in the hold of the *Maidenhead*, newly slipped from the Pool of London, the hangman is working his passage to the New World. With not even one execution from the November treason trials (treason in itself), he has thrown in the rope and will try his luck in America. The first job given him by the ship's captain is to lash down a pianoforte, bought in London for a New York family of musical girls. His familiarity with knots is turning out an advantage.

In the hold is a veiled girl, waiting for him to finish. Annie boarded early. She already knows she will find no utopia in the New World, since the Pantisocratics cannot get themselves past Bristol. Nevertheless, she will make the voyage. Throughout the entire crossing, she never leaves this pianoforte. At first, she cannot bear to play Bach, then she cannot bear to play anything else. The dreadful storms of the Atlantic are welcome. The pianoforte groans while Annie howls, clutching Alathea's ring, secured to her for ever by a chain round her neck. When the storms subside, Annie is calm because she is now empty.

Disembarking at New York, she clutches her veil and does not speak. It is left to the captain to explain her attachment to the pianoforte as best he can, which, since he has no idea of Annie's story, is no explanation. The mother of the New York girls, making far too prosaic an assumption about the wedding ring on the chain, senses tragedy. She takes pity and a risk. She invites Annie to their home. And there Annie remains, silent for the most part and nearly always veiled, until people no longer ask where she came from and must content themselves with the one thing they do know about her: that she belongs to the pianoforte, which she plays every day, for most of the day. The family come to believe that Annie blesses them through her music, and through their unquestioning, continued welcome, Annie believes they bless her, so far as blessing is possible.

Annie's heart never heals. Music is just enough to keep her sane. When she dies – a sudden stroke – the New York family bury her in their own plot, her veil secured, her secrets intact, the wedding ring still on its chain around her neck. At her funeral, at her request, the aria from the fourth part of Bach's *Clavier-Übung* is played. Her tombstone is plain and the inscription simple. It reads ANNIE 1777–1843 and, underneath, PIANIST.